THE MAN AT THE GATE

HILARY NEWMAN

COMBIS PRESS

Published in 2020 by Combis Press

ISBN Paperback: 978-1-8381129-0-5
Ebook: 978-1-8381129-1-2

Published with the help of Indie Authors World
www.indieauthorsworld.com

IndieAuthors
World

In Memory of George. 1941-2019

ACKNOWLEDGEMENTS

The author wishes to thank Clarissa Cairns, Dorothy Goldman and Catherine Eady for their constructive advice and support. In addition to acknowledge the loving encouragement given by George and their three children, Ben, Matt and Clarissa.

PROLOGUE

SUMMER 1944

The tall, well dressed man passed through the gate and turned down the path, bracing his shoulders as he walked. A short distance away, the two brothers stood on the tow path, watching the river. It was an ordinary day, a little grey, but the morning rain had stopped, and later the sun would come out. Their name was Rinaldi, the older one, Andre was 22, the younger, Pierre, had just turned 18. They were very alike, dark hair, tanned skin and well built, their bodies accustomed to the hard physical work of the family farm. They did not speak, while Pierre drew deeply on his cigarette, cupping it in the palm of his hand. They wore heavy dark jackets and the flat, black berets typical of Gascony, waiting impatiently, and scuffing the path with their boots, as they stared at the fast flow of water.

After an hour had passed, Andre too was smoking now, they saw who they were waiting for, the tallish man walking briskly toward them. Tapping the ground with a smart cane, he was accompanied by a little dog who, trotting slightly ahead of him, stopped repeatedly for a sniff. A wide brimmed hat shielded his face. His coat, with collar turned up, was a good brown tweed, and his brown shoes were highly polished.

He too was looking at the river, while carefully skirting the puddles. As he came up to pass them, he was surprised to be spoken to…'Monsieur!' it was Andre Rinaldi who spoke, 'we've been waiting for you!'

'Why? What do you want of me?' The man looked at the two brothers, noticing now their menacing stance. He went to pass by, but they blocked his way. Andre spoke again, 'You, Monsieur,' he spoke loudly, 'are an enemy of good loyal French men!' Pierre, who though he was younger, was taller and heavier, moved a step closer, and the man looked at him for the first time. His little dog, alarmed at the loud voice, came and stood beside his master. A spasm of anxiety passed through the man. He was tall, but slight of build, and these two men were heavy and muscular and rough looking. But he was not to be intimidated, 'Let me pass. I don't know you. I've nothing to say to you!' He gripped his cane more tightly, weighing it in his hand. They were now standing very close to him, he could smell their breath.

'You don't know us. We know you! We know, who you are, Monsieur, where you live…and,' Andre spoke quietly, 'your young wife, and child…' He flicked his cigarette into the river, and raised his voice, 'You're a traitor to your country! An enemy of France! Good men have died because of you.' His face was now livid, contorted with anger.

Bertrand du Pont looked at the brothers, standing together now, side by side, blocking his path. He too was angry, and not yet afraid; he stood very straight, his cane raised, 'Get out of my way!' He shouted.

The little dog barked as he heard his master's loud voice, then barked again. Andre, with no hesitation moved nearer, and his sturdy boot caught it in the ribs. 'Ouf' he said, 'such a little dog!' he lifted his boot again. Bertrand lunged forward and the struggle began. It was very one sided, two brothers against one man, Andre struck him on the shoulder as he tried to raise his cane. Bertrand staggered…Pierre struck a heavy blow to his face close to his right eye …he fell back… and then another blow at his chest … The dog whined, whimpered… as the brothers closed in… Bertrand, afraid now, and trying to dodge the blows, stumbled, as he sought vainly to shield his head, and slipped on the muddy path, falling back, unable to save himself, and fell down the shallow bank and into the river.

His cane lay on the towpath. Andre picked it up and threw it into the river and they both watched, as his body rose and fell, and then disappeared. There was very little movement on the surface of the dark water, they saw only the cane. It floated slowly away, turning in the current. Pierre, horrified, looked at his brother. 'Shall I go in? Should we help?' He motioned at the water and continued to stare at the river, but the body was gone.

Andre, overwhelmed by the sudden speed of the struggle, and the violence of their behaviour, made no reply as they stood side by side. It had all happened so quickly, he couldn't think clearly. But the body of Bertrand du Pont was beyond help. A few moments later, without a word being said, they turned towards the town and returned home. After a few weeks their memory of the event began to fade, an unspoken agreement had been made to never speak or refer to it. The following month, Pierre now nineteen, was taken off under the forced labour scheme he was absent for two years, working in the east of Germany. Andre remained to work the farm and look after the family, there was a younger brother and a sister, to support and care for. In the autumn he noticed that the home of Bertrand du Pont, at Les Palmes, was closed up, but thought little of it.

Bertrand's body drifted slowly down until it became caught at the millrace, above the town. Eddies circled it gently. Sometime later in the afternoon, an old man, walking back from visiting his sister saw the body. He called out to the men below the race, who were fishing at the millpond. None of them was young, and it took them several minutes to scramble up the path and reach the scene. They hauled him out with some difficulty, grasping his sodden coat and fine shoes. Finally, laying the body on the bank, they turned him over. His face was swollen and badly bruised, water leaked from his mouth. There was a nasty cut below one eye.

'Monsieur du Pont!' one said, 'I know him. We need to get him home.'

They made a stretcher from a length of wood lying on the path, laid him on it, face up, hatless now, his clothes smelling of the river. It took four men to carry him up the tow path, it was not far.

'He lives here!' the man who had recognized him said, 'We'd best carry him in!' They pushed open the gate and carried him down the path toward the house, it was heavy work, and from an upstairs window, a little girl was watching. The little dog returned later, but never recovered from its injuries, its loss subsumed by the anguish resulting from its master's death. There was no inquiry into the drowning... It was wartime... Sudden death, disappearances had become normal, accepted. There had been no witnesses to explain why a fit and healthy man had fallen into the river, and his young wife, now a widow, was too distraught and shocked to ask many questions. She accepted their account for it was easy to slip on a muddy path. The damage to his face was ascribed to the millrace where his body had been trapped and held, banging no doubt, against the stout wood pillars.

His widow took an unexpected decision to leave the family home, which lay in the depths of rural Gascony, where food was scarce, but still available; there were eggs from their own chickens, and fish in the river beyond the garden gate. There were apples and pears from the old canker ridden orchard, edible if cooked, though sugar was now hard to find. She closed up the house, said goodbye to the gardener Jean, who agreed to keep working there, and packed two baskets of clothes. It was a hazardous journey; they travelled erratically by bus and train, north across the 'Line', passing out of Vichy France, into occupied France, the 'zone nord' as it was called. It took the mother and her young child three days, sleeping in bus shelters, speaking only to the uniformed soldiers, showing their identity cards quickly, averting their eyes. They were to live now outside Paris, with grandparents, whom the child hardly knew. For the young grieving widow and her father-less daughter, it was a time of uncertainty, far away from the home, Les Palmes, and the life they had previously known.

CHAPTER 1

SEPTEMBER 2000

Marthe turned her car slowly into the circular drive, edging between the two tall stone pillars. The heavy wrought iron gates had been pushed back, and glancing at them she noticed their rusty condition. She drove up to the flight of shallow steps which led to the heavy front doors, and stopped. There was another car parked there. It had been a long drive from Paris, and, despite her early start, it had been barely light as she set out, it was now nearly two o'clock in the afternoon. Marthe was tired and hungry, but excited. A light rain was falling now, disappointing as it had been sunny all week in Paris.

She picked up her bag from the seat beside her, pushing aside the map which she had not needed, and got out, stretching her arms and legs with pleasure. She looked up at the house; the shutters were open, and there were lights on in the ground floor. She stood for a moment feeling the rain on her head, it smelt fresh and sweet.

As she began to walk up the steps, the big double doors opened and her son, her only child, Felix stood before her. 'Welcome back!' He was smiling, and came forward to kiss her. Felix! She was delighted to see him. They embraced and he led her into the hall.

'How was the journey? Do you have luggage? Are you hungry?'

'Long, yes, and yes!' she answered as she looked around. It was a large hall with a high oak-beamed ceiling and a dark oak staircase leading to the upper floors. It was illuminated by some decorative wall lights of wrought- iron placed high on the brick walls, and Marthe had difficulty seeing further into the house. The only natural light came from the landing above, whose long windows rose above the entrance. It always gave a sombre impression at first.

To her right, there were the double doors that opened into the salon, and a matching pair to the left which led into the dining room. They were closed. Felix and Marthe walked down four steps to the lower hall and turned into the spacious beamed kitchen. There was a large, scrubbed table here, and Marthe put down her bag, and inhaled appreciatively. 'It all looks very nice and clean. Thank you.' She spoke with some formality. It was a lovely room. South facing, enjoying a long view through two deep casement windows into the garden. There was a wide, brick hearth, very tall with a mantel above, and, on the wall facing the windows a fine, pine dresser displaying china on its shelves. The room smelt lightly of bees-wax. 'I shall hang lavender, from the beams.' She said standing at the table. 'There are some elderly bushes I remember lining the terrace. And in summer, the door can stand open, and the sunshine will pour in!' She grimaced at the grey day outside. Felix was watching his mother, 'Goodness, you've got it all worked out! But you're right- this is the friendliest room. Even on a day like today.' He felt gratified that her first response had been appreciative, Felix had been looking after the house for nearly two years, having moved to Toulouse, a short distance away. It had not been an onerous responsibility;

he had enjoyed driving out of the city into the landscape of that part of France, with its wide fields and small woodlands, and red brick farm houses set on the low ridges of the hills. He had, at his mother's request, visited once a month, missing rarely, and enjoyed the quiet, dusty rooms; opening shutters, leaving the high windows ajar in the summer, running the taps, sitting on the old fashioned sofas, checking the gas in the kitchen. Sometimes he brought a picnic, sitting in the sun as he ate his ham baguette and drank a beer at a rusty table on the terrace. He liked the old house, but he could not imagine himself living there.

Marthe walked across and peered through one of the windows. The rain was now falling heavily, it all looked very green outside. She turned back,

'How's Valerie? Working?'

'Yes, she sends her love of course. She works hard…long hours.' He paused, then continued, 'Would you like some lunch? Or a drink? Or a pot of coffee? It's all here!' He indicated the pantry which led off the kitchen.

'No, not for the moment, I'd like to walk around first.' She said, 'remind myself of what I've undertaken. My new life!' There was a brief silence, she led the way back into the hall.

This house, Les Palmes, had been the home of several generations of the du Pont family. They originated in Alsace but had fled the German invasion of 1871, abandoning a prosperous brick making factory. They set themselves up outside Toulouse, using the local clay sourced from the river Garonne, and a new factory grew up. Wise investments and a growing demand for bricks enabled them to increase their wealth. They enjoyed the warmer, drier climate and settled with pleasure at the home they built and named. Bertrand was an austere figure, regarded as a fair employer, though few people knew him personally. While keeping a vigilant eye on the factory, he preferred to read in his salon, mostly history. He developed a formidable knowledge of French history and the great figures of the past: Louis XIV, and Napoleon, and deplored the moral collapse, as he saw it, of France in the twentieth century.

*

Felix watched his mother as she led him up the stairway. He saw a slim, upright figure, neat in her smart Parisian clothes. Her grey hair was stylishly short which suited her small face. A moment of doubt flickered. She looked incongruous in this large house, with its many rooms. They toured the rooms upstairs together, walking through slowly as Marthe ran a critical eye over the furniture, all of which had stood untouched since her departure so many years ago. It was mostly dark and heavy, oak and walnut with some mahogany. The beds were high and large, and in every bedroom there was a tall armoire. The fireplaces were guarded by screens, some were tapestries, worked, she assumed by one of the du Pont family. There were gilt mirrors and high backed chairs and thick red rugs. 'All very nineteenth century!' she said, 'I'll enjoy making some changes.' They paused on the landing, a gutter was dripping water against a pane, it drew Marthe's attention and she looked again at the garden.

'Has young Jean been working? I've paid him every month!' Felix joined her,

'He's very irregular, I'm afraid. I've hardly seen him.'

Marthe was cross and disappointed, 'I'll chase him up then. His father was so different, loyal and hardworking. This son is…well, not so satisfactory.'

Bertrand's gardener had been employed for nearly fifty years to look after the large garden, but ten years previously his son 'young Jean' had taken on the responsibility. A man of few words and sour expression, he hadn't the interest of his father, the garden had steadily deteriorated. It was now an overgrown and neglected wilderness. Nothing had prepared Marthe for the sight of it. Trees had fallen, brambles had grown high into those that were still struggling for life, the paths that had once divided the neat beds were lost in weeds. The shrubs had not been pruned and had lost all shape, and the lovely old walls were smothered in ivy and overgrown climbers. Standing at the window, she could only sigh, 'How big it was!' She had forgotten. She turned to Felix with a grimace, 'This will be a challenge, and I know so little about gardens!'

'You can find someone to help… clear it out… prune!' His voice faded away. He had lived all his life in apartments in Paris and now Toulouse, barely caring for his balcony. What did he know of gardens?

Felix felt his mother's spirits drooping, she had already driven for some five hours and was looking exhausted. He spoke briskly and took her arm, 'Come, let's eat. The fridge is full and a glass of wine will revive you!'

They retraced their steps as Felix listened to the creak of the new radiators, heating the house, wisely installed by Marthe in preparation for her return. He saw the rain was running through other gutters; many needed repair, and water was spouting on to the terrace. It did feel rather desolate. But the kitchen was warm and dry, and Felix opened the wine and gave his mother a large glass. They sat together eating a cheese omelette, one of Felix's specialities, with bread and salad. It helped to restore their spirits, but a silence now lay between them, each wary of their thoughts.

CHAPTER 2

Marthe's new home stood on the edge of farm land. It had a sweeping entrance, and a walled garden running down to the river. The quiet road led to St. Girou, which like the city of Toulouse, was built of red brick, with narrow streets and a large cobbled square. The houses in this part of Gascony were heavily shuttered against both the cold winds of winter, and the blazing sun of summer. Small windowed, they presented a blank face to the world, their occupants hidden in the dark rooms, kept warm in winter by open fires. The people were small in stature, rather square-bodied, and many were of Italian stock.

Marthe had described her decision to leave Paris and take up a new life in her father's home, some five hundred miles South of where she had lived all her life, as an 'adventure'. Her closest friend, Patricia, a lively widow whose husband had died some years ago, thought it a mad cap scheme. She repeatedly urged Marthe to stay in Paris. 'Whatever will you do in an old family house? It will be dark, cold and lonely. And rural life? You are a city person, the countryside is tolerable in summer, but boring for the rest of the year! Please ...' But Marthe was not to be dissuaded. Her happy marriage had ended very suddenly, when her husband, Xavier, died of a heart attack on the Metro. He was just sixtyfive and due

for retirement that year. The unexpectedness, the unprepar-
edness left Marthe in a state of shock for several long empty
months. She had married at twenty one, having fallen in love
with a lively, intelligent and outgoing young man, a teacher
of music at the prestigious Academy. She was delighted to
get away from the stultifying life in her grandparent's home.
The marriage was a great success. She became Mme Xavier
le Brun, and moved to a sunny apartment in the sixieme
arrondissement in Paris. It would be her home for nearly forty
years. Their son, Felix was born soon afterwards, and Marthe
embarked on a new life as a wife and mother. Xavier taught
her to play the piano and she led an interesting and stimulat-
ing life, within the musical circle; concerts, supper parties and
visits to exhibitions and galleries. She was a devoted mother,
but her own upbringing had had a profound influence on her;
she had no experience of the rough and tumble of family life,
and found it difficult to join in Xavier's games with his son.
Felix thrived nonetheless, having inherited his father's easy
disposition and sharing with both parents a love of music.

As Felix grew up, she recognised that one day the house in
Gascony would be his, and the family made several visits, driving down in the summer. They enjoyed exploring the flat lands
around Poitiers, Chartres cathedral, and the Dordogne region
with its caves and hill towns. They purchased bone china in
Limoges, and tried boating near Moissac. But Xavier was a
Parisian through and through, country life quickly bored him,
and he found Les Palmes, with its large dark rooms depressing.
Yet increasingly the house intrigued Marthe: she liked the many
rooms, such a contrast from the Paris apartment, and the walled
garden. She found it mysterious and it connected her to her past;
her mother, who had moved there after her marriage, and the
father who she never properly knew. As the years went by, she

began to make independent visits, she enjoyed the drive, and looked forward to the last few miles as the now familiar landscape opened up before her, the rolling hills, and if the weather was dry the long view south to the Pyrenees. She persuaded old Jean to open up the house for her, and it too began to feel familiar. She would stay longer and longer, once even a week when Xavier was also away. She continued to appreciate the spaciousness of the house, and, although she only used a few rooms, nonetheless it was a pleasure to open the shutters, and let in the sunlight, to wander about admiring the high ceilings and the family portraits. Despite its sorry state she felt happy and calm in the garden. By 1990 Jean was a bent old man, very deaf and his speech had become difficult to follow. She had one last conversation with him, thanking him for his long years of service to the family. He was the only person who had known her parents and she was sad to see him go. He spoke slowly and reluctantly, nodding his head with the effort. 'Your father was a fine man, it was an honour to work for him. Very respected.' He paused, 'But it was your mother who loved the garden.' This was quite unexpected. 'I didn't know that!' Marthe responded.

He continued, 'She pruned the orchard every spring, and loved sitting there in the summer, with the fruit hanging high in the trees about her.'

Marthe tried hard to imagine the scene, the young wife and mother enjoying the orchard. Had she, Marthe, played there, beside her, as her mother sat in the shade? She had no memory of it. She looked at the old man, 'Thank you Jean. That gives me great happiness.'

He had smiled slightly, it was a good memory for him too, better than many he had of the war years. She touched his shoulder lightly, his jacket was old and threadbare. It was the last time that they spoke.

Young Jean, one of his sons, now took over. He was a taciturn man, dark haired and swarthy. He agreed to work, for more money, while listening to Marthe with an indifferent air, which bordered on rudeness. With a garden costing more, yet deteriorating year by year, her visits were less happy and Marthe began to consider selling. It was, surprisingly, Xavier who counselled against this. 'It's family, you can't do that. Property is valuable and should never be sold. Leave it empty, visit when you feel like it, spend some money on the heating, remember that it will be Felix's one day, he may feel differently. You can afford it!' he said with a smile. She took his advice, and was delighted when in 1998, Felix announced that he was moving to Toulouse, to work on the local paper as their music critic. Xavier was eager for Felix to expand his career, and took his son to lunch to celebrate. 'It's a fine city, you'll enjoy living there... good buildings, warm climate and a long musical tradition.'

'I think it'll be a challenge, criticism is something new for me, and I shall take up some teaching, young students preferably.'

'And Paris isn't far away, a quick flight or an easy drive, as I remember.' Felix sipped his wine, listening to his father, he was looking forward to the move needing a change from his present work in music publishing.

'And Valerie will join me there. She's been offered promotion in her accountancy firm, we'll move together!' Xavier patted Felix' hand,

'That's good. She's a lovely girl, you're a fine couple.' Neither of them referred to Les Palmes, both assumed that Felix and Valerie would live in Toulouse, no doubt in a smart modern apartment. In the summer of 1998 they left Paris.

*

Felix was simply astonished when Marthe announced her decision to settle permanently in Les Palmes. They were in his apartment in Toulouse. It was a lovely spring day in the year 2000, some six months after Xavier's death.

'I've been thinking about it for some time. Living at Les Palmes was out of the question when your father was alive. He had no connection with the house and, as you know, he had no real affection for it. Imagine him living in rural Gascony! He would have hated it! Without friends, or concerts, or supper parties and lunch appointments.' She looked out of the window across the river Garonne, to the large houses on the opposite bank. Lights were coming on as people returned home from work, and it was a pleasing view.

'No, you're right, father wouldn't have been happy there.' Felix was still trying to digest the shock, 'But can you live without all that? You love Paris, it's been your life.'

'Without your father everything has changed. It's different, and difficult. I need to move away, and Les Palmes offers me an opportunity, to start again. I can't continue as I am, sad, and always thinking of the past...expecting the door to open and your father to walk in. Friends have been kind, but most of them are couples. My life is too painful, going out on my own to concerts and galleries.' She stared out of the window, avoiding Felix's eyes, they were both uncomfortable with any reference to Xavier's death.

Felix said, 'But to move to Les Palmes! It's a huge decision. Have you,' he paused, 'well, really thought it through?'

Felix looked at his mother who continued to stand at the window, where the lights were throwing up a reflection off the water. The ceiling of the flat danced with the movement. Marthe turned, she had a look of quiet determination. 'I have thought about it, Felix. I'm not a fool rushing in!' He blushed slightly, 'I wasn't suggesting such a thing.'

'No of course not. But I'm not acting in haste. I have relied all my life on the support and direction of others: my grandparents, my mother, and your father. But I'm on my own now, and this is my decision. I shall move into Les Palmes as soon as I can settle my affairs in Paris. It won't take long. I hope to arrive in September. Now let's have supper shall we? We can talk some more as we eat.' She walked towards the door, picking up her jacket and her bag. Felix observed her with a mixture of admiration and trepidation, realizing how little he really knew his mother.

They enjoyed their supper; Felix was a familiar figure at the restaurant, and the maitre d' seated them at a good table by the window. Though it was nearly dark, they could watch people strolling past: lovers arm- in- arm, an elderly couple talking earnestly, a single man carrying a little dog. Marthe looked away, she missed the companionship of her husband acutely, and while it was enjoyable to spend the evening with Felix, later she would be returning to Les Palmes on her own. They talked briefly about the issues surrounding her move, storing her furniture, which for the moment she would leave in Paris, and sorting out some of the financial changes. But Felix was unable to relax, he felt uneasy, and apprehensive. Having said goodbye to Marthe, he returned to his flat, where Valerie had returned from work, and was watching TV while eating a salad. She had found the wine which he had opened for Marthe. There was very little left.

'Shall I open another bottle?' He joined her on the sofa. 'I've got some news!'

Valerie nodded her head, her eyes were fixed on the large TV screen, some animal seemed to be eating another animal. It looked very gruesome.

'Yes.' She had not heard him properly, there was a terrifying noise as a pack of wolves appeared. Felix could not bear to look, and rose to find a second bottle. Valerie seemed unperturbed at the gruesome scene in front of her, she was wrapped up in the scene of death and violence.

He passed her a fresh glass 'So. My news!' he said. She held up her hand, 'Wait Felix!' She still hadn't looked at him. The programme finally ended, but Felix, disappointed and rather annoyed, had gone to take a shower having decided to tell Valerie another time. He failed to do so for some time.

SEPTEMBER 2000

In the city of Toulouse another family, mother and son were also busy. It was Friday, Annie taking two supervisions at the university and Charlie clock watching at school. He was nine years old. They had been living in Toulouse for a year now. Charlie had accepted the uprooting of his life from rural Somerset to this southern French city without complaint. In one year he had become fluent in French, absorbing the incessant swear words of his new friends. He had grown, and become very independent, walking to school every day, leaving promptly at eight o'clock. Annie loved to watch him go, from her fourth floor windows; listening first as his steps faded down the stairwell which all the apartments shared. Then she would see him walking down the narrow street, brick paved, heavily shaded by the tall, close built buildings. This was the very heart of the city, and she could glimpse the spire of the cathedral of St.Sernin if she leaned very far out from the high casement window of her kitchen. Charlie, backpack containing few books, more pencils than necessary and his sports shirt, continued past the boulangerie… There was a pause here, as he admired the display of bread, croissants and pains aux chocolat. Inhaling deeply he continued his way, skirting the great plane trees on the corner (always important to watch one's feet here) and then…lost to view. She imagined him walking on, through the square where already the old men sat, drinking coffee, or grappa, reading their newspapers, scratching their dogs. Past the great entrance to the indoor food market, always cabbage leaves and parings of vegetables at the entrance, and down the narrow alley that ran past the market, now he turned left and in through the gates. Jostling the other children. Awake now, laughing. Annie was thirty two. Married. Separated… now making a life in a city far from her former home.

She had been invited to join the university's horticulture department by a colleague, who had settled in Toulouse some years earlier and who was eager to help her. Adventurous by nature, and seeking to distance herself from her collapsed marriage, she jumped at the offer, and with few misgivings moved herself and her son, then eight years old, eight hundred miles south to a new life. It was the autumn of 1999. It had worked out well and, once the language difficulties were overcome, Annie proved a popular teacher, whose classes were rarely missed. She had rented a flat as near to the great Place du Capitol, the centre of Toulouse, as she could afford. She wanted life all around her; to see across the narrow street to the flats opposite, to hear the buzz of traffic circling the square and to listen to the regular chiming of the hours from St.Sernin. 'No more empty fields, dark afternoons and listless sheep,' she said to herself as she hauled her shopping up four flights of stairs, pushing the door open with her shoulder as she turned the key in the old brass lock. Unconcernedly she would observe the lives of the families in the apartments opposite: movements around windows, adults crossing rooms, sitting at tables. She would even interpret the TV programmes they watched every evening. It was sometimes noisy with arguments, babies crying, and children arguing, but it was company and she never grew bored or lonely.

The apartment was shabby but spacious, with high ceilings and plaster mouldings. Long light windows, and beautiful wooden floors, uneven and worn. She loved the doors most of all: tall double doors into every room with great metal fastenings and smooth handles. She left them open that first summer (until the heat of the street forced her to close them) so the air flowed through and the flat felt as large as possible. Charlie had the quietest and biggest bedroom at the back overlooking the communal courtyard, but his books, pencils, scooter, clothes, shoes were in every room. They were both untidy.

At first she was teaching only two days at the College, but soon after arriving, she had secured a contract with Toulouse council to oversee and design the annual planting of all the urns, tubs and planters of the parks and squares and communal gardens. Her MA from the University of Bath had been a study of Mediterranean flora and specifically plants for dry climates, and it was this that had recommended her to the city authorities .This city work kept her out of the flat almost daily, which suited her well. Annie was an active and lively woman.

Her move to Toulouse had been made against an unhappy background of strenuous opposition from Ralph, her husband, from whom she had been separated for four years. The rows over the phone had been exhausting and continuous, and continued after she and Charlie had settled in their new home.

The question of contact with Charlie was the ongoing problem. On this particular Friday it had rained in Toulouse and both Annie and Charlie had returned home wet and irritable. Charlie had thrown his damp shirt on the floor, and Annie had forgotten to pick up fruit for supper. Annie started cooking their evening meal, and looked at her son who was sitting at the table. 'Charlie, phone your father now, it's a good time. He'll be at home.'

'No- he won't. He'll be at the pub.'

'Try now. Please. Don't make me cross, do as you are asked.'

'No.' Charlie who was building a complicated Lego space-ship got down from the table, and disappeared into his room. Annie sighed. She found her hands were shaking. Nothing distressed her more than these battles with her son, it was simply that Charlie hated talking on the phone. It seemed to underline his distance from his old life, and he could never think what to say in answer to his father's questions. Normally a chatty child, he became tongue tied and shy. It all felt artificial. Their conversations followed a familiar pattern:

'How was your day?' Ralph asked,

'Ok.'

'What have you been doing at school?'

'Usual stuff.'

'And tomorrow? Is it chess?'

'Yes.'

and so on. It was frustrating for both of them, and Annie tried very hard not to listen. Charlie stayed in his room until supper, and they did not speak again about Ralph.

Meanwhile in England, Annie's mother, Claire, was writing a letter to her daughter. She was conscientious, filling the pages with gossip, weather and news of the dog, Annie's dog, left behind to Charlie's anguish, as life in a city flat was clearly unsuitable, or so Annie said. It still caused Charlie a hard knot in the stomach to think of Arthur.

Claire, a widow, was now in her sixties and living happily with a man she had met at a Christmas party. Tony proved a happy choice and he moved quickly in to Claire's cottage, taking over responsibility for the vegetable garden. The only cloud on Claire's horizon was her daughter's decision to move to Toulouse. Claire had not approved. 'It's risky and if I may say so, selfish!' she said firmly, 'really Annie, how many more times are you going to change course?' This struck deep and Annie flared up, 'It's a great opportunity for me and Charlie, I need a new challenge.'

'And where is this place? This Toulouse?'

'In France! The south west. It's not far, Mother! An hour and a half from Gatwick- you could do the journey from here, door to door in half a day. It's probably nearer than- Scotland! We can telephone.' Annie added rather lamely.

'And what of Charlie? You're uprooting him too. He's already coping with losing his father. You should consider him.'

Annie flared up again, she felt it was an unfair comment. 'He has not lost his father. We are,' she emphasised, 'separated: Charlie can see him for holidays and at half term.'

'Well I think it's selfish.' she repeated. 'There must be perfectly good opportunities nearer to home but maybe you haven't looked.'

Annie had sighed. She realised that her mother was thinking also of herself- she would miss Charlie- and he would miss her- but Annie was convinced that the opportunity was too good to miss. She needed a fresh start, and her interview in Toulouse had encouraged her. The city was lively and had fine buildings, and she was drawn to its cosmopolitan atmosphere. After her interview, she had eaten a delicious lunch sitting at a little table on the pavement outside a café. In the sun! It had all felt very different from life near Bath and the job would be a real challenge. Annie liked challenges. Mother and daughter continued to talk, with Annie trying hard not to become exasperated, 'Charlie will learn French, and the education is far better. With my salary we can live quite well and…it's an opportunity mother- be pleased for me… for us…'

*

But Claire was unconvinced and had not felt able to give Annie much help as she packed up of her English life. She leaned on Tony in Annie's last weeks, and kept herself busy organising jaunts, and planning a holiday. Tony tried to keep her spirits up and was secretly looking forward to the arrival of Arthur, a dog of steady manners and loving disposition. Tony loved living with Claire, especially working in the garden; he was growing vegetables at the far end, behind a low wall, where there was a bench, and she sat and watched him, as he dug, and lifted, and tied in.

'Always something to do,' he waved at her as he carefully stepped over Arthur. 'We'll be eating peas soon, and then the strawberries!' Claire knew that she was lucky; they both liked the same things- walking Arthur, going to the cinema, visiting local gardens, returning with a plant that that had caught their eye. Claire had much to be grateful for, and she knew it.

Tony knew that he would miss Charlie. His only child, a son, had lived in New Zealand for many years and he hardly knew his grandchildren. He had enjoyed teaching him to fish, in the stream that drifted slowly past the bottom of the garden, and to play chess, at which Charlie showed great potential.

'Goodbye old chap.' Tony hugged him a final time. Charlie tried to smile,

'Look after Arthur, won't you.' He said, his voice a little wobbly. Claire stood with Tony by her side, holding back her tears. 'Bye darlings! Good luck! Phone when you get there!' She turned away and went into the cottage. 'I hope it turns out well.' She thought to herself as she filled the kettle for a restorative cup of tea. But Annie had made mistakes before, and Claire was not too optimistic.

The next day Annie and Charlie flew out to Toulouse, and Tony took Claire and Arthur for a long weekend to the Isle of Wight. They were all trying very hard not to think of each other.

CHAPTER 3

The first weekend after his mother's arrival, Felix stayed at Les Palmes, helping her to settle in. He enjoyed sleeping in the large oak panelled bed with its thick mattress and heavy linen sheets. The room was down a long corridor at some distance from his mother's- she had chosen the best of course- but his also over looked the garden. It was peaceful and quiet and a great contrast from his flat in Toulouse where there was always traffic and the endless hooting of car horns. Here it was dark as well as silent. Felix was not sure that he would like to live in the country, though he had enjoyed the eerie call of two owls during the night and had listened to the collared doves in the morning in the garden. Propping himself up on the rather old, lumpy pillows, he admired the dark red, flowered wallpaper, the deep crimson rug, the old fashioned heavy furniture. An over large mirror crowded the marble mantel- badly marked, it reflected his image back at him as he prepared to get up. Felix was a tall man, now in his mid thirties, his hair was dark and straight. He had a tendency to keep it rather long, sweeping it out of his eyes with an impatient gesture. He wore expensive clothes with unconscious grace, and attracted much attention from the young women of his circle in Toulouse. Valerie enjoyed his style and often bought him clothes.

After two days Felix felt able to leave his mother and return to Toulouse. 'She'll be fine!' he assured Valerie as they walked to their favourite restaurant.

'I am sure she will, it's her family home. It's a coming back for her isn't it?' Valerie did not know Marthe well but saw her move from Paris as a logical step in order to be near her only child. She took Felix's arm as they entered the restaurant. She knew that they were a good looking couple.

*

By early October Marthe had settled into the rhythm of her new life. She enjoyed the now fresh mornings, -breathing deeply as she opened her bedroom shutters. It all felt very different from Paris! The garden lay green, tangled, uncared for below her. She admired its high brick walls, still covered in neglected roses, and climbers that she could not identify. There was a path meandering away from the house-much covered in moss and weeds-but still discernible. It gave a little structure to the neglected planting. Two wide borders lined the walls at each side, with shrubs, now full of bindweed and tall thistles...or was it something else? Marthe cursed her ignorance. Something would have to be done. Her first priority was to clear the orchard, where she had been told her mother liked to rest, but it was a dispiriting sight. It had once been planted in straight lines, and she identified cherry, apple and pear, much of the fruit now humming with wasps. Brambles had entangled and smothered the branches. At the centre there was a fine quince, its boughs hanging with yellow fruit almost to the tall grass below. She had tasted the apricots and peaches, but their fruit was small and hard and covered in ugly black spots, and not even the birds were interested.

She had by now explored the whole garden, pushing through the brambles and high nettles, and uncovered a pair of tumbling brick sheds, their tiled roofs gaping in part to the sky, and a greenhouse, also in poor condition. There was an old fig here, with black fruit that was tempting. She pulled one from the tree, it almost fell into her hand. She tasted it expectantly, it was sticky and delicious! Beyond the sheds was the high wall that separated the garden from the river.

The house was lovely from this, the furthest point. All of the six windows on the first floor had balconies, wrought iron, once painted black. The centre window, wider than the others, consisted of two glazed doors, designed to flood the upper landing with sun light. The ground floor was shielded from view by the long pergola of the terrace, it was overhung with a wisteria she thought and maybe a clematis. Their flowers were long over so she found them difficult to identify. She wondered if her mother had stood where she was now, enjoying the warmth of the brick wall, looking at her house. Perhaps collecting the apples as she held Marthe's hand, guiding her through the orchard. She shut her eyes, trying to force a memory...nothing came.

*

Tracing the warm brick wall with her hand, she found the raised wooden frame of a garden gate hidden by ivy. She walked to the nearest shed, and entered cautiously, but could find no useful tool. Frustrated, she walked briskly to the house, stumbling on the uneven path and pulled open the drawer next to the sink, took her gloves and grabbed the scissors. She felt strangely excited as she approached the gate. The scissors, hardly suitable for their task bit uneasily into the ivy, but she hacked and cut into it, and into the branches of an old honeysuckle, pulling both away as she tugged, scratching her arms. It was a green wooden gate, the paint, mostly peeled away and flaking at her touch. It was bolted. Despite pulling hard at the old bolts, she could not move them, they had not been pulled back for years, and stood firm. Vexed, Marthe abandoned her struggle, standing back to look again at the gate and its frame. She needed help in this garden, she reflected. Young Jean having failed to turn up for the last two weeks, had been dismissed. He left scowling, ungrateful to the end, Marthe reflected. She tried not to think of the money she had paid him over the last years.

Marthe decided to walk into the village, it was a crisp sunny morning. She enjoyed the exercise and it gave a structure to her day. She carried her basket on her arm and wore a straw hat against the autumn sun. She was becoming quite tanned, and her Parisian clothes now hung, unwanted, in the cupboards. She wore a cotton shirt, pale grey to match her hair, and linen trousers. A deep blue sweater was draped around her shoulders… She looked much taller than anyone she met, and was conscious of the glances of the men drinking at the pavement tables of the cafe by the fountain.

The town did not boast a wide range of shops, but sufficient. There was an excellent charcuterie; whose cool, white-glazed tiles and air conditioning were welcoming on a hot morning. There she bought local ham- sliced thin on the cutter, brown eggs and for a treat, the black boudin sausage. There was also a small supermarket, two pharmacies , an ironmonger and two butchers. There were three boulangeries, a post office, and a surprising number of hairdressers, one of which doubled as a ladies' dress shop. Marthe glanced in the window, there was a selection of clothes, none of which she could imagine herself wearing.

There was a wide central square with a solid brick fountain- once used by cattle on their way to the market- now ' restored 'with summer geraniums still in flower in pots, on the rim.

The Hotel de Ville was situated here, the tricolor hanging from the first floor, and there was a war memorial with a low wrought iron rail. Three cafes lined the wide street, which ran straight through the town and circled the square. It was always busy in the morning. The town 'died' as the tall brick church chimed the noon alarm. The shops rolled down their shutters, the traffic disappeared, the tabac owner dragged in the newsstand, and the bank put up its solid door. Lunch! Marthe looked wistfully into the restaurant next to the fountain-still serving meals outside, under a spreading mulberry. She would have loved to eat, in its shade but hesitated- feeling out of place. She ate alone at home every day, with book and radio for company and could not quite see herself sitting in a restaurant. Solitary. A widow. (How she hated that word). Still, no time for tears. Marthe walked briskly home, feeling the morning sun now warm on her shoulders, her jumper tucked into her basket. She began looking forward to Felix's arrival on Sunday, with Valerie she believed. She would enjoy planning and cooking the lunch.

In St.Girou she had not gone unnoticed. She was so clearly not a local born resident: her clothes, her haircut, her accent all marked her out. The local traders soon recognized her, as she purchased expensive cuts of meat, and the best cheese, and her choice of wine was not limited to the cheap local reds. She was seen walking in the afternoons, upright and full of energy, even as far as the next village, some four kilometres away. But few people thought anymore about her once she was out of sight. All the same news gradually circulated in a town where newcomers were a rarity, the mayor being the chief informant. It was quickly established that she was Mme Le Brun and had moved into 'Les Palmes', the house shut up for many years. Who was she? Where did she come from?

The gossip drifted around, but no one was that interested. It was known that she had 'sacked' Jean the gardener, but most people thought he was lazy and a bad lot, so his dismissal raised few eyebrows, and the gossip did not last long.

That same warm October day welcomed Felix as he strolled into the Place du Capitol from his apartment beside the river Garonne. He was as usual smartly, but casually dressed. It was Wednesday, he had no plans for the day. Maybe a little shopping for the supper he had promised Valerie: fish, possibly some squid if they were available. He would buy everything from the daily market in the Place St.Georges. It would be full of autumn produce, apples, mushrooms, walnuts, toma-toes, zucchini, peppers. But first a late breakfast.

Arriving in the Place du Capitol he took a seat at the front of his usual cafe, ordered a café crème and a croissant. Stretching out his legs, he looked at the world around him. There was the usual flow of traffic edging its way slowly around the square, mostly heading for the underground car park. An exceedingly pretty girl, a sleeveless summer dress exposing her brown arms, passed in front of him glancing not so discreetly at him; she gave a faint smile but didn't stop. There was a large flat backed truck, on the other side of the square, its platform filled with tall shrubs and grasses. It was parked at the foot of the steps of the town hall. He watched it idly. Workmen were unloading some of the taller plants, also heavy bags of compost, and shouting to each other. They were, he realised, the city gardeners- planting up for the winter. He drank some coffee, ate his croissant (he just might order another) and let his eyes wander again. The traffic continued to move slowly, scooters weaving in and out their horns hooting. He wondered idly if the pretty girl would pass by again. Pedestrians completely ignored the traffic, walking unconcernedly across the narrow cobbled street. The whole square pulsed with life, and the glorious brick facades of the Place du Capitol glowed. He admired opposite him the Capitol itself, with its long rows of windows, edged with raised brick- the French flag fluttering proudly on its roof. To his right was the Hotel Opera, with its green awnings and smart glass doors, their brass handles shining in the sun. Following his move to Toulouse, he had eaten there frequently with his father, who stayed there in preference to Les Palmes. That was before Xavier's sudden death. Felix could still hardly believe what had happened; he missed his father almost painfully. They had enjoyed much together: music and conversation about concerts, discussing the performances they heard, always over a good meal and good wine. Xavier had been responsible for developing Felix's musical talents, encouraging him to attend the conservatoire, and hoping for his son to have a career as a concert pianist. Felix now missed his guiding hand and gentle presence and for many months he had been unable to work properly or enjoy his time with Valerie. He and Marthe grieved but separately, neither able to discuss their feelings with the other, and the distance between them, one in Paris the other in Toulouse, made sharing their grief difficult.

Avoiding looking at the Hotel, Felix had raised a hand to summon the 'garcon' for a second croissant, when a sudden noise and movement caught his attention. The garden truck, had lurched forward, dislodging several bushes, a lot of earth and a small figure off the back.

Oblivious to what had happened, the truck moved slowly forward. Felix jumped to his feet, no one else appeared to have noticed that a boy was lying immobile on the cobbles. Ignoring the traffic he walked rapidly across the square, and found the child, both knees bleeding, earth on hands and shorts, struggling to his feet. He was clutching a chessboard and bending down to pick up his chessmen.

'Can I help you? Are you hurt?'

'No, I'm not. I just need to find my chess men.' (The boy hadn't looked up.)

'Let's look together, shall we?'

Seeing that the injured child was near tears, he squatted down, rummaged quickly in the spilt soil, and pulled out the little figures. The boy helped him, sniffing, his cheeks were very pink. Within a few moments, the job was done. Felix stood shaking the soil off his hands. 'Was this child on his own?' he wondered. No one else had come to look for him. He stared at him and without much thought, asked,

'What about a drink? A chocolat chaud? I am sitting just over there. We could wipe your knees and hands too, and your face.'

The boy looked at him for the first time and saw a tall man with a brown face, and dark eyes, smiling.

'Yes. Thanks. I am Charlie'-helpfully-'I'm English.' He held out his right hand, very French.

'Well. I'm Felix. Hello.'

He led the way across the square, carrying the board, and Charlie followed, the chess men cupped in his hands. They sat down and Felix asked,

'What will it be then?'

'Chocolat chaud, please.'

'With a croissant?'

Charlie smiled for the first time,

'Yes, please.'

The chocolat and croissant arrived, with a second coffee for Felix, and Charlie sat back in his chair. His knees, rather grazed, had stopped bleeding, but were still sore and earthy. Felix offered the paper napkin instead of his own white handkerchief, and Charlie dried his face. They sat in silence, the boy picking up the pastry flakes with a wet finger. Felix watched him. 'I used to do that,' he thought. He was musing quietly when he heard an angry shout. A woman, in workman's dungarees, hair flying behind her, was racing across the square, waving her arms. She had a trowel in one hand, and Felix looked up with alarm. She reached the table in record time. Stopping in a whirl- she grabbed the boy by both shoulders.

'Hi, Mum!'

'What are you doing? I thought I had lost you. How dare you wander off? You know you must never never do that.' She paused briefly for breath.

'I'm ok. Mum. Look, I've got a croissant.'

This incensed her further. She seemed not to have noticed his dishevelled state, but continued, 'But why are you eating here?' and for the first time looked at Felix. People at adjacent tables were now staring. Felix eager to deflect her wrath, from, he assumed her son, interrupted,

'Please, let me explain...'

'Who are you? '

Felix was rather surprised by her manner; he had after all acted out of kindness, but continued, 'Please, calm down.' His words had the opposite effect.

Annie, exploded again. 'I find my son' (so he had got that right) 'eating with a total stranger, who had presumably enticed him with an offer of food.' Charlie, rather pale now, tugged at his mother's arm,

'Mum! Listen. I fell off the truck and he... his name is Francois,'

'Felix, actually.'

Charlie nodded, 'Felix, picked me up, and helped me find my chessmen. I was all bloody!' he continued dramatically. He pointed at the table, where a soiled napkin lay, and the chessmen, covered in earth.

Annie looked at the table, nodded her head, slowly calming down. Felix noticed her hair, very blond and curly; she had a rather artless manner and wore blue dungarees with a tee shirt tucked underneath. Looking more carefully now at her son she finally noticed the grazed knees, dirty shorts and hands.

Felix tried to take the initiative. 'Please, sit down. Your son was very shocked. He seems to have fallen off the lorry! He pointed to where it stood at the far end of the square.

'Yes.' Annie said, 'I am working there, we are planting out for the autumn.' Felix did not entirely follow this, but held out his hand: 'I am Felix.'

Annie, pulling a chair close to Charlie's, sat and held out her wrist. Felix touched it lightly, he noticed that her hands were very muddy. 'I am Annie.' And, after considerable thought, 'Thank you. I owe you an apology I guess.' She turned back to Charlie who was draining the dregs of his chocolat and sorting out the chessmen.

'You should not have left…it is as simple as that…I did not know where you were …and for a moment, well…. Anyway no harm seems to have been done.' She looked at his knees and hands, 'we had better go inside and wash those now.' They both stood up, Charlie gave Felix a rueful smile, 'Thanks, the drink was nice. And the pain chocolat! Goodbye.' he extended his hand politely. Annie looked again at Felix, noticing for the first time his pleasant smile, and his expensive linen jacket.

'Yes, thank you, sorry about the misunderstanding. How much do I owe you?' Felix watched as she dug about in her dungarees.

"No, no! My treat.' Felix smiled at Charlie.

'Well thank you. That is very kind. Goodbye.' She turned away, pushing Charlie in front of her and gathered the chessmen into a capacious cotton bag. They disappeared into the cafe.

Felix was alone again. The truck continued to circle the square, the new plants were dug into the huge stone urns. The angry mother, he now realised was overseeing the men. He watched as she returned to work, firmly holding the boy's hand. She was a small, slim woman in her work clothes, yet apparently, the 'boss'. An unusual situation.

Felix rose and walked back across the square, carefully avoiding the workmen and their fiery director. It had been a surprisingly eventful start to his day.

CHAPTER 4

Annie had not left England on a 'whim' the word Claire used when describing it to her friends. She continued to bemoan their departure. 'So selfish, really… throwing up her life here, Charlie's education, her home, her job and,' disloyally, 'her dog.'

Claire had taken over this responsibility with a great show of reluctance. But, in fact, it had worked out rather well: the dog, a middle-aged spaniel, was quite content with his new lifestyle, indeed, he appreciated a stricter routine especially a daily walk, which Annie had not always managed, plus regular meal times and an early bed. Tony, rather a sedentary man, bought some walking boots and, to his surprise, began to enjoy more regular exercise. They had now explored the countryside in their part of Kent, the narrow paths, open heathlands, small woodlands. Even on the worst of days, when the rain had made every route a mud trail, they set off together after lunch, determined to 'give the dog a run.' It did them all good, though the car now smelt of wet dog.

Tony enjoyed walking along behind Claire, admiring her steady gait, the swing of her arms and her round bottom. It was a time for silence between them; only occasionally did the dog need calling to heel. Arthur was not an adventurous type- sniffing along, quite content, head down.

Claire's happiness was partly clouded by the anxiety she always felt about Annie and Charlie, the current issue, it was October, was, 'Are they coming home for Christmas?' It was the thorny problem for them all.

It was the week of Charlie's tumble off the lorry, and Claire was sitting at the kitchen table, writing to Annie. She felt that her grandson should have Christmas in England with her, doing all the traditional things. Not so Annie. How could it be? It was not simple at all; she had Ralph demanding that Charlie join him in his flat near Bath, and now her mother pressing her in a letter. The day that she received her mother's letter, Annie looked across at Charlie. They were having supper. He seemed fine; he had a chess match at the weekend and would be busy all day Saturday. He was, so the school told her, very promising for his age, with a power of concentration, that was not apparent to her. She saw no sign of it at home, where he flitted about with lego and books and homework in a disordered manner.

'So are you looking forward to Saturday? Will it be fun? Who else is going?' Charlie answered her enthusiastically. His rather solemn face lit up as he explained, 'Mum, it's a tournament against the clock. There will be kids from,' he waved his arms, ' all over. And medals, for the winners!' Annie smiled at him, 'You already have several of those! Maybe a cup?'

'That would be great. I am going to practise now.'

'Hold on a minute.' Charlie was already getting down from the table- clearing his plate, scraping back his chair.

'We need to think about Christmas. I've had a letter from Grandma, and she and Tony are very keen for us to stay with them.'

'Mum, it's October.'

'I know but,' she paused, seeing the weakness of her position, 'people like to plan.'

He was a nine year-old boy. Plan? This meant nothing to him. Practice for Saturday was in his head. 'You decide! You always do.'

He pushed the dishes away, and got out his chessboard. Silence fell.

Annie passed a quiet evening, trying not to get depressed. She concentrated on the priorities in her life: Charlie, work, home and friends. Rather few.

But the negatives were there too. Ralph! Ralph! Ralph! His name bounced off the walls at her. Even at this distance and with little contact- she thought of him, almost daily. How could she not? They had lived together for five years. How could he be forgotten?

She thought about their early years. They had met at horticultural college- each following the three year degree course. Annie- straight from school and home- 'hit' college running. It was her first taste of independence, having lived at home until then. She was eighteen, pretty in a tangled way, her blond hair tied back but escaping from its band, her clothes rather 'bohemian.' Full of interest in her work, she was talented and ambitious. In her first year she shared a flat with fellow students, enjoying the freedom from her parents and their tidy ordered home. She ate chaotically: pizzas, pasta, raw salad, sliced bread, milk from the carton. She drank beer, and cider and smoked occasionally. She sang in a mediocre band, her soprano voice barely audible against a booming background. Gigs. Parties. It was Fun! Fun!

She fell in love. Ralph, 3 years older, more experienced sexually, led Annie into a completely new world. The Course interested and stimulated her and she rarely missed her lectures. Her tutors were encouraging and her course work won regular praise. She knew that she was 'good', recalling the complicated names of plants with ease, and building up a portfolio of work. She worked very hard, even following a late night with the band or love making with Ralph. She lived happily in the student lodgings and then in her second year moved in with Ralph into a draughty attic flat above a newsagent. She had not told Claire about this. Smitten with love, Annie waited for Ralph's foot on the stairs up to their rooms, watching the way he entered, smiling, shabby and long limbed. She loved the smell of his clothes, the way he rolled his sleeves up, his long strides as they walked to the pub.

They had a shared interest in their courses, helping each other with projects and research, though Annie was more serious, identified as an ambitious and able student. Her grades were always higher than Ralph's, who had almost drifted into the course. His school results had not been good enough for the University course that his parents had hoped for him. He did not lack ability, but stamina. He was easily distracted, and, good at sport, had devoted much school time to football and cricket. Tall, with blond hair, he began going out with girls. A distraction that explained his poor results. He shrugged off the disappointment of his grades, and light-heartedly looked around, and signed up for the course to be ...a gardener. He spoke to his father, who stared uncomprehendingly at his son,

'It takes three years... To be a gardener...?'

Ralph stuck to his guns, 'I'm not going to be a gardener. I'm going to be a landscape architect.'

'Ah.' He doubted whether Ralph even knew what that was.

Ralph and Annie were an established 'pair' in their final year. Her chief interest had become dry Mediterranean plants- plants for hot climates, which with water shortages and global warming gave her a very up to the minute edge. Ralph could not compete and did not try to.

'You must get a good degree Ralph. It's so important.' She was cooking some rice and courgette for supper- her hair almost falling into the pan. She had been thinking that day of the options open to her, after the summer exams. She needed a job, but long term, it would have to have a future. 'Oh leave off Annie, I'll be fine. Stop fretting.'

He leaned over, took a courgette, gave her a kiss on the neck, lifting her hair.

The pregnancy hit them like a thunder clap. It was unex-pected, overwhelming, a frightening piece of news. Untimely too- they were in the thick of their exam preparations. They looked at each other, appalled. It was too momentous an event for them to be able to discuss it. They acted as though nothing had happened, but both of them were in near panic, and Annie was overcome with anxiety. She had thrown everything away- the work, the plans, her future. She could not see beyond the prospect of a ...baby. She tried not to blame Ralph, but she looked at him with fresh eyes. 'Was he able to care for her and a baby? would he be a good father? what would life now be like for her ? and money...how would they live ?' Worries consumed her, and the exams passed in a kind of fog. They packed up the flat and left without saying goodbye to tutors or friends.

Annie returned home. Claire after one look at her daughter, and understood. She took control, immediately, recognising that Annie was once more her responsibility. Ralph she refused to see. Throughout the months of pregnancy, Annie lived at home in Kent, she and Ralph spoke on the phone, and met when they could, without a car, it was difficult. Their college results came through, Annie had missed the top award: her papers were not as good as expected, which Annie rationalised was not surprising. Who else amongst her fellow students was reeling with shock? But she had won high praise for all her course work, so all was not lost.

Ralph had done badly, but seemed not to mind. His father would support him for a further few months, and then he would have to find work. They did not discuss his imminent fatherhood, Ralph was still only twenty four, and it was hoped that he could make a career for himself in spite of every thing.

Annie and Ralph married quietly. The baby arrived safely, 'a son!' exclaimed Ralph, as though that made all the difference. They settled together in a rented cottage, a short drive away from Claire. (Who is paying for that? Claire asked.) She knew the answer of course. She was now reconciled to the situation, and the arrival of a grandchild enabled her to put aside her earlier hostility to Ralph.

'How's Charlie?' was always her first question, in her regular phone calls.

'He's on solids! I've just fed him. Opens his mouth like a bird!' Ralph could not hide his pride and enthusiasm. Annie was relieved to hear them chat, Charlie it seemed had healed the rift, and she smiled to herself as she heard them exchange baby talk. Life was going well; Charlie thrived and Ralph found work with a local landscape garden outfit. The pay just about met the bills, and Ralph seemed to benefit from the routine of daily life. He adored Charlie, rushing home in time to bathe and bed him. He liked the chaos of their cottage, baby clothes, wipes, toys, bowls of mashed peas, and little muslin cloths smelling of milk. It was great he thought, holding the baby over one shoulder, gently patting his back, listening for the burp. He and Annie were joined together in parenthood- a much closer bond than any that had gone before. They talked endlessly about Charlie, watching his every move, noting every change. They had no social life at all now, no pubs, no gigs for Annie, and no football with his mates for Ralph. It was all about Charlie.

This lasted for about nine months. By which time they were both ready to look further than the walls of the cottage and Annie was missing the challenge of study or work. Claire came over weekly, bringing lunch and a new toy, she tried hard not to notice the untidiness of her daughter's home, but could not stop picking up clothes, piling dishes in the sink, throwing open windows. One day Annie found her scouring the bath, 'Mum. Stop it. Please. If you want to help, start heating up Charlie's lunch!'

Claire was hot and vexed. 'How can you live like this?'

'Because I do! I like it! I'm not like you!' Annie stormed through the narrow kitchen, her arms full of wet washing. In fact, Annie did not want to live like this for much longer. She was planning to return to her studies. She tried discussing this with Ralph, 'I need to work, it's really important to me. This life is not enough for me.'

'Well it should be.' Ralph looked at her, 'My mother never worked, she looked after my father and her children.'

'It's different now. You know that. I want a career, and I've worked hard for it. It's not about not loving you or Charlie, but there has to be something more.' He listened but could not agree; he was bitterly disappointed, for him life in the cottage was just fine.

Difficult years followed. Ralph changed jobs regularly, but managed to pay most of the bills, and Annie balanced caring for Charlie with studying; she was determined to work for a further degree. The marriage held together, and Charlie was the main reason for this, but in her heart of hearts Annie knew that the love she had felt for Ralph had been based on a weak foundation and was slipping away. She managed to secure a

Masters' degree, working in the cottage at the kitchen table when Charlie was asleep, and then secured a post at Bath in the horticultural department. But as her marriage broke down, and she and Ralph separated, she began looking for a change, talking to colleagues at her work place, and scanning the university courses for possible openings. She had never thought of Toulouse, but when a good friend suggested applying, for a teaching position there, and as it met her special area of knowledge, she filled in the application form. Annie hadn't consulted either her mother or Ralph. She liked a challenge.

CHAPTER 5

Marthe drove into Toulouse, following the now familiar route. It was mid October, and she now knew her way to the carpark in the Place St. Georges. She was going to have her hair cut at a hairdresser recommended by Valerie. She waited impatiently for her stylist, leafing through a copy of the interior design magazine which had been passed to her. Her attention was caught by an article on the restoration of a grand chateau in the Loire valley, and in particular a photo of the large salon. It had a striking wall paper, cream with green climbers, eglantine and ivy, she thought. Marthe stared. 'Could I copy this idea? It might be the first step in changing the salon!' her mind began working busily. She had been thinking, since her arrival, of redecorating the two main rooms, that led off the hall, but had not felt much inspiration. But this wall paper set her imagination running.

'Madame.' The girl was waiting for her. Marthe took a further look at the photo. She had made up her mind, she would find a design shop as soon as her hair was done. Two hours later Marthe was sitting in a décor shop in a commercial part of Toulouse. She had found it easily, there was a life-size, cut out figure of a man; in a painters' smock, beret and red scarf, carrying a ladder, standing on the façade. The shop was large, it supplied paints, brushes, rollers and a wide selection of cleaning materials. There was a strong smell of turpentine. The section for wall papers was at the rear, where there were chairs and sofas and tables. A pile of wall paper sample books was now in front of her. They were large and heavy. She called to one of the assistants, he came over eagerly, 'I saw the paper I am looking for in a magazine.' He nodded. 'It might be a Zoffany.' She remembered the name from the article. Several minutes later he had found a sample of the paper, it was a lovely combination of green and deep cream. 'That's it!' Marthe was delighted. She was already thinking of curtains, rugs, lamps and sofas. The assistant agreed to visit and measure the room the following day. Marthe drove home with her head full of ideas, her new project would occupy her for several months, and in time transform her home.

*

Felix was sitting quietly in the cathedral of St. Sernin, a notebook on his knee. He loved both its fine architecture and its many concerts. It was cool, almost dark in summer. Now in early November it felt more chilly. He had been there for over an hour... listening to the choir, who were singing Monteverdi's Vespers. His attention was very focused. Felix was a music critic, writing for the widely circulated regional newspaper. His review would be with the editor in twenty four hours, and published by the weekend. The conductor Jacques Martin was a friend; Jacques was a distinguished music scholar, who also composed church music for his choir. Felix often drove him to the concerts which Felix had to review. Both men enjoyed Felix's fast car and despite a thirty year age difference in age, they enjoyed each other's company. Performances were generally followed by a good supper, good wine and good conversation. Neither was married, both had 'attachments' from time to time.

The music came to a close. The audience, some one hundred people, stood up, the choir withdrew to a vestibule. Felix put his notebook and pen into his jacket pocket. He was already planning what he would write, and walked to the west door. He chatted briefly to an acquaintance, and then strode out into the cobbled street- straight into a slim figure hurrying toward the square.

He apologized quickly, 'Sorry I wasn't looking.'

The woman stopped, clutching sheet music to her, and her handbag, which Felix had knocked out of her hand, fell to the ground. Felix, bending down to pick it up, caught her eye as he stood up: 'Do we know each other?'

'No. I don't think we do.' He handed over the bag, wiping it briefly on his sleeve. She began walking away, but Felix was sure that he recognized her. He spoke again, 'Yes, we met in the square. You have a son... He plays chess. He also falls off the back of lorries.' He now had Annie's full attention. She looked at him closely. 'Yes of course. Francois. Wasn't it?'

'Well, an easy mistake.' He held out his hand, 'It's Felix. Were you singing?'

They shook hands, but Felix was not rewarded with a smile. 'Oh yes, I was there. Second row soprano.'

'Can I walk with you to the square? I enjoyed the concert so much...'

Annie relaxed a little, carefully putting her music in her bag, she replied, "Really? That's good. We've worked hard on it.'

'Yes, Jacques always works his choir hard! But the results are there for all to hear. It was really very good. Maybe the tenors were a little strong.'

'You know Jacques?' She had frowned a little at his name, but Felix moved smoothly on.

'Yes, we're old friends.' They were walking side- by side-now along the narrow, cobbled pavement, dodging other people, it was a busy night.

'And do you go to all his concerts?'

'It's my job' Felix shrugged, as if it were of no importance. Annie stopped walking and looked, more carefully, at him.

'Your job? To listen to music! How wonderful!'

Felix felt very gratified- most people responded to his 'job' with surprise, or worse, indifference. Writing about music lay outside most people's lives and interests. He had always been somewhat solitary in his work.... Attending concerts, travelling to venues, flying to festivals, then writing his 'review' for au editor, who did not know Mozart from…anybody!

Felix, much encouraged, impetuously suggested, 'Let's have supper shall we? Here? Something light, after all that singing?'

Annie was surprised, but hungry. She looked about. 'Good. Yes. That would be good. But not,' she pointed, 'perhaps there.' Following her gaze to the café where he had sat with Charlie, he smiled, 'No. Best avoided!' They both smiled now. They sat at a nearby café, looked at the menu and ordered bowls of mussels, and Felix added a bottle of red wine. The bread came, and Annie started chewing, she was indeed hungry.

They chatted lightly about music, singing, the acoustics of St Sernin. He watched as she relaxed over her food and wine. She was younger than he had thought, and when not shouting angrily, quite attractive. Large eyes, in a small face. She had enjoyed the wine he noticed, and they had almost finished the bottle.

'So' he said, they were now into coffee. 'What brings an English family to Toulouse? Is it your husband's work?'

'No- it's mine!' She did not correct the 'husband' assumption. She briefly outlined her work for the city, not expecting a music critic to find her love of gardening of any interest. Like Felix with his music, Annie often became defensive when talking about her passion.

Felix listened carefully, but was unable to ask any relevant questions, he knew next to nothing about this world.

He deftly changed the subject. 'And you live here? In the city?'

'Oh yes. Right in the centre.' She waved her arm. 'I can see the Cathedral spire, if I lean out!'

'Sounds good. Life in the heart of Toulouse.'

'Not for Charlie. He's a country boy. He misses his old life. Running about in the fields, riding his bike, making a camp.' She brightened up with an effort.   'But he has developed a passion for chess, so that helps at weekends. He is happy, on the whole.' There was a slight pause, then glancing at her watch, she rose and opened her bag. 'I think it must be about €35 each. Here,' she dug out some notes and change, passing it to him. 'I need to go- Charlie's baby- sitter will be worrying. Thank you. I don't often eat out.' They shook hands again. Felix rose too. Afterwards, thinking back on it, he never knew where the idea had come from, for he looked at her and made a suggestion.

It took a little time. Annie was too surprised to answer. She stared at him, 'I need to think about that! Goodness. What an idea! Are you sure? Do you mean it? We've only just met!'

Felix dismissed this. 'Yes, but it might work!'

He wrote a number on the paper napkin. 'Think carefully and phone me. Please.'

She smiled again, looking at him, an open smile which lit up her face. 'I'll think about it… very carefully. Goodness !' she repeated. She walked away swiftly, pushing the napkin into the bag with her music.

Felix paid the waiter, and walked slowly home. It had been a good evening.

*

Felix phoned his mother immediately. It was a long conversation. Their relationship had never been that close, her own lonely childhood had not equipped her for displays of affection, and she found it difficult to demonstrate her love for Felix. When he was growing up she was cautious, afraid that an excess of affection would embarrass them both. But Felix was now an adult, and they had drawn closer since the death of Xavier. He had helped her with the sorting out of the details of his estate, and the terrible days that followed the funeral. Marthe now much enjoyed his easy company, his humour, although there was a vague feeling of disappointment that his career as a musician had not developed. Felix had been very fortunate in life, but the loss of his father had hit him hard; he now deeply regretted all the conversations they would never have, the advice he would never receive, and Felix continued to mourn the father with whom there had been so many hours of pleasure.

Felix's phone call had given Marthe much to think about. He had spoken to her about Annie. He called her the 'English gardener', and said that he had encountered her by chance. Marthe had now been at Les Palmes for over a month, and the 'wilderness' as she now thought of the garden, was her most urgent problem. She swiftly realized that professional gardeners did not exist in this part of France. The farmers managed their own patches of flowers and vegetables, working on them in the evenings. Hiring someone for this work would not have occurred to them. She had made it known in the local shops that she was looking for gardening help, but no one had come forward. She began to think herself rash for dismissing Jean, whom she saw regularly hanging around in the square and cafes. He never acknowledged her. Marthe determined to look around at the alternatives and one wet afternoon she drove to the large out of town garden centre, which sat incongruously between the supermarket and a factory outlet selling shoes. Wandering inside the enormous building, she realised garden centres sold many items not immediately connected to plants. It was all very interesting for a woman who was naturally curious, and who had never set foot before in such an establishment. There were aisles of workmen's clothes, dungarees, waterproofs and overshoes, flowery women's aprons, and racks of grey and green trousers and sun hats. She examined all these with fascination. 'Were these what she needed to become a gardener? Surely not!' Glancing outside she saw that it was still raining, so she continued wandering around. It was really quite fun! She found shelves of various poisons, all marked with danger symbols, and traps for mice and rats and moles, 'I had no idea that there were so many vermin,' she said to herself. There were great balls of twine, hemp and plastic, thick gloves in various sizes and an enormous display of tools. She sat on the plastic garden furniture, opened up the parasols and perched, cautiously, on the edge of a hammock. She continued to look about. No one seems to work here, she mused, or no one seems to care about me! Finally she found what she needed: strong gloves, secateurs and shears. For good luck she added an unwieldy looking hoe, and a heavy hand fork, and at the last minute some waterproof boots, these were to prove her best purchase.

The following morning, instead of setting off into town for her daily shopping, Marthe donned some old trousers and a warm sweater and set off to garden. It was a dry day and the sun was almost hot, but the previous' days rain had dampened all the plants and shrubs. She put on the new boots, and walked towards the back wall, where she had cleared previously. Ignoring the nettles which had sprung up even higher, Marthe, using her new secateurs, tackled the brambles that had grown up through all the trees in the orchard. Within an hour she had cleared an apple tree, whose fruit was badly cankered, and was surrounded by a pile of long, prickly stems. She now needed a barrow but neither of the sheds yielded one, and Marthe, sighing, sat down. 'I really need help here. This is a huge task.' She tried not to think of 'young' Jean, but felt very discouraged. 'I'll make more enquiries in the town. There must be someone who knows about gardens and needs work.' She tackled another tree before lunch, and returned to the house suprisingly hungry.

She was therefore delighted to receive a phone call from Felix who, in some rather confusing way, seemed to have encountered an English woman who was a gardener. And not just any old gardener, he was very insistent on that. 'An expert!' he insisted. 'She teaches here in Toulouse at the university!' If Marthe agreed, he proposed that she should come to Les Palmes and meet her. 'I am sure you will like her, and you can show her your garden and see if she is interested.'

'What sort of an expert?' Marthe enquired. Felix was not sure, 'She is ...well, why not wait and see?' They agreed that the following Sunday would be a good day and Felix promised to arrange it. He was relieved when in two days Annie phoned and said she was also interested. It all seemed to be falling into place.

CHAPTER 6

A nnie was eagerly looking forward to a Sunday outing (as she described it to Charlie.) It was an expedition with a possible future for her, and the money would definitely come in handy. She relished the possibility of getting her hands on a garden. She missed the feel of damp soil, and its earthy smell. Working in Toulouse was interesting and varied, but she missed the activity of a garden: loading a wheelbarrow, on her hands and knees planting, pruning an overgrown shrub- all the satisfaction of a day's work out of doors. She also knew that she wanted much more than gardening: she wanted to design a garden from scratch, and maybe, just maybe, this was her chance.

She was also thinking of Charlie who, fretted around the apartment, at weekends, restlessly demanding space, space and more space! The prospect of a train ride, a picnic, meeting new people and being outside had raised him to a pitch of excitement. Annie tried to calm him down. 'This is a job interview Charlie. You'll have to be quiet and not interrupt. If the lady doesn't like us,' she looked at his eager face, 'we won't be asked to come back! Ok?'

Charlie was not deflated. How could anyone not like his Mum! She was pretty and energetic and… wonderful. He had forgotten the arguments that had been flaring up between them. 'I'll bring my chess set and sit with that. So I'll be as quiet as quiet can be.' He reassured her. Annie gave him a hug.

Felix was also feeling hopeful and rather pleased with himself. He believed he had come up with a tremendous idea, he liked Annie and felt certain she could do the job. He decided to drive out on Sunday with Valerie to bestow his blessing on a new enterprise.

The Sunday morning meeting, after an akward start, went well. Marthe was both anxious and eager, she was also, though she was determined to hide it, slightly desperate. There had been no response to her further enquiries in the town and she felt her options were running out. She had rarely dealt with those who had worked for her in the past, allowing Xavier to tackle the issues of wages, holiday allowances, days lost to sickness. So she was rather abrupt with Annie, acknowledging Charlie with a quick nod. Annie had never before, been inside such a large, austere house and she and Charlie walked in a subdued manner, through the dark hall and down the steep stairs to the kitchen. Servants' quarters! Annie thought to herself. She also felt tense, this could be an important day for her, she was eager to make a good impression.

Marthe spoke quickly, 'Would you like a coffee? Or something to drink?'

Annie nodded. But then not wanting to delay, 'Can we look first at the garden? I am very interested to see it!'

'My wilderness! Of course. That's what you are here for! Why not go and have a look.' She pointed to the heavy door that led outside, but made no move to accompany them.

Annie and Charlie went outside. Charlie had not yet opened his mouth, but had shaken hands politely and smiled. He had also managed to take a good look around as he waited in the kitchen. What a huge room! It was almost the size of their apartment! She must be very rich!

Half an hour later, Charlie, itching for his picnic, was tugging Annie's hand, 'Can we eat please, Mum, I'm starving.' They were back in the kitchen, at the long wooden table with his mother and the lady, now talking non-stop.

'Charlie, be quiet. Be patient.'

Marthe looked at him for the first time-what a nice boy she thought. He had been no trouble at all. He was very like his mother, the grey eyes and wide forehead, but his hair was darker and his nose much straighter. She guessed that he was about ten. She smiled reassuringly at him.

'Let him eat. Have you lunch with you?'

So while Annie and Marthe discussed the garden, Charlie ate most of a baguette, all the ham, a large hunk of cheese, and a pear. While exploring the garden, keeping well out of the way of his mother, who was frowning with concentration, he had noticed apple and pear trees, mostly covered in brambles, at the far end near the sheds. There were many 'fallers' and he had given a 'waspy' feller a mighty kick. It had made a pleasing mess.

Sitting at the table, Annie negotiated her deal with the experience that Marthe lacked. The terms were vital to her, and though Marthe seemed surprised at the daily rate she thought appropriate, so was her need. In later months Marthe would acknowledge that this deceptively young woman was pretty tough in reality. And so it was decided.

Annie would draw up a plan for the complete renovation of the whole garden, she would work for six hours there every Sunday, weather permitting. It would be a 'Mediterranean' garden, laced with gravel paths, beds of dry loving plants and shrubs some cacti and lots of grasses, with three full size palm trees in the centre. A focal point, Annie emphasized for the view from the house. She would retain part of the orchard as Marthe wished and the wild area beyond it. All the paths would be of a soft pink gravel, typical of the region. Annie would hire extra labour, as she needed it, calling in her contacts from her city work. She would choose, buy and plant and Marthe would pay. Annie would have one hour for lunch- Charlie perked up at this bit- and use both sheds for her tools, if she needed them. If it was cold, she and Charlie could eat in the kitchen. These negotiations took nearly an hour and left Marthe slightly breathless. She had intended to discuss any proposal with Felix, but Marthe could hardly believe how quickly it had all been decided and agreed, it felt as though a whirlwind had blown through her kitchen. She felt lightheaded at the prospect of the garden transformed. Her 'wilderness' gone.

Annie could hardly believe her luck. She returned to the garden with Charlie in tow. Marthe sat at the table and watched the two figures, walking hand- in- hand, as Annie pointed out things to her son. She felt amazed at what had been suggested, but excited at the enormity of this English gardener's ideas. Leaning towards the window she tried to imagine three full size palm trees, their great leaves moving in the wind.

Grabbing what was left of the picnic, Annie took a heavy measure from her bag, and a pencil and pad: 'You stand where I say and put your foot on the end, Ok.'

Charlie was keen to help and, trying to avoid nettles, brambles, rose thorns, broken branches, did his best, and after nearly an hour, Annie's pad was full of measurements, sketches and Latin names. She turned to the boy,

'We're done. You were great, Charlie, not even one little moan.' She hugged him. She was excited above anything she had felt for a long time. What a challenge! How interesting! A whole garden for her to rework. Her mind was racing with ideas. Nor could she ignore the opportunity it offered to both of them to be outside, away from the flat. She could see Charlie muddling about, with trees to climb and sheds to explore. Annie had also spotted the gate in the wall, maybe he could walk there or ride his bike.

They said goodbye to Marthe, both very formal as they shook her hand, and walked back to the station, it took only 10 minutes and more relaxed now, they enjoyed looking around at the small French town. It was quite shut up now though earlier it had been busy with people buying their Sunday lunches. 'Did you like her Mum?' Annie shifted her backpack and turned to him. 'Yes I did. Very much.'

'And the garden? Did you like that too?'

Annie stopped walking, 'Yes I liked that too. It'll be a wonderful place for me to work. I shall transform it!'

'Is that what she asked for? Is that why we came?' Annie started walking again, 'Well Charlie, she didn't know that that was what she wanted. A transformation. But she is going to be delighted, thrilled with it when it's done. We're going to have great fun here, hard work, but fun. You and I.' Charlie sighed with pleasure, he could think of nothing better than playing in that garden with his mother nearby. They caught the train home, both slightly hungry, Annie had forgotten how appetites were stimulated by fresh air and exercise. Charlie was quiet as he watched the landscape pass by him, fewer fields and trees, more apartment blocks and warehouses as they approached Toulouse, he was already looking forward to the next Sunday.

Back at the apartment, Annie got out the tools of her trade, squared paper, ruler, coloured pens and some very large and

heavy horticultural books. She was calmer now and analyt-
ical. Professional. Charlie, having grabbed some bread,
watched TV, lying on the sofa, one eye on his mother. He
continued to reflect on his day, the train had been fun, the
walk to the lady's house not too far, the picnic was yummy
and the garden… well it was a garden. It was outside. He
had run around, seen some very promising trees for climbing and looked inside two spidery old sheds. Perhaps, if she
worked there, he could have a penknife for scratching things,
and cutting, and digging up snails. His mind drifted happily
along. An hour passed,

'Mum! I'm hungry.'

Annie had completely forgotten supper, so absorbed was
she in her task.

'Right, let's celebrate! Supper out! Yes?'

'Yes! Steak and frites!'

He raced to put his shoes on. Annie felt like hugging him
again. But didn't. He would only tolerate so much…

Later that evening Marthe phoned Felix, who had not come
in the afternoon. 'He's got a busy life,' she said to herself,
'Valerie probably had other ideas.' She was annoyed to reach
only his answer phone and left a brief message, 'It's agreed ! I
liked her a lot, she's a pretty tough negotiator, but convincing
and wonderfully enthusiastic! She will start next Sunday. So
here I go!' She poured herself a large glass of wine and felt
more relaxed than she had done for some time. She sat and
thought about Les Palmes, she was now committed to a great
deal of work, both indoors and outdoors, it was going to be a
busy year of changes in the old family house.

Looking out at the garden, the next day, Marthe sipped
her hot tea. It was Monday morning. She had much to think
about, but was confident that she, or rather Felix, had found

the person to resolve the garden problem. It was a cooler day, but still sunny and bright. Marthe took her usual route into town, it was a pleasant enough walk under a long line of plane trees now dropping their crispy brown leaves. She enjoyed the crunch of the rough gravel path, as she strode along, there were no other walkers. She was now a familiar figure in the family run shops- the boulangeries, the charcuterie, the tabac-these now greeted her with a polite welcome. Deciding to celebrate her new ventures, Marthe crossed the street beside the fountain, and approached the restaurant whose menu she had often admired. She would have lunch! She would eat at a table in the shade of the mulberry tree. It was turning hot... It was early November! This southern sun had caught her by surprise. She entered the café. It was dark inside in contrast to the brightness of the streets. Approaching the bar, she saw Jean propping up the far end, and she glanced across and nodded with a faint smile. Jean responded with a surly look. Marthe ordered a glass of white wine and, sitting down at a table laid up for lunch, she threw off her cardigan, put down her basket, and looked about her. The only other occupants were men... also under the shade of the tree. Two were playing a board game, noisily slamming down pieces, and the rest, perhaps six in total, were talking, smoking and throwing glances at her. She smiled, turned away.

She drank her wine slowly. It was delightful, sitting in the shade, just enjoying the town and feeling part of the life here. The café owner came to the table, and handed her a menu for the wine and food. 'There is a Special today' he spoke with the strong local accent, 'rognons de veau, in a cream sauce' Marthe did not bother to look any further,

'Thank you. That sounds delicious, just right for lunch!'

'With carrots and green beans, perhaps?'

'Yes.'

'Good. I'll bring a salad while you're waiting.'

They exchanged a smile and he went towards the kitchen. Marthe sat quietly, and realized that she had forgotten to order water. The two men had finished their game; they looked older than her, in their late sixties, dark skinned, tanned by days spent on the land, both were dressed in worn jackets and faded denims. They walked slowly towards her table and then, suddenly, with great force the taller man, kicked her basket across the cobbles, spilling out her shopping. Apples rolled slowly into the gutter, and a carton of milk oozed wetly onto the street.

'Get out! Leave! Traitor!' he hissed, standing now very close.

Marthe, who had jumped up from the table, raised both hands to protect herself, she could smell the wine on his breath, she was rigid with fear. What was this? Who was this? No one else moved. An awful silence had fallen- all the men both inside the bar and outside were watching her. Her hands were shaking. She sensed the tall man and his companion- still standing near her, watching. Again she smelt the wine on his breath. 'Who are they? Why? Do they know me?' Her head was buzzing. Feeling very vulnerable, she stepped away from the table, picked up her sweater, which had fallen onto the dusty cobbles and walked unsteadily out into the street. She ignored her basket, its contents now strewn into the gutter. Her little punnet of late strawberries lay amongst a pile of cigarette ends.

Standing now at some distance, she turned,

'Do I know you?' She was feeling a growing anger, 'How can you speak to me so rudely?'

'Yes Madame, I know you! You are the daughter of that traitor, Bertrand du Pont. I curse him and all his family!" He spat horribly on the cobbles. His companion tugged at the sleeve of his jacket, pulling him back toward the café,

'Come, Henri, enough.'

But Henri stood facing her, his face contorted, almost purple.

'Get out! You're not wanted here.' He raised his fist and shook it.

Marthe was astonished, confused but no longer frightened. She watched as he and the other man returned to the café and disappeared inside. The other men had vanished and the café owner, who had appeared briefly to see what the shouting was about, had also gone. The incident seemed to have ended as abruptly as it had started.

Marthe was left alone with her spoiled basket, she was very shocked and quite mystified. 'Who was the man, Henri? What did he mean? Her father, a 'Traitor!' She turned from the café, the square was quiet, Marthe walked directly home, trying to slow her racing thoughts.

Entering the house, she closed the door firmly behind her and reached the chair in the hall. She sat for a long time, trying to blot out the man's hot breath, his violent kick, his appalling words. She did not recognize him, he was a stranger. Why had he attacked her? Insulted her? Who was he? She went through to the kitchen and stood there, her head was pounding. She drifted aimlessly though the house, but could settle to nothing. A headache developed rapidly, and brought with it a sense of great unease.

This was not the first violent experience for Marthe. The previous year, walking back to her apartment from supper with friends she had been 'mugged' in the street next to hers. It was a warm June evening, still some pale light in the sky. A group of young people were walking towards her, but she had paid them no attention. As their paths crossed, two of them, a girl and a boy deliberately pushed into her, and as she protested, another, a girl she thought, snatched her shoulder bag and ran off. Marthe was left standing, surprised and then angry. She had shouted after them, but they were young and fast and had disappeared around the corner. She could never catch them she realized and cursed them for stealing her bag, which contained her flat keys and a fair amount of cash. The affair had shaken her up and was one of the prompts to her thinking about her life in Paris, its difficulties now that she no longer had Xavier. She did not report it to the police; such muggings she knew were now a feature of life in the city. They would probably have thought her careless, walking at night, unaccompanied, with a bag on her shoulder. She became more careful, and managed to put it behind her. But she no longer walked home on her own, taking taxis even for short distances.

Marthe reflected constantly on the scene in the café, but she could make no sense of it. The man was drunk possibly, and knew her...how? Was Jean involved? He bore a grudge, she knew, had he encouraged the violent outburst? He was at the bar, maybe he had spoken to Henri. But what did he mean about her father? That was the mystery. Marthe determined to search the house for anything she could find that would help her to understand.

*

Two days later, Marthe, received Annie's plan in the post. She took it to the kitchen table and studied it carefully. She very much liked what she saw. Annie had sent a complete design, measured and detailed. There was a long, very long, list of plants, shrubs and trees each with its botanical name- in Latin. But, she had also included a coloured sketch, which showed Marthe what the design would look like in its maturity. Annie included a letter. She explained that while the full effect would take some four to five years to achieve, nonetheless Marthe would gain great benefit within a very short time, by next July certainly.

The plan was a good distraction from the thoughts that had pursued her and Marthe phoned Annie later that morning. Annoyingly there was no reply and she grew increasingly impatient, with an irrational fear that she would miss her opportunity, that Annie might have found another project. Her anxiety was groundless.

CHAPTER 7

It was early evening. Annie had just concluded a fractious conversation with Ralph. She was cooking supper. The phone rang again, Charlie who was reading a book on chess moves, sighed very audibly and looking at his mother with a cross face, picked it up, 'Hello.' he said loudly. It was Marthe. There was a pause. Annie, recognized the voice, and found her heart beating fast as she snatched the phone 'Hello!'

'The plan looks wonderful. I would love to go ahead. Can you start this Sunday? I have several questions, and there are things I do not entirely understand, but the design is perfect and ...well, thank you very much.'

Annie waved a big spoon at Charlie. She spoke to Marthe,

'I'm so pleased and excited. Yes. Of course this Sunday will be fine and we'll be there at 10 am. I'll photocopy the plan, so that you will have one and I will have my own. Goodbye' she paused, 'And thank you!'

Charlie looked up from his book, hearing the excitement in his mother's voice, her mood had certainly improved since the conversation he had overheard with his father.

'Will we be going back then, to the garden?'

'Yes, every Sunday, from now on.'

'Wow!' The length of time was a little beyond his grasp. 'Until when?'

'Until I've finished it! Maybe- yes- definitely July. A long time, a lot of work!'

'And will I always go with you?'

Annie gave him a big, lovely smile, 'Well, I can't leave you behind, silly. We'll find things for you to do. It won't be 'boring'. I promise.'

Charlie returned to his chess book. But his mind had drifted away, he was thinking about spiders, snails and a penknife. Annie dished up supper, her row with Ralph put on hold, for the moment. The news from Marthe was too exciting to allow anything to spoil it.

Back in England Claire was vexed. It had been a bad day... wet and cold, Arthur's dirty paws across the kitchen floor, Tony had forgotten to find the towel, and at lunch the lamb was nearly raw, and the broccoli had been boiled too long. Nothing had gone right and now- she threw the paper away, there was nothing good on TV. Tony knew better than to try to appease her. He had already settled on the sofa, the offending dog at his feet, when the phone rang. He could hear Charlie's voice. Claire had a gentler tone when talking to her grandson, they chatted and laughed together,

'Arthur's fine, good as gold. You don't need to worry about him! We love him as much as we love you!' She looked at the dog who obligingly rolled onto his back. 'How are you? Tony misses the chess, he says I'm rubbish!'

Charlie wanted to tell her his news, 'Mum's got a new job, in a garden. We'll be going every Sunday, there are sheds and trees to climb, and I can play.'

Claire listened attentively, 'Another job! She's already got two! But it sounds very exciting. Hand her over to talk will you?' She held the phone waiting, looking at Arthur, she saw his paws were still dirty. Annie explained at length her new job, Claire listened carefully but could not entirely understand why her daughter wanted to work every Sunday in a garden some miles outside Toulouse. Wisely she kept her reservations to herself. There was another argument about Christmas and so the call ended.

Tony, looked up as she stomped back to the sofa 'Trouble?' he asked.

Claire felt her shoulders go down as she looked at him. He was a good man. She even managed to smile at the dog, who lay oblivious, now farting a little.

'Oh! It's the endless Christmas argument. She just won't commit! Is she coming? Is Charlie? If not, are we going? Or is Charlie coming to England on his own? If so, is he staying with Ralph? Or are we to share him? It's the uncertainty that I can't abide!'

'It's difficult for her.' Tony spoke gently and gave her hand a squeeze as she joined him. 'Be patient. She'll make her decision soon. No doubt Ralph is making demands.'

Tony was very fond of Annie, she was the daughter he had never had, and he dearly loved Charlie, but he though he had met him rarely, he had a poor opinion of Ralph. Ralph had not prospered in life since the breakdown of his marriage. Initially he had moved into a flat above the garage where he kept his motor bike, and continued to try to establish himself as a landscape designer. His efforts had not been rewarded. He was now a jobbing gardener; he maintained several local authority care- home gardens, cutting lawns and hedges, but it was very part time work, and seasonal. He kept himself afloat through contacts, often made in the pub, 'regulars' for whom he laid paths, built small walls, dug ponds. But again, it was often 'seasonal', and in winter, his funds ran very low. He still owned his motor bike and 'tinkered' with it happily, but he had been compelled to buy a van for work, an expense that left him in debt. It contained all his tools and work clothes. He kept them there permanently as he had no shed or storage, so the clothes were often damp. His father despaired at this hand- to- mouth existence, and was disappointed at the departure of his only grandson to France. He had invested large sums of money in Ralph, but it seemed to have bought him little.

In the year following Annie's departure for France, Ralph had moved again into a smaller flat over the Indian newsagent. It was fine for him, and much cheaper, but when Charlie had come to visit it felt small and poky. It was the summer of 2000 and Charlie had stayed for two weeks. After a few days Ralph and Charlie decamped to a friends' place in Devon. Ralph piled their clothes into an old duffle bag and threw it into the back of the van among his gardening equipment. Charlie sat in the front, his seat was held together with gaffer tape. Their stay had been a mixed success. They shared the Devon cottage… dark, low and oddly cold… with Sam- a 'mate' from the bikers' club.

Sam expected Ralph and Charlie to spend their evenings in the pub, which was a nice enough place, but not for a father with a young boy. So, on the whole they went to the beach, sitting on the sand and Charlie swimming a little. It was sunny, but a stiff wind from the south west, kept the air cold and Charlie found the water chilly. 'Too cold for my old bones!' Ralph grinned, ignoring his son's pleas. On grey days, and there were several, they walked the cliff paths, but the weather had deteriorated. Twice they had a real soaking, always, Ralph noted when they were furthest from home. They returned to the cottage, with wet clothes, soaked shoes and chilled- it was very difficult to dry things out and Ralph's trainers were damp for the whole holiday.

Charlie found the erratic nature of their holiday unsettling, but enjoyed the food: a two-week diet of crisps (cheese and onion, please), pork pies, Cornish pasties, chips (just for the change) and no green vegetables. He drank a lot of fizzy lemonade, and fruit- every now and then. They found early blackberries in the hedges and he and Ralph ate greedily on their walks. He also watched TV in the mornings at the cottage, and in the evening at the pub- English TV- football and cartoons, and one night, half asleep on the sofa, a very unsuitable film. Charlie became quietly homesick and began thinking of Toulouse and the flat, even the green salads and spinach which Annie gave him almost daily now seemed attractive. Neither father or son was too sad to leave Devon, and Charlie was handed over, plus a mountain of dirty, damp clothes to Claire and Tony.

'Phew!' Thought Ralph as he gave Charlie a final hug. 'Even work seems attractive.' He had not realised before what hard work caring for a young boy could be. He phoned Annie.

'He's with your mum and Tony. We had a great time. He's such a great kid. I'll have him any time you let me- I suppose Christmas is next.'

Annie suppressed a feeling of relief- knowing that Charlie was now at her mother's home. She didn't respond to the Christmas remark.

'Well, I'm glad you had a good time- Devon can be wet. I was surprised that you took him there- quite a risk!'

'It was okay- just a hint of a shower.'

Annie was a little perplexed- what had they done in a Devon cottage for ten days?

CHAPTER 8

Marthe struggled to understand what had happened at the café. She remonstrated with herself for having retreated from the scene, 'Why didn't I confront them? I'd done nothing wrong!' She saw her behaviour as 'weak and pathetic'. At other times, Marthe defended herself, 'I did what any woman would have done... Two angry men, strangers shouting at me.' She went over the scene continually, there was no explanation. She wondered also at the failure on the part of the other men- there were four or five of them, she wasn't sure exactly, who hadn't intervened to help her.

Two days after the event, she walked into town, returning to the café. It was mid-morning and there was no one sitting outside under the mulberry tree. purposefully she walked in and up to the bar. The owner was standing polishing tumblers, and setting them on the high shelf behind him. He looked at her.

Marthe greeted him, 'Do you know the man who assaulted me, here, in your café the other day?'

He put down his cloth and paused, 'I saw nothing.'

'But you must know them, who they are.'

'I have many customers, Madame, this is a busy place.'

Marthe was both amazed and angry at his attitude. 'How usual is it for a woman to be treated like I was in this café?'

She insisted, 'You must have heard the raised voices, the commotion.'

He looked at her more carefully now, seeing a woman of smart looks and determined demeanour. He was not an unkind man and had no reason to refuse her request.

'Yes I know him,he comes in here from time to time. His name is Henri, Henri Carrere.'

'And is he local?'

'Outside town a little, he owns a farm, a market garden, on the road to Auch.'

Marthe stood for a moment. 'Thank you, Monsieur, I shall seek him out! Now, if you would, a café crème, I will sit outside.'

Marthe went to the table where the' incident' as she called it had occurred, and took the same seat as before. She drank her coffee, pleased with her information and planning what she would do next. A visit was her intention, to the market garden on the road to Auch.

Her afternoon was taken up with a visit from an interior designer from Toulouse. Her name was Nicole. She carried in to the house swatches of upholstery and curtain fabric, and a large portfolio of her work. Marthe shewed her a piece of the wall paper which was now on order, and she looked at it. The salon was a large room, with long windows, facing west and north, and a fine walnut fireplace. The floor here, as throughout the ground floor, was of brick, it shone rather dully. The heavy dark furniture had been removed, it was in an antique store in Toulouse, and Nicole called the room a 'blank sheet'. She was clearly excited. The two women spent a long time browsing through the heavy books of samples, and Marthe began to make her selections. Nicole agreed to measure the room, and return in a week, with a sketch of the room and the fabric that had been chosen. As she was leaving, Marthe opened the door to the dining room, 'Would you also be interested in this?' Nicole looked in and then walked across to the fireplace. Turning she said, 'I would love to do up both rooms, they are splendid.' Marthe thought about that as she ate her supper, 'I'm lucky to have come here, it's going to be a wonderful home…after some changes. The garden plan was also an excellent diversion, and the following Saturday she took the car and drove to the out of town garden centre again. It was bustling with activity. This time she felt more part of the world of plants and shrubs, closer to the rural life which she had chosen. She walked through the huge 'shop' and outside, where rows and rows of plants were on display. She had 'the plan' in her handbag and began the task of identifying some of Annie's chosen plants. The Latin names were not always attached though, so her task was difficult. She spent a happy half- hour wandering around, bending down to read the labels, identifying as many plants as she could. It was an entirely new world for her, and one she found increasingly interesting. 'How could I not have learnt about all this before?' She asked herself 'I have been missing out!' She thought of Xavier, he had had no interest in the world of nature, living all his life in Paris. He never went for a walk, or sat in one of the many parks, and he could hardly identify a tree. He purchased flowers for her frequently but could not have named one. Perhaps he might have recognised a rose, but she wasn't sure. She thought of him affectionately, but acknowledged that he was an urban creature, unfamiliar with the life outside streets and squares, at ease in boulevards, and pavement restaurants. She sighed and bent to read another label, it was very long though the plant itself was small. She smiled to herself and walked on. Returning inside, she bought an expensive and detailed Glossary of Garden Plants. That evening she continued her task of identifying the plants on Annie's list and staring at the illustrations, she couldn't wait for Annie to start.

Sunday arrived. Marthe was up early. It would be a change to have voices around and see the little boy running about. She looked anxiously at the cloudless sky, all well there then.

Annie and Charlie were sitting on the train by 9:15. The journey was some thirty minutes out of the city through the tall white apartment blocks, like sugar cubes Charlie said, and then an ugly commercial area of low, factory made buildings and huge lorry parks. After this, the train passed through open countryside, rather flat as it was the valley of the Garonne, but in the distance the low hills, still in early morning mist. It was beautiful Annie thought, as she sat beside Charlie, and what a lovely way to start the day. The fields were golden at this time of year, orderly rows of vines stretching away. Tractors were working on one side, it was the autumn ploughing season and Charlie remarked on the dark soil with deep ridges. He enjoyed sitting by the window, surreptitiously pulling the end from his lunch baguette, chewing. They had shopped for their picnic near home, joining the queue of families buying bread for lunch. Annie had taken from the fridge some slices of salami, and some cheese. She carried everything in her haversack, with water and fruit, along with her plan and some gardening tools. Charlie carried the bread.

The little railway station of St.Girou was close to the centre of town, a short walk for Annie and Charlie, it was not without interest. They walked past the garage, where a man in greasy overalls looked up and grinned at Annie, and winked at Charlie, and then up a slight slope to a run of shops. They were doing a brisk Sunday morning trade. Charlie noticed a tabac, and eyed the comics on a stand outside; he would try his luck next Sunday he decided. Turning beside a high wall that led up to the church where families were gathering, they continued now on a cobbled street, through the main square. The cafes were already open and several men were drinking at the bar in the largest. Charlie nudged his mother, glancing at them disapprovingly, like many small boys he was something of a Puritan about alcohol. They took the road for Les Palmes, Charlie walked steadily, he had picked up a stick, a useful tool, or was it a weapon? He waved it like a sword, catching Annie on the arm as they turned into the drive. Annie pushed open the wrought iron gates.

'Be careful! Ouch! Really Charlie...'

She stopped and rubbed the place.

'Sorry Mum- it wasn't hard was it?' He looked at her, slightly repentant.

'Throw it away- now!'

He did so- there were plenty more in the garden anyway.

'And you've eaten half our bread!' Annie was exasperated.

'I'll go back and buy another- if you like!'

Charlie had remembered the boulangeries.

'No, we'll manage.' Annie was heaving off the haversack as she walked towards the side gate.

'You'll just get less!' Her mood softened as she walked into the garden.

'What a challenge! What an adventure- this is.' She thought. Her mind emptied of all other thoughts, as she dug the plan from inside the haversack. She glanced back at the house but, surprisingly, Marthe was nowhere to be seen.

Charlie shot off throwing his jacket on to the rusty table on the terrace. He was frantic to explore, this time thoroughly. His goal was the sheds. In the first whose door he pushed open easily with his shoulder, he found some large piles of moveable items covered in dust: catalogues, twine, nails and hooks, many empty glass jar stained brown inside. 'Were they poisons ?' Wisely he put them aside. He continued to pick things up, trying on earthy gardening gloves, stiff with age and much worn, and dislodging a number of old seed packets, which he would shew to Annie. The best thing was a wicker chair, which he heaved outside, and sat on cautiously. Annie was nowhere to be seen. He glanced back at the house. It was the largest house he had ever visited, its numerous tall windows, balconies, high tiled roof and wrought- iron veran- dah deeply impressed him . 'Did she live here alone? It was very large for one person!'

Returning to the sheds, he entered the second one, which was more solid. Here he found the bigger things: hoes, saws, heavy spades, rusty wire, a stack of wooden stakes, several leaning precariously against each other. There were also large tins of paint, dark bottles and oil cans, which he knew better than to touch- for the moment. His next best 'find' was an old radio, which he thought he might borrow for his bedroom- and then something that looked like a hammock.

While Charlie kept busy, Annie was hard at work. She devoted most of that first day to marking out that part of the garden, which would not be changed. She put stout red tape around the orchard and sprayed the trunks of several trees. She began pegging out the areas that would be planted and delineated the paths that would criss cross the spaces. A large central circle was 'red taped', it would be the home for the three tall palm trees that would provide the height that Annie needed. She was preoccupied with work, and ideas, and as the morning passed, it became warmer and then hot; she threw off her work jacket and enjoyed the sensation of the sun on her thin tee shirt. Charlie too kept busy. He continued to explore the wooden sheds. Moving between the two, he was quite oblivious to the calls from his mother, who occasionally needed a helping hand. In the second shed, on a low shelf, he dislodged an old wasps nest, very large, paper light- it crumbled as it fell to the floor. Warily, he touched it. There were plenty of insects, desiccated flies, weevils and spiders on the dusty ground. These he kicked with his foot. He returned to the wicker chair and sat on it carefully. The seat had many holes, and he surveyed his new 'kingdom'.It pleased him very much! It was the best morning he had had for a long time. By noon both Annie and Charlie were equally dirty and hungry.

They picnicked on the wide brick terrace under the pergola that ran the breadth of the house, grateful now for the shade it provided. The rusty table wobbled as Annie tore the bread and shared out the ham and salami. Neither talked much, Annie was absorbed in her plans, Charlie was thinking about his afternoon. Marthe joined them, 'How was your morning?'

'Great fun!' It was Charlie who answered. 'You've got some very interesting sheds!' Marthe looked at him and laughed, 'Have I?'

'Yes! I'll show you, if you like.'

'Maybe later. After your mother has walked me around her work. I've been watching from the window of the kitchen, I confess.'

Annie was delighted, 'Let's go now, lunch seems to be over.' She pointed to the empty table. 'I seem to have forgotten how much boys eat, when they have been outside all morning. I must buy more next Sunday!'

Marthe addressed the little boy, 'Charlie, you might find some apples and pears still worth eating if you look at the far end.'

Charlie who had already seen them on his first visit looked at her politely, 'I will. Thanks. Would you like an apple or a pear?'

Marthe smiled, 'Yes. That would be kind. Perhaps one of each?'

Marthe and Annie walked out into the garden, and Annie showed her carefully what she had done, the marking of the trees, the positioning of the paths and beds, the site of the palms.

'And you've kept the orchard haven't you?'

'Yes, of course. And the wild area beyond it, up to the wall. It's a wonderful space, that you have here, and the walls create such an atmosphere.' Annie smiled, 'I wish it were mine! But it will be a joy to make it really special. Really extraordinary. I am lucky to have this opportunity.'

Her little speech broke the ice between them. Marthe touched her arm lightly,

'Well. I won't hold you up! I'll go and see the sheds now, and get my apple and pear.'

Later Marthe returned carrying two slices of seed cake that she had made the previous day. She found Annie surrounded by a huge pile of brambles. 'I'll start a bonfire before we leave. Would that be allright?' She poked at the brambles with a heavy looking fork. Marthe supressed a sense of alarm, 'Of course! Will that clear all this?' It looked a dangerously high pile.

'Yes! It'll burn away quickly, it's very dry.' Charlie appeared from nowhere the word 'fire' had miraculously reached him. 'Can I help? With the fire.' he saw the plate of cake. 'Is one of those for me?'

'Yes, to both those questions.' Annie grinned at him 'And then we have to start packing up.' She smiled at Marthe, who was hoping that the bonfire would be dying down before they left; she had never had one herself.

Returning to the kitchen she phoned Felix, 'She came and it's started! She's a real hard worker- barely stopped. So strong for such a slight person!'

'I'm glad the first day went well. One of many! I hope you're prepared for that… Not just the money, which you can afford, but the presence of others around the house every Sunday...'

'I look forward to it, the house is empty with just me. Also, the little boy was no trouble. He is very well behaved, he even gave me one of my own apples!'

Felix was relieved. His optimism about Annie now seemed justified. That's good. I'll be over next Sunday to see how it's all going.' He had intended to go to Les Palmes in the after-noon, but had been prevented by Valerie, who had organised a lunch with friends. He felt mildly put out that he had missed the first day.

'Traitor!' The horrible word echoed in Marthe's head. She woke with a start, damp, sweating… It was early morning, grey light seeping through the half open shutters. This was the second nightmare that week, and the same scene, it was the café and the two men were shouting at her. But when she rose she could not walk away, something had happened to her legs. They were caught up in her basket. She was trapped!

Marthe felt oppressed and very much alone. She had by now filled her bedroom, the kitchen and the parlour with familiar possessions, brought down from storage in Paris. It made those rooms feel more like home with paintings, lamps, rugs and some photos in silver frames. They were the accu-mulation of a long, and happy marriage. The small uphol-stered sofa and matching chairs, which she and Xavier had bought together while on holiday in Provence, now sat in the little parlour, adjacent to the kitchen, and which had a small fireplace. The chimney 'drew' well, and she had carried in some of the logs from the orchard which old Jean had stacked many years ago. They were apple, and smelt delicious on the few evenings when it had been cold enough to light a fire. She liked this room, it was sunny until tea time and had some low bookshelves. The deep blue rug that had previously lain in her bedroom, looked better here, with more space around it and she matched it with the blue cushions from her old drawing room. 'Things seem to work here,' she said to herself, 'maybe it's the sun and light.' She had positioned her photos here, mostly of Felix and Xavier, though there was one of her mother too, a slight figure standing by a window. She was not sure if it was taken here, or in Paris, at her grandparent's home, she did not recognize the room. The figure was in shadow, which, sadly was how she often thought of her...a fading image.

Marthe had ruthlessly cleared out the furniture that was not to her taste, it dated back many years, acquired by the du Pont family in the course of time. The dark, heavy dining room furniture, a long table for maybe twelve people, surrounded by ornate chairs, with dark velvet seats, and a huge carved sideboard. It ran the entire length of one wall. She had opened the cupboards and laughed to find so many plates, bowls, dishes of all sizes and huge serving platters. There was also a quantity of table linen, folded in deep piles, with a lingering scent of lavender. After all these years! She lifted out a napkin, once crisp white linen, it had yellow stains down the folds.

She wondered if the du Pont family had been very social that they owned so much. The 'salon' had likewise been emptied, creating the 'blank space' that so pleased Nicole.

Marthe kept a fine mirror on the mantel and some elegant upholstered chairs but the rest of the furniture had gone. For the moment, she kept the clocks, the paintings, and the rugs, intending to ask Felix if he wanted any of them; it was 'family' stuff after all.

On the first floor there were also changes – the dark armoires, which dominated every room, were destined for the removal men, as were several beds and all the mattresses. Marthe had contacted an Antique dealer in Toulouse who assured her that he could sell the best furniture, and gave her a not too generous sum for him to take it all to auction. She had not yet heard back from him. Marthe had no regrets about discarding so much. She checked with Felix who was quite clear.

'No thanks! I live in a modern apartment and none of it would fit. Not my style at all. See what you can get for it! May be less than you expect though.' His warning was not encouraging, but the dealer had already warned her that dark furniture was unfashionable. Felix could imagine Valerie's face if a load of old fashioned furniture was delivered. She would have thrown it out instantly. So that was that, and it all went one afternoon in a large van. She kept the the family portraits that lined the stairway, serried ranks of her father's ancestors, men in high stiff collars and dark jackets, solemn and unsmiling. They took themselves seriously that was clear. And their wives and mothers, low bosomed and corseted, festooned in pearls, their hair piled high. She thought she could see Felix in some of them, something about the forehead and eyes, Marthe nodded at them as she walked up and down the wide stairs. They eyed her back.

She got up to rid herself of the nightmare, still vivid with the sensation of being trapped, as the two men confronted her, shouting horribly. She crossed to the tall window. It was a misty autumn morning, very soft and quiet. Holding the low sill she looked out...The garden was below and... what was it ? A memory flooded her head. A memory! But of what? She held her breath. It was another morning, long ago. A group of men carrying a heavy burden, through the green gate in the wall at the bottom of the garden. They were carrying... a door or a sort of stretcher, and, she could hardly breathe, a grey body lying on the door. It lay very, very still. Slowly they came up the path and into the kitchen, there was a terrible shouting. There were awful tears, sobs reaching up to her. She was standing at this window, looking out...she was little, could only just see over this sill.

Marthe collapsed on to the chair. What was this memory? When was it? Who was the grey figure? Why the shouting? But the memory was gone. She could not progress it. She sat for a long time, thinking, thinking. Had the nightmare caused the memory to surface? Were they linked? Or was it all fancy and the fears of a woman, alone in an old house?

Forcing herself to be calm, Marthe dressed and went down into the kitchen, all was normal here. She made coffee, sat at the table, wrote some letters and toyed with the idea of phoning Felix. She glanced through the newspaper, but it was of little interest and she failed to see Felix's article on a concert in Albi. After lunch she went out into the garden, which now looked very different, with areas marked out with tape and a large bonfire still smouldering from the previous Sunday. There was not much that Marthe could do here, which was frustrating. She walked down to the far wall and gazed at the gate. It was the one that her memory had brought back, she was certain of that. She had decided that the nightmare and the memory were not connected, that it was coincidence, but it was upsetting that the two had come so closely together. She now stood before the gate. It was painted green though much faded. Annie had forced it open with Charlie's enthusiastic help, but Marthe had not explored the towpath that ran parallel to the wall. She pushed the gate open and walked outside. The path was quite wide, the width of a pair of horses in harness she supposed, pulling the barges beside the slow moving river which linked the two towns. In previous times, the river was an important part of the local economy, now it was only used by fishermen, whose voices she sometimes heard when she was in the garden, and the occasional dog walker. Marthe turned toward St. Girou, there was no one else about. It was very quiet and still, the path was lightly gravelled, and there were willows trailing into the water; it was a pleasant place to walk. As she drew nearer to St.Girou, she could see other houses which, like Les Palmes, backed onto the towpath, they were all hidden behind high brick walls. Her neighbours she realized. She had not met any of them. She stopped and admired the tall church spire. The church itself was dark and gloomy, and very cold. She had stepped inside soon after her arrival, had not been tempted to linger, but the spire was fine and a local landmark. From within, it tolled the hours and she loved its sonorous chimes. As she drew closer to the town she walked round a gentle bend, and reached a very wide pool, where the water was held back by heavy wooden supports and an old brick wall over which the water was passing. It formed a weir which controlled the flow and there was another pool some fifteen feet below it. Several men were fishing here on low stools. Marthe stopped and watched them from a distance. They paid her no regard.

She returned home calmer and pleased with her explorations. She had decided to search out Henri Carrere the following day, she wanted to ask him what he had meant by the word "traitor" and the cause of his anger against her. She knew the road to Auch, she would find his farm she was sure, and then she could find an explanation. She would confront him.

But she woke in the night with a fever and a horrible headache. As soon as it was light, she knew that she was ill. Forcing herself downstairs, she felt worse and was unable even to make herself breakfast. Marthe had flu.

CHAPTER 9

A nnie was thrilled to have a new challenge and interest in her life. Making a garden almost from scratch was a rare opportunity for any gardener and added to this was the prospect of putting her ideas on planting into practice. She had made a copy of the plan that she had laid carefully before Marthe, and this copy was now pinned to her bedroom wall. She looked at it frequently, jotting down ideas on the wide margin, and testing colours against each other. She was particularly concerned not to mask the lovely rose brick walls that led the eye down to the far end. Climbers were needed, but not ones that would overwhelm or intrude, and they would have to tolerate the dry soil. She decided on apricots and some vines- both would thrive on the warm south facing side and for the opposite, north wall, she selected some hardy pears and apples. With this, she was able to distract herself from the problem of the coming holidays. It was already late November and Charlie was beginning to count down the days until school ended. Annie sighed as she prepared supper, waiting to hear his step outside as he climbed the last flight of stairs. He was returning from his weekly chess practice- a high spot in the week for him. He took real pride in his play and showed a competitive edge, looking forward to the monthly tournaments organised by the city chess club, which made him eager and bright eyed, failure or disappointment he found intolerable…

Charlie came in, flushed from his climb. He carefully put down his chess men and sniffed the air: 'Mum I'm starving! What's for supper?'

Annie was pleased to see Charlie back home safely, she looked up from the stove, 'How was it?'

'Very good! I won my group and they are discussing pushing me up. I'll be playing with much older boys.' He shrugged. 'That will be Ok, though', he tried to dip his finger into the dish of beef casserole.

'No! It's hot! Wash your hands and then it'll be on the table.'

They sat and ate, and Annie drank some red wine left over from the previous evening. It helped her unwind and she felt content, sitting with Charlie who chattered on. It was dark now, but Annie liked to keep the shutters open and see the lights from the windows opposite. The autumn was closing down the days earlier now, and the street lights sent a yellow glow that made the cobbles shine. The café opposite her windows had already taken its round metal tables in for the day. Toulouse though was never quiet. People were strolling by, traffic was accelerating around the square, heavy entrance doors were slamming and St. Sernin tolled the hours. Annie loved the activity, hustle and noise, and most of all the bells, a sound she now associated with 'home.' She thought briefly of the choral concert at St. Sernin, and her supper with Felix; she had not really seen him since then. But she thought of him with gratitude, it was entirely due to him that she had met Marthe. She cleared the table, but did not seize the moment to discuss Christmas with Charlie- he was tired now, it would not be fair. She delayed again. Charlie got ready for bed.

The following Sunday, Marthe did not appear at all which disappointed both Annie and Charlie, but Felix's car was in the drive and Annie assumed that he was taking up Marthe's attention. Having worked hard all morning, and eaten their picnic, she walked to the local garden centre. She left Charlie in the garden, playing in the shed, which he was quietly transforming into his 'den'. He was under very strict instructions to 'be good'.

'I'll be about an hour. Ok?' Charlie nodded, preoccupied.

Annie wanted to see which of her many plants she could obtain locally. The centre was not one of the large 'chains', but a family business, entirely devoted to growing and propagation. The 'boss' was an elderly man, in his late sixties she estimated, very tanned and leathery of skin, with large knuckled hands. He wore an old straw hat, though it was not sunny, and his eyes were very dark, he had a pair of secateurs in his hand. He gave her a quick nod, but paid no attention as she walked up and down the long, carefully labelled rows.

Annie tried not to linger as she made notes in her pocket book, she was, she thought, being paid to work not enjoy herself, and was admiring a line of climbing roses, when a dark haired woman of about her own age in dungarees and heavy shoes approached. 'Bonjour! Can I help you?'

Annie looked up. She was also brown eyed. The daughter? Maybe.

They began discussing the climbers and as Annie spoke, her enthusiasm spilled over and she found herself talking about what she was doing, what she was looking for. The woman listened with a growing interest,

'Goodness what a plan! How exciting! Lucky you.' She put out her hand: 'I'm Sylvie. You may have seen my father already? He's busy pruning.' She pointed, at the old man. 'Where's your garden?'

'Oh it's not mine. I am the planner and the labourer! I'm Annie.'

'Ah, you are working then for...'

'Mme Le Brun.'

Sylvie said,' I don't know the name. Is she new to the town?'

Annie explained that Marthe had arrived in the last months and they had found each other by chance. 'It's a wonderful opportunity for me. I am very excited!'

'And where's this walled garden?' Sylvie asked.

'Les Palmes? It's the last house on the road to...'

'I don't think I know it. But, you say, shut up for many years?'

'About fifty I think. Extraordinary! There's been a man working there, off and on, but it's badly overgrown, and needs a lot of work. So I'm going to restore it- with an entirely new design! But will you be here next Sunday?'

Sylvie nodded her head 'Yes. I'm always here. Wait, can I give you our card? Perhaps you would give me your list? I'll show it to my father. We would love to supply some of these. I'm sure we can come to an arrangement. For so many plants!' She drew a little card from her jacket pocket and Annie put it in hers. They chatted a little more, while Annie admired the plants and trees all about her, but she couldn't delay and said goodbye.

She walked briskly back, and felt the card again, and drew it out 'Sylvie Carrere' It read. 'She seems nice, a good contact and their plants were excellent.' On her return she could not find Charlie anywhere. She checked both sheds. She admired the 'den' he had created in the smaller one. Then, she pushed her way down through the orchard, the nettles dying back now, to the far wall. She stopped at the gate, and, trying not to panic, she called his name- urgently. He did not appear, nor did he answer. Annie ran towards the house, her heart beating horribly fast, she pushed open the rear door that led into the kitchen, and walked in.

'Charlie? Charlie?' she called.

He was there of course, at the table, his back to her and holding his head in both hands, concentrating. Opposite, equally engrossed sat Felix. Neither of them looked up. They were playing chess. Annie was swept with relief, Charlie held up his hand in recognition, requesting silence, and touching the board said softly 'Check!'

Felix moved in his chair and put a finger to his lips regarding the board in silence, and then he looked at his opponent: 'Well done! I had not spotted that! You're a very good player, young man!' He stretched out his arm and shook a delighted Charlie's hand.

'The victor!' he proclaimed. Charlie sat back, grinning. He picked up one of the Queens- looking carefully, 'Are they old? Are they yours?'

"No. Not mine. I found them in the cupboard. They are indeed old, but who did they belong to? I don't know.' He and Charlie both looked at Annie, who was standing by the table now, pink and flustered.

She spoke first, 'I always seem to be in crisis! You and Charlie together- first in the square, now here.' She smiled at them. Felix smiled back,

'He looked a little lost on his own, so I invited him in. We had a good game, I haven't played chess in ages. It's good for the brain!' Charlie stood up, having finished putting the pieces in a dark wooden box.

'Thank you. Shall we have a return match?' He was eager to win a second time. Felix who had thoroughly enjoyed the game too, replied, 'Why not? Maybe next week! We'll see. The box lives in the dresser- there- the left hand cupboard.' Annie looked around her, it was such a lovely room and Marthe had made it feel very homely, there were roses in a jug on the table, a little marked by the rain, and some branches of beech in front of the fireplace. It smelt faintly of soup,

'We must pack up Charlie. It'll be dark in an hour.' She turned to Felix, 'My outing was a success. I've found an excellent local horticulturalist, growing many of the plants that I'm looking for. A very helpful woman too, the daughter of the owner, she thinks she can supply most of what we need.'

Felix felt guilty that having 'found' Annie he had paid little attention to the changes planned for the garden. Today he had walked around rather quickly with Valerie before lunch, carefully avoiding Annie's red markers and staring rather in awe at the bonfire . He could not make head nor tail of it all. He had not ventured as far as the sheds. Valerie had briefly accompanied him, but her high heeled shoes prevented her from walking beyond the terrace. She had set herself up after lunch in Marthe's parlour with her newest book, and when Felix went to join her she was dozing. He had opened the salon door; the room was stripped almost bare, ladders lay on the floor, the mantel and the mirror were shrouded in dust sheets and there were many rolls of wall paper propped against one wall. Felix was amazed, his mother had told him nothing of her plans, but he was pleased that she had ideas for the inside of the house, not just the garden.

'Well, that sounds good. It is useful to buy locally...' He stopped. 'Really I know so little about this garden, I'm sorry.'

'Is Marthe about? I've some questions for her.' Annie was surprised not to have found her in the kitchen or parlour.

'No. She has been unwell all week. A touch of flu, nothing serious, you'll see her next Sunday I'm sure. She is resting now, but she did manage some soup for lunch, so she's picking up.'

Annie expressed her concern, but Valerie was eager to be off, and in a few minutes they had left. Annie could hear the roar of Felix's engine as it set off for Toulouse.

On Monday the outside work, began in the garden, for four days she endured a digger. This machine started up promptly at eight o' clock, squeezing through the side gate, and continued to exactly twelve noon. It restarted at two o'clock and shut down at six in the evening, though it was by then nearly dark. It had effected a transformation, grubbing out tree roots, piling up their trunks and branches into a great heap. A huge bonfire had been lit, burning through the fallen trees and consuming the brambles, nettles and green material that had been cut down. The machine had levelled the garden, creating a flat, planting area stopping only at the orchard, sheds and far wall. Marthe watched its progress, marvelling at the work it could achieve. She compared the area with her 'plan', trying to imagine what Annie would be doing next. The paths? Obviously. And the beds which were to be edged with red brick. On the last day, a Friday, a delivery was made of topsoil, manure, and bags of compost, all carried from the front drive on wheelbarrows by the digger driver. He stacked them around the garden in large piles, ready for spreading.

Marthe went out to thank him, but he was un-communicative and merely shrugged. Just another week's work for him, she supposed. He left promptly soon afterwards.

The noise outside was matched by the sounds from the salon and the dining room where two men were stripping the wall papers, talking as they worked. Marthe tried to ignore their radio, which played endlessly. She welcomed a visit from Nicole who brought the samples of fabrics, which she had chosen. The new wall papers would go up the following week. It was all very exciting.

*

It was Sunday and Felix was coming to lunch on his own. She looked forward eagerly to this, and the arrival of Annie and Charlie, their voices, their laughter, the sounds of the shed door banging and the wheelbarrow squeaking. Annie was delighted to see her coming out of the kitchen door, 'Let me shew you what will happen next, if you'd like that.' She said. Marthe found her jacket and followed her into the garden.

'The paths will cross here, and the beds will be of different sizes. You've seen that on the plan? Yes?'

Marthe nodded, listening, trying to see it all. 'It'll be both formal and informal!' Annie added.

Marthe said, 'And the three huge holes are?'

'Your three palm trees.' Annie waved her right hand to indicate, 'I'll have the plant list for next weekend, and I've found an excellent local source at the garden centre. Sylvie, the owner's daughter will help me. The planting is a huge task, and I really want to get in as much as possible before Christmas. The soil will be cold and heavy in the early part of the year. We're looking at the first two Sundays in December. In the mean time I'm going to finish spreading the topsoil and mulch.' She paused for breath. Marthe looked at her, impressed.

'That's heavy work. Do you want some help with that?'

'Have you got someone then?'

'No, I'm afraid I don't know any 'locals' yet. There was someone, but he well... He no longer works for me.' She remembered the last time she had seen Jean, at the café that dreadful morning, and tried to blot out the memory of his insolent face. Annie saw the change in Marthe's expression, but pressed on thinking quickly, 'I'll have a word with Sylvie, she must have local contacts. Would that be all right? A couple of days would really help at this stage and free me up for more, well skilled, work.'

It was agreed. Marthe returned to the house, it was a damp morning. She put a chicken in the oven for lunch. Looking over the sink, she saw Charlie hauling an old wicker chair out of the shed. She watched him with interest. What was he up to? He seemed perfectly absorbed.

Charlie also looked forward to Sundays. The whole day was an adventure for him, and he was proud to be part of the 'plan'. He enjoyed the brisk walk from the little station and then through the town, chatting to his mother, whose undivided attention he could enjoy. He liked walking in through the stone pillars, admired the red brick house with its formal windows and door. He had learnt quickly to run down the side path, between the high wall and the house and out into… Well, today it was chaos and mess really! The digger was waiting to be collected and the garden resembled a building site.

'Mum! It looks awful!'

Annie agreed. Indeed, it did: 'Not for long. Patience. Gardening is a slow business, preparation, planting, waiting! Not unlike your chess really, it's all in the patience- the planning. Move slowly.'

Charlie looked at her- warm quilted jacket, old jeans, red socks, heavy shoes, and her hair already escaping from its band. She looked great, he thought, and taking the picnic bag, he offered, 'I'll put this somewhere safe.'

'No eating please, Charlie. I'll be hungry later. We'll stop at Noon. You'll hear the church bells.'

Charlie shot off, swinging the bag, heading for his den. He stopped to look at the bonfire now a great circle of ash, and bent to test it, it was disappointingly cold. Today, he thought, I am going to throw out everything I don't want, and have a good bonfire myself, then next week I'm definitely going to ask Mum for a knife. The bonfire itself was a step forward for him, Annie was trusting him to be sensible. The morning passed. Felix arrived for lunch, on his own, and came out to look at the progress. The garden was no more! It had been replaced by, as Charlie had said, 'chaos.' Annie was bending over a fork and heaving manure, she looked very hot and pink. He walked gingerly over, 'Good Morning' he said. Annie stopped and stood up slowly, 'Gracious Felix! Don't creep up on people.' She felt a little put out, she didn't know why.

'Whatever has happened?' Felix felt compelled to ask.

'Progress!' Annie replied defensively. 'One step forward...'

'Yes. And several back!' he laughed. They stood together for a while and Annie explained what the digger had done. Felix thought he understood but it was so far removed from a 'garden' that he was quietly bemused. 'She seems to know what she's doing.' He thought as he walked back in for lunch, 'It'll be on my head if it all goes wrong!'

He enjoyed his lunch with Marthe, who, looked better he thought, with a slight glow back on her cheeks. 'Country life is suiting her' he decided. Relieved Felix drank a small coffee in the parlour, recognizing the Provencal sofa which had been a great favourite of his father. The salon was much changed; without the old wall paper, it felt light and airy. One wall had now been hung with the cream and green paper, 'This is lovely,' Felix complimented Marthe, who was arranging swatches of fabric by the window.

'See what I have chosen for the curtains. What do you think?' They discussed the room for some time, then Felix left for a concert that he would later review. Marthe wondered about Valerie, who Felix explained, had been working hard and preferred to spend a lazy day at home. He had promised to take her out for supper when the concert was over. Charlie was disappointed to hear his car accelerate out of the gate, he had been hoping for a game of chess. The score between them now stood at two wins each, Felix had shown himself to be a keen competitor.

Before she packed up, Annie went to look for Marthe who was reading but happy to be disturbed.

'I thought it would be a good idea to go through the plan in some detail with you. It would be helpful to me before I order the plants.'

'I think that's an excellent idea. It would be helpful to me too… to understand the concept and the detail. I'm quite a learner here. I've never owned a garden before!'

Annie supressed her surprise. This was quite an undertaking for a novice.

Marthe invited her into the kitchen and they spread the large plan out on the table. It was meticulous and covered in Annie's red writing, each plant, shrub and tree numbered, with an accompanying list down the margins. Annie stood before it and took a deep breath.

'The principle is, as you know, to use the whole garden within your three brick walls. The new planting will stop at the orchard, which you tell me you want to keep. I think that's a good idea, it will preserve a historic part of what you have here and, apart from those trees which are too old and damaged to be worth keeping, I'll leave it as it is.' She looked sideways at Marthe, who nodded her head.

'I aim to create an atmosphere within the walls that is tranquil and peaceful. Where possible the plants will be Mediterranean, and they should need little or no watering. A dry garden, is the technical term. There will be gravel paths, using the local pinkish gravel, winding around beds of varying size and shape. It should look natural and 'painterly'. That is the colours will tone and blend.

The hot colours should be nearest the house, beds of orange, yellow and red. They should be at their best in the summer. So there will be Californian poppies, red salvias, golden crocosmia, yellow and red kniophia. All in big drifts. I'll include several prolific- flowering Californian fuschia, which are red, and some yellow achillea. To give height we can grow lots of sunflowers from seed, and put in a Sumach which will give deep red autumn colour. And a Sambucus which has red autumn berries. There will be tall grasses, they'll give a lovely effect with the wind blowing through them.'

Annie paused, 'Are you with me?' Marthe felt slightly breathless as she tried to take in what Annie was saying.

'Go on!'

'So the hot colours give way about half way down the garden, at the point where the three palm trees will be, circled by a path. The colours now will be blue and silver, and the atmosphere cool. It will look best in spring but many will continue right through into summer. Lots of lavender, though I am afraid your bushes will have to go, they are too woody and straggly. I'll find some young upright plants instead. Also lots of bulbs: alliums, blue iris and agapanthus, though they may well be in pots. Also there will be nepeta near the paths, and silvery santolina and blue campanula. Some stately yuccas for height, and verbena bonariensis, which will spread everywhere!

I have planned the garden to be very scented, not just the lavenders and nepeta but beside the paths, thyme, and juniper, and rosemary.

I advise you to invest now, while prices are down, in some good stone and terracotta urns, large and small, and lots of benches and maybe a table. It's important to create the atmosphere of a garden to rest in and enjoy!'

Marthe pointed to the plan, 'I don't follow this. Is it a pond?'

'No. Not exactly. You may not want to go ahead with this, it will be expensive, very. I haven't included it in the overall price.'

'So?' Marthe continued to point at the plan.

'It's a rectangular brick basin, about hip height, with water flowing in from a spout set into the wall. Clear water, no plants and a gentle flow, almost a trickle. The basin should be surrounded by low pots, and we can change the planting here every year. I want to create the coolest spot in the garden, so I have to site it carefully on the west wall, for maximum shade, and as near to one of the tall palms as is practicable.'

Neither had noticed Charlie who had entered quietly and was listening intently. 'I think a water thingy would be great...'

Annie interrupted him crossly.

'Charlie this is nothing to do with you. I'm sorry.' She was blushing.

Marthe wasn't put out. 'It's fine, all opinions are valuable. I think he's absolutely right, a water,' she paused, 'thingy, sounds the best idea of all!'

She stood up, and touched Annie lightly on the shoulder as she rose from the table,

'Thank you. You have made it all very clear. I now understand why I'm paying you so much money! You're a designer of great vision.'

Annie blushed again, and gave a slightly awkward smile, 'It'll be very special. I promise!'

Annie was ready to present her plant list to Sylvie, she was delighted that Marthe had agreed to everything, even the basin. She and Charlie walked there after their picnic lunch. It had been a sunny morning, and Charlie had entertained her in his 'den'. He had spread out the food on an old wobbly-legged trestle table, placing two wicker chairs, with gaps in their seats, outside the shed door. Annie placed a very old green tarpaulin on the ground. Now they were walking quickly to warm up, Charlie gabbling away.

Sylvie took the list, looked at it carefully. 'This should all be OK. Some will do better if planted in March or April, but most of them we could get in now. Should be with you in the next two Sundays, is that still what you want?'

Annie offered her deposit and, in return, negotiated a reduction on the total price. Sylvie smiled broadly at her, 'This is a big order for us. My father will be pleased to give you a discount, so I'll show it to him later.' They discussed Sylvie assisting in the planting, which she would do happily for payment.

'Of course, you are a professional.'

'What does that mean?' Charlie interrupted 'Are you one too Mum?'

Sylvie looked at him. 'Yes, she is ...definitely.'

Henri Carrere was checking the supports and ties on young fruit trees. They grew in long straight lines, each labelled with care. Most were four to six years old, ready for replanting, and their roots were strong. He worked steadily, the autumn sun warming his back through an old blue serge jacket. His pockets, deep and earthy, were full of broken ties. His nails were uneven and dark with soil. He whistled tunelessly, stopping every now and then to look up at the sky now beginning to darken. It was, he reckoned, about three o'clock, another hour and his day would be done.

Sylvie walked rapidly down the line, her eye appraising her father's work. She had been working alongside Henri for eight years now, having, after lycee, spent a year in the local college, studying horticulture. But most of what she knew, had been learnt here, on this land, working under her father's direction. The family had owned the land, sloping in the lee of the hill, for many years. Once it was a market garden, growing vegetables and fruit for Toulouse. But her father, in his younger years, had transformed it into one of the best centres for trees, shrubs and plants in the whole area. He had overcome competition from the big new centres, which had sprung up outside of town, by supplying home grown stock and earning the support of many of the local gardeners. His reputation was well deserved. Sylvie was his only child. She interrupted the tuneless whistle, 'Here is the order I spoke of before. Can you check it over? I think we have many of the plants and we can order in the rest.' Henri, glad to stand up, reached out a grubby hand. He ran his eye expertly down the long list, it ran to nearly three pages. It was a substantial order.

'She has offered a deposit of 10-15 %, but I indicated we could give a discount for such a big sale.'

He nodded in agreement, 'That's fair.'

Sylvie was delighted. 'It's getting cold. Papa. You should stop and come in, I can finish off here.'

He nodded again, 'I'm nearly done, always finish a job if you can.'

Sylvie smiled to herself. Her father never stopped giving advice. A rather gruff man, all his life had been centred around this business and his daughter. He had lost his wife many years before, when Sylvie was twelve, and had never thought of marrying again. He was solitary by nature, with a passion for growing, and planting, and nurturing. He had never considered any life other than this one, and watched with pride as Sylvie followed in his path. All this would one day be hers.

'Who's this English gardener? Where does she live? It must be a very large place!'

'Oh, it's not hers! She is a garden designer, from Toulouse. She's very nice, about my age, English with a boy of maybe nine or ten. She's the designer, and will be responsible for the planting. She hopes to work here until July next year at the earliest, she plans a transformation.'

Henri felt in his pocket for a pencil and paper, 'So give me her name, in case she comes and you are busy.'

'She is called Annie, and the house is Les Palmes. It has been shut up for nearly fifty years, and the garden is neglected and overgrown. It is on the outskirts, the road to...'

Henri held up his hand. His face was white, his eyes were wide and staring. He gripped Sylvie's shoulder. 'Les Palmes did you say?'

Sylvie was surprised by the look of agitation on the old man's face. His grip was hard, and painful. 'Yes! Why, do you know it?'

Henri's face was contorted with anger, and his breathing was short, and hurried. He spat the words out. 'Mon Dieu ! I will never forget it ! It's the Du Pont house.'

Sylvie stared at him, she had never seen him so agitated, she spoke hurriedly,

'The owner is Madame Le Brun.'

But Henri was not listening. He turned, releasing his grip, and walked up the narrow path, abandoning his work. Sylvie was concerned, she pursued him back towards the shed that was their office.

'What is it? Who is she ? Papa, speak to me!'

Henri sat on the only chair in the office. He was shaking. Sylvie pressed him again. 'Speak to me! What is it?' She was now alarmed; her father looked very old, and his face had turned grey. Sylvie stared at him. 'What is it?' she asked again. Chapter 10

Henri extended an arm along the wide table which they used for accounts, catalogues, lists, and orders. He slowly flexed his fingers, thinking. After what seemed a long time, he raised his head and looked at his daughter, 'What is it? A tale from the past, the family... History.'

Sylvie leant against the wooden side of the shed. What tale could her father have to tell. Henri spoke very quietly, very deliberately. His mouth felt dry, and he repeatedly ran his tongue over his lips. He continued to flex his fingers as he spoke, so softly that Sylvie strained to hear him.

'It was 1944, war time. Our family was here, growing vegetables and fruit, we were a close-knit family; my father, my mother, and myself. I had a sister too, older than me. We looked after each other, neighbours and friends, everyone struggling to survive, for life was tough; there were shortages of food and fuel, and a night time curfew. One needed a travel pass, and an identity card, while we saw Germans and Italians, walking boldly in our towns. There was the fear of being rounded up for 'service', as they called it, which meant forced labour in the German heavy industries, or worse conscription into the German military machine. Life was uncertain; people were demoralized, and intimidated. Our family tried to live as quietly as possible, there was work every day. Food was rationed, but there were vegetables, fruit, and chickens, and eggs, and a pig.' He pointed out of the narrow wood framed window at the old stye, now reinforced with heavy planks and used for storing bags of compost.

'The war had interrupted everything, though in the early years, the family was not much affected. We were in Vichy France, still under French rule. My parents knew nothing of international affairs, but they hated the Germans and their presence on French soil, they could not accept the fall of Paris. How had such an event happened? And the government at Vichy, soon hand in glove with the Nazis, a great shame had spread over France. But down here in the south, at first, life went on, as I say, much as before. People read of the events in Paris, and the fighting in the East, and from 1942 in Africa. The Germans were everywhere, with new orders, and fresh demands. He paused and stared at her, then continued,

'My father was young, and a patriot, he loathed the Germans and their supporters here in the South. Especially the Milice who rounded up those who dared to voice opposition, and those seen as undesirable: the Jews, and the gypsies and the handicapped. He joined the Resistance. These men were brave and foolhardy; they knew nothing of armaments, but learnt to blow up bridges, and disrupt railway lines. They met secretly, and devised ways of making life difficult for those who aided the government. Devoted to France, they helped many who were fleeing Nazi rule, Jews and communists and British airmen, who had been shot down over France. They knew the routes over the mountains, they were dangerous but passable, and on the other side was Spain and hopes of freedom. Your grandfather worked in the local Resistance, he was one of many, sneaking from home at night for rendezvous on farms, where men and women and children were being hidden. They were spirited away to safety, many were saved, others were less fortunate...'

Sylvie had never heard her father speak for so long, she listened, trying to imagine life as it was on the farm at that time. It all seemed such a long time ago, but for her father it was still a raw memory.

'But the Nazis had their spies, and their informers and my father was betrayed. One night he was arrested, here on the farm. Taken off in the darkness, he was never seen again. The family could do nothing to protect him, to save him…

He 'disappeared', as did three other men, all taken on the same night, with no time to give a warning. He is remembered, as you have seen, on the plaque in the wall beside the church, the inscription records his name and that of the other three. It is a part of the history of the town. I told you all this, when I thought you were old enough to understand.'

Sylvie had never forgotten the story, though it was never spoken of again. She had been perhaps twelve years old, too young to appreciate the impact on the family of the loss of her grandfather. 'Yes,' she spoke as softly as her father, ' They were taken first to Drancy, then, after several weeks, loaded on trains heading East. They were destined to work in the mines, and factories of Poland.'

Henri interrupted her, 'Or to fight, to be forced into the German army.'

Sylvie took up her story again, 'But they never reached the East, they died on the train, in a railway siding outside Strasbourg. They died without water or food, and in the heat of summer.'

'So. You know the story?' He looked at her, 'You remember what I told you?

'Yes. What more is there?'

'The man who gave the names of the four men to the Germans, who betrayed my father and the other three, lived at 'Les Palmes.' His name was Bertrand du Pont. He was a Nazi sympathiser, and worked actively for the Germans. He was a wicked man, and a betrayer of true French men.' There was a long silence. The past, Sylvie reflected, is always part of the present, we can never escape it. She looked at her father. He was a boy at the time. She calculated he would have been about twelve. 'Betrayed', it was a terrible word.

Henri looked very old and pale sitting there, and Sylvie did not know what to say. He looked hard at Sylvie, 'This Madame Le Brun is a descendant of Bertrand du Pont, I know he was married, and had a daughter. And now she has returned and is living in his house. Well, I will not do business with her and nor will you. She should never have come here, stirring up unhappiness and sad memories. I have seen her in the town, walking about, not a care in the world. She should go back to where she came from. She is not welcome here.' His face was red, and angry and contorted. Sylvie had no words, but reached out her hand towards him, but Henri rose from the chair, and walked out of the shed, ignoring her gesture, and went to the farm house. Sylvie lingered in the shed, thinking about the story that Henri had related, she hated to see her father so distressed and angry about events so long ago. It was 'History' as he had said, of the town and the family.

It was early the next morning, and Marthe picked up the phone. She did not recognise the voice... It was that of a woman.

'Madame? My name is Sylvie. Sylvie Carrere. You and I have never met, but I need to talk to you.'

Marthe jumped at the name, she recognized it immediately. Was this the wife of Henri? Had she phoned to apologize? Before she, Marthe, could search him out? Marthe agreed that the woman should come to the house the following

morning, alone she assumed. She woke with a sense of expec-
tation, she had not forgotten the café incident, and the thought
of it made her angry. So that, by the time the doorbell rang,
promptly, as agreed at ten o'clock, Marthe was in a state of
eager anticipation.

Sylvie had dressed carefully for her visit. It was a cold and
bright day and she had put on her blue wool coat, and a dark
sweater,and she wore a skirt and leather shoes. She wanted to
look respectable.

Marthe welcomed her, quickly realizing that this was not
the wife of the man she had seen, and led her through to the
kitchen. Sylvie glanced about her, taking note of the large
comfortable room. There was a large table with a white table-
cloth, on which stood an arrangement of winter leaves in a
big brass jug. A good log fire was burning in the hearth, and
a smell of coffee came from the pot on the stove. It was very
homely and welcoming. Sylvie felt a sharp spasm of anxiety,
which compounded with her great sense of unease, reduced
her to sitting down very abruptly.

'So you said your name was Sylvie? Are you the daughter
of Henri Carrere?'

Sylvie was surprised. 'Yes. He's my father. I didn't know
that you knew him.'

'I do indeed know him,' Marthe paused, 'he assaulted me,
in the café in St. Girou. Called me a 'traitor' a strong word to
use to a stranger. Have you come to speak for him? Can't he
apologise for himself?'

Marthe brought the coffee pot to the table, and took her
place opposite Sylvie, confronting her. Sylvie was astonished,
she knew nothing of this, really had no idea what Madame le
Brun was referring to.

'You must be mistaken,' she replied.

'No! not at all.' Marthe interrupted her quickly. 'The café owner confirmed your father's identity. He was quite sure. Henri Carrere.'

Sylvie sat silently, she had come to tell a story from the past, which touched her family, and that of the woman sitting opposite to her. Now she was hearing of an assault by her father! It did not seem possible.

'Perhaps you could tell me what my father has done.'

Marthe gave her account, as calmly as she could. It did not take long. There was a long silence. Marthe spoke again, 'So he told you nothing of this? Indeed why would he? It is not something to be proud of!' Marthe almost felt sorry for the dejected woman, who was a complete stranger to her.

Sylvie remembered why she had come, she looked carefully at Marthe,

'I have to explain something to you,' she gripped her coffee mug, 'of events that occurred years ago, during the war... It is not easy for me to do this... We are strangers...But I know when you have heard it, that you will understand why I must tell you.'

Sylvie carefully recounted all that Henri had said, of the war years, the work of the resistance and the disappearance of Henri's father and the other men. The room was unbearably still, as Marthe watched her, listening intently. Finishing her account, Sylvie felt exhausted. She sat back and slowly looked at the face that had been concentrating on hers. Marthe had spoken not a word, she had not interrupted as the awful events were described.

They sat silently. Marthe eventually, her face now very pale, stood up and walked to the window. The sun shone, the sky was blue, a bird was singing. But Marthe's world had imploded- she could not for the moment grasp the details, but she had the heart of the events clear in her mind. Four men betrayed... by her father. All dead. In a train. 1944. She was 4 years old.

Sylvie knew she had to leave. She went to the door, picking up her coat.

Marthe turned, she wanted to be absolutely clear. 'And one of these four was?'

'My grandfather, Francois. I regret Madame, that my father behaved as he did. That was wrong, but it is difficult for him, to forget, or to forgive. Our family has lived with this loss but it was not, is not easy. Even now.'

Marthe bowed her head as she spoke, 'These events ...I was not part of them. Your father Henri and I were children. I cannot bear responsibility now! It is nearly sixty years ago.' She felt overwhelmed, trying to digest what she had just learnt, that her father an active friend of the Nazis!

Looking at the familiar kitchen, the golden dresser, the blue and white china, the vase of leaves, it all seemed the same, but everything had changed horribly...She escorted Sylvie to the door, and the two women parted, as she left Sylvie remembered the rest of her mission,

'I regret that my father will not, does not feel able, to supply your plants. I am sorry.' Marthe hardly knew what she was referring to, her mind was so taken up with what she had just learned. Sylvie climbed into her work van and drove through the heavy gates, but she did not for a moment believe that this was the end of the story.

Marthe went up to her room and lay on her bed, looking at the familiar furniture, the silver framed photo of Xavier, holding a baby, Felix. Shutting her eyes she could hear a bird singing on the wisteria outside her window, a blackbird maybe; she knew that they sang in the late autumn. It all seemed the same, she thought again but it was not the same. She felt sick and weak, her head spinning as thoughts flooded in. She lay still for a long time and then exhausted, fell asleep. It was mid-afternoon before she woke, then the events of the morning immediately returned.

What should be done? Felix? How could she tell him? She would have to, but what would he say? It was his grandfather. A man he never knew. A collaborator, and a friend of the Nazis, and responsible for the deaths of four men, maybe more. She got up slowly, washed her face and changed her blouse. She went down the wide staircase, glancing as usual at the du Pont faces, in their ornate frames. She felt a surge of dislike and distrust.

Within the next hour Marthe, forcing herself to address the garden plant issue, had phoned Annie who fortunately was working at home. She told her that the supply of plants should be obtained at the big Garden Centre, as the family firm could not assist. Annie, surprised, attempted in vain to question Marthe, but getting nowhere, agreed to make contact and put the order through that afternoon.

'This may cause a delay, and set the planting back.'

'You must do the best you can.' Marthe responded and rang off.

The rest of the afternoon hung heavily on Marthe's hands, she could not settle, and wandered around the house, moving objects, tidying and poured herself a brandy as the light outside faded. She wandered into the salon, which was empty, waiting for the new furnishings... Marthe stood for several minutes, admiring the cream and green wall paper, it was a good choice, and she felt calmer. She picked up the phone repeatedly, but did not dial Felix. She simply did not know what to say. Her thoughts were in turmoil; she remembered very little about her father, her mother had rarely spoken of him, and her grandparents, not at all. 'Did her mother know about Bertrand's Nazi sympathies? About his activities? The disappearance of the four men? Their deaths on the train? Was it a secret that she took with her, when she moved to Paris, after Bertrand's death? Is that why she had left? And after the war ended did she tell anyone? Her own parents? The hardworking doctor and his strict wife? Or did she know nothing at all?'

There was no one now to answer her questions. It was all so long ago! But Marthe knew that there must be an answer to some of it.

Sylvie's story helped her to understand Henri Carrere's outburst, and his strong words, 'I'm not to blame!' she repeated to herself. 'I was four years old.' It gave her no comfort.

It was Saturday afternoon and in Toulouse Annie was tidying up the flat, doing all the mundane tasks of daily life; sorting out the laundry, being her least favourite. She had much on her mind. She was juggling a demanding job with the Toulouse City Council who employed her and pestered her endlessly for accounts, details of staff, and their holiday allowances, and other time consuming paperwork, plus her teaching at the college, and her garden Sundays and family life with Charlie. Now she would have to photocopy another three page plant list and present it to a garden centre that she did not know. It was not good news, and she was piqued that Marthe had asked, almost ordered, her to go there. The door of Charlie's room flew open, she looked at him, 'Goodness, is it four o'clock already?' He came across to the table where the plant list was carefully spread out, and began fiddling with it,

'Come on! I hate being late. Let's go now!'

'Hold on please. I need to finish this.'

'Oh come on, Mum.' Charlie's face was getting red with frustration. Sighing Annie stood up, she grabbed her bag and scarf and checked that Charlie had his warm hat on.

'Where to exactly?'

'Mum! I've told you, it's the big school at...'and then remarked, in a mocking tone, 'Do you never listen to me?'

Annie smiled at his cheek. 'And how long will you be there?' They were out on the street now, dodging other pedestrians, Charlie clutching his chess set and bumping into people.

Tentatively Annie broached the issue of Christmas. She had been avoiding it for too long.

'So I'll fly back to England on the 23rd, and stay first with Dad, then at grandma's? And Dad will meet me?'

'Yes, if that sounds right to you. Dad will have you for Christmas Day and Boxing Day. She boxed his ears lightly 'and then drive you over to grandma's for the rest of the week, so they all get to see you.'

Charlie looked at her sideways, they were nearly at the lycee, other children were arriving and it was busy. They crossed the road, and Annie stopped at the gates. 'What will you be doing? I mean not now, but when I'm away?'

'Oh goodness. I have so much to do. I'll be really busy.' She patted his shoulder, no kissing in public now; she knew that. Nor hugging.

'Play well. Have fun. See you later!'

Charlie walked in. What would his mum do on her own? Would she miss him? He found the big notice board. With his name in Group B, room twelve, and all thoughts of his mother, Christmas, Dad- vanished. He climbed the stairs, looking for room twelve.

CHAPTER 11

Annie was not troubled at the prospect of a solitary end to the year. She would enjoy a week free of the city work, the teaching and she thought, guiltily, a break from Charlie. She was to sing with the choir after Christmas, and would meet with friends for St Sylvestre. If the weather was dry, not wet which it could be, she would sit in the square to watch the world go by. And she would, she hoped, take a few good walks. Life is fine she thought, as she strolled home; Toulouse was full of people, shopping, sitting outside the numerous cafes, planning their evenings. She returned to the apartment and phoned her mother. It was a relief to have made her decision, and Claire was pleased. She fenced off any suggestion that she too should visit England and stay with her mother, 'No Mum. It's good for me and Charlie to have a break from each other, and I've lots to do here.' Claire was surprised but not too much so. Deep down she loved having Charlie on his own. She began making plans.

Another Sunday, and Annie was eager to get to les Palmes, during the week she had organized for one of her freelance labourers to work in the garden, restoring it to some sort of order. Charlie was also keen , hoping to see Felix and show him the medal that he had won the previous day.

Annie, turning the corner of the house, saw the hard work that had transformed the garden: gravel paths now intersected the beds that were neatly edged in brick. There were large holes for the three palms, they looked enormous. The heavy, claggy soil had been broken up and compost dug in. Even Charlie noticed.

'Wow that looks great, Mum! You can get going now, for sure.'

Annie was delighted. She looked back to the house, where Marthe was standing in the window. Usually she came out immediately, but not today. She hoped that the change of supplier had not caused a difficulty between them. Annie set to work, placing her labelled sticks on the beds, each representing a plant or shrub, working to her plan, which she had carefully placed on the old garden table, weighed down at each corner with a stone.

'I'll help if you like.' Charlie was standing beside her, suddenly very enthusiastic, so Annie mobilised her new volunteer and between them, they were half way through the task, when Felix came out. Charlie was, as always, pleased to see him. He rushed up.

'Hello, bonne jour!'

Felix looked at his brown, rather muddy face and extremely muddy hands, knees and boots. How wonderful childhood can be… No responsibilities, no worries, all life in front of you. He smiled at the boy, then, 'Can I have a word, Annie?' He spoke over Charlie's head.

Annie walked over. She too was muddy, and her face was damp with effort, 'Welcome. We have a garden, of sorts.'

'Yes, it's looking good. What are all the little sticks?'

Charlie still eager to be involved, answered, 'They are the plants. Look,' he pointed proudly, 'they tell us exactly where to put them.'

Felix, suddenly, felt rather foolish, almost out of place. He was wearing a very fine new blue sweater, with dark trousers and expensive leather shoes. He had a black scarf around his neck. Dressed, for Toulouse, he thought, then remembering why he had come out...

'Annie, Marthe says: please use the kitchen for your picnic- it's getting cold. If you want to, I mean.'

'That would be nice. It's lunch time now, isn't it?' Charlie said.

'Always hungry. So get the bag then.' She turned to Felix, 'We seem,' she smiled at him, 'to be going to take up her offer.' She put her muddy gloves next to the plan, and prepared to go in- leaving their boots neatly at the door. It was warm in the kitchen; but their picnic did not take long, they were both hungry, and keen to press on with the work outside. Felix and Marthe had lunch later, in the small parlour. Marthe liked to use it once a week as a dining room, she had not eaten in the large formal room which was now empty and looking very bleak. The long table and heavy chairs, and the sideboard with its contents had been dispatched for sale in Toulouse. She enjoyed sitting at the little round parlour table, set with her better china and good glasses. She had made a confit of duck, cooked vegetables and opened some wine.

As soon as they were seated, Marthe began relating the account of Sylvie's visit, she spoke steadily, sipping her wine occasionally. Felix did not interrupt, he was listening with mounting horror. At last she stopped, her lunch still untouched before her.

'And you knew nothing of this? Your father a collaborator?'

'No. Nothing.' They both sat silently, Felix avoided eye contact, he had never felt so shocked. 'Who knew this story?' he wondered. There were so many questions, that he did not know where to start. They ate a little, then Felix prepared a pot of coffee, the sun filtering through from the terrace onto the table. Marthe sat in its light.

She had not told Felix of the incident at the café. She still saw herself as having failed on that occasion, allowing herself to be intimidated and walking away. Of as much concern to her was not just the violence, the unexpectedness of the attack, but the failure of any of the bystanders to protest. Did the whole town hate her? It was too horrible to contemplate. Was there a communal consciousness of hatred, lying beneath the surface of the town?

'Have you looked at this plaque?' Felix interrupted her thoughts.

'Well, no, not properly. I've seen it, walked by it, but not stopped and properly read it. I didn't know that it had any connection with me... us.'

Felix was quite unfamiliar with it. He always drove in from Toulouse, and could only just place it on the wall outside the church. He silently resolved to stop and read it, later that day. 'Of course you don't carry your father's name, and nor do I.'

'Well, I realise that!' she replied impatiently. 'But I'm his daughter, living in his house, his family house. It is obvious to all that we are connected with Bertrand.'

Felix thought about this for a moment, he tried to get the timing of the past clear in his head. 'You were a small child, Mother, you weren't involved. You can't be blamed for any of this. These things,' he finished his coffee, 'are in the past.'

Marthe sighed, 'Yes, but not buried. As we now see. Memories have not faded, obviously.' They looked at each other carefully, neither sure of the other one's thoughts.

'Do you think this is why your mother took you away?' Felix said. 'Did she know of his role, his sympathies? He had died suddenly, that is all you told me.' Felix continued to try and establish the sequence of events.

'I imagine so. She was probably fearful of staying here, if she knew that is. Her husband was effectively,' she shuddered, 'well…a murderer. I cannot believe she did know, how could she go on living quietly all those years, with a secret like that!'

Felix looked at her, he had been told very little about his grandfather, and had not thought to enquire. He now regretted that deeply.

He spoke again. 'Bertrand was acting, as he thought, in the best interests of France. Many people sympathised with the occupation, supported it, gave help. It was not a crime-just a different view of France. His actions would have been supported by some."

'Wasn't it? A crime. To betray four local men?' Marthe was almost angry.

They stared across the table at each other. They both knew that it was wrong, terribly wrong. 'And grandfather?' he asked her again, 'When did he die? Exactly?'

'I know so little,' she thought to herself 'Why is that?' She turned to Felix,

'You ask me questions that I cannot answer. Mother never spoke to me. I just understood that, after her husband died, she couldn't go on living here… It was wartime, the house was too big, there were food shortages, and life was difficult; especially now for a widow with one small child. So as I understood from her, she brought us both to Paris and we lived with

'Yes, I know. She returned to her parents' home. She had little choice I'm sure.'

Felix stood up and crossed to the window. He watched as Charlie, pushing a wheelbarrow, nearly wobbled off the new path. Why has this history entered our lives? He thought, almost resentfully. Annie was packing up. It had turned cold and storm clouds threatened rain. Felix looked at the clouds, his whole life, he knew, had changed. The afternoon dragged on, neither Marthe or Felix could think of anything else, and every attempt at conversation ended in silence. Felix left early, and drove to the wall, where the plaque was. It was a quiet Sunday afternoon, a light rain was falling, there was no one else about, families were resting after lunch, the little road empty of traffic. The church itself rose above him, its tall spire throwing a dark shadow onto the damp cobbles. He parked alongside and walked over to where the plaque was set into the wall, he bent down to read the inscription. He read it twice, pausing at each name. It was deeply sad…commemorating four men, with their names, and ages, and the date of their deaths. All four were young, two obviously Jewish, a third was named Rinaldi and the last Carrere, Francois Carrere.

Felix drove home his mind filled with what he had learnt. Entering the flat he saw that Valerie was preparing to go out.

'Do you like it?' she gave a little twirl. She had had her hair cut, very short and sharp, falling at an angle beside her face. Felix looked at her, he did not like it, it was not feminine he thought.

'Yes. It's fine.'

'Fine?' She pursed her lips.

'It's good…suits you.' he walked towards the bedroom. Valerie turned away, she was disappointed in Felix, who had always admired her looks.

'We are meeting Sophie for supper.' She called after him, 'Is that Ok?' She emphasized 'that'.

Felix detected the dissatisfaction in her voice. Emotionally drained, he had been looking forward to a quiet supper in the flat. 'Of course, if that's what you have planned. I'll take a shower.'

Felix took his shower, as the water streamed down his face, he shut his eyes thinking again of the story Marthe had told. He realized that he would not share it for the moment with Valerie, but could not explain to himself why not.

On Monday morning Marthe woke with a sadness in her heart. Life at Les Palmes had suddenly become very testing, and she was not sure that she wanted to face its challenges. She lay and thought about her mother, now long dead. They had never exchanged confidences and unlike the lively mothers of some of her school friends, her own was a pale, shadowy figure. Marthe wondered if she too had lain in this room staring at the high ceiling, alone with her thoughts. 'Why had she left? What had she known?'

For the moment to lift her spirits she went into the garden. It was no longer raining but still grey and cool. She went outside after breakfast and looked around. She saw Annie's hard work in close up now, and was excited to walk the new paths, stooping to read the labels for all the new plants. The ground smelt fresh and earthy, she found it delightful, and understood for the first time Annie's enthusiasm for her work. At the far end of the garden there was an old and decrepit greenhouse. It stood against the right hand wall, next to the two wooden sheds, which she now rather generously thought of as 'Charlie's, and close to the back wall. This too was wooden, once painted white, the paint now peeling and flaked. The further door had fallen, it lay amongst the last of the nettles, but the nearer door was still in place, and a large handle held it fast. Marthe gingerly turned it, and then putting her shoulder against it, gently eased it open. It had once been used and cared for, there were wooden racks all along the outer side, piled high with seed trays. Though weeds had established themselves on the gravel base, and the windows were green with algae, Marthe could almost feel the plant life that had filled this space. She imagined tomatoes, and courgettes and aubergines, strings of onions drying and garlic too. She thought of the scents of summer, of basil, and parsley and thyme. 'I must do something with this!' she thought and continued to look around. Some of the glass panes were missing, others cracked, but all could be repaired. The back wall had once supported peach trees and a fig- only the latter remained, holding on determinedly, its supports long fallen away. Looking about, Marthe felt great excitement, her own greenhouse! She could easily restore it, with a bit of help with the glass. Quite without experience, and now sixty, she knew that the heavy work of a garden, the digging, clearing, planting, cutting down were beyond her. But, seeds and their cultivation attracted her. It would be a challenge, and interesting to see seeds become little green shoots and then plants for her garden, and food for her kitchen. Money savers too, she was not averse to that. She could afford the large expense she had agreed to, but even so an economy was not to be ignored. 'Annie can teach me,' she thought, 'and I can make a gardening start in here. It is warm and rather soothing, out of the wind and rain, a world of its own.' She liked that idea.

That afternoon Marthe drove to the garden centre, the Carrere business, she was looking for Henri. It was easy to find, and she parked on the verge, beside the entrance gates. She stood beside her car, and looked at the prosperous garden centre: extensive green houses, and a large area devoted to planting pots, and long lines of trees and shrubs. She could see bags of manure and compost, and an old shed whose door was shut. No one was about and the big security gates were locked. She stood uncertainly, the wind was cold and she was turning to leave, when she saw Henri emerging from behind a long line of trees. He was stooped, and encased in a thick jacket. He was carrying a long hoe and had been working on the weeds at the foot of the trees. She recognized him immediately as the man who had shouted at her, but today he looked very harmless. Marthe stared at him. She could hear his low whistle. He was making his way back to the house.

And this was the son of Francois Carrere, the young resistance fighter who had lost his life because of her father. She was overwhelmed by shame. How could she now berate him for his rude conduct? What was her brief moment of fear to his loss? She understood his angry outburst, as he saw her sipping her wine and enjoying the autumn sun, and at peace with the world. Marthe returned to her car, and sat with her head resting on the steering wheel, she felt quite unable to reproach Henri. She hoped that having abused her once, he would be satisfied and let the matter rest. It had after all, she reasoned, been some months ago.

Marthe drove home and as she did so, she found herself thinking of Xavier, and how she missed his steadying hand, and his unfailing good humour and lively mind. She knew what a gift her happy marriage had been, how lucky she was, but that made it worse. The missing of him. She dreaded Christmas which was approaching.

Marthe told Annie the following Sunday that she was now going to 'take on' the greenhouse. 'That's a good idea. We can easily make it usable, the roof is sound, and we can clear out all the old trays, and attack the weeds.'

Marthe was pleased at Annie's enthusiasm. 'And, of course, I shall need your help and advice on growing, 'thinning out' she used the phrase cautiously, 'everything really!' Annie suppressed a tiny feeling of disappointment, she had owned a greenhouse many years ago, when she and Ralph had rented a cottage with a bit of a garden. She remembered the feeling of satisfaction at harvesting the food she had grown, the pleasure of herbs for soups, and casseroles, and salads.

Charlie was also rather sad to hear that Marthe was going to take on the greenhouse, he also swallowed his disappointment. 'And I can learn with you!' he said. 'It's right next door to my sheds so we can work together!' Marthe smiled inwardly, it amused her that Charlie had so taken over the control of 'my sheds'. She determined to find him some chairs, and perhaps a better table for the picnics she saw them sharing.

Marthe looked at him. She could not recall ever sharing a project with Felix when he was young, he had always been a quiet boy, busy in his own world, making models, reading, music. It was above all music with him, and he became a good pianist, practicing regularly without complaint. His father had encouraged him and enjoyed taking him to concerts. Living in an apartment in Paris, Felix had been very much a city child, though she remembered sharing some afternoon walks in local parks; it had always been rather an effort, and both mother and son were content when they turned for home.

'That's a good idea Charlie!' Marthe said.

Charlie grinned at her, 'I'm only really good at chess you know. I can always beat Felix now.' He turned away and went into one of the sheds, returning to shew her a green glass which he had filled with snails. 'I'm doing an experiment,' he said 'testing to see how long it takes them to crawl out!'

'Are they edible?' Marthe asked.

'Definitely not!'

Marthe made no further comment, she presumed that he had not seen the snail farm in the valley, just beyond the slaughter house. She had thought of stopping there, she liked snails very much.

Marthe turned to walk back to the house, and thought of what he had said about the chess. She looked at Charlie with a smile, 'Yes, Felix told me that. But he's going to improve. You must beware!'

Felix, now came for lunch most Sundays, alone, it suited him to see his mother, without Valerie who seemed to some-how inhibit him. He liked to get out of Toulouse, and to drive his car, which otherwise was parked underground near his flat. It was a fast car, an indulgence bought when he moved from Paris and he loved driving it. Sunday was a day he anticipated with pleasure. The roads out of Toulouse offered him an opportunity to test the car; negotiating the narrow streets, accelerating around the many roundabouts, he drove the dual carriage way with speed, steering confidently into the fast lane, until he veered off suddenly for St. Girou. He admired the countryside as he passed through; the wide open fields, and dark woodlands and red farm houses. There was a stone castle too, with four towers, almost hidden by the poplars that had grown up around it. He was not sure if anyone lived there, it looked neglected. Felix soon entered the little town. He slowed down now, there were always people, emerging from Mass, queuing at the boulangerie, clutching their bread and Sunday tarts. Every Sunday, he stopped and bought something for Marthe, a seasonal fig tart was their present favourite. The locals were getting used to this well dressed young man with his quiet demeanour and ready smile. They could not ignore his car, which they looked at enviously. He also looked forward to seeing the changes in the house and garden, and the progress Annie was making. Annie! She had become part of the Sunday routine and Felix was not indifferent to the pleasure he got from talking and laughing with her. She was invariably casually dressed, but she was attractive, with her hair pulled back and her fresh, open-air style. He often went straight out into the garden, while Marthe busied herself in the kitchen. He now remembered to wear his older shoes and a thick brown sweater, trying to look more 'country'.

After the first flush of interest in Marthe and Les Palmes, Valerie preferred to remain at home. She had never lived outside Paris before, and unusually had no family who lived in the country. Her friends disappeared every summer to stay on family farms, or beside rivers, or up in the mountains, returning home, tanned and full of enthusiasm for their outdoor life. Valerie was not in the least envious. She passed her time in the museums and galleries of Paris in the company of her mother, a talented artist. She learnt to sketch whilst still at school and accumulated a portfolio of drawings, watercolours and dreamt of art college. But nothing came of that idea, and Valerie found herself pressurised by her father into accountancy, a profession she enjoyed once qualified. Now in her twenties she was independent, and sophisticated. Her choice of Felix, whom she had been with now for over two years, rested on a mutual love of city life, and a shared interest in the cinema and holidays abroad and good restaurants. The move to Toulouse had been, so far, a success. They had chosen the flat together, and both liked its space, and the clean white walls and modern fixtures. Valerie was not interested in cooking, but Felix enjoyed it, so the smart kitchen was his alone and he spent a lot of time ,whilst Valerie was out earning her large salary, making new and interesting dishes. He was a familiar figure in the covered market near the Place St. Georges browsing for fresh fish and vegetables. Now it was

Autumn they were eating game, which Valerie liked, knowing that it was healthy and good for her figure.

'What's Valerie doing today?' They were having a glass of wine, and Felix was looking down the garden, he answered over his shoulder, 'A massage, and seeing a girlfriend for lunch.'

Marthe looked at Felix, 'Was everything Ok?' She wondered. They talked of other things. The story of Bertrand had been left hanging in the air for the moment, neither wanted to raise such a difficult subject. Felix still thought daily of the four men, whose names he now knew, but it all seemed so long ago. In his heart of hearts he hoped the problem would just go away.

After lunch, Felix wandered outside, and found Annie staring up at the sky her hands deep in her pockets, he startled her.

'Oh are you looking for Charlie? He is busy today with a bonfire, but has not had much success! Could you stoke it up a bit?'

She looked at him more carefully, 'Maybe not a good idea. You're not used to bonfires are you?' Felix shrugged,

'Perhaps if not a bonfire, a game with him? Chess I mean? It's pretty chilly.'

He and Charlie went into the kitchen. But Felix found himself watching Annie through the window, as she continued her work. 'She is remarkably determined', he thought, and thus quite quickly found himself in an impossible situation on the board, where a delighted Charlie closed in for the kill.

'Check Mate! Felix! You weren't concentrating properly! You have to, you know. Or you will never improve.' He looked with great earnestness at his vanquished opponent.

Felix pushed his chair back, stood up, and made a great show of disappointment. He was standing when Marthe came in, 'Can you ask Annie to come in? I have tea for us all. She must be frozen out there', she said to Charlie, but Felix, already on his feet, moved first.

'I'll go and find her. Deep amongst the nettles!' He grinned at Charlie. He went to find Annie.

CHAPTER 16

Charlie spent three happy days over Christmas at Ralph's flat, though it was a bit of a muddle. Ralph had invited another couple for Christmas lunch, which was planned for three o'clock. They arrived in good time, and Charlie, who had peeled some potatoes, and laid the table at one end of the living room, was excited. They ceremoniously put a turkey, unstuffed, into the small oven, and then went to the pub while it cooked. Charlie enjoyed the pub: a packet of crisps, a fizzy drink, and lots of people to watch. But he became anxious that his father and his friends would never leave, as they settled into a number of beers, and became the life and soul of the busy bar. By three o'clock, Charlie had given up hope, comforted only by the present that he had brought with him on the plane from his mother. It was a proper penknife, dark red and shiny. Ralph had showed him how to open the blades, they were very stiff and Charlie had gasped with excitement. 'We'll find you some wood and you can practice, cutting and making notches... it's a really good knife Charlie. Look after it!'

The Christmas lunch was finally eaten at nearly four o'clock, it was a success; with crackers and the pudding set alight and some sparklers. The flat became busy, it was a meeting point for many of Ralph's pub friends, and a jolly stream of people passed in and out, all eager to meet and chat with Charlie. The weather was wet, and he hardly went out for the three days; occupying a small space on the sofa, with his presents around him. A great deal of television was watched, programmes which his mother would never have allowed.

'You're a great little chap!' Ralph said, as he packed up Charlie's stuff and thrust them into his case. 'We've had a good time!' Charlie nodded, he was always sad to leave his Dad, the days had passed in a blur of people, meals and TV, but he was also looking forward to moving on, to staying with Grandma and Tony and Arthur.

His grandmother greeted him with a kiss, ruffling his hair, Arthur ran around, barking and sniffing. Charlie bent down to kiss him, his eyes filling with tears, he did not know why.

'My goodness! that needs a wash!' She exclaimed, looking at his shirt.

'Are those your best clothes?' She stared at him. Charlie remained preoccupied with Arthur, while Ralph moved swiftly towards his van. He turned,'Bye, old chap. I'll see you soon. Work something out with Mum.' He paused at the gate. Then walked swiftly back, bent down and hugged his son closely, 'Bye, be good!' he said. Ralph drove off, and Charlie waved goodbye, his hand resting on Arthur' head. He bent down and kissed the dog's nose, a flood of love poured through him.

Claire phoned Annie later in the evening. She had been waiting for the call,

'Oh Hi Mum! Everything all right? How's Charlie?'

'Oh, he was pretty hungry, ate a huge tea, thank goodness I'd made a cake...'

'Chocolate?'

'Of course. He always loves it. And how are you? What are you doing for New Year's Eve? Not on your own, are you?'

'No! I'm meeting choir friends at a restaurant. Then, well, fireworks at midnight... Jumping up and down. Alcohol!' She laughed. 'Bye Mum. Thank you for having Charlie. I know he'll have a great time with you. Give him a hug from me.'

Annie had enjoyed some time on her own; the weather was cold and rainy, and she was happy not to make fresh air expeditions every day. On Christmas Eve she stocked the flat with food from the market, bought some good red wine and began preparing a supper for the friends she had invited to join her. She dug out some CDs and located a selection of Christmas carols recorded at Kings College, Cambridge. The service on television was a favourite event for her mother, who always watched it sitting on the sofa, in hushed silence. Annie sung quietly to herself, she knew these carols by heart. She felt "Christmassy" for the first time. Decorations? She wondered. Just for herself? Why not?

She bought a tree in the market, dragging it home and up the stairs. It stood now just inside the door, decorated in silver and gold, and some little animal figures of painted wood that she and Charlie had chosen together for their first Christmas in Toulouse. It gave her a bit of a wrench to put them on the tree without him. Her guests would enjoy the tree and she'd leave it up for Charlie. The afternoon passed quickly; glancing at the clock she realised it was after five o'clock, already nearly dark outside, only the street lights giving a yellowish glow. She looked at the street below, hardly a person about, all the shops closed and shuttered. Christmas Eve was a traditional family celebration, and the city had already turned to the important business of preparing food. It was quiet as Annie chopped and stirred, laying the table for six, and digging out her best table cloth and napkins. She had enjoyed her afternoon; the flat grew warm as the heating slowly creaked into life, the warm cinammon cake rested on the rack, filling the air with its sweet smell. She touched it cautiously and it sprang under her finger. Reassured, she smiled 'You look good' she thought and fetched the round decorative plate to rest it on. 'I could eat you right now.'

By 8 o'clock, the party was in full swing; and Annie, now in a relaxed mood, looking at her friends enjoying themselves, felt pleased. They had all bought gifts, a contribution for the meal: oysters, wine and chocolates. The oysters took some time to open, and caused much mess, but they were traditional, an almost indispensable part of Christmas Eve. Annie sighed with pleasure as she sat down to enjoy them. They oozed the salty smell of the sea. She forgot Charlie, and concentrated on her guests. Later getting ready for bed, Annie felt suddenly lonely; what could she do tomorrow? She had never spent Christmas day itself on her own, and she tossed and turned for a short time, until, the good food and wine sent her to sleep.

On Christmas Eve, with the sky already darkening, Felix drove out of Toulouse. The traffic was bad, with numerous other cars; impatiently the drivers jostled for position at traffic lights, and roundabouts, harassed fathers sounding their horns, and anxious faces staring from the rear windows. Cars packed with families returning to the homes of grandparents and parents, their boots full of wine and food: cheeses, and foie gras, and oysters, and lobsters, the specialities purchased for the fete. It was a serious matter the Christmas Eve meal, and in many kitchens families prepared dishes all day long. Children were bursting with excitement, for, not only was the meal one of the best of the whole year, but after the last plate and dish had been cleared, there were presents to give and receive. The dark afternoon made the warmth of family houses even more desirable, as the cars drew up and occupants spilled out.

'Bonne fete! Bonne fete!' The words never changed. Doors flew open as children were embraced, grandparents, hot from the stove, beaming a welcome. 'Come In!' Hands grasped the baskets of food, and boxes of wine, the presents rustled in their paper, long journeys were forgotten as families gathered together, easing off their coats, smiling at each other, anticipating the meal.

Marthe and Felix tried hard to celebrate but the house was in the midst of decoration, smelling now of fresh paint. It felt too large for two people. Nonetheless they enjoyed the preparation of the meal laughing as they struggled with the oysters and lobster that Felix had brought with him. Marthe had bought champagne and, with the help of that, and then a good Burgundy they made themselves quite jolly, and lingered over the cheese to see Christmas day in. They felt relieved to separate at their bedroom doors, Felix knew that the heavy red wine would be followed by a headache the following day. He contemplated phoning Valerie, he envied her in Paris with all the variety that city offered for a good fete, but decided not to risk interrupting her, she was staying with her parents.

Annie walked to the cathedral on Christmas day, for a midmorning Mass. She was no believer, but enjoyed the singing. She recognized the conductor Jacque, but avoided him. She thought briefly of Felix, hoping that he and Marthe were enjoying their fete. It was a bright morning, and the streets were still wet from the overnight rain. After Mass, she sat in the square. It was lively again, as residents began to 'surface' from the indulgences of the previous night. Annie had a café au lait, then a croissant, she had a slight hangover, like most people around her. 'I'll go for a good walk,' she decided.

'Without Charlie, I can go as far as I like.' She enjoyed a long walk beside the Garonne, and then made a wide circle back into a quartier, whose narrow streets and little squares were almost empty. She looked about carefully at the planting of the urns, tubs and gardens, which had so preoccupied her back in September. They now looked, dull and straggly. 'I must revive these next week,' she resolved. She wondered how the garden at Les Palmes was doing, she had not been there now for over ten days. Later, she sat on the sofa, her feet up, and watched a film on television.

Felix left Marthe on December 27th, just as Charlie was being deposited by his father at Claire's home. He was pleased to get away. The countryside in winter he found bleak and depressing; empty fields, muddy farmyards, leafless trees and dogs barking on chains. No life, no activity… He hoped that his mother would be able to endure it, she had lived all her life in a city. These winter days were joyless and grey.

They had avoided the subject that dominated both their minds, in an unspoken resolve not to let the past spoil a festive day. They had not gone to Mass, but took a long walk together beside the river. It was their best moment. Felix had kissed his mother goodbye. She then finally raised the issue.

'How do you feel Felix? About all this?'

'About Grandfather? Some days, I feel angry thinking about what he did, what he believed in, angry that his actions, probably ruined, destroyed grandma's life and those of four families. And now threatens yours, even mine. At other moments I feel it is all a long time ago and that it has to be set aside. You and I cannot make amends, we cannot' he searched for a word 'atone'. Nor should you feel any guilt, you weren't responsible for any of this, you hardly knew your father', he paused, as Marthe interrupted,

'Well, that's exactly it! He was my father, and I'm living in his house, I'm enjoying his garden. I can'tt ignore that. Henri has every reason to be angry. Doesn't he?'

'Angry? Maybe. But not to blame you. That's where he's gone wrong. We all have to move on…terrible things happened during the war here and elsewhere.'

Felix was climbing into his car, he felt he could say no more. Marthe bent to give him a kiss, 'Go on, off you go, enjoy St. Sylvestre!' She waved as he drove through the gates, wondering not for the first time, whether she should tell him of the incident in the café. That too seemed a long time ago.

Felix felt able to leave as Marthe had organised a trip away for herself… She was flying to Paris, to spend four days with her old friend, Patricia. It would be the first time she had left the house and she tested her emotions as she prepared to leave. 'It has been more eventful, than I expected!' was her rueful conclusion. 'Hopefully the New Year will bring me better luck.'

Felix was not in a rush as he left Les Palmes. He decided to look again at the church wall and the plaque. It was cold standing there, but he lingered like a grieving man at a grave side. Where were they buried? Did they even have a grave? What had his grandfather intended? Did he even think of the families left behind? What drove a man to betray his fellow French men ? Felix was overwhelmed with the wrongness of it all, the choices of the man, the man he had never known. Yet this man was his grandfather… He drove home. Standing at the tall window of his flat, he looked out onto the river, wide at this point, quite shallow in places- little gravelly islands with grass popping up from the silvery water. 'It all seems so long ago' he thought 'What was life like then? Were there collaborators, here in Toulouse? There must have been, and members of the Resistance.' He thought about the bravery of the men who stood up against the occupation, risking their lives for others. 'Where would I have stood? With Grandfather? Or with Francois Carrere?' It was impossible to know. He could not find any answers to any of it.

The flat was warm and he lingered, slowly feeling calmer. Felix poured a glass of wine and tried to remember all that he knew about the war. It was school boy stuff and he, like most of his class, were not encouraged to ask too many questions. They learnt the basic facts: the German invasion, the fall of Paris, and the division of France into two zones. They learned of the difficulties of life in both the Occupied Zone and the area under the Vichy government: rationing which brought hardship to every family, and the travel passes, and the persecution of anyone who resisted the Nazis, the deportation of Jews, communists, and gypsies. They also learnt of the Resistance: the heroism of the men and women, who risked their lives working to undermine the German occupation, and who helped the escape of many who were 'undesirables'. But, Felix, born in 1966, 'missed' all this. It was history, recent, but still history. His parents, like all their generation, barely spoke of it; they had survived and determinedly looked to the future. The past, of course, had happened, but much of it was unpalatable.

Felix watched the light fade in the flat, he had probably drunk too much. He grabbed his coat and walked to his favourite bistro, he thought of Valerie, no doubt enjoying meeting up with old friends, enjoying Paris. And also of Annie. He wondered what she had done over the festive period.

It was New Year's Eve and Annie was eager to go out and have some fun, without worrying about getting back to an expensive child sitter. She rarely went out on her own, and spent some time getting ready. Before leaving the apartment, she phoned her mother and wished everyone a 'Happy New Year.' She spoke briefly to Charlie, who was staying up late, but not till midnight. He was watching a movie, and his attention was on that, and the prospect of pizza which he could smell from the open kitchen door. He spoke distractedly,

'Hi Mum! Fine! Yes! Ok! See you soon. Yes. Bye.' And that was that.

Their party in the restaurant, one of several large groups, was loud and lively. There was a huge tree with flashing lights, streamers from the ceiling, and balloons suspended from the walls. Music played constantly. Annie found her table, and set about enjoying herself, she knew everyone well, and it was fun to laugh and chat over the long drawn out meal. They danced between each course, changing partners every time. But the man who showed increasing interest was Jacques, the choir director, and a friend of Felix's. He took choir rehearsals, but they had never really spoken. She knew his name, and he hers, and that was about it, or so she thought. He danced very well, holding and releasing her to the tempo of the music. She loved rhythm, and he responded to her movements- hips, arms and shoulders all moving to together. The restaurant filled up, it was hot and crowded, and Annie threw off her jacket revealing a pretty red dress, low cut. She was oblivious to the attention she was getting, dancing and drinking like everyone else.

There was a sudden break and the dancers reformed- the midnight conga was starting up. Everyone piled onto the floor, making a winding queue which snaked its path through tables and chairs, some overturned as people pushed their way forward. Annie grasped the man in front of her, whilst from behind, someone held her hips. They were all dancing now, together, legs stretched sideways to the rhythm, heads thrown back. Laughter filled the hot room. The band played louder, until there was a great shout, 'Midnight! It's Midnight! Bonne Annee. Happy New Year everyone!' The balloons were released, and bobbed above the dancers, streamers were seized and whirled, catching in hair and clothes.

The room was now full of jumping, shouting people, their arms waving aloft, and their hands holding bottles. Everyone kissing and hugging. 'Bonne Annee!' shouted Annie and pushing her hair back from her face, noticed,

Felix! He was quite drunk, holding a glass, empty she noticed, his face shiny, his hair wet with sweat. He too had thrown off his jacket and loosened his tie, he looked unusually dishevelled.

Annie, delighted to see him, and sensing that Jacques was closing in, grabbed his shirt and kissed him on both cheeks. 'Felix, you're here! Have you just arrived?' The noise in the room was too great for Felix to hear her words. But he saw her and seized her hand. ' Let's dance!' he shouted.

'You can hardly stand up! I don't think you can dance!'

'I'll have a good try' He pulled her into a space and holding her close, still clutching his glass, they swayed gently together. Annie closed her eyes, it was very pleasant, dancing with someone who she felt had no ulterior motives. She liked his gentle, if drunken, embrace.

They were interrupted by another great shout; someone, to escape the heat of the room, had opened the large window by the band and they could hear the sound of the church bells. They were ringing in the new year. Annie stopped swaying.

'Quick! Let's go and watch the fireworks. I love them. Come on Felix.'

Pushing him forward to the open window, they saw the magic of exploding stars, bright colours falling across the river. Rockets soaring up, radiating light.

Annie, not yet fully drunk, but very gay and bright- gave a great cry of delight: 'Oh my God! How wonderful!' She spun round and kissed Felix on the mouth, he held her there with his hands round her face.

Felix was entranced. Someone pushed them aside, as the last of the fireworks shattered the night sky and the fireworks ended. The crowd returned to their tables or the dance floor.

The heat, music and dancing continued for a considerable time. Annie was carried off by Jacques, and she danced with him for a while. The wine continued to be poured. Felix lost sight of her and returned to the group with whom he had arrived. Valerie had gone home early. She had returned from Paris two days earlier, with a heavy cold which now looked like flu, and had left the party half way through supper, urging Felix to stay.

Felix sobered up, and felt dry mouthed and depressed. He knew a hangover would be the price of his careless drinking. The euphoria vanished as quickly as it had come. He could see Annie across the room, dancing in her red dress, but she was taken up within her own party and he left her to her fun. He left the party alone, walking back amid the detritus and litter of the streets. People were still singing and shouting as he opened the door to his flat. Felix drank a large glass of water as he prepared for a bad night's sleep. Valerie was snoring and her cheeks were flushed. A number of pills lay beside the bed.

*

January! Annie reflected as she prepared breakfast for Charlie. A hopeless horrid month, to be endured as best as one could.

She too had lost the euphoria of St Sylvestre. She looked at Charlie, home safe and sound, after a happy holiday. Annie put his cereal in front of him, 'Do you want toast? An egg?'

'Grandma always made me eggs. Two boiled, like she does.'

'Well I'm sure I can boil an egg. I'll try my best!'

Charlie, not sure if she was teasing, looked up: 'How's the garden? Have you seen Felix? Are things growing now?'

Annie remembered New Year's Eve, but not very clearly. She had seen Felix, she knew that, and they had danced. She remembered kissing him, and enjoying it. She had got home in the early hours, walking through the crowded, noisy streets, stepping over fireworks, and bottles, pavements strewn with coloured papers chains. It had been fun, she had had a good time, but she had detached herself from Jacques and ignored his messages. He was not for her.

'The garden? No, maybe next Sunday, if it is not too wet…I can't work if it's wet. January is often difficult.'

Annie was right. January was wet, cold and miserable. She phoned Marthe to say, 'Let's wait till next month. It should be better, drier. It's a waste of time and your money for the moment.'

Annie got on with her work in Toulouse. Towards the end of the month Charlie became unwell, a winter cold, had settled on his chest, and he missed a week of school. Annie had her hands full, looking after a fretful boy and continuing work. She badly missed her Sunday trips with Charlie, they had already become an important part of their lives. They both became increasingly disgruntled as the month wore on.

Marthe was also finding the start of a new year difficult. She had enjoyed her stay with Patricia, they had seen friends for supper and gone to the cinema twice. She had fitted in two exhibitions and bought some new clothes. But Paris too was wet and cold, and they had found themselves thinking of the spring and summer months ahead. She returned to find an estimate from the interior designer, Nicole, who was eager to proceed with the two rooms. Marthe brightened at the prospect and phoned her. They agreed that the salon, with its new wallpaper and fresh paint was now ready for the furniture and curtains. Nicole planned a visit in the next few days to discuss ideas for the dining room. Marthe had decided on red as her colour here; the room faced east and needed warm tones.

But the days were grey and long, and Marthe was increasingly haunted by the memory of the body being carried through the gate and into the garden. She knew that she and her mother had left Les Palmes towards the end of 1944. When she was four. But little girls… could they remember any event at such an early age? To revive her spirits, she set to work cleaning out the greenhouse now fitted with new panes. The activity was a pleasant distraction. She had never done physical work like this before; she was slow, but methodical. It was quiet inside the green house on grey mornings, the rain pattering on the roof. It felt almost cosy in her new warm anorak and boots. After a few days the greenhouse was ready, its new panes glittering in the occasional bursts of sunshine. It needed only a freshly gravelled floor. Annie could help her with this she thought, looking at her achievement with pride. She sorted out her packets of seeds, impatient to start planting. Following Annie's plan she bought packets of sunflower seeds, and nasturtiums, and some forget me nots for the cool area. One afternoon returning from Auch, she noticed a garden reclamation centre, it looked very run down and there was a fierce barking Alsatian in a cage beside the entrance. Undeterred, Marthe parked her car, as far away from the dog as she could, and walked about. The centre was full of statuary and benches, urns and water troughs. Against a wall at the back she found a stone basin, its edges chipped but otherwise it looked very handsome. There was water trickling in from a tap in the wall. She walked on, and into a shed where there was a man looking at a ledger, he glanced up.

'How much for the basin?' she pointed across the site.

He rose and then smiled slowly.

'Show me.' They walked out together. For the next quarter of an hour they walked around, Marthe indicated what she was interested in and the man, he was the owner, made a note in a little book taken from his pocket. He was tall and grey haired with an easy manner.

Marthe made her choices carefully: the stone basin, three large, hip height terracotta urns, and a matching pair of stone urns, much weathered. The owner agreed to deliver them the following week, and Marthe agreed to pay him cash when he did. It was a satisfactory deal for them both.

He walked her to her car, shouting at the dog who was again barking furiously. 'My security!' he said, 'you'll be surprised at the folk who would carry this lot off!' Marthe was not surprised, she had already realised that this was a large, and prosperous business.

It was the last Sunday in January, and Annie was desperate to get back to work at Les Palmes. It was now five weeks since her last visit. She phoned Marthe, 'I'm sorry. The weather is drying up, and I yearn to get back to work, but Charlie is poorly. I don't think I can come. He shouldn't get chilled.'

Marthe tried to hide her disappointment, she had been looking forward to seeing them back in the garden.

She was also eager to show Annie her work in the green-house. 'He could play indoors if that would help. Bring his chess set maybe? I am expecting Felix.'

Annie leapt at the offer, 'That would be great. If you don't mind a floppy ten year old in the house.'

Charlie brightened up at the prospect of seeing Marthe and Felix, he made a determined effort to walk to the station and then again through the town. Annie indulged him, and stopped at the patisserie. 'You can choose one little tart for me and one for yourself.' Charlie joined the queue of people, all looking at the tarts, which were set out behind the glass counter. Reaching the head of the line, Charlie spoke clearly but pointed for emphasis,

'One pear and one cherry please.' He carried them carefully in a small box to Les Palmes. Annie left him in the kitchen, where there was a good fire burning and Marthe was busy at the table, chopping vegetables.

'Don't let him get in the way! He's got his book, and his chess set so plenty to do. He has some school work too, he has missed two weeks!' Charlie grimaced and waved her out of the room. Marthe made a space beside her and he opened a book. She smiled at him and gave him one of the carrots that she was chopping, and he munched it as he read. Annie went out and sighed with pleasure, 'It's good to be back' she said to herself and began walking around looking for any frost damage.

Sunday worked well for everyone. Annie checked all the new plants, putting in support stakes and tying up…she turned some manure into the soil in the new red bed, the ground was hard and cold. Marthe cooked lunch for everyone, and Charlie perked up; he finished his maths project at the table in the kitchen, savouring the scent of roast chicken and rosemary and watching Marthe. She reminded him of his grandmother, though Marthe was much quieter. He thought briefly of Arthur. Earlier he had shown her the two tarts and she was now making two more, one for her, and another for Felix. He watched as she carefully rolled out her pastry on a marble slab and filled the two tarts with some apple. She gave him some trimmings, and he rolled them into a ball. 'We can bake this too,' she dusted it with sugar, 'it'll be a biscuit.' He waited for Felix, who arrived and greeted him with surprise. 'Hello stranger.'

'I've been ill!' Felix patted him on the back, 'Hope you can manage some lunch,' he took a deep breath, 'It smells delicious.'

Charlie and Felix got the chess board out after lunch had been cleared away. It was the first time they had all eaten together, and Annie had felt a little strained, though it was a relief to see Charlie looking better. He and Felix played a couple of games, but Charlie was not at his best and Felix won the first and then 'allowed' him to achieve a stalemate in the second. Marthe suggested, tactfully, a little rest. Charlie agreed, stretching out under a rug in front of the parlour fire. He was asleep immediately.

'I'll go and have a walk outside.' Felix rose, stretching. He went to find Annie. She was up a ladder, her thick coat, buttoned up, tying the peach trees against the wall. They had been damaged by wind and frost, and she was considering cutting them down and replanting in the spring. She was preoccupied, humming quietly.

'Oh Gosh. You made me jump. Could you foot the ladder? It's slippery!'

Annie looked pretty in spite of her ungainly position. It was a cold afternoon, and her knitted hat was pulled down almost to her eyebrows – her pink face glowed. She smiled down at Felix as he footed the ladder. Her task did not take her long, and she climbed carefully down.

Annie asked, 'Have you beaten him then?'

'Yes. I couldn't fail today. He's not on top form, is he?'

'Oh he'll be all right. Winter colds- they linger.'

They chatted, and Annie explained what she was doing, and what she expected to happen in the coming months to the garden. He tried to imagine the spring changes, the burst of green, trees unfolding their leaves, birds nesting and singing. He suddenly threw back his head and sang the opening of Vivaldi's Spring, from the Four Seasons. Annie stared, laughing at first, then, joined in. They followed the soprano and tenor lines, listening to each other.

'You've a lovely voice Felix! Why don't you join the choir?'

'I can't do that! Sing and write a criticism.'

She shrugged, 'Silly of me. I always forget your professional side!'

'Well it's not so important really is it.' He gave a short deprecating laugh.

'Felix! You should make more of yourself. Your talents. Your interests.' She immediately regretted what she had said, and to cover it up began to sing again. She sang for quite a time, Felix staring at her. His heart had missed a beat, not of music.

Annie stopped. 'That was fun! I haven't sung solo for ages... No one supporting me, it's both easy and difficult!'

She talked about the music. Felix listened, but his mind was elsewhere. He remembered their last meeting at New Year. While he had been pretty drunk, he still had a clear memory of a kiss, and Annie dancing in a red dress.

Marthe came out into the garden. 'Felix would you drive Annie and Charlie home today? Charlie is warm in the kitchen, he's fallen asleep Annie, but it is too cold for a walk back to the station.'

Annie was grateful, the temperature was dropping steadily. 'That would be kind, is it OK with you Felix? We should leave soon, he has school tomorrow, hopefully.' Annie woke Charlie, who sat up in surprise. She told him they were leaving with Felix. 'We're going home with Felix, in the car! Wow!' He had seen the car in the drive many times. It was much faster, and smarter than any he had been in before. Felix was secretly flattered. He was absurdly proud of the car.

They left quickly. Charlie dozed in the back seat as they drove through the almost empty town. As they passed the church wall, Annie, who was enjoying the comfort of the front seat and had begun fiddling with the radio, heard a loud bang and felt the car shudder. Something had hit the car! She looked out, seeing a figure behind, watching them... A man, his face hidden by a large beret. Felix braked hard and the car stopped.

'What was that? What did we hit?' Charlie had woken with a horrible start.

'What's happened? Why are we stopping?' his voice was anxious.

Felix pulled to the side of the road. He got out. They had not run over something, no dog or cat lay beneath the wheels. But walking around to the rear of the car he saw immediately that there was damage there. A very large dent just above the number plate and below the back window. The paint was already peeling back. A brick or stone he concluded. Annie was next to him now, they looked about, further back, in the direction from which they had come, and Annie saw the brick. It had fallen into the middle of the road. The man in the beret was no longer there. She spoke in bewilderment, 'How extraordinary! He threw it at us... At your car Felix!'

Felix was thoroughly shocked but improvised swiftly. 'He must be the local drunk! What a thing! On a Sunday.' he tried to laugh it off. Annie was confused, perplexed at Felix's words. 'I saw someone, in a black beret. Watching us. I think he threw it... The brick. Goodness,' she looked alarmed, 'what if it had come through the window? Charlie was in the back!'

This was what Felix was also thinking, not of the damage to his car, but the danger to the sleeping boy. He tried again to make light of the incident, 'Well, I'm sure it was not deliberate. Let's get back in the car, shall we?'

He drove them home. Annie was very quiet and Charlie had gone back to sleep, Felix pushed back his fears and suspicions, but he was convinced now that the man in the beret had singled them out, had recognised the car, that it was no accident. No drunken attack.

In Toulouse it was getting dark already. Felix followed Annie's directions and found himself in the narrow street in which she lived. Charlie now awake, sat up. He looked rested, with colour back in his cheeks. 'Stay for supper, Felix. Mum has made lasagne and I helped... A bit.' Felix was taken by surprise, unaccustomed to the impromptu manner of a young boy. He looked at Annie, who nodded her head and smiled. 'Yes. Do. It would be very nice to have your company!'

Felix parked and they gathered up Annie's haversack and Felix carried the chess set. In the apartment and instructed by Annie, Felix opened a bottle of red wine and slowly explored, guided by Charlie. It was very different from his own, and he was amazed that two people could live in such a disorganized state. Annie watched him while she cooked, as he put books into little piles, picked up two sweaters, and began sorting out all the pencils and pens on the table. He poured another glass of wine, aware that he had drunk the first rather fast. 'Slow down!' he said to himself.

'We are pretty chaotic, but we manage!' Annie smiled, and Felix felt embarrassed. 'Can I help?'

'Help Charlie to lay the table would be good.' She was busy making a salad now, and slicing big chunks of bread. 'How can we be hungry again?' she laughed, and Felix realized that indeed he was hungry, and lasagne was just what he felt like. Charlie lifted glasses down from a cupboard and placed them carefully beside the place mats. Annie moved a vase of tulips and positioned them in the centre of the table, and supper was ready. Felix relaxed, pushing the memory of the brick hitting the car from his mind. The lasagne was very good, it was not the kind of food that Valerie would eat, and Felix enjoyed it. They chatted lightly, and no one mentioned the car and the brick. As Charlie was getting ready for bed, Felix began shaking. His hands, and his legs trembled violently. He sat down. Annie at the sink, turned to look for the plates off the table, 'God. Felix. What is it?' he was very pale and sweaty. 'I'm sorry. I have to sit down. I don't seem able to stand up!'

Annie, her hands still wet, put one on his forehead. 'You're very clammy. It's shock I think. Delayed shock. Sit there, it'll pass.'

Struggling to keep calm, Felix did as she said. 'Was it the wine, had he drunk too much.' he remonstrated with himself.

Annie pushing anxiety away, said, 'I'll first see Charlie into bed. Stay where you are.' She gave him a glass of water. 'Try not to faint please. I am 'no good' in emergencies.'

Felix recovered while she was out of the room, but he felt idiotic. Annie returned, looked at him carefully. 'There's something going on, isn't there? It wasn't an accident, was it? I recognised that man, it was Sylvie's father. M.Carrere. I have seen him twice at the garden centre.' Felix did not want to lie, nor did he want to explain. He said nothing.

'Felix, listen. You don't have to tell me- but it may help... to talk.'

'Can I have a strong coffee? I need fortifying!' He tried to smile.

She made two espressos, taking her time, giving Felix time. She pointed to the sofa, 'let's sit here'. She concentrated as he spoke, he told her all that he knew, the full account that he had learnt from Marthe. The account she had heard from Sylvie. He looked straight at her as, for the first time, he told the story out loud.

'In 1944, my grandfather, Bertrand du Pont, gave the name of Francois Carrere and those of three other men to the Milice here in St. Girou. They were arrested and taken to the railway station and put on a train to Paris. They were destined for Germany, and waited in a camp, unable to communicate with their anxious families. Several weeks later, and already hungry and fearful, they were moved east to Strasbourg, it was August and very hot. The train waited there for two or more days, and when it was opened up, to take on more prisoners, many of those inside were dead of heat exhaustion and asphyxia. Francois Carrere and the three other men were amongst the dead.' Felix paused, Annie had not moved. 'Have you seen the plaque on the wall? Down from the church. Near where the brick was thrown?'

She nodded her head. 'I've not read it.'

'It commemorates the four men. Henri Carrere is the son of Francois, and has a burning hatred for Bertrand, and now for his daughter, Marthe.'

The room was very quiet and dark. They had finished their coffee and Annie looked at him. 'It's a sad and terrible story. And I'm so sad that you and Marthe have learnt it.'

Felix continued, 'It was Sylvie, who went to Les Palmes and told Marthe. Henri refused to supply the plants that you had ordered.' Felix stood up. ' So you recognized him earlier?'

'Yes. It was only a glimpse but it was definitely Sylvie's father.' Annie tried to be reassuring. 'He had probably been drinking…saw your car…and impulsively picked up the nearest thing to hand, a brick, and threw it. He is now probably at home regretting his foolishness.'

Felix was grateful for her common sense, though he was by no means convinced by her explanation. They talked on, but both were tired and Felix prepared to leave. 'I'm sorry that you've become involved. At least Charlie wasn't hurt!' he grimaced at the thought, and Annie gave his hand a squeeze, and touched him lightly on the shoulder, speaking quietly,

'This is France, in the twenty first century. The past, we all have to be reconciled to it. But it does shadow us perhaps even to the present day. Hopefully Henri has made his gesture, refused to help with the garden order and chucked a brick. That should be enough. Stay strong Felix!'

Felix walked home, he had drunk too much to drive, reflecting on what a special person Annie was. She had insight and sympathy…she was a listener. He felt more positive, but deeply uneasy. On the table in the flat he found a terse note from Valerie. He had forgotten that they were dining with friends and she had left without him. She would be both cross and disappointed with him. Grabbing his coat Felix ran down the stairs, 'Maybe I can get there in time for coffee.' He found them as they were paying the bill. Valerie hardly looked at him. They walked back home in silence and she went to bed ignoring his attempts to apologise. She blamed his forget-fulness on his increasing involvement with his mother, who Valerie thought had become very demanding.

CHAPTER 14

February was cold and sunny. Marthe kept herself busy, in a determined effort to distract herself from unwelcome thoughts. She had bought several books in Paris, on the subject of World War ll and the occupation of France, and was reading with growing interest the history of the Resistance. It was a revelation, and she was horrified by her ignorance of the events which had occurred in her early years. She thought about her school days, had she just not paid attention? Or, was this dark period of French history deliberately not taught? The Resistance, she learnt, had been active throughout France, recruiting support from all manner of people, many were women, and adolescents. Their extraordinary bravery and steadfast determination made Marthe feel very humble. And one of them was Francois Carrere. She thought about her father too, and wondered if she would ever be able to understand and accept his role in the events of that time. She had some very dark moments.

The stone and terracotta ornaments were delivered and she had them positioned. They looked very large standing in the empty beds, and the basin too looked out of place. But Marthe was confident in her choices and the owner assured her that they would look well. She walked him around and he showed great interest, which Marthe found flattering.

'Come back in the spring and see how it looks then!'

He nodded gravely and thanked her, searching in his jacket he drew out a card and gave it to her.

'Claude Mangeard.' it read and a phone number.

'I would like that. Thank you.' He drove out of the gate with a small wave.

The following Sunday, she was pleased to see that Charlie had recovered his spirits. He had shown her a red pocket knife and then raced out to look for sticks. Near lunch time Charlie heard Felix's car, and went out to say 'hello.' He found Felix and Marthe together talking, in the drive way, Charlie interrupted them. 'Hi Felix! How's the car? Did you get it fixed? Was it expensive?' Charlie walked around looking for the damage. Felix held his breath,

'Have you had a crash?' Marthe looked at Felix in surprise. Charlie spoke eagerly,

"No! No! It wasn't Felix's fault. A man threw something at us as we were leaving last Sunday. It hit the back... a big bang. It woke me up!'

Marthe looked at Felix. She turned to Charlie, 'And did you see him? This man?'

'No, not really, but Mum did.'

Marthe stood thinking rapidly,

'Did you know this man?'

She had turned to Felix and was looking at him intently,

Felix paused, 'Let's go inside,' he pretended to shiver, 'It's cold here. Charlie are you having a picnic today?'

'Yes we are! Mum has brought some sausages, and we are going to cook them in my bonfire.'

His face was a picture of enthusiasm. Marthe and Felix walked up the steps to the front entrance, Charlie went back to the garden.

There followed a long conversation at Marthe's kitchen table.

'It was just an old man, who had probably been drinking.' Felix tried to play it lightly.

'But you knew him?'

'No, not immediately. Annie saw him more clearly.'

'And she knew him?'

'Yes,' he paused again, 'It was Henri, Sylvie Carrere's father.'

'And the son of Francois Carrere. This was no chance happening was it? He recognized you, and your car, and tried to do you harm.'

'It did little damage. And it's now fixed.'

Marthe looked at him angrily, she stood up,

'Felix! Listen to me. He could have done far more, he could have broken the windscreen, caused you to crash. Anything!' and then momentously, 'This is not the first time!'

Felix felt a pain in his stomach, he looked at her,

'What? What are you saying?'

Marthe sat down. 'I need to tell you something…maybe I should have told you before…but I chose to keep it to myself. Let me make us a pot of coffee, you look cold, and this may take a little time.'

Five minutes later, Marthe began her account of the incident in the café the previous October. She spoke slowly, leaving nothing out, she could remember the details with horrible clarity.

'And you kept all this to your self ?' Felix was astounded.

"It seemed so extraordinary at the time. Yes. I was frightened, and then cross with myself for fleeing the scene. That's what it felt like afterwards! I only understood when Sylvie came to see me, the very next morning and I learnt the connection between this man, Henri, and our family. Then when you learnt the story too, I got caught up in the horror of Bertrand and the war and the four men and the deaths on the train. I tried not to think about the café…it seemed so little in comparison.'

Felix drained his coffee, and went to look out of the window, to calm himself. He turned but his face was angry,

'You should have told me immediately! That is what I am here for. To support and advise you. That's what sons do!'

This was a surprise for them both. Marthe had never before needed Felix to play a role of advice and support, she had had a husband who played that role for many years, and since his death her relationship with Felix had been loving, of course, but she had not turned to him for advice or needed 'support.' She had decided to move to Les Palmes without referring to him, and had tried hard to be independent and selfsufficient.

'Have I been foolish?' she wondered. 'Was I too determined to stand on my own two feet?' Her adventure, as she had thought it, her attempt to take control of her own life for the first time, seemed to be going horribly wrong. She turned to Felix, 'Maybe I was foolish. I'm sorry if you think so. But it is difficult being on one's own, after so many years. I don't want to lean on you, or anyone now,' she looked at him, 'You have your own life, your music, Valerie, your lovely flat.'

'Yes and I have you!' He touched her arm as he returned to the table, 'we are the family now, you and me…we cannot have secrets. So let us now think where we are,' he emphasized 'we'. 'As I see it the picture is this: this man Henri recognised you in October and took the opportunity to distress, humiliate, and frighten you. He may have been encouraged by young Jean, you mention that he was drinking in the café, and Jean had a grudge. Henri seized his opportunity, maybe he was a little drunk, and you were an easy target. It was cowardly and contemptible. Then he refused to supply you with the garden plants. His daughter Sylvie explained to you the connection between our two families. Then he saw me in my car passing through the town and took the opportunity to try and harm me.'

Marthe was by now extremely agitated. Felix had drawn a very clear picture of a man who seemed to have developed an obsession with her and her family. Marthe said, 'We need to act slowly. He is rash and angry and, maybe violent, but we need to be calm and considered. He does,' she paused, 'he does have a reason for his anger. Think of what Bertrand did…'

They continued to talk about Henri and the implications of his behaviour and Marthe persuaded Felix to do nothing for the moment, but he was by no means convinced. She told him of her visit to the Carrere business, watching him as he worked, 'Goodness, I wish I had spoken to him then! But he looked old and harmless! What a mistake I made!'

'Well.' Felix responded, 'It's my turn now! I will go and see him. He cannot behave like this and get away with it!'

'No. No. Not today Felix, please. I will go back and talk to him.' Felix agreed reluctantly; his mother was very insistent. He drove home in an angry mood, too preoccupied to say goodbye to either Annie or Charlie, who, he could see were still enjoying their day in the garden. Annie glanced up as he left, surprised to see him go without saying goodbye.

*

Marthe had noticed the sign on her route up to the big town of Auch some thirty miles to the North . The city was the old capital of Gascony. It occupied a very fine position on a hill, rising up on steep banks from the river below. It was dominated by its imposing cathedral, and there was a large cobbled square in front of the heavily carved west door. This square was the site of a weekly market; in summer it was busy, and full of colourful sun shades, in the winter it struggled a little, the vendors wrapped in thick coats and scarves and woolly hats. There was a pungent smell of sausage and warm wine from several stalls, but when the prevailing north west wind blew, the market felt cold and miserable.

The stone façade of the cathedral was much damaged in the sixteenth century, for the province became fiercely Protestant, but the beautifully carved wooden choir stalls had survived the Protestant iconoclasts. The cathedral had an impressive neighbour. It was but a stone's throw from a defensive castle, used until recently as a prison. There was a tall statue of d'Artagnan overlooking the river.

For Marthe it was a useful centre for shopping and she had purchased the larger items there: beds, pillows and duvets, some lamps and electrical items for the kitchen. In the narrow cobbled streets near the square, there was a bookshop, with a friendly, dishevelled young man who did not mind her browsing. It was part of a very old building and inside it was dark, with oak beams supporting the low ceiling. The books were well displayed with clear signs for History, Art, World Affairs etc. The fiction was set out on wide tables in piles. Next to the till, there was a section that sold CD's, and Marthe lingered here too. The young man played jazz quietly, he was casually dressed in a sweater and jeans, and his hair was shoulder length. He was reading as she approached with a book in her hand. 'Found what you wanted?' Marthe showed him, 'It's just what I was looking for. About gardens...in Gascony.' He wrapped it up. She enjoyed chatting with him, and wondered whether the books were an indulgence, and that he made money elsewhere. She had never seen anyone else buy a book.

Marthe enjoyed her drive, and while her car had none of the glamour of Felix's, it gave her a good all round view of the landscape. She drove through some small villages, where there was rarely anyone to be seen, this always surprised her, the emptiness of the countryside. It was a little used road, following a high ridge which gave lovely views. She never tired of looking out for signs of life, a tractor ploughing on a hill side, a line of washing blowing in the wind, dungarees and tea towels and linen. On one farm there were horses grazing, and on a steep slope a field of grey and white ducks sitting in the sun, so fat that they could barely move. On this particular day, following her conversation with Felix, she wanted time for reflection, so she turned off the road after leaving Auch, following a sign for a convent.

Marthe had been brought up a Catholic and had attended Mass every Sunday with her grandmother. She had been confirmed in the company of her school friends and enjoyed for many years the sense of belonging to a group outside her family. She took part in religious processions and attended several summer retreats. But in her twenties, married to a man who had no faith, and away from the influence of her family, she found herself missing all the Festivals, even the Easter and Christmas Mass. Felix's birth had for a while changed this, and she enjoyed sitting beside him as he watched the rites and studied his missal. But this did not last beyond his early teens, when he picked up his father's indifference to religion and refused to accompany her. She had turned back to the church after the death of Xavier, finding consolation in the familiar rites. But she would not have called herself a believer. She attended rarely after the first year of mourning.

The Convent was set on a slight hill approached up a winding road, rather narrow and steep. This ended in the hamlet which had grown up around the Church and the community of nuns. They were an enclosed order who had settled there, several centuries previously, in what was once an isolated place, driven out during the Revolution, they had returned soon after the fall of Napoleon and once more taken up a life centred around their faith and a rule of self sufficiency. Wearing workman like overalls, their heads covered modestly, the nuns farmed their fields, tended a variety of animals, and produced honey, jams and soft cheeses, which were sold at local markets. They employed no one, and had the skills of brick layers, glaziers, plumbers,and even electricians. It was a surprise to visitors to see a nun driving a tractor, her habit tucked into serge trousers, as she negotiated the heavy machine on the steep hill sides.

Having parked carefully on the verge beside a large duck pond, Marthe entered through the arched entrance. She saw a number of children of all ages, playing in the garden, running about and shouting noisily, they were enjoying a week's retreat, away from a rough suburb of Toulouse. A young nun was watching them, her face almost hidden in her habit. Some villagers were walking slowly to the church, which was located behind the convent itself, and she followed them. Inside it was dark and cold; a few chairs were set out in the narrow nave. The ceiling was very high, and the lighting relied on several windows which did not give much illumination. The congregation, none of whom were young, slowly stood and Marthe, who had taken a seat at the back, watched as a procession of nuns entered from the cloister to the left. They wore mostly black, with white cowls shielding their faces, though some, novices she thought. were in grey.

Glancing up, Marthe spotted Reverend Mother in a high alcove some twenty feet above the nave, she was old and bent and watchful. Taking their places in the choir stalls, the nuns stood with their heads bowed in an attitude of submission, as a very old priest entered, through an arched door, and taking his place, stood before the altar. He began the Mass in a frail voice which Marthe strained to hear. About her the congregation moved their lips saying the words in unison. It was like the murmuring of bees. Marthe glanced at the old woman who was sitting nearest to her, she had a thick shawl around her narrow shoulders and on her feet a pair of tartan slippers. Her hands were purple and mottled. She had not noticed Marthe.

At certain moments, small groups of nuns formed a circle before the altar and sung unaccompanied, with one of them gently conducting. A thin rope hung above them and was pulled, making a silvery chime. At this the nuns bowed very low in the choir stalls, their backs quite straight and making a line of black and grey. The elderly people around Marthe did not kneel but bent forward on the hard chairs. It was very cold.

Marthe sat in awe at the solemnity of the Mass, and the evidence of faith all around her. She tried hard to concentrate but her mind drifted away and she was almost startled when the bell was tolled to signal the Eucharist. She felt unable to go up for Communion, but sat with her head bowed trying to focus on the meaning of the Mass. A last hymn was sung by all the nuns, their light voices drifting up into the high ceiling, their offering to God. Several of the congregation joined in, their voices were very weak. And it was over. The nuns bowed as the priest withdrew, and then making a neat crocodile filed out in silence. From her lofty perch Reverend Mother continued to watch them, until she too disappeared through some hidden door. The small congregation gathered up their hats, gloves and shawls. There was one solitary man, Marthe noticed, and he was the most bent of all.

The garden which surrounded the church was empty, the children had disappeared, they had not attended this Mass and Marthe assumed that they had been in church much earlier. It felt very quiet and still. Marthe experienced a brief moment of hope, the experience had indeed calmed her and restored her spirits. She walked back to her car, determined to return frequently, though she knew that her faith, her child-hood belief, was gone forever. As she drove back down the hill, she reflected on the life of the nuns, who had turned their backs on the outside world, living a spiritual life of prayer and seclusion. She could not comprehend it in any way.

She turned the car toward home and the garden business of Henri Carrere.

*

Sylvie had never regarded her father as an angry man, but following their conversation about the death of Francois, and his refusal to do business with Marthe, she began to think about him afresh. They were close, especially after the death of her mother when Sylvie was thirteen. Just the two of them, drawn together in grief, and later by their shared love of plants and horticulture. She had spent so many hours in his company, working alongside him in the business and at home-eating, talking, planning the year. But how well did she really 'know' him? Henri was a quiet, self-absorbed father- loving of course, but undemonstrative. He had few close friends in the local town, though she would see him drinking at the café, but no one ever came to the house, socially. Their neigh-bours were hardworking farmers, absorbed in the endless daily routine of their lives; they might stop work for a family celebration: a marriage, a funeral, a first communion, they all had a dark suit and collared shirt for that, but overalls, a warm hat, stout boots, thick socks were what they put on, day in day out. They were in tune with the rhythm of the year, the progression of the seasons and for some, with their advancing years, the slowing of their gait. The steep slopes on which many farms were set began to be noticed in a new way, as did the north wind which rattled the barn roofs and forced itself into their old farm houses.

She and Henri had not spoken again about his refusal to supply Annie's plants. Sylvie had been disappointed at the time, it was an interesting order and she had looked forward to the possibility of working with a professional garden designer. She had been very impressed by Annie's knowledge and new ideas. But hearing for the second time, Henri's account of the events of 1944 had shocked her, while her visit to Marthe, had been difficult and traumatic. She had not told Henri of this visit. It felt somehow like a betrayal of Francois, to speak to her. Which it was not, she reasoned after several days. But she did not want to upset her father whose mood seemed unforgiving. Sylvie knew nothing of Henri's behaviour in October at the café, nor more recently, of the brick that he had thrown at Felix's car. It was therefore with some surprise that she saw Marthe walking into the farm. Henri too was taken aback. He was briefly alarmed. He and Sylvie were standing outside the office and there was little opportunity for him to avoid her. Marthe had a clear idea of what she wanted to say to him, and had no hesitation in approaching. They did not shake hands. Marthe did not hesitate. 'I have come to tell you to leave me and my family alone. We are not your enemy and will not be treated as such. You have twice abused us, in a way which is wrong and criminal. I am not here to threaten you, but if anything further happens, I shall go directly to the gendarmerie,' she paused, looking at him, ' the past is the past, and neither you nor I can alter what has happened. Wrong as it was. I am sorry for the death of your father, and the part that my father played in it...'

She was prevented from finishing,

'Wrong! Wrong! Your apology is nothing to me!' he spat on the ground, 'Get off my property! Your family has no place here, you are as unwelcome as he was!'

Marthe stood her ground, 'I repeat, I played no part in any of this, and I will not be driven out of my home by you or anyone. Be warned, the law is on my side. One more of your disgraceful actions and the Gendarmes will be here!'

Sylvie was listening to this in horror. What did she mean? What had her father done? She looked at him, he was shaking and pale, but angry beyond anything she had ever seen. Marthe turned to her, 'You should control your father, this has to end now! I shall be true to my word.'

Sylvie turned to Henri, 'What is this? What have you done?' He stood defiantly in front of them both, shaking his head. Sylvie spoke fiercely,

'Whatever has happened, there will be no more of it! I give you my word!' There was a brief silence, then Marthe without looking again at Henri, walked briskly back to her car. It had not been a pleasant experience, but she was confident that Henri, and Sylvie, understood her. Henri watched her leave in silence. Later Sylvie was able to force a reluctant Henri to explain what 'disgraceful actions' he had been guilty of. He gave a brief outline and refused to acknowledge that his actions had been wrong. He continued to blame Bertrand Du Pont for all the problems of the Carrere family, and maintained his right to 'drive the family out'. Sylvie could make no headway with him, while she was very aware of the promise she had given to Marthe. She did not know how she could keep it.

On the first Sunday in March, Felix took Marthe out for lunch, it was her birthday. It was a warmer day, Spring well established, and before they set out, they went to see what Annie was doing. She was working on the newly planted grasses, thinning them carefully to allow maximum light to their roots. 'I'll be leaving at four o'clock today Marthe, if that's all right. Charlie and I are going to the cinema. I hope that's OK?' Charlie put down his pen knife, he was trying to cut the stiff stems that Annie had thrown aside, 'We're going to Star Wars! With my friend, Jean!'

Felix looked at Annie. She had a smear of earth above one eye, and was, hot and sweaty, her shirt sleeves were rolled back, and already her arms showed an early tan. Her dungarees had been replaced with a pair of blue jeans and her hair was pushed up under a sunhat. Felix found himself staring at her, and stopped abruptly. A certain shyness had come on him. He knew that he found her attractive and interesting, but she was very different from any woman he had known before, and he was uncertain about his feelings. She had an aura of self-sufficiency and independence, yet she could also be light hearted and amusing.

'That sounds terrific! Enjoy it Charlie.' He said and wished momentarily that he was going too.

Quick to spot an opportunity, Charlie replied, 'You could come too… if you're back from lunch. It's for grown ups, you know.'

'Well,' Felix was flattered, 'if I'm back, perhaps I will. Annie?' She nodded, 'That's good with me! We always go for pizza after! Or maybe two meals a day… Too much?' she looked at him. 'Pizza? What is that then?' Felix said.

Charlie gasped, 'It's pizza of course!'

Annie laughed, 'He's teasing, Charlie. Even Felix knows what pizza is.' Felix was not sure who had won this little exchange. Marthe had watched this with amusement. Annie was sharp, but kind. A little on the defensive sometimes, but bright and spirited, and she was a good mother. As Felix drove her to lunch, she looked at the landscape, going past, rather fast, and turned to look sideways at her son. He seemed fine, 'But how did one know?'

Felix was silently wrestling with uncertainties; it was not just Annie who was on his mind, but more seriously his life with Valerie seemed to have run onto the rocks. She was restless and distracted. They did not 'row' but nor did they communicate. They had not made love with any passion for several weeks. Not really since her return from Paris after Christmas and the New Year party that had been ruined by her heavy cold. He blamed himself. In truth they had little in common, she worked hard and was tired by the time she returned to the apartment. Their evenings had lapsed into a regular pattern, he listened to music, cooked supper, and wrote reviews of the concerts that he attended. He would have liked to play the piano too, but his playing irritated Valerie. 'Too loud! I need peace after the day I've had!' she would interrupt on the rare occasions when he played. She preferred to eat watching TV, her plate balanced on her knees and a glass of wine on the table between them. Their lives were increasingly separate, and Valerie knew nothing of Marthe's troubles. 'Why haven't I confided in her? She should be told. Am I trying to protect Marthe or her?' Felix did not know the answer, but it was an aspect of his life which he continued to keep hidden. Valerie was away in Paris for the weekend, seeing her sick father; it again made any real conversation between them impossible. Marthe's birthday lunch was a welcome change.

A Sunday market was still up and running, a small affair-mainly stalls selling fruit and vegetables, but there were chickens roasting on a spit outside a van selling meat. The smell was delicious as Felix and Marthe parked and walked by. Marthe inhaled deeply, 'I don't think I've eaten all week-goodness that smells so good.' She quickened her step 'Did you reserve, Felix?'

They ate in the restaurant set in the arcades that formed the square. It was busy, several large families eating together, but also couples like themselves, quieter. The food was 'local' and good, Marthe sat back with her small coffee cup and looked at Felix.

'You seem quiet! You're not worrying about me, are you?' She had been conscious that he had avoided anything but light, gossipy conversation throughout the meal. 'No. I'm a little tired, that's all.'

'Why? What makes you tired suddenly?' her voice was sharper than intended.

Marthe believed that Felix's work was full of enjoyment, listening to concerts and writing about them; she thought it was an easy way to earn a living. She had never regretted her family wealth- it had allowed both her and Felix to live without any financial concerns, but she also felt that it had prevented any real ambition in Felix. If pressed, Marthe would have conceded that she was disappointed that Felix was not more ambitious. He was delightful, attentive and good company, but where was his career leading? Nor, at this lunch, did he seem particularly happy.

'Is it me? Because if so, it is the very last thing I want! I have been to the Carrere farm and confronted Henri, he won't cause any more trouble I am sure. I told him clearly that I would go to the Gendarmes if he approached you or me. His daughter assured me that she would control him from now on.'

Felix expressed surprise, impressed by Marthe's decisive action, 'Well I am sure that you're right. Did he mention Francois and the war?'

'I was not there to discuss that. He was not interested in any apology! They are separate issues, the past and the present.'

Felix looked at her, she seemed very confident. He hoped that she was right.

'Anyway, back to you, Felix, why are you tired?'

'Sorry, I used the wrong word!' Felix answered, 'I'm just a bit... Flat! Down! Maybe, well I'm missing Valerie a little, she seems to be away a lot and is always tired in the evening. We are going skiing soon with some friends of hers, so that should be nice...'his voice tailed away.

'You don't like living alone?' Marthe suggested.

'Something like that,' he smiled, 'don't fret, it'll pass- perhaps a change of scene... I love skiing.'

They left it like that. Felix stood up, his coffee half finished- paid, collected their coats, ushered Marthe out. Standing outside, they briefly watched as the stalls closed up; their awnings were put away. The crates of unsold produce were loaded into the vans, the area was untidy with cauliflower leaves, cabbage stalks and the green fronds of carrots strewn in the gutters of the square.

*

When they got back it was nearly four o'clock and Annie was packing up, Charlie impatient at the gate, eager to catch the train home. Annie was running her eye over the garden, 'I'm done for today, Marthe. It's all going really well, I am sure you've noticed the signs of Spring.' Marthe nodded, 'Of course! I inspect it every day!'

Annie smiled at them both as she packed her tools into her backpack. She shrugged it onto her back, and gave Charlie her purse, 'carry this please! So Felix, are you coming?' Felix hesitated…. And failed. His mind more occupied with thoughts of his mother and Henri.

'No I'm not sure that will work for me… I have some writing to do, by Tuesday. But thanks, perhaps another day." Marthe was disappointed, she thought some fun would do Felix good, and Charlie was also put out.

'It's a good film! You'll be missing it!' he said looking hard at Felix.

Felix was already regretting his decision, he looked at Annie, but she was adjusting her coat and had turned away. 'Maybe another time, Charlie,' he repeated. The pair walked away now ready, and eager to be off, and back to the station, Charlie waved at the gate, Annie did not. Felix stood watching, remembering a previous Sunday when Annie and Charlie had joined him in the car. The day Henri had thrown his brick. He remembered her kindness after supper, that she had listened as he told her the family history. Offered him her support. She was not like Valerie! Was that part of the attraction he felt? Felix's confusions continued to trouble him. 'Why didn't I, at least, offer a lift?' He was angry with himself, remembering how attractive Annie had looked in the garden in her hat and jeans, her hair rather adrift.

Annie was more disappointed than she had shown when Felix turned down the invitation to join her, Charlie and his friend for a film and pizza. She would have liked some male company. She felt sometimes that she was becoming too solitary. It would be nice to have someone else to dress for, to cook for, to talk to. She looked out of the train window, Toulouse was coming into sight, its tall buildings catching the last of the afternoon sun. She was looking forward to the film and a pizza, but essentially it was a Charlie treat, though of course she would enjoy it, but through him, rather than for herself. 'I must liven up, or I'll get dull!' She looked at Charlie, he gazed back- such uncritical love! Annie wanted to hug him. 'Are you ready? We need to be a bit quick now- the film starts at five!'

She and Charlie had a fun evening, but as she began getting things ready for Monday morning, Annie reminded herself to think more about herself in the future, not just about Charlie, work and Marthe's garden.

*

To make up for a sense of having failed in refusing Charlie's invitation, Felix resolved to do something that he had been avoiding for some time. Marthe had told him of her visit to the Carrere farm, now as he left Les Palmes, he found his way there. It was easy to spot, there was a large wooden panel beside the road, somewhat faded, and printed on it in green letters, 'Carrere et Fils'. He parked and approached. Henri was startled to see the car he knew to belong to Felix parked outside the heavy gates. He stood back in the small window of the kitchen, watching as Felix got out. What does he want? Henri felt oddly apprehensive. Felix was now at the door, lifting the old knocker. He knocked loudly. Henri was unsure what to do. He could stay still in the dark room, unseen, or pull himself together and see what Felix wanted. He had no time to decide, for Sylvie, hearing the noise, had left the kitchen and was opening the door.

Felix had not realised that Sylvie also lived in the farm house, he had prepared himself to talk to Henri. He was as surprised to see her- as she was to see him. They looked at each other, Sylvie with a sense of alarm, spoke first.

'It's Felix? Yes?' She also had recognised the car, and she stood in the doorway, barring it. Felix nodded. 'I've come to speak to your father, is he in?' Felix wasted no time. Sylvie thought quickly,

'Can we speak first? Let's go to the office- shall we?'

She guided Felix away from the door and the house, where she knew Henri would be listening. Somewhat disconcerted, Felix found himself agreeing- they walked together down the gravel path, now lined with spring tulips, to the wooden building... the office. They sat down in the office and Felix voiced his concerns. Sylvie tried to reassure him, 'I'll call in the Gendarmes if he does anything more! He understands that, and the threat will stop him. He has never been in any trouble before, and has his good name in the town to preserve. Our business depends on it! I'm just sad that your mother's return has been made so difficult.' Felix accepted her apology, he had little choice.

It was dark by the time Felix left the office. 'Trust me, please, he will give all this up. He knows it was wrong. He's tired, old, foolish.' Sylvie managed a small smile as they parted. Felix felt he had done as much as he could.

CHAPTER 14

Marthe woke suddenly, she had been dreaming of a little brown and white dog, a terrier, digging in a garden. This garden she thought. Had there been a dog in the house when she was a child? She lay still trying to remember. The room was quiet and dark, only a light from the hall downstairs filtering under the door. A little dog? She cursed the fading image of her dream. She reached for her watch- it was five o'clock, at least two more hours before she would get up. She was wide-awake and slightly cold. The open window was allowing in too much chill air. She rose, closed the window and looked down the garden. There was darkness everywhere. She tried cautiously to access her other memory, the one that she had supressed, of a figure being carried in through the door in the wall... Who was it? She climbed back into bed, it was still slightly warm, and lay on her back. Marthe tried to piece together everything she had been told by her mother and grandparents about her life in this house. She had been given little information and everyone was dead now. Frustrated, she turned on the light, wrapped her dressing gown around her and went down the stairs and into the 'salon'. There was a smell of paint still, and the newly laid carpet was soft under her bare feet, she switched on one of her new lamps, it created a pool of light. Her mother's desk stood by the wall, untouched since her mother had departed for Paris. It had a strange, musty smell as she pulled open the drawers. There were papers, documents, certificates among old photos and discarded letters: all the paraphernalia of a life. Marthe turned on the lamp, sat at the desk and began carefully to examine the top drawer on the left. She was looking for information, anything about her father and mother.

She searched slowly and carefully. There were photos, much faded to a sepia colour of her grandparents, she supposed, posing beside fireplaces and chairs. Very formal, a record of an occasion, perhaps a celebration. And in better condition, photos, in black and white of her father. He stood very stiff and formal, unsmiling, posing rather, his clothes as uncompromising as himself. Was this how he really was? Marthe could not remember. She stared at his face, seeking some resemblance to herself, searching for some sign of...what? Kindness? Compassion? But the face gave no clue to the character behind it. Marthe felt a deep sense of frustration. She was delighted to find some pictures of herself, as a little child, in laundered dresses, with bows and sashes. They too had been taken to commemorate an occasion, perhaps a birthday, she stared solemnly at the camera, a slight figure, with soft pale hair. None were snap shots like those Xavier would take of her and Felix on their annual family holidays, on a beach or at a café, the sun shining. She tried hard to push the memory away. There were photos of her mother, gentle looking, with a hat that shaded her eyes. She seemed always to be in the background. But there was one photo which caught her attention: her father standing, not in the salon, but in the garden, posing a little, under a fruit tree and behind him the gate that led out to the river path. And there, next to him, waiting impatiently and attached to a lead, was a little bright eyed dog, it was brown and white. Marthe stared at the photo for a long time, but she couldn't summon up more from her memory. She now knew that there really had been a dog, it was not just a dream, but a memory. Time passed, Marthe continued to sift through the papers, she didn't know what she was looking for. She had grown cold, but her patience was rewarded, for searching now with her right hand in the middle drawer, she found … Her father's death certificate. A faded yellowing paper. She read it carefully. It gave the date, October 1944, and the place, the department of the Gers, and the cause of death: drowning. The word leapt off the page. She read it again and a third time, 'drowning'. She had never heard that before… Why not? Why had her mother not told her? Marthe stared at the certificate, it told her so little and yet so much. She looked again at the date. Why had her father drowned? He was relatively young, in his forties. And where? Marthe tried to think calmly about this quite unexpected information. Bertrand had drowned! She sat back in the heavy chair, closed her eyes and shivered. To drown was a horrible death, the struggle for breath, the water flooding one's lungs, the body gasping and sinking. Did it become dark as one sank? Did the body rise and fall?

With a sudden revelation she recalled her nightmares, she tried to think calmly, 'Was it possible that Bertrand had drowned here in St Girou? Even, horrible thought, at Les Palmes?' She thought of the river, beyond the garden gate, where she liked to walk. It was little more than a sluggish stream, but deep, and after rain it flowed with strength. But why would a fit man in his forties fall into it? Maybe Bertrand was a poor swimmer? Maybe he could not swim at all! Or was it suicide? That was the worst possibility! Marthe's thoughts were uncontrolled, the questions coming one after another.

She stood up and, leaving the desk and its contents, moved across the cold Hall and down the back stairs to the kitchen. It was a comfort to be in this familiar room, where a pale morning light was filtering through the shutters. The wisteria banged gently against the window. It distracted Marthe for the moment. She made a pot of coffee and warming her hands with her cup, she returned cautiously to the memory of the nightmare. It was a body, she was sure of that, being carried through the garden gate, carefully and slowly by several men. Taking their load through the garden to the house. From the river. Was it her father whom she had seen then, looking out, as she was from her bedroom window? She had heard her mother's screams, but had not gone down the stairs, she felt sure, but had crept back to bed, hating the commotion, the unfamiliar voices. Hiding in her bed, not understanding.

Marthe nagged at her elusive memory, but she could bring out nothing more. She kept thinking about the death certificate and its implications. If she was right and it was Bertrand, then had that caused her mother to abandon the house and flee to her parents? A horrible accident having made her a young widow?

Marthe returned to the desk, she looked again at the photos, all of them over fifty years old. She held up one of her father for a long time, 'Who were you? Did you realize what you had done? Were you ashamed, full of remorse, repentant?'

Marthe felt overwhelmed. To have no answers to so many questions was exhausting. She laid the photos and the certificate carefully on top of the desk and left the room, returned upstairs, and lay on her bed. The heating was creaking into life, but it was still cold. The thought had returned to her; the dates of her father's death and those of the four 'betrayed' men were close. Just five months apart. Was there a connection? Had her father committed suicide? Would she ever know?

Felix was playing the piano in his apartment in Toulouse. It was very pleasant with the sun coming through, and the traffic noise not too loud. He was also listening for the phone. It was early evening and he hoped to hear from Valerie. He was 'practising' or so he persuaded himself, but his thoughts were more on Marthe than the Schubert in front of him. Felix combined a career in music criticism and journalism, with some steady teaching work. In his heart of hearts, he saw himself as a failed concert pianist; one of the many who had graduated from conservatoires and music colleges, hoping to establish a glittering future as a soloist, but after a short time, had settled for something more ordinary. He was in fact a very good teacher: patient, encouraging and firm, at his best with young students, teenagers who were hoping for a career in music. His next student, a promising boy of thirteen, was due in half an hour. He had set him the Schubert that was now laid out on the piano. Felix had covered it in 'fingering' notes. He jumped when the phone rang- picking it up in a rush. It was Marthe. Felix swallowed his disappointment and listened as she spoke rapidly. He was slow to follow what she was saying- it all seemed so extraordinary. 'Slow down! I can't follow you.' Marthe repeated herself, and when she had finished speaking, there was silence.

Felix said, 'So it just says 'drowning', no more?'

Marthe replied impatiently, 'I've told you! That's what it says!'

'It must have been an accident. Maybe he couldn't swim, he would have got into trouble very quickly.'

He closed his eyes trying to envisage the scene, a man dressed for autumn, out for a walk in a heavy wool coat, probably also a jacket, and thick trousers. All would quickly become water -logged. He wondered where it had happened. In St. Girou, or maybe near the family brick works, the river Garonne was fast and deep there. It was certainly no place for swimming. Marthe pressed on,

'There is something I haven't told you.' She paused,

'Mother! You said I knew everything, that you had told me everything. What else is there?' He was angry now.

'It seemed silly...a dream, a nightmare...Iv'e had it several times. It didn't worry me much. But now, the drowning takes on a new significance.'

"You are talking in riddles. What nightmare?"

'I dream about a body on a stretcher, or a door, being carried into the garden, here at Les Palmes, through the gate in the far wall. A figure, flat and unmoving. And then screams and terrible sobbing. From my mother I'm almost sure. I'm standing at the bedroom window, looking out. No one knows that I'm watching.'

'And you think that the body, might have been your father?'

'Yes.'

'So, it's a memory.'

'Yes. A memory. I think I recovered it, by returning here.'

Felix felt his stomach lurch, with apprehension. Could his mother recover a memory? And if she could what else might she recover? He stood gripping the phone, so the drowning of Bertrand had happened, if Marthe was right, in the river beyond the gate. And Bertrand had been carried home, dead or near to death. He felt a wave of pity and sorrow for the grandfather he had never known. To drown was a terrible fate. Marthe spoke again, softly, 'But it seems ...do you think it might not have been an accident? He was a youngish man, mid- forties it seems unlikely that he would drown, the river is not fast flowing is it?'

'What are you saying?'

'Well, the date is 1944 just a few months after the men died. Is that coincidence? Suicide is possible!'

'Mother! Stop this! Now! You are letting your imagination run haywire.' The bell of his flat rang. It was almost a welcome distraction.

'I have a student at the door, sorry, I'll phone you later. Try to calm yourself, please!' Felix was relieved to end the conversation, his mind, like Marthe's, was in turmoil.

It was a difficult lesson. Felix couldn't concentrate and the boy had not practiced sufficiently, 'You'll play this to me again, next week!' he said, closing the piano lid. The boy nodded his head meekly, Felix was not often angry, and he knew that he had been a disappointment. He trailed off down the stairs.

But Felix did not phone Marthe after the boy left. He was cross that Valerie had still not phoned and he wondered if all was well. She had flown to Paris early that morning for a work meeting and he knew it had been important to her. Felix was disappointed that she seemed to find it unnecessary to keep him up to date with her life. He was piqued. So, needing to talk to someone, Felix phoned Annie, who was as usual cooking supper while watching Charlie at his chess board. He hoped she had forgotten the pizza upset; he had already tried to make amends.

'Felix, hi! Thank you for your message. I'd love to come.'

There was a slight pause, Annie continued,

'You asked me to a concert! On Saturday. The message… have you forgotten! Am I still invited?'

Felix, who was still thinking about his conversation with Marthe, relaxed, relieved to think about something else, 'Good, I'll pick you up in the car, about six pm?' Annie looked for a pen to write down the time, and inadvertently knocked over a chess man. Charlie scowled at her. 'Will that give us enough time?' She asked, ruffling her son's hair. She was rewarded with a faint nod, as he bent to pick the figure from the floor.

'Six o'clock will be fine. I've got the tickets, in the front row or nearly, the conductor is an old friend. We can eat afterwards.'

'Sounds good. I'll be ready. Thanks. Just ring the bell, I'll run down. Are you Ok? You sound distracted.'

'I'm fine. Just distracted.'

Felix was in a confused state of mind. He thought about what Marthe had told him, but had no means of interpreting the phrase, 'death by drowning.' Had he fallen into the river? If so why? Was he unwell? A blackout? He dismissed Marthe's suggestion that it might have been suicide. Felix had become impatient with the past, and his ignorance of the family who had lived at Les Palmes. Suddenly their history had entered his world, and seemed ready to crowd him out. He resolved to ask Marthe for the papers that she had found in the desk. He wanted to look at them himself. The phone rang again. It was Valerie, finally. 'Felix?'

'Of course! Who else!' His tone was impatient,

' I'm going to stay in Paris for a few days more, I'll be back on Sunday. Work is so busy at the moment …'

'Was she subtly trying to justify her longer stay?' Felix was thinking. Valerie rattled on, but Felix was hardly listening. He realized that in inviting Annie to the concert, he had been subconsciously anticipating that Valerie would return later than she had said earlier. He was not sorry; Valerie had never attended concerts with him, she regarded them as 'work' and felt no obligation to join him. Valerie was not shallow, she was intelligent and successful, and worked long hours. She saw her leisure time, evenings and weekends, as well deserved opportunities for pleasure. She earned far more than Felix, and this had given her something of an upper hand. She made her life as she wanted it, and while she was not exactly 'bossy', she generally got her own way with Felix.

It was March and the winter was over. In the south west corner of France, the sun was giving real warmth, and most people began looking forward to better days. The afternoons lengthened, the air smelt of new foliage, birds sang and nested, the crops began shew, and tractors were out in the fields. Even in the city of Toulouse the change was evident... Terracotta pots were placed on the balconies, ready for spring planting, and sun umbrellas reappeared in the pavement bars and cafes. The shops filled with bright coloured clothes, shoes and bags. The markets had spring flowers for sale.

Annie had a new spring in her step as she organised the work of her team. She felt life was looking up for her and Charlie, his class were going on a school walking trip in the Pyrenees, and he was anticipating having fun in what she nicknamed 'the great outdoors'. Her work in Marthe's garden had provided Charlie with great opportunities for spending time outside, and she realised how dependent they had both become on these Sunday trips. 'I will have to find something else, somewhere else, once July is over,' she said to herself, as she stood in the square feeling a warm sun on her back. Annie was looking forward to the concert on Saturday, even more so after an excited Charlie had rushed off to join the other children on the large coach, which was blocking the street outside the school.

Felix picked her up as agreed at six o'clock. He was determined to put behind them the awkwardness that had developed since the pizza debacle, and made a fuss of settling her in the car, pushing back the seat and adjusting its angle. Annie was pleased to be travelling in his car; the smell of the leather seats, the state of the art sound system, his smooth acceleration at junctions. She tried to put out of her mind the memory of the last time she had been in the car, but she remembered vividly the loud bang and the man in the beret, watching. She looked at Felix, who drove confidently one hand on the steering wheel and the other resting lightly on the little gear shift. He felt her looking at him and turned slightly, 'You look different today!'

'Well, I am not wearing heavy boots, a woolly hat and dungarees? Might that be it?'

'Could be. It's certainly different .'

Annie laughed and began fiddling with his CD's 'Do you want some music? You've got so much here.'

'No. I prefer to keep my mind clear before a concert. I have to focus when I get there.'

They joined the autoroute, heading for Carcassonne. The traffic thinned, and the car moved effortlessly into the outside lane as Felix accelerated. 'He really loves this car,' Annie thought 'he shows quite a different side of himself when he drives.' The afternoon darkened as the green valley of the Garonne slowly changed into a more 'Mediterranean' land-scape: dry soil, and rocks, and pines, a scent of 'maquis', of myrtle and heather, wild broom and mint. She looked at the tall poplar trees that lined the tow path beside the Canal des Deux Mers, and noticed that they were flashing past very fast. Annie avoided glancing at the speedometer. 'Have you ever taken a canal boat there?' she asked, she thought it looked fun, and remembered a trip on the Norfolk Broads when she was a child. Her father solemnly steering the narrow boat through endless locks, while she and her sister walked alongside staring at the rising water.

'No. But I've eaten at several of the good restaurants which border it.' He pointed towards one of the hamlets that edged the water. 'It's lovely on a summer's evening. Valerie loves it here.' He regretted it immediately, but Annie seemed not to have noticed, she looked again at the poplars,

'One of my favourite trees, tall and proud.' she said, but the light had faded and they were, rather like Valerie, a ghostly presence. They arrived in Carcassone, parked and walked together to the Hall. Annie had visited once before with a uninterested Charlie; they had been taken by some friends, it had not been a success. 'It's not a proper castle which is what you promised.' He had moaned and ruined their expedition in a way that only a sulky child could. It was not a happy memory, but now with Felix, Annie appreciated its towers and walls, cleverly flood lit, wishing that they had set out earlier with time to explore.

The concert was interesting. It was devoted to French music, some of which was modern and unfamiliar to Annie. She glanced at Felix who was surreptitiously making notes and concentrating. As promised, they were in the second row. Annie enjoyed the sense of occasion, because since having Charlie, she rarely went out in any style, and it was pleasant sitting next to Felix who looked smart, but not too smart. In Toulouse she had work and choir friends, but they preferred a quick meal in a brasserie, which she enjoyed, but was nothing 'special.' She knew that she looked attractive that night: hair washed, black coat setting off her skin, and a blue scarf, a Christmas gift from Claire, setting off her grey eyes. She glanced around in the interval, aware that Felix was looking at her. He nodded to several people as they stood drinking a glass of wine, but she could see that he was preoccupied with the music they had been listening to, and again reflected that Felix had a side which he kept hidden. She did not interrupt his thoughts.

Later they came out into the cold night air and walked briskly to a restaurant set into the city walls. 'Smart,' Annie observed to herself, 'expensive' and was relieved that she had chosen a dress, and not the blouse and skirt as she had originally intended.

The Maitre d showed them to a side table and handed Annie an enormous menu, while opening her napkin with an impressive flourish. She looked at the menu with astonishment, it was very extensive and each dish was described in loving detail. The prices were not shewn. Annie looked at Felix,

'What do you recommend? What are you having?'

Felix, for whom a menu like this was not unusual, looked at her in surprise. He noticed that she was rather pink. 'How about the lobster to start with? Then the fillet of beef?'

'Too much! But yes, the lobster would be a treat, then I would like the risotto.'

They settled to enjoying their dinner, Annie could not remember when she had last eaten lobster, and forced herself to take small mouthfuls to savour every morsel. Felix's choice of wines, a crisp white followed by a light red, put them both into a lively mood. Annie was relaxed, perhaps even a little intoxicated by the time the coffee was ordered. Her eyes sparkled as she chatted away, and laughed at Felix's accounts of his pupils and their lessons. 'Do you take beginners? People who can read music, but not much else?'

'No, not really. I'm too impatient,' and he grinned, 'too expensive.'

Annie looked at him, 'What about Charlie? He would work hard, practice, you know how committed his is, if he likes something.' She smiled at him across the table, very appealingly. Felix sat back and regarded her. 'Annie you are shameless! Playing on my affection for him!'

'So will you think about it?'

The coffee had arrived and Felix swallowed his cupful in one quick gulp, 'Oh that's good! Yes. OK. I will. But Charlie must want to learn, otherwise it will be no use,' he reached forward and took her hand, 'it's no use, if it's just you who wants it.'

They sat quietly, Annie left her hand in his- it felt warm and dry. She felt happy to be sitting here, not exactly drunk, but content in his company. Was she drawn to him? It was nice to flirt a little, it had been a long time since she had enjoyed a man's company.

'You have a very good 'ear' did you realise?' Felix said. Annie stared at him in surprise. 'Oh. I am nothing special! I can hardly tell' she thought for a moment, 'Borodin from Bartok.' Felix laughed, 'How about Beethoven from Brahms?'

'Easy!' She was laughing too.

'So...'Felix said, 'Name six composers beginning with S ,in ten seconds.'

Annie frowned, her competitive spirit roused, 'Start counting. Now.' Felix began slowly counting out loud and Annie said, 'Schubert, Sibelius, Schumann, Shostakovic,' she paused 'Saint Saens,' Felix urged her on,

'six seconds, seven, hurry up!' Annie began to panic, she looked hard at him 'nine' he said slowly, was he willing her to succeed or fail, she wasn't sure. Then out of nowhere came, 'Scriabin!' Felix said, 'ten', and then, 'well done. Scriabin is very clever.'

Annie was delighted with herself, 'Ok. Your turn.' she thought for a moment 'Sing something by…Puccini!'

Felix made a shew of thinking deeply, and said, 'You must lean forward, everyone is looking at us. We're too noisy!' Annie complied and, with Felix still holding her hand, leant forward 'You too' she said, and Felix leant across the table, and then very softly began Rudolfo's aria at the beginning of La Boheme. 'Che gelida manina…..'though he did not sing for long the moment seemed to last a long time, when he stopped he leant further across the table and gently kissed her. That too seemed to last a long time. Drawing apart they both sat back and stared across the table. 'What is this?' they were separately thinking, 'what am I feeling?' An observer would have been in no doubt -they looked like a young couple in love.

They walked out into the cold night air. He drew her to him as they walked to the car, and they drove home in silence, comfortable with each other, full of good food and wine. Each enjoying their private thoughts. It had been a lovely evening. He kissed her at the apartment entrance and she did not draw away. 'It was a lovely evening, thank you,' he said softly. He stepped away, and walked back down the dark street to his car. Annie walked into the flat, it felt empty without Charlie, but she slept very well.

The weekend after his evening with Annie in Carcassonne, Felix and Valerie went skiing with friends whom they had met on holiday the previous summer. They were eager to spend some time together away from work, and the grey days which hung over Toulouse. Felix was in a state of some conflict; he had been pleased to see Valerie return from Paris, she was looking very lovely, her eyes sparkling as she talked about her time there. Her work was clearly going well. But he had also experienced sudden and unwanted flushes of guilt, when the memory of Annie washed over him. He found her very attractive and he did not know how to get her out of his mind. He hoped that time with Valerie would erase Annie and was intending to ski hard, eat and drink well, and make love every night. It was not to be.

They all flew to Megeve and settled into a lovely hotel, which Valerie had chosen. The week promised to be fun; the snow was at its best with all the runs open, and the forecast was for sunshine the whole week. The resort was busy but pleasantly so, lively and stylish just as Valerie liked it. The school holidays had not begun, so the lifts and cable cars were uncrowded and there was no early morning queuing at the ski stations in the town. Felix had learnt to ski at a young age, he was fast and confident, but Valerie was rather tentative, very cautious. It was unusual for her not to be the leader of a group, and her mood deteriorated. She was soon holding Felix back and he became increasingly impatient: the easy blue runs quickly bored him, and with superlative powder snow on the top slopes he was itching to go higher after the first day. He could not abide pottering about, watching her snowploughing, as she turned carefully avoiding the steeper slopes. He spent a lot of time waiting for her at the bottom of the lifts. Valerie refused his requests to go higher, prefer-ring the lower levels, 'I might fall. No. Let's go this way.' She looked at him appealingly, her pretty face surrounded by a white fur hat which was a recent acquisition. Felix knew that he pandered to her too much, his easy going nature normally prevented him from attempting to get his own way. But on this holiday they found themselves arguing all the time. Felix spent four days, skiing on his own, twice failing to meet for lunch, a sin of great importance in Valerie's eyes, loving as she did to pass a long afternoon, sitting with a glass of wine in a comfortable chair, admiring the slopes on which she refused to set her skis. Returning late in the afternoon, Felix found their room in the hotel empty as Valerie devoted herself to shopping or massages. Nor did they make love every night as he had planned, Valerie had developed a coolness to punish him for his neglect. As the week drew to a close they both realised how unhappy they each had been, and Felix's hopes of a restorative holiday had come to nothing. They returned to Toulouse and their increasingly separate lives. Valerie quietly decided to visit Paris for Easter; her father was unwell, and her mother had become anxious. And, though she had not told Felix this, she was to be interviewed for a more senior position within the firm, which would enable her to return permanently to Paris.

At Les Palmes, Marthe was busy, with the changes in the house. The salon was transformed, with its new furnishings, and furniture, and was now a light and comfortable room. She had arranged the transport of Xavier's piano, which had been in store since she left Paris, and had positioned it near the windows on the west side. Its arrival would be a surprise for Felix, who had played many duets with his father on the instrument. He had always said it was better than his own. The dining room had yet to be finished, but she hoped that this room to would be a success. The designer from Toulouse had introduced her to several art galleries where she planned to look for paintings for her new red wall papered walls.

The garden was taking shape. It was March, and Annie's plan with its paths, beds and plants could now be appreciated. Marthe wandered outside every dry day, always finishing up in her greenhouse, now stocked with trays of seedlings. She checked carefully for slugs, and lightly touched the potting soil- testing it for dryness. It was very quiet and still here, near the wall and the gate to the river. Marthe frequently pushed the gate open and stood looking at the murky water, it all seemed so peaceful, and unthreatening. She tried to imagine her father walking here with the brown and white dog, did her mother join him on his walks? Or did she prefer the orchard? Reading in its shade? She would hear occasional voices- fishermen mostly, passing by to their favourite spots. They would sit patiently for hours on their low stools staring into the dark brown water- waiting, waiting. As she worked in her greenhouse, she liked to think of them there smoking, chewing a baguette perhaps, solitary but content.

She had heard no more from Henri, but had seen Jean several times in the town, hanging around near the café, he glanced at her malevolently, averting his gaze if she returned his stare. Was he behind all this? He was not a Carrere, but maybe his family had also been affected by Bertrand. She knew this could not be, Old Jean had served the du Pont family for many years and had always spoken of her father with respect and admiration, he had been a most loyal employee. Young Jean had no reason to dislike her father, he was just a disgruntled man whom she had sacked as a bad worker. Marthe dismissed him from her thoughts.

CHAPTER 15

Annie and Charlie returned to England for Easter, and stayed with Claire and Tony. It was good to be looked after again after such a long time, Annie lay in her old bed, indulging herself,whilst Claire prepared a proper breakfast (Claire's words) and Charlie discussed football, a growing passion, with Tony. Arthur lay beside her, pushing at her hand for attention, he seemed pleased that they were back. She got up late, a rare luxury, and had a long bath. She could hear Tony downstairs getting Charlie ready for a walk into the village, they were off to buy sausages, his favourite lunch at the moment. The weather was colder than expected and Annie thought back to earlier Easters with Ralph, who had been impatient to get out into the cricket nets, ignoring her requests for help in the small garden, where the winter vegetables needed clearing. Determinedly she put him out of her mind.

Annie joined her mother for some walks with Arthur, Claire seemed fitter and was less critical of her daughter, which made the holiday easier. Tony took Charlie to a science fiction movie, which he hated, and Charlie enjoyed. Her mother's small cottage was warm, and the garden was full of early daffodils, crocuses and the last of the snowdrops. 'England' Annie sighed, 'Why did I leave?' But after a week of too much television for Charlie, heavy meals and no space for herself,

Annie's mood changed. She missed her large airy flat, the noisy bells of the cathedral, and the smell of the boulangerie. Her mind had turned back to Toulouse and work. She found herself thinking of Marthe and the garden which was becoming increasingly interesting. She looked forward to returning the following weekend and seeing Marthe and maybe Felix. She had thought about him more than she wanted to, wondering where he and Valerie were. The Carcassonne evening was still a vivid memory, the meal and wine, the French music, the fast car powering down the autoroute, Felix's kiss. She did not know what it meant for her…or him. Toulouse is home, she thought, she could not imagine living as her mother did, a quiet country life in a village with few diversions. But Claire was well and happy and that, she thought, was a relief, Annie no longer felt any guilt about living in France.

Ralph was busy and had not pressed for a long visit from Charlie, which Annie found strange, he had gone to see his father for just two days. It was their last morning. 'Time to pack, Charlie' She called down the stairs, 'and don't forget to wash the mud off your shoes, before you put them in your bag!'

Charlie had enjoyed his holiday in England being thoroughly spoiled by his grandmother, and had enjoyed watching English TV and playing with Arthur. He and Tony had played lots of chess and Tony had taught him some card games and tricks. The two nights he had spent Ralph were Ok, but his father seemed pre-occupied, and Charlie got bored. Like Annie, he was not too sad to say goodbye, already looking forward to being back in his room with all his 'stuff' as Annie called it. There was chess the following weekend, he would be travelling by coach, which was always fun and he liked his new team. Also Annie had told him that Felix was going to give him piano lessons, and he really liked Felix. He would be going to Felix's every Friday after school, for one hour. Charlie and Annie said their farewells and flew home to Toulouse.

Felix too had gone away for Easter, but not with Valerie, who was with her parents. Finding himself at a loose end, he was delighted when a fellow critic on the paper offered him her holiday flat in Perpignan. He jumped at the opportunity for a change of scene. He drove along the road past Carcassonne-trying to forget as he did so, the evening he had spent there with Annie. Perpignan was perfect, sunny, busy, and full of life. The flat overlooked an old square where the chestnut trees were now in leaf. Sitting at a table on the small balcony, on the first floor, Felix ate breakfast every day watching the people below him. He took long walks, ate wonderful fish, explored every street and bought a present for Charlie, a not too battered leather case for holding music. After five days, the weather turned rainy. The sea was rough, and green, and the streets were cold. Felix packed up his few possessions, and drove back, past Carcassonne again, to Toulouse.

His phone was ringing as he walked in, his heart leapt (Annie or Valerie? he was uncertain who he was hoping for) but it was neither. It was his editor complaining at his absence. The flat felt cold, and there was no food in the fridge, but Felix was pleased to be home.

Felix realised after just two lessons, that Charlie had little aptitude for the piano, in spite of his enthusiasm. He was delighted with his music case- holding it firmly as he climbed the stairs to the fourth floor. It was his second lesson and Annie had left him at the entrance, unwilling to be too involved. 'I like your flat,' he remarked, looking out across the river. 'But it's not as old as ours.' Felix wasn't sure if this was a compliment or a criticism. 'Well you're right there. My flat is very new- 'modern'- he tried not to sound complacent, but yours is…'

'Yes, old.'

Charlie crossed to the piano and settled to his task. He quite enjoyed the feel of the keys, stretching his fingers, trying to 'hear' the sounds as Felix taught him. The time passed slowly, Felix tried hard not to look at his watch. Just before six o'clock, he heard Annie coming up the stairs, and he jumped to his feet, while Charlie plodded on through his scales. He opened the door and Annie stepped in. It was the first time she had been inside and she was curious to see where Felix and Valerie lived. They kissed rather politely and then Felix gave her a hug. Charlie watched them out of the corner of his eye, he liked seeing his mother being hugged by Felix, it made him sort of happy. Felix turned back, 'much progress,' he said and patted Charlie on the back. Annie wandered around the airy room, it had a wonderful view of the river, the light enhancing the pale furniture and wood floor. It felt quite unlike anywhere that she had lived, and she suppressed a smile. How chaotic he must find us, she thought, as she admired the books and sheet music, carefully placed in alphabetical order on the open shelves. There was an impressive sea scape over the fire place, very blue and grey, and on the mantel a collection of coloured glass, from Venice she thought. Felix watched her cautiously, he was used to visitors, he and Valerie had several good friends and entertained frequently, but somehow Annie was different and he felt uncertain. He went to the large fridge and took out a bottle of white wine, pouring two glasses, but he had nothing for Charlie. By good luck there was a packet of nuts and he put those in a bowl, Charlie was quickly devouring them, it was his supper time and he was hungry. Annie sat briefly on a huge sofa and tossed back her drink,

'We can't delay! Charlie is, as you see ravenous, but thank you. Same time next week?'

'Yes, and maybe I will see you both on Sunday.' They all said goodbye as Charlie headed for the door and home, clutching the music case to his chest.

Annie had come up with an idea which she found very exciting. It had come to her in England when she and Claire had visited a National Trust garden famous for its collection of Spring flowers and shrubs. Returning to the flat after listening to Charlie's faltering notes, she phoned the number now familiar to her, 'Have you got a moment? There's something I want to propose!'

'How mysterious!' Marthe responded, she was in the salon and had been sorting through her mother's desk.

'No! No! It's just an idea.'

'Well tell me all about it!' She took the phone and sat on one of her new sofas, adjusting a cushion. Just let me sit down.'

'Is this a good moment?'

'Yes I have finished supper, I eat terribly early... on my own!'

Annie spoke rapidly, 'So I propose that we have a Garden Day! An opening, where people, who are interested in gardens can come and see what you and I have done. It will look very good by the summer and we can show it off. It is quite an unusual garden, with the wonderful walls and all the new 'dry' plants, trees and shrubs. People would be interested to see it I am sure.' She waited expectantly for Marthe's response. It was immediate and enthusiastic, 'What a good idea! A garden opening, do you have a date in mind?'

'Maybe July the fourteenth? It's the holiday weekend so there will be lots of people around... free to come and have a look!'

'All day are you thinking?' Marthe was trying to keep up,

'Yes, with a break for lunch of course. Perhaps ten o'clock till six in the evening, unless you think that would be too long. For you I mean.' Marthe was reflecting on this, her thoughts were interrupted by a voice , in the background. 'Can I help ?' Charlie had been listening, while eating his pasta. It sounded great fun to him, a garden opening, and he could invite some school friends to admire his shed.

Annie and Marthe continued to discuss the plan, it would require considerable organisation and planning and the day itself would be hard work, but as Annie said, 'It would be a challenge and give them both a goal. I think the garden deserves to be shown off and it will be lovely for you, Marthe, to see the appreciation and interest of others.'

'I'll check with Felix,' Marthe said, she had begun to realise the implications of opening up her garden to 'locals.'

'Yes, of course. Maybe he'll be able to help.' Annie imagined Felix moving smoothly about amongst the plants, elegant and friendly; she pushed the image aside, trying to concentrate on Marthe, who was now full of questions. The phone call lasted several more minutes as they aired their ideas, and Marthe agreed that, provided Felix approved, the opening would take place in July.

*

Henri had been confined indoors throughout March- a bron-chial infection having settled on his chest. He coughed pain-fully, endlessly, complaining as he did so. Sylvie was worn out with him. She was working alone now in the nursery at a very busy time, and caring for an irritable, and impatient father at the end of a tiring day, was exhausting. Henri seemed unable or unwilling to help around the house, but sat beside the kitchen fireplace, stoking the fire, doing nothing, and watching the sport on their small TV. It was a long month for both of them; they still had not talked again about the 'past.' Sylvie could not face another argument, and her father's grey face discouraged her from raising a topic which had caused them such upset. She hoped that her father's anger had subsided under Marthe's threat of summoning the gendarmes. After Easter, Henri seemed better, wearing his thick old coat and a beret, he sat, whenever possible, in the porch in the now warm sun, out of the wind. He looked at seed catalogues and farming magazines, showing interest now in the business, questioning Sylvie as she ate her supper. His health improved. He got in the car, one morning, and drove down to St.Girou, 'I need to get out, change of scene,' he explained. 'I'll buy some bread, maybe have a 'fine' in the bar.'

Sylvie was pleased to see him go. She found his constant gaze at her work in the Nursery and his accompanying comments very tiresome. She had enjoyed the greater independence his absence had provided for her. Increasingly she felt ready to strike out on her own, but had no idea how to set about this. She couldn't buy her father out, but nor was he likely to retire. None of that generation ever really retired. They just did less and less, working more slowly, staring across their fields as they paused for a rest, and started later in the morning. But outdoor work was all they knew and they loved the land in a way incomprehensible to other folk. Sylvie knew this, and she had no solution to a problem exercising many young farmers. How to get their hands properly on the controls, make changes, 'modernise'. She watched the car move slowly down the road towards the town. 'It'll do him good,' she thought kindly.

Henri sat on the wall beside the church. He was horribly breathless and slightly cold. He had bought a newspaper and some fresh bread, nodded to some locals, and was watching some children playing in the little square. He intended to have a brandy in the café before returning home. Suddenly he saw Marthe, who had finished her daily shopping and was turning for home. The sun caught the shine of her belt buckle. Henri, in a flash, changed to a state of great agitation. To see the woman, for whom he felt deep hatred, walking in 'his' town was too much. He was enraged and he stood up and began waving his bread at her, shouting abuse. But a long month of sickness and idleness had made Henri weak, and when he tried to run after her, his breath coming in gasps, his legs gave way. Henri fell down heavily onto the hard cobbles, lying there for some moments, and only slowly got to his feet. Marthe had walked on around the corner, the traffic had blocked out Henri's shouts. Henri was trembling in anger and shock. His trousers were dust covered, his jacket torn at the elbow. No one had seen his fall, and he felt grateful for that. Marthe had disappeared. Throwing the spoilt bread into the gutter, he returned slowly to his car, limping heavily and drove straight home. Sylvie was nowhere to be seen. Henri poured himself a large Armagnac and went to sit by the fire, he shut his eyes. But his anger prevented him from resting. He said nothing to Sylvie when she came in for lunch. His bitterness consumed him for the rest of the day.

Meanwhile at Les Palmes plans were being made. Following her conversation with Annie, Marthe phoned Felix and described the garden opening idea. She could not keep the excitement out of her voice, Felix listened cautiously. He saw the advantages of a new project for Marthe, yet he balanced that with a sense of unease. He worried chiefly about allowing strangers into the garden, 'who might come? Henri?' Also if no one came, or just a few, it would be disappointing for everyone. He tried to add a word of caution, but Marthe would have none of it.

'Don't be negative Felix! This will be a showcase for Annie, and an opportunity for me, to become involved with the town.' Felix said no more, he bowed to his mother's new interest. So it was decided: the second Sunday in July from ten till six, as Annie had hoped.

Marthe had invited a friend to stay. Patricia was also a widow, a little younger, and full of life and energy. She had lived all her life in Paris, and was eager to see how life in the country suited Marthe. She brought a little dog with her, a black poodle, Gaston, and the two friends passed a happy week exploring the area, eating lunches out, and walking. Marthe took her to Toulouse, where they were entertained by Felix, who provided a day's tour of the city, and cooked them an excellent lunch in his flat. Patricia thought that Toulouse would have made a more interesting home for Marthe, as yet, she had not seen any advantages in rural life. She kept her reservations to herself, while enjoying the weather which was fine and warm. She enjoyed the garden, and took an interest in the new design; she and Marthe walked with Gaston beside the river, and Marthe took her to visit the Convent. But Patricia remained unconvinced, privately wondering if Marthe would 'last'.

It was the penultimate day of her stay. Patricia was standing by the greenhouse, peering in, she could not understand her friend's new passion for growing little plants, which could perfectly well be purchased at any garden centre. She suppressed a sigh. Marthe was pulling the hose down one of the gravel paths, she watered the urns nearly every day. The little dog, tried to eat the hose as it snaked down the path, he was fascinated by it. Marthe played with him, wriggling the hose and making the little poodle jump about.

'Gaston. Laisse!' Patricia called out. Gaston continued to leap about, then, distracted, he started barking furiously. The garden gate had opened and a man in a heavy jacket was standing there, looking in at the two women and the little, agitated, dog. Gaston ran up, he stopped just short of the man's trousers- growling. Marthe and Patricia, caught unawares, stood looking at the visitor. Patricia, assumed he had made a mistake and had pushed open the wrong gate. She walked towards him, calling to Gaston as she did so. 'Monsieur! Are you looking for someone? Are you lost?' Her voice was friendly.

Marthe, however, knew that this was no mistake. Henri- for it was he- was discomfited to see the two women in the garden. He had acted on impulse as he walked beside the river. He knew full well that this was Marthe's house, Les Palmes. He had no plan when he opened the gate, he wanted to see in: to find out more about the garden and how she lived, he wanted to see Marthe. He now glanced about, taking in the paths, plants and trees. He ignored Patricia and the dog.

'Gaston! Be quiet!' Patricia looked apologetically at Henri. He was carrying his wooden walking stick and leant on it, as he looked first at Patricia, then the annoying little poodle, and lastly at Marthe. 'A weapon,' Marthe thought, she had not moved, and looked at Patricia, who continued to smile in a friendly and helpful manner. Patricia spoke more firmly, 'Gaston, ici!' she called the dog to her. 'Monsieur, this is Les Palmes, you must have made a mistake…or are you looking? she indicated Marthe.

Henri faltered, he continued to look at Marthe, who was moving slowly down the path towards him. She had picked up a hoe. Henri continued to lean on his walking stick, ignoring Gaston, who was growling. It was the first time he had seen Marthe since his fall in the town, and he was struck by her upright stance and confident walk. 'She is younger than me' he realised with some surprise.

Marthe was enraged to see him inside her garden...trespassing. Her initial shock had gone and she was ready to confront him again. Her heart was pumping wildly, but she continued firmly to walk toward Henri clutching the hoe.

'Get out! How dare you! I shall call the Gendarmes!' she shouted, Patricia was astonished and alarmed. She had never seen her friend so agitated. Henri panicked, he turned abruptly and hurried back through the gate, leaving it ajar, and turned left down the towpath hastening away towards the town. The gate stood open and Gaston stood uncertainly at the entrance. Patricia walked to close it, glancing as she did to see the man, limping a little, but still hurrying, as he passed under some willow trees and out of sight.

'Whatever was that about? Do you know him?'

They stood together while Marthe struggled to recover her composure. She had known at once that it was Henri, though it was only the second time she had seen him. She was horrified that he had dared to enter the garden. What was he intending? And worse what if she had been alone. Abruptly she walked into the house. As Marthe hurried in, Patricia felt confused and worried. Had something happened here? to Marthe? She called to Gaston, and returned to the house. Marthe, made her excuses and went to her room to collect her thoughts. She came down, somewhat revived, but still pale, and found Patricia reading in the little parlour. She had opened a bottle of red wine, and although it was not cold, she had lit the fire and the room was warm and smelt of the apple logs that were burning. Marthe sat on the sofa that faced the fire, and took Gaston onto her lap. Hugging him she turned to

Patricia, and spoke quietly. 'You are one of my oldest friends. I need someone to talk to.' Patricia sat down joining Marthe on the sofa, and put her feet up. 'Tell me, Marthe. Tell me! Who was that man?

The following morning, Patricia prepared to leave, as she settled an excited Gaston into the car, she urged Marthe to secure the gate as soon as possible. 'You must feel safe in the garden, that's urgent, don't delay.' Marthe assured her that she would buy bolts and padlocks that morning, and Patricia drove off. Marthe was sad to see her go, she was a good friend, and her presence in the garden on the previous day, had been very fortunate. She walked into the house and phoned the hardware shop, they promised to visit later in the morning and bring all the equipment that she wanted. In the afternoon she walked down to the gate and tested the new bolt and lock, whose key she hung on a hook. It all felt very secure. She listened to the familiar sound of the voices of some men passing by, going fishing, she assumed. Marthe was angry that Henri had spoilt her last afternoon with Patricia, but was undecided as to what action she should take. 'Should she follow up her threat and go to the gendarmes?' They might interpret Henri's actions as an innocent mistake, and would see her as a foolish, and nervous woman. Also she would need to dredge up the café and the brick incident, and she was not sure what they would make of those. 'Would these actions been seen as harassment?' She needed to tell Felix, as she had promised to keep nothing from him. But she was in a predicament, for she was angry also with her father; she was ashamed of him and that was painful.

It was early evening by the time Patricia opened the door to her apartment. It had been a tiresome drive, the traffic was diverted by road works around Limoges, and the detour had been lengthy. As she approached Orleans the light drizzle had intensified and a heavy rain set in. Gaston whined and whimpered, impatient at the long journey, and Patricia grew exasperated. She spoke to him sharply. They finally arrived home; Gaston scampered up to the lift, he was as pleased as she was. What a relief! Home! She stood still, looking about, she was on the fourth floor- just above the level of the plane trees that lined her street. 'I've not a garden' she thought 'but I have sunshine and a quiet square and...' she felt fortunate, and lamented Marthe's decision to leave Paris for Les Palmes. 'I pray she won't regret it,' she said to herself, throwing her bag on to the bed, and adding her keys. But she was full of doubts. Gaston ran to the sofa by the window and jumped up, wagging his tail, barking at the people walking below, then rushed to his bed and lay there looking at her. Patricia regarded him affectionately 'and I have you for company!' she thought, throwing him a toy, and reached for his favourite dog food. She had forgiven him for his restless behaviour.

Henri walked away in a state of anger and disappointment. He had opened the garden gate on impulse, and was caught by surprise when confronted by two women, only one of whom he recognised. He was angry with himself for backing away- he had missed his opportunity to further frighten her. Henri's obsession had returned, he had no forgiveness in his heart, no thought of accepting the past. Revenge for what he saw as the murder of his father drove him , 'let her suffer as we all have,' was his only thought. It was of no importance to Henri that Marthe had taken no part in the crime, had known nothing of it. That she was a little child at the time. Returning home, Henri hung up his coat, and slammed the kitchen door as he walked in. Sylvie looked up. She had been working on the budding fruit trees and was washing her hands at the old sink.

Henri stood facing, the fire, with his back to his daughter, 'Do you still see that gardener- from Toulouse?'

'Not really, her name is Annie, father.'

'Next time you talk, tell her not to bother with that garden.' Sylvie stared at his back, 'Papa! What are you saying? Why should Annie 'not bother'?'

Henri spat out his words, 'Because I shall destroy it. That's why!' He told her of his visit that afternoon, his 'entrance' and encounter with Marthe. Sylvie could not believe what he was saying. 'Papa! We have discussed this. Marthe has done nothing, nothing wrong. She was a little child. This is unfair! Ludicrous! I will not allow it. You trespassed into her garden? Entered off the tow path did you?' Sylvie was standing now, facing Henri who had turned to confront her.

Henri scowled, shrugged. 'My family and her family cannot live together. She has to go. I will drive her out!'

Sylvie felt like slapping him, shaking him. She was angry now. 'How could you be so... Stupid! Vengeful! Any harm you do will be wrong. This hounding of her has to stop.'

Henri scowled at her, unrepentant, 'Our family...' he began,

'Don't say that! I don't want to hear again about the past, the war. WE are the family now, all that is left, and I'm against you on this.' She stood in front of him, she was taller and blocked his path out of the room.

'Now listen! You're going to do nothing in relation to Marthe. Nothing at all. You're not to approach her, speak to her, or make any attempt to seek her out.' Henri tried to push past her but Sylvie grabbed his jacket. 'If you do, I'll do what I said. I'll contact the Gendarmerie and have you arrested for harassment! If Marthe has not already done so! This 'family' is not going to be disgraced, and lose its good name because of you, and your desire for revenge. I mean it! I'll have you arrested!'

She released her hold and Henri stumbled towards the door at the rear of the house. He released the chained up dogs and strode down towards the stream. They barked with pleasure, bounding beside him as he walked them down to the lower field, where the stream formed a boundary with his neighbour, and stood watching, as they roamed and splashed in the cold, clear water. Several resting duck flew up in alarm. Henri slowly calmed down. It was almost dark by the time he struggled back up to the house. Sylvie was nowhere to be seen. There seemed to be no supper for that day. For the first time Henri began to think about the seriousness of his position; he feared any contact with the Gendarmes, was uncertain as to the law on harassment, and believed that Marthe was more than capable of turning to the law. He could not afford to lose his 'good name', the business was all that he and Sylvie had. He began to appreciate that he had to give up his vendetta against the family of Bertrand du Pont, or his business could indeed be ruined.

CHAPTER 16

On returning from seeing her parents at Easter, Valerie dropped her bombshell. Felix learnt that her ailing father had been only one reason for her stay in Paris, the other was Valerie had been 'head hunted.' She was thrilled to be given a new career opportunity and had accepted without even referring to Felix. 'How exciting to return to Paris! Toulouse has been fun, but two years is long enough.' She said to herself. She was flushed and happy as she told Felix her news. He was sitting at the piano. 'So... what do you think?' Valerie sat next to him on the piano stool, 'We can move quickly! I am to start at the beginning of the month! Ooh Felix! To be back in Paris for the spring!'

Felix looked at her in astonishment. 'But you never asked me ! How could you be so thoughtless.' Valerie was genuinely surprised, 'But aren't you pleased? We've been here long enough surely?' Felix felt rising anger, 'And why should I want to leave?' he said.

'To be with me, silly!'

It was a disastrous comment. 'So you are all I have in life. Is that what you think?' Valerie realised for the first time the extent of her miscalculation.

'I'll give up my life, my work, my interests and follow you to Paris...like a faithful dog?'

Felix slammed down the lid of the piano, she jumped off the seat and stood up, a sinking feeling in her stomach.

'Sorry Valerie, but no! I have a flat that I like, a job that interests me, I have pupils to teach and finally I have a mother who needs me.' Valerie felt her world implode. She had moved from euphoria to emptiness in a matter of seconds. But she was not going to change her mind. Walking towards the bedroom she gave herself time to think. 'So that's it? I'll go to Paris' she concluded, 'and you are happy, it seems, to let me go!'

'I am not happy! At all. I am sad. It's you who are leaving...' They looked at each other across the room, already distanced from each other, both thinking silently about what had happened. Wisely Valerie did not refer to Marthe, though she blamed her presence at Les Palmes for Felix's refusal to leave Toulouse. There seemed no more to be said, they were both shaken at the speed with which this had come about.

Valerie went to bed early, she two tranquilizers from beside the bed, and slept deeply. Felix lay carefully on his side of the bed avoiding any contact. He gazed at the ceiling where the lights of cars below sent flashes of brightness. He asked himself, 'What was really stopping him from going with her?' But he knew in his heart that the love he had felt for Valerie had been dying for some time. He had behaved disloyally, he knew. He thought again about Carcassone, recalling the evening with nothing but pleasure. 'Who was really holding him here? Was it Marthe or Annie?' Sleep came slowly.

They lived together for a further fortnight in awkward companionship. They spent the final weekend emptying the flat of her possessions and packing them into her car. Felix felt miserable after she had gone- with a rather formal kiss and goodbye. The flat looked bleak. The cupboards and drawers that were normally overflowing with clothes, bags and shoes, now stood open and blank. The bathroom was the same-devoid of all feminine bottles, jars and soaps. For the moment her perfume lingered, but he knew that that too would soon be gone. He had not lived alone for nearly three years and did not look forward to it. He closed the door and went onto the balcony- the river was full- fast flowing, silvery in the morning light. Felix felt that his life had turned a corner, but had no idea of what direction it should now take. He looked at his watch, it was nearly noon and he would be late for lunch at his mother's. Grabbing his keys, he left the empty flat.

Despite her earlier promise, Marthe had not yet told Felix that Henri had trespassed into the garden, and he did not initially notice the new bolt and padlock. But Charlie of course did, he was an observant boy and the gate was near the old sheds. Entering the house to wash his hands, it was lunch time, he asked Marthe, 'Did you fix the new locks? Or did someone do it for you? They are very strong!' Marthe replied, swiftly, 'I had a man do it for me. I'm not much good at things like that!' she changed the subject, 'Are you having a picnic now? I had not realized it was lunch time!' she turned back to Felix. 'Let's have a drink outside shall we? It is such a warm morning.' Charlie dried his hands and went outside.

They sat on the veranda. Felix asked about the new gate locks, and Marthe could not deceive him. She gave an account of Patricia's last afternoon and her shock at seeing Henri inside the garden. 'He got no further than the gate?' Felix asked. 'That's right, Patricia spoke to him and her dog was growling, and he stopped.'

'But if you had been on your own, what then?' Felix's face was angry as he spoke. 'That's why I have bought the lock and bolt, he won't be able to get in again.' Marthe replied, 'I'll go to the gendarmes tomorrow and report him. If you agree. I threatened him with that as you know.' Felix stared down the garden, thinking carefully, 'Yes I think you must, or your warning will mean nothing. He's an opportunist, that's clear. We have to stop him seizing his chances. He is up to no good, and the law is there to protect us.' Marthe knew that Felix was right so, in spite of her reservations, she agreed to go ahead the following day. After lunch, Marthe said, 'I've a surprise for you!' She led him to the salon, 'Go on, have a look!' Felix looked around at all the changes: the green sofas on either side of the mantel, the lamps with cream shades, the new carpet and rugs, it was fresh and charming. Then turning towards the windows he saw, finally, his father's piano! The lid was open and he walked across the room and sat on the stool; he ran his hands over the keys. The familiar feel of the piano and its special tone moved him deeply. It was as though Xavier was in the room! Felix sat there for several moments, and then slowly began to play a Chopin Nocturne, a favourite of his father. Marthe sat and listened, she understood why he had chosen this particular piece. As he finished, he said, 'Thank you. I've missed this piano very much. I'll play every time I'm here, it is a beautiful instrument.' The music had helped to restore their spirits.

Two days later Felix set out to attend a concert at the cathedral in Albi, it was an organ recital, devoted to twentieth century music. He had heard much about the young organist, who was regarded as up and coming, and he was looking forward to it. He was pleased to have the opportunity to get out of Toulouse. He was finding the flat lonely. He settled contentedly into his journey, his was his one true indulgence, and the prospect of driving it, never failed to give him a boyish thrill. It was an escape in every way, to get out of the city streets and it was relaxing to be able to drive fast while enjoying the passing scenery.

He knew the route well, having taken it frequently with Valerie who had a cousin in Albi. They had enjoyed several weekends there, though he found it rather dull compared with Toulouse, while the area around the cathedral seemed dark and sunless. But the acoustics of the cathedral were good.

Felix accelerated past a line of lorries, moving smoothly into the fast lane and turned on his music system. A flood of Beethoven filled the car, and he turned the volume up as the flat countryside flashed past. He left the motorway at the Albi exit slowing down for the toll booth. There was a police car at the side of the road, and Felix held his breath. Were they waiting for him? He glanced across as two figures, in uniforms with guns, holstered at their hips, eased out of their car. They wore dark glasses.

Felix remembered guiltily an earlier speeding conviction and gripped the wheel as he slid between the barriers at the toll. The police were watching him, he could feel it. He concentrated on extracting his money for the payment, smiling at the girl in her booth. She looked at him indifferently. Slowly he drove the car forward, the two men continued to stare at him but neither moved. 'They're admiring the car!' Felix sighed with relief, 'thank God!' He drove into Albi with care.

After the concert, which was indifferent and would be difficult to comment on in any positive way, Felix strolled around looking for the restaurant where he had eaten with Valerie several times. They did a particularly good cassoulet and had some excellent local wine. He found it with difficulty, but they were shutting up and only reluctantly allowed him a table. The cassoulet was finished, but he ate a steak with frites and salad. He began thinking about Annie. His main concern was that she thought him a playboy. Am I? he tried to see himself in her eyes. He was wealthy, and lived well; he had a spacious apartment in the best part of Toulouse, he went on frequent holidays and his clothes were expensive. He had a fast car, and his job was pretty much a hobby. He had been living with a lovely girl for nearly three years but they had split up and he was on his own. So what did all that mean? Felix' spirits were sinking fast. He caught the waiter's eye and ordered an espresso and the bill. It was after eleven o'clock and the staff were packing up. Felix downed his coffee in one bitingly hot gulp and paid the large bill.

Driving back the road was empty, and the night clear. Perfect conditions for a fast car, but Felix had had one escape and dared not risk his luck. He continued to think about himself and his life, but was tired now and his reflections were negative. He parked in his usual spot and walked slowly home, 'I must try to focus my life in a more serious way.' he said to himself . He thought of Marthe and realized how much his life had changed recently, with his increasing involvement in her affairs. He was happy for that, it had brought them closer together, and he felt a certain pride in the support he had given. Try as he would he could not understand Henri Carrere's anger, the all consuming desire for revenge. The past has to be accepted was Felix's view, and should not be relived by the next generation. It was too destructive, too backward looking. But he remembered the phrase used after the French defeat in the Franco Prussian war, the war which had seen Strasbourg fall to the Prussian army, and forced his father's family to flee,

'N'y parlons, N'y oublerons' (we do not speak of it, we do not forget it), keep and cherish your memories. That was what history taught. Henri was in that mould. Unforgiving.

Marthe had visited the Gendarmerie and filed her complaint. It was a time consuming morning as the elderly gendarme wrote down her words in long hand. The room was cold and uncomfortable, and Marthe struggled impatiently with his questions.

'So you did not know the man who shouted at you in the café?' he asked, and then, 'You were not in the car when this man in a beret threw a brick? You did not see him?' Marthe could understand the gendarme's confusion; her story was unusual. She struggled on with her account; her visit to Henri, and her threat to him, but she did not tell him of the connection, through Bertrand of the two families. She did not tell him why Henri hated her presence in the town. The interview finally ended, 'I will report your concerns to my Superior in Auch. He will decide what action, if any, should be taken.' And it was over. Marthe returned home full of uncertainty.

*

It was Sunday evening and Annie was tired, she had worked hard in the garden and had spoken lengthily with Marthe about July. They were both equally excited and their relationship had become more a partnership. She was able to speak more freely, though they only discussed the garden. They walked the garden together after lunch, a time of mutual benefit. Marthe asked questions and Annie gave explanations. It was all changing so fast and the colours that Annie had planned were now easily seen. The reds and yellows giving way to the blues and silvers. The three palms were the strongest features and the water basin one of the most pleasing. Marthe and Annie sat beside it on the brick edge, their hands trailing. 'Why does one do that!' Marthe laughed.

'It is impossible not to. Water has some magic attraction! We have to touch it!' Annie continued to trail her hand. She looked about her, 'Is there anything that you don't like? Want to change?'

Marthe shook her head, 'No! It is all coming together. I can see it all. How it will look in…'

'July!' Annie said and they stared at each other. 'Not long is it?'

Back in Toulouse, as they walked into the apartment, the phone rang, it was Ralph, he wanted to discuss Charlie's next visit at half term. Annie was impatient, 'Charlie can't keep flying over! It is expensive and disruptive. His life is here now- home, friends, his chess world. He doesn't think of his old life, as you call it, he has grown away from it, his friends there have forgotten him. His holidays are so short too…'

'Your mother… she misses him too!' A sensitive point, Ralph knew how to upset Annie.

'I know that, but we are discussing Charlie and you. We need to think long term Ralph. I want a divorce.' There it was said.

'What? Why? We can go on as we are Annie. I'll make more effort, the money…'

'It's not about that. I need to move forward. I have a new life here, I like Toulouse, I like my job, Charlie has settled.' Ralph was appalled,

'So- you are fine. Charlie is fine. And I am irrelevant? Is that how it is?'

'No. Don't be stupid.' Annie's frustration was boiling over. "Charlie must always see you, must have a father. A divorce merely clarifies the position, it won't make any difference to Charlie, your relationship with him… We have been separated now for two years, and living apart for even longer. I'm not exactly rushing.'

'You think not! Of course it will make a difference. It's so final, Annie, it's as though we don't exist.'

'We' she echoed him- 'we' don't exist Ralph. It's over. You need to move on too- maybe find someone else? I don't know.'

Ralph grimaced, he had no plans to find someone else, having enjoyed the freedom of the last years. He liked going to the pub, drinking beer with his mates, working when things got tight. Drifting? Well, that was all right. He had no desire to travel, see the world. He liked his bit of England. It suited him... He had his football, though he was getting slower and cricket every summer. He was still the best spin bowler on the team. He was fine! But he also loved Charlie above all else, and he was not going to let him disappear out of his life.

They continued to argue. Annie resented the way in which Ralph made her feel mean and selfish, but she stuck to her decision.

Claire welcomed Annie's decision, she wanted Annie to move on, even find a new partner, as she had herself with Tony. She phoned her lawyer the very next day. Claire had loved having Annie and Charlie in her home over Easter and wanted to build on it. When she was shopping with Tony, she broached cautiously the idea of a French trip. He was, as she had expected enthusiastic. 'Ah! La belle France! Why wouldn't I want to visit you !'

'Don't be silly Tony. Here,' she handed him the heavy bag that she was carrying, 'Take this please and put it in the boot.'

Undeterred Tony continued speaking in a rather good imitation of a French voice. 'Comme je t'aime, mon petit choux!' Claire began to go pink, 'Oh do stop it Tony, people are staring!' She closed the boot with a bang and made to get in the car.

'Pardonnez moi Madame!' Tony swung open the door and bowed low. Claire looked at him and laughed, 'If you're going to behave like that, well, I won't take you!' Tony stood back and eyed her ,'You are not going on your own! How can I trust you with all those French men.' Tony drove home, he was already planning to dig out his French guide books and look up restaurants in Toulouse. Claire, her mind quite made up, hastened in to phone Annie.

'Shall we come over? Would you like a visit? Quite soon? Now the weather has warmed up.'

Annie was excited at the prospect, shewing Claire and Tony her part of France would be fun and Charlie would be thrilled. Claire had visited briefly when Annie first arrived, it had been all about helping with furniture removals and they had both been very edgy.

'That sounds nice! I'll pencil it in the diary, shall I?' Annie spoke eagerly.

Claire was excited, 'We can stay in that rather nice hotel... A bit of a treat, celebrate the end of the winter.' Claire's thoughts rushed along. The trip would be a good excuse to go shopping- a nice light wool coat, new shoes, a smart shirt perhaps. Mentally she was sitting in the square, enjoying a glass of wine, her lovely grandson sipping a pink drink through a straw.

'Whatever is that?' She had asked, on her first visit. 'It's what the kids drink here, grenadine- cherry!' Charlie answered and sucked at his straw.

Claire had looked disapproving, 'I suppose it's all going to be very French now! I'm sure it's full of sugar!'

*

So it was agreed. Claire and Tony would come out for a long weekend at the end of May and everyone would have something to look forward to, especially Claire... and Charlie. The divorce was progressing slowly, and Annie had not yet mentioned it to Charlie.

The following Sunday, Annie arrived at les Palmes early, focusing now on her garden plan and putting everything else out of her mind. The walk through the town had been calming, she enjoyed observing the French going about their Sunday mornings. Some people were getting to recognise her and Charlie, and several had smiled in recognition. The fat woman in the tabac now handed Charlie his comic without him even asking, sometimes she added some sweets.

'Bonne journee!' he smiled at her. He ran ahead as they entered through the old gates, scuffing the gravel deliberately with his new sandals. Annie walked round to the rear of the house, it was a real spring day- warm, even hot in the sun. The garden was turning green as one looked at it. Annie almost purred with pleasure. She had put a great deal of time and hard work into this project, and she was thrilled to see it coming to life. 'I must take photos for my portfolio,' she thought, 'it's changing so fast.' Later she found Marthe and the two women mapped out the timetable for July and the possible programme for the great day.

Annie said, 'We will need some extra hands if it's going to look good, there's always last minute hitches. We will need trestle tables, chairs dotted around in the shade under the trees as well as several here on the terrace. I will draw up a plant list with explanations as to what we have tried to do and get them photo copied at work. If we are going to have a plant sale, it has to be for charity! Any ideas on that ?'

Marthe was listening with mounting enthusiasm fused with anxiety. ' I hope we're not trying to do too much...

'Of course not!' Annie was quick to allay any fears, 'It's a garden we are showing, just for locals, though there may be interest from local garden centres, and growers. We could, I hope, be setting a trend, a new way of planting for all new gardens!'

Charlie had joined them and took a seat next to Marthe, he interrupted,

'I think tea is very important too. Everyone will be thirsty so we should make lemonade and iced tea and have cake and sandwiches…like in England.'

Marthe looked even more horrified "What do you think Annie? It sounds like a lot of work!"

'I think food and drink is important, but we can order it all locally. There are several patisseries in town, and one of them will be happy to be involved -it is advertising for them.'

'I'll definitely help with tea,' Charlie touched Marthe's hand, 'You'll see this is going to be great fun. And Grandma can come and help, she is very good at food…cakes and so on.'

Marthe looked down the garden envisaging it full of people, wandering the beautifully laid paths, pausing to read the little labels, admiring the palms which now dominated the central avenue, exploring her greenhouse and buying her plants. And eating an English tea. 'It's going to be fun, as you say,' she said and Annie grinned, 'Oh yes, fun and just a little hard work!'

Ideas came popping up,and after an hour most of it had been brought together, and Annie had the programme in her folder.

Felix arrived later, he had been delayed by a long, tearful phone call with Valerie, whose return to Paris was proving more difficult than she had expected. Felix was angry to be called in as her prop- feeling that, having opted to leave him, she should go elsewhere when things did not work out. His mood was rather quiet as he walked in. He found Marthe humming in the kitchen with her back to him- she was arranging the table for lunch. They had spoken only briefly during the week, she turned and walked forward- kissing him warmly on both cheeks. 'We've worked it all out! July I mean! You'll be needed on the day!' She did not pause, but rushed on, explaining the plans and ideas that she and Annie had put together.

Felix felt pleased for his mother, but slightly left out. He would have liked to have been part of the planning, he knew he was being foolish, and he had arrived late. He sat at the table and carefully arranged the roses he had bought in Toulouse. 'So I'm to be a helper?'

Marthe looked at him sharply. 'Felix! What is this? Of course I want you to help, be involved, this is more to me than a garden opening. It's an opportunity for me, and you, to open our house to the village, to meet people... even those who have...' She left her sentence hanging in the air, and looked at him, he was still moving the flowers about. He said, 'Of course I want to be involved, to share all this with you, it will be something special, for us. Also I like the idea of you and I working together, as a team.' Marthe was pleased, 'Look at this!' She picked up Annie's folder. 'Tell me what you think, start at the beginning.'

He sat down, and Marthe put a glass of white wine next to him, he smelt lamb roasting in the oven and glanced out of the window. Annie was not in sight.

Reading the roughly drawn up plans, Felix felt better and his earlier row with Valerie was slowly forgotten. 'She has made her bed and she must lie on it!' he thought ungenerously. He was no longer missing her, and had made changes in the flat to suit himself: there was now an even larger television, and a huge cream sofa on which he lay when listening to music. His sound system too was new and expensive, 'work' he said to himself, as he carried it carefully through the entrance. He intended to visit a friend who owned a gallery and seek out some prints for the large empty wall space where Valerie had hung several paintings. Something modern of course.

Over lunch Marthe gave Felix an account of her visit to the gendarmes, he was pleased that she had kept her promise. It had obviously been a trying interview, but it was done. They agreed to wait now for a response from the gendarmerie in Auch. He went to play the piano, something he had been looking forward to all week. In the garden Annie heard the music, stopping to listen for a few minutes, it was a happy moment, 'He really is very good.' She thought 'I had no idea!'

Before leaving Felix told Marthe some news. Earlier in the week he had been interviewed by his boss, a man who usually gave him a wide berth, and to his surprise had been offered a wider role:

'I want you to cover jazz Festivals! There are lots coming up- summer etc.' He looked at Felix. 'Manage that? Yes?' Hiding his surprise, for Felix knew nothing about jazz, he accepted the offer, and was even more surprised when he was offered a salary increase. He would have to read up a bit, listen to recordings and the radio late at night, but that wouldn't be a problem. He had no one to disappoint now, if he went to bed late. Marthe was pleased for him, giving her congratulations 'So that'll keep you busy, well done! Do you like jazz?'

'I don't know! But that doesn't matter, I write about classical music that I don't like. It's about criticism, not personal taste.' Marthe thought about this later, she had enjoyed the jazz in the bookshop in Auch, maybe Felix would like it too. She hoped so.

On Wednesday morning, she received a letter from the Gendarmerie in Auch; it said that they had decided that there was insufficient evidence to proceed with a harassment prosecution against Henri Carrere. Marthe was not surprised, she hadn't been able to identify Henri at the café, and hadn't been present at the incident with the brick. But, the letter said, an officer would visit the business of M.Carrere and speak to him about his actions in entering Marthe's garden, and her allegation of trespass. She determined to be hopeful, there was no more she could do.

Henri was frightened to see a Gendarme walking into his business, and looked anxiously for Sylvie, he was glad that she was not there. He led the officer into the house. The man spoke slowly, and gave him a serious warning. Henri was thoroughly alarmed. He was compelled to admit that he was wrong to open the gate, and walk into the garden, and the officer accepted his promise that he would stay away from Les Palmes. The Gendarme drove off, satisfied that he had dealt with the matter; he thought Henri was a harmless old man.

CHAPTER 17

During the week Felix decided to go for a drink in a café, beside the river. He was pleased to see Annie walking towards him. She looked preoccupied, hurrying along with a scarf over her hair, and a large canvas bag on her shoulder.

She saw him and stopped, hastily pushing her hair back, 'Felix! Hello.' They kissed in the normal way- left side, right side- not actually touching. They had become guarded with each other since their supper in Carcassonne, Annie blaming the wine for what she saw as harmless flirtation. She had expected it to lead to nothing, after all there was Valerie. She had tried not to think about him and had managed quite well, though seeing him regularly at Les Palmes, made it difficult. Felix had allowed himself to think of Annie a great deal, but he was held back by caution, and a sense that he would look shallow if he tried to start a new relationship too promptly. Nonetheless he seized the opportunity. 'Have you time for a drink? I've read the garden opening plan, from Marthe, I've got some suggestions!'

'Not working then?'

Felix replied, 'No! I'm done for today! Do come, I've some ideas for the garden day, and it is too lovely to be indoors!'

She had no reason not to join him: 'Ok. That sounds like something I would like to hear. Which way?'

They found a table on the quayside, at a café Annie had seen, but never visited. It was pleasantly stylish with round glass- topped tables and wicker chairs. Felix pulled one back for her as he took her jacket, and put her cumbersome bag on the floor. He sat opposite allowing her the view of the river. A waiter arrived almost at once and smiled at Felix. 'He knows him.' Annie thought, 'Perhaps it's a Valerie place.' she felt an irrational moment of jealousy.

'It's nice to see you Felix, but I'm afraid I'm looking rather... scruffy... for this place! I've been working... Obviously!' The waiter was putting olives in a deep dish at their table, and pouring the wine that had been ordered. She now felt uncomfortable and wishing she had refused Felix's invitation.

Ignoring her remark- Felix, who had noticed her work wear, and thought nothing of it, sipped his wine and took an olive – 'let me tell you what I think.'

Annie listened as he outlined his ideas for advertising the July event. She sat back in her chair, suddenly at ease. She asked a few questions- mainly about the cost of the publicity he was proposing. She was excited at the thought of proper advertising, an area she knew nothing about and was delighted that Felix had been thinking about the opening independently. Felix continued to expand his ideas, 'I can use the printers I know, who work for the paper. It won't be expensive...'

'Well that sounds excellent, let's do it as you think best.'

'I'll surprise Marthe. Get it all done...'

'She'll be thrilled. I am too! Neither of us had even thought about this side of the day, of course we have to tell people about it. Properly I mean.' They watched the river- the lights were coming on across the water which sparkled with the reflection. For the first time in ages, Felix felt happy. He looked at Annie, she was checking her phone. 'She looks pretty without that awful jacket. I would love to dress her up a little!' The idea immediately alarmed him, he could imagine her response to any suggestion from him. But still he said, 'You look good in red. Did you know?'

'I do like red. I wore a red dress that evening we went to Carcassone.'

"Yes I do remember.' They looked at each other and Annie blushed.

'It was a happy time,' Felix said 'Would you do it again? I have some jazz evenings coming up. Do you like jazz?'

'Jazz! I certainly didn't know that was your scene! I had you down as a pure classicist.'

'Oh it's part of the job…well to be truthful, it's a new venture. The Editor's idea.'

'In answer to your question; my husband liked jazz, and I played a few gigs at college, singing . But that's about it.'

'So' Felix pressed her, 'Would you like another evening out? with me?'

Annie thought carefully, 'What about Valerie? Doesn't she want to go?'

Felix looked down at the table, and then across at the river. Then he looked at Annie, 'We're over! Valerie has gone back to Paris, a promotion. She left some weeks ago. She assumed I would go with her. She's angry now.'

Annie said nothing for a moment, this certainly changes things, she thought, no Valerie! But what does Felix want? What do I want? She could feel Felix looking at her, but she resolved to keep her emotions in check.

'I'd like that. The jazz. If it's possible.' Her phone rang, 'Sorry it's Charlie, someone's returning him for me.'

'I never have her full attention,' he thought 'there's always something, someone else. How can I be jealous of Charlie? It's absurd.' But he was.

They finished their wine, Felix paid. Annie accepted gracefully. "I have to get back now- supper and all!' She indicated the canvas bag, and then impulsively and against all her earlier sentiments, 'Do you want to come, it's not pizza?'

Felix grimaced at the memory, 'So she remembers it too.' he thought. He smiled, 'Well, if it's not pizza, that would be more than nice. Yes.'

He took the bag from her and peered in seeing lots of fruit and spring vegetables, 'Looks healthy!'

'Oh yes, we eat well. One of the reasons I love living here.' Annie thought about Valerie as they walked together back to her flat. She had found Valerie to be cold and selfish, not prepared to give up any of her time to Marthe. She had rarely visited Les Palmes, and when she did was quite uninterested in the garden and the project which was exciting Marthe. Walking in as the light finally faded, Felix glanced around. It was his second visit, he tried not to recall the evening of the brick incident and his emotional collapse, hoping that time had helped to erase it also for Annie. The flat was cool and untidy, there were flowers on the table, which was covered with Annie's work. Felix looked for somewhere to hang his jacket, and finally laid it carefully on the chair nearest the door. Annie had thrown her jacket on the floor and was already busy opening the fridge. She had kicked off her work shoes, and was walking around bare foot. 'Could you do the wine? Though there's not much of a choice.' She looked at him over her shoulder and smiled, 'It's good to have a man about the flat,' she thought and then stopped herself.

She quickly assembled supper as Felix opened a local red wine and put a glass next to the sink where Annie was washing spinach vigorously. 'We'll have to wait for Charlie- he's already late. He so loves the football that he forgets the time. I think they have to throw him out in order to shut the gates.'

'And the chess?'

'Oh that's his real love- long may it last! Felix, I've been wanting to mention it...'

'The piano!'

'Oh! You guessed. Yes. He has no aptitude- I can hear that. Would you mind if we abandoned the Friday lesson?'

'He tried, but you're right- he doesn't hear. He's not like you.' There was a pause, 'I shall miss seeing him!' Annie waited for Felix to say some more, but any thoughts that he had were interrupted by the door being flung open, 'Hi Mum.' He saw Felix, 'Oh I didn't know you were here ! Are you having supper? I'm starving!'

'And late!' Annie shouted from the sink. 'Go and wash your hands.'

Charlie grinned at Felix, pulled an 'I'm cross' face, and went off to the bathroom. They sat at the table- waiting- and talking. Felix enjoyed the mood of Annie's flat, which was so unlike his own. Here it was an untidy mix of two people's lives; Annie's work laid out on the desk where the computer sat, her cardigan on the back of her chair, her bag, overflowing, had fallen on to the floor, and Charlie's football kit now lay beside it. The table had been roughly cleared of books, pencils, a scarf, - leaving a space up one end for the mats and crockery she had put out for supper.

'I suppose this is how families live,' he thought, 'order and chaos side by side. His own upbringing in Paris had been formal and organised. They only ever ate in the dining room, and meals had been eaten with his parents talking quietly. He had to ask permission to leave the table. Marthe was a loving mother, but wrapped up in her husband's busy life, and he could not recall many impromptu moments. His parents had entertained a great deal, Marthe was a good cook, and there were frequent suppers and formal dinners; but these events were planned well in advance, with careful choice of menu and wines. Nothing was ever last minute, like this evening. Tonight by good luck, Annie had bought some local sausages, she now added a jar of white beans, some garlic and red wine. It was delicious, and reminded Felix of the cassoulet he had not eaten in Albi. The three of them ate the whole pot full, with a frsh salad of spinach and rocket and huge chunks of bread. The wine disappeared fast. The evening passed quickly, Charlie went off for his bath and Felix washed up at the sink. Annie watched him as he carefully wiped each plate, knife, fork and bowl and then rinsed them carefully under the cold tap. He is very… meticulous, she thought, unlike Ralph. It had been an enjoyable evening, a change for her and Charlie, they had all made an effort for each other, she liked that. She seriously wondered if she meant anything to Felix, or was she just a grubby gardener? There seemed indications to the contrary and she didn't think Felix was a flirt, but was he on the rebound and just feeling lonely? He seemed to enjoy her company, but Charlie was always there, and the mood was more family than anything else. Again she thought of Carcassonne and kissing him across the table. She had liked that.

Annie tidied up, a little, after Felix had left. She was glad that he seemed more cheerful. She decided to be a little smarter in future. Like her mother, she was not averse to a little spring shopping. Maybe they might browse together when she arrived.

Felix was pleased to have found a role for himself in the opening day, one that no one else could undertake. He began for the first time to look forward to July and made a start on contacting printers and a friend in design. His life suddenly felt busy, and he realised that he had little time now for a coffee and croissant in the Place du Capitol.

Marthe was standing on a ladder, trying to hang two small water colours that she had bought in Toulouse. She wanted them on the wall, above the piano, but was fearful of damaging her new wall paper. The doorbell rang. On the step stood the man from the reclamation yard; he was keeping his promise to return in the spring. Marthe was pleased to see him, 'Come in, Claude isn't it? It's good of you to remember.' She put down her hammer, 'I'm trying to hang a picture, difficult on one's own.'

Claude offered his help. He glanced around the salon, 'Your changes? It's a beautiful room. And the piano, do you play?' He walked over and had a closer look, touching the keys lightly.

'No, it was my husband's. My son plays it now.' Claude continued to look around the room, 'You've done a lovely job here.'

'It's not too designed I hope, not too like a magazine.' She suddenly doubted what had been done.

'Absolutely not! It's full of harmony and style...chic. It reflects your personality.'

Marthe looked at him in surprise, she was flattered. 'Well that's kind, I did have a designer from Toulouse. One can sometimes doubt one's taste.' Claude paused, 'Now where do you want this hung?' Marthe shewed him the spot, and Claude hesitated, 'Too much sunlight, they are pale and gentle paintings. Maybe they would look better' he looked about carefully, 'there, to the left of the mantel. They discussed the positioning of the paintings for some time, but Marthe was undecided. 'Oh, let me think some more, let's go and look at the garden. That's why you came.'

'I've something for the garden in the van, come and see.'
He said.

He had brought with him two Grecian style statues. They
were a little chipped, and worn. About the same height as
Marthe, they represented the goddess Athena. She smiled
when she saw them lying, prostrate, in the boot of the battered
van. Claude unwrapped them from their sacking, and said, 'I
thought they might stand on either side of the basin. What
do you think?' he stood them upright. Marthe was delighted,
'What a good idea, they are charming and somehow fun!'

'I'll leave them here and come back later with my helper,
Luc. If that's all right?'

'Luc?' Marthe paused,

'My son. He's a bit of a layabout at the moment.' He
grimaced, 'A degree in art history, followed by unemploy-
ment. So he has to help me, when I need it!'

'Bring him over then, and we can site these two ladies.
About four o'clock?' It was agreed.

They were sitting on the terrace later, the two 'ladies'
successfully positioned. They gave a definite charm to a
part of the garden that was already one of Marthe's favourite spots. Marthe and Claude chatted as Luc, a shy young
man with long flowing hair, explored the garden. She could
see him wandering the paths, pausing every now and then,
stooping to read the plant labels. Claude lingered and at
six o'clock, Marthe suggested an aperitif. He followed her
into the kitchen, to help carry the glasses. But Marthe was
soon showing him the rest of the house as he expressed
such interest. They forgot all about Luc, as they wandered
through the house, carrying their glasses. Claude stopped
at the foot of the stairs, 'And they are?' he was looking at
the family portraits.

'My father's family, but I didn't know any of them. I left this house when I was a child. But I do say good morning to them every day!' Claude listened gravely, sensing that Marthe was lonely in this big house.

'A brave decision,' he said, 'To move here. Without knowing us. I mean the local society.'

'Local society?'

'It does exist! There are several families, who have lived here for many years. A little scattered about. Some are interesting, worth getting to know.'

They returned to the garden. Luc was sitting at the table on the terrace, sketching in a small pocket book. He looked at Marthe, 'Is this your design? It's very clever.'

'No. I can't take the credit at all. It's the work of an English woman who has moved to France. I was fortunate to be introduced to her. Pure luck!'

They drank their aperitifs as the light faded and the air grew cooler. Father and son were easy company and Marthe was sorry when they prepared to leave. She had enjoyed their conversation. They walked back to the van, and Luc climbed in; Claude turned to her, 'There is a garden and house I think that you would enjoy. Not far from here. It's not open to the public, but I know the owner, an elderly lady, and she would welcome a visit from a person such as you.' He bowed very slightly.

Marthe was pleased at the opportunity to see another private garden, she could compare it with Les Palmes. Claude said that he would make the arrangements and pick her up one afternoon. Marthe waved as the van turned out through the gates, and thought about what he had said, 'local society.' It sounded interesting.

They visited the elderly lady the following week, she was resting when they arrived. Claude led her to the garden, he seemed to know it well. Marthe saw that the house had been built on a steep slope, leading down to a meadow and woodland. The garden had been landscaped many years ago, to form a series of terraces, supported by stone walls. The feature that was most pleasing was a small stream that flowed down the slope; it meandered through the garden, occasionally being checked by small ponds and waterfalls. A path ran beside it, with bridges and stepping stones. As she walked down this path, Marthe looked for a planting pattern, 'was there a hot bed? Or a blue and silver bed?' she asked herself. It was difficult to determine, for many of the terraces were overgrown and neglected. In some places the stream had overflowed, and the surrounding area was wet and boggy. She saw Claude, he was carefully crossing the stream on stepping stones a little above her. He was dressed in dark blue and wore an old straw hat, and she wondered how old he was. He had lifted the urns and statues easily. He joined her at the meadow, and she saw that his shoes were muddy now. The stream formed a large pond here, it had been planted with gunnera, which were already taller than Marthe.

'The family used to keep fowl,' Claude said, 'I remember coming here as a child, and chasing them: guinea fowl, and various sorts of ducks, and pheasants. They had a pair of peacocks too, terrifying animals!'.

'How many years ago was that?' Marthe asked. 'Too many! But the memory is still sharp. Happy times!' Claude replied. They walked slowly back up the path and across the bridges. Marthe picked off a sprig of lavender, it was in flower now, 'as is mine!' she reflected. They took a last look before entering the house, 'I can see why you brought me here, this garden is very different from mine! she said. 'I like it very much, it is full of the past, and there are plants here which I don't even know.'

'Of course' Claude said, 'Yours is a dry garden, and it's new and experimental. And equally interesting.'

It was an interesting visit though the lady was rather deaf and vague; she was very fond of Claude and delighted to see him. They had many mutual friends, and the conversation turned around them and the past. 'We live on our memories' Marthe thought as she listened to them, and, unexpectedly the image of Henri Carrere, came to her. She pushed it firmly to one side.

Later as she prepared supper, she thought about Claude's kindness in organizing the afternoon. She envied him a little, he had lived in this part of France all his life, it had given him a depth of knowledge and a wide circle of friends which she could never hope to equal. She found him easy company and hoped that they would become good friends.

CHAPTER 18

Claire had found a lawyer for Annie and almost without anyone realising... and certainly without input from Ralph, papers were prepared, forms filled in and they moved inexorably into a divorce settlement. There were heated arguments on the phone, as Ralph remonstrated angrily, throwing accusations at her, but he was resigned to losing her, accepting the inevitable. Annie hated the whole business, but kept firmly to her decision... By the summer the divorce would be final. Her marriage would be over. She explained the changes to Charlie, he listened silently and then went to his room. Annie waited and then went in, Charlie was playing chess on his computer, and he refused to talk to her. Annie felt sad for him as she watched him from his bedroom door.

In the end Claire and Tony came to Toulouse for five days, coinciding with Charlie's spring break. 'After all there's no point in flying all that way and spending all that money if Charlie is going to be in school all day!' Claire announced. Annie tried to listen calmly. The visit turned out well, and Claire and Tony revelled in their smart hotel right in the heart of the Place du Capitol. Charlie joined them on his own for breakfast each morning. He enjoyed wandering up and down the buffet- eating the sort of food they would not dream of having at home. He went back and forth- with little amounts, trying out cheeses, jams, pastries, and salami, before settling into cereals and milk-his usual diet. Claire watched him proudly. 'Don't eat too much! We'll be having lunch !' She was talking as much to Tony who had disappeared again in the direction of the food.

They had two expeditions as Annie was eager to show off the opportunities that her new life offered. She hired a car, and drove them up towards the Pyrenees, it was a sunny bright morning and they were all in a good mood. Claire smoothed down her new coat and counted her blessings as the country side sped past. Tony, who was sitting in the front, asked Annie lots of questions about the farming, and the landscape which steadily changed as they left behind the flat valley of the Garonne and drove up into the mountains. The huge fields of maize and sunflowers gave way to pasture and woodlands. The farm houses were no longer brick built with sloping red tiled roofs, but grey stone, sombre with long low walls enclosing them. Claire spotted a large field of ducks sunning themselves, they were all sitting down. 'Why aren't they eating? The grass looks good.'

Annie watched her mother's face in the mirror, as Charlie explained, 'They can hardly walk. They're too fat. Their livers are huge. They're for foie gras. It's delicious, but I'm not allowed it!' He held his hands wide apart to demonstrate.

'I love foie gras.' It was Tony speaking, 'Can we have some please Annie?'

'You can have some for lunch, it will cost you though.'

'But how do they get so fat?' Claire persisted.

Charlie replied, 'They stuff them. With corn. Down a tube. We learnt about it at school.' Claire was astonished. 'Is that allowed? It sounds horrible!' She tried to look back but the ducks had disappeared behind a curve in the road.

Tony turned around and winked at Charlie. He resolved to slip some foie Charlie's way at lunch.

Annie stopped in the mountain resort of St. Lary, and parked by the river, which ran under the old stone bridges. Charlie leant over the wall of one,

'Oh I wish I had a rod Mum. I bet I could catch you a trout!' There was a busy market in the narrow streets and they wandered through, ducking their heads to avoid the stall holders sun umbrellas. 'Who eats all this? It's only a small town!' Claire asked, she and Tony were fascinated. He took advantage of the many opportunities to taste the local wines, winking unashamedly at the women who caught his eye, and tasted the local aperitif, a strong drink based on plums. He also bought a black beret which did not altogether suit him. He wore it for the rest of the day..

Annie and Charlie took a walk after lunch, following a foot path which led them to a viewing point, beside a little church. It was shut which was a disappointment but the view was worth the effort. It looked back down the path to St. Lary and then up towards the mountains which suddenly seemed very close.

Claire and Tony had found a quiet bench and were dozing in the sun. Charlie gently woke them up, 'Mum is getting the car. We're going home.' They returned, with Claire now sitting beside Annie, she glanced at her daughter. She looks prettier, a good hair cut, and a bit of colour in her cheeks, she thought, and reached across and patted her hand as it rested on the gear shift.

'Was the car expensive? to Hire?' she asked.

'No. Cars like this are not too expensive. But I don't do it often. I should really, Charlie would love to go roaming more!'

After a while both her mother and Tony drifted off to sleep. Annie spoke to Charlie who was looking out of the window and humming quietly. 'Your father phoned yesterday- he'd like to see you in the summer.'

'Where? Here?'

'No, in England.'

Charlie was silent. Annie regarded him, using the mirror- he had turned away from her and was looking out of the window. 'What do you think? You don't have to go, only if you want to. You could fly back with grandma.'

It was their last day, they were all saying goodbye at the same time, as they waited for the taxi for the airport, when Claire slipped an envelope into Annie's hand, 'Open this later,'

'Mum what's this ?'

"Just something I want to give you. To make life easier. My shares have done well and I don't need a windfall. Please don't make a fuss!'

Tony waved from the taxi as it disappeared around the square. Annie sensing that Charlie was sad, took his hand, 'How about a nice hot chocolate?'

'Yes, in Felix's café!' He had called it this ever since their first encounter, and it was still his favourite spot. They sat at almost the same table, and Annie ordered two croissants as well. 'We'll see them in the summer and grandma is coming in July.' He nodded, flakes of pastry settled on his shirt, and he smiled at Annie, 'What's in the envelope?'

'Goodness I had forgotten it! When did you notice?'

'I saw her. That's all. Go on Mum. Look!'

Annie looked and gasped. She went very pink. She looked again. It was a cheque for Six thousand Euros. There was a card too. 'Buy a car! Love Mum.'

She showed it to Charlie. He had never seen such a big amount, 'A Car is that enough?'

'Good heavens yes.'

'Can we have one like Felix's?'

'Absolutely not. I need something practical, with loads of space for all our stuff. Come on, we need to buy some food.'

Charlie was hugely excited as they walked to the market, he pointed to every car that passed calling out their makes and sizes. He emphasized their qualities with enthusiasm, 'Look Mum that one has a huge back, plenty of room for your plants and tools. Ooh look at that!' he pointed, 'it's red like Felix's and, wow it has a roof rack and huge wheels.' Annie was almost as excited as Charlie, she had never chosen her own car before, having inherited hand- me- downs, and the vans that Ralph insisted on. She too cast surreptitious glances at the cars, as they edged through the streets.

'We'll go and look on Saturday,' she promised Charlie, who was all set to go 'right now.' She wondered if she should take someone with her to help; not in the choosing, but negotiating the price. As if reading her thoughts Charlie said, 'I think Felix could help. He knows all about cars.'

'Flash ones, yes. But I am not sure he has ever bought the kind of car that I am looking for! I'll phone and see what he is doing." Charlie felt reassured. Cars were, a 'man' thing and he felt certain that Felix would be a great help. He overheard Annie that evening talking to Felix, 'Well if you could. It would be sort of reassuring. Shall we say ten o'clock then? Here?'

Later she phoned Claire, who cut short her attempt to express her gratitude, and asked only what she would buy. 'We're taking Felix with us, he can help with the choice.'

'Yes and deal with the smooth talking salesmen!' Claire replied.

Charlie continued looking at cars all week, as he walked to school. He was still hopeful that Annie would choose something fast and red. He was in for a disappointment. Felix was prompt on Saturday. He carried some motor magazines and, had high-lighted some showrooms, that specialised in second hand cars. Charlie's face fell but Felix was full of encouragement. 'You never want to buy a new car, Charlie. Mum needs something with low mileage, and that is what we will look for. I suggest we start,' he pointed at the Saab garage. ' It's out of town, they all are. And next door is the VW showrooms and beyond that the Renault. So we can see what they all have to offer. Let's go shall we?'

Annie was impressed both with Felix's organisation of the morning and with his eagerness to help her. They drove there in his car, Charlie again in the back, fiddling with the electric windows. Felix tried hard not to notice.

'I hope we don't look too smart! You, I mean, and this car of yours!'

'It is a very good idea to impress salesmen, or they take control and dictate to you!' Felix said.

Annie kept silent and tried to smarten herself up a little, tying the belt of her coat and putting her hair up with a band. She told Charlie to zip up his anorak.

'Help!' she thought 'we look like a family!'

Felix was thinking the same thing as he guided Annie into the vast showroom filled with new Saabs. A strange warm glow infused him, he had never done anything like this before, but was confident that he was going to help Annie in an important investment. They were soon outside again, inspecting the used models, and Felix began a close exam-ination. He asked technical questions about servicing, and fuel consumption, and insisted that one always looks under the bonnet. Charlie was most impressed, and stood close to Felix, gingerly touching the oily parts and listening to the salesman's patter. Annie sat in the driver's seats, fiddling with the gear levers and inspecting her hair in the vanity mirror.

Felix caught her looking at herself, and winked. He was thoroughly enjoying his role and pleased that Annie, for once, was deferring to him.

After two hours he and Annie had exhausted their possibilities and Annie felt fairly certain that she had made her choice. 'Which would you choose?' she asked him.

'No No! It's you who must decide! It's your car and your money!'

'It's actually Claire's money! That's why I have to get it right!'

Charlie who had become a little bored, interrupted, 'Well, if anyone is interested I think we should have the dark blue car. I can see out of it easily and it has a huge boot.'

'The VW?'

Charlie nodded, 'Yes, I like that one.'

Annie looked at Felix, 'Well?'

'A wise choice. It'll never let you down. Now you and Charlie go for a little walk around and I'll negotiate the price.'

Annie was astonished, 'Felix! I can't let you do that!'

'Yes you can. There is a coffee shop across the road, take Charlie, and I'll meet you there.'

And so Annie acquired a car. It never let her down, and she owned it for four years until, unexpectedly, she needed a bigger one. On Sunday drove it to Les Palmes. She and Charlie were very excited to show it to Marthe for whom it was a surprise. Marthe insisted that they went out for a 'spin' before Annie got down to work,

'Where shall we go?' Charlie was sitting in the back and leaning forward down the middle, 'What's your favourite place?'

Marthe thought carefully, 'My favourite place is about 20 minutes away so that would do well. Turn right Annie and then left at the cross road. She took them to the convent. They drove up the hill and Annie looked about with interest. There was a fine view at the top of the farm land below. Many of the fields were bright yellow with rape, which shone so brightly it almost hurt the eyes.

'There,' Marthe said, 'Park there next to the wall.'

'Can we get out? Or is it private?' Charlie was already pushing open his door,

'Yes you can get out, but the nuns live mostly in silence, this is a convent, as you can tell, so not too much noise!'

Annie could immediately see why Marthe had chosen to come to the convent. It had a gently calming atmosphere as they walked into the gardens surrounded by the high walls. There were some fine trees and wooden benches set under them. Annie walked across and sat down to admire the old buildings that formed the convent and the church. There was no one about, the nuns were at Mass or at work. Charlie was quietly exploring, following the gravel paths to the vegetable garden, and to where there were some cages and wooden hen houses. He stared at the chickens pecking about. He had never been inside a convent before and was quite in awe. A nun was working inside the chicken wire, she was dressed in grey and her head was covered, her face hidden. She wore a black overall, it was muddy. Carefully shutting the door to the huts, she came out carrying a large bucket, full of eggs, Charlie guessed. He watched her respectfully, there was a pungent chicken smell. Sensing Charlie looking at her, she turned around. He smiled slightly, conscious that he had been staring. She acknowledged him with a slight bow and moved away. 'Does she ever speak? Charlie wondered, he was fascinated, 'Why would one choose to live like that!' But it was very peaceful in this garden, and he thought that that was probably the answer. A complete absence of noise…apart from the chickens and further away some cows and a tractor. He walked back slowly.

Marthe joined Annie on the bench and they sat silently for a few minutes.

'Thank you for bringing us here. It's lovely,' Annie said, 'a sense of calm but one feels the activity also. Not just the faith and dedication of the nuns, but their hard work and attention to even the smallest detail. It's full of love: the pots filled with geraniums, the pruning of the roses, the raked paths, extraordinary!'

'They're quite self -sufficient.' Marthe explained, ' Behind that wall' she pointed, 'there's a working farm. They have cattle, and sheep, and pigs, and sell butter, cheese and honey. They provide holidays for the poorer children of Toulouse, and care for the elderly of this little village. It is a life of service to the community and devotion to our Lord.'

They were interrupted by the return of Charlie, 'Can we go back to Marthe's now?'

The rest of the day passed busily. There was no sign of Felix, and Annie felt a mild sense of disappointment. She realised that seeing him was one of the attractions of working at Les Palmes. Also she wanted to thank him again for his help with the car. It had made the whole purchasing business very easy for her. She wondered how she might thank him.

They went to say goodbye to Marthe, she was reading on the terrace.

'It's a very nice car Annie. Well chosen.'

'Felix helped. Mum doesn't know much about cars.' Charlie was loading gardening tools into the back, 'Where's Felix?' he continued.

'Charlie!' Annie exclaimed. 'That's nothing to do with you.'

'He's in Paris, Charlie, for a few days.' Annie felt an odd sinking sensation.

*

Claude had become, as Marthe had hoped, a good friend, and he called regularly to see the garden. He was interested in its progress. Marthe quickly realized had a 'good eye' and she enjoyed talking to him. Now in the early summer the urns that he had sold her looked splendid; they had been thoughtfully placed by him, some in full sun, planted with Marthe's nasturtiums and marigolds, and others under trees in the orchard, or at the junction of two paths. The two largest were yet to flower, they contained blue agapanthus. The urns, benches, statues and basin gave the garden a new 'settled' feel.

They enjoyed each other's company and liked the same things: the cinema in Toulouse, and once the opera in the Capitol. During the interval they had a drink at the busy bar, and Marthe looked expectantly for Felix, she wanted him to meet Claude. She was disappointed, she would have liked Felix to see her, dressed up and in the company of a man. 'Silly of me' she thought, 'but they have to meet sometime.'

They had lunch with some of his cousins, who were particularly welcoming and appeared delighted to meet someone new and from Paris. It gave Marthe a certain cachet to discuss exhibitions and concerts that she, and not they had attended. They were now seeing each other regularly, often just for lunch, and Marthe began to dress more carefully, having retrieved her Paris clothes from the wardrobe. She had lost weight and they hung loosely, she resolved to go on a shopping trip.

Claude lived in the wing of a chateau south of Auch. It was 'family' he said, an aunt occupied the main part but was rarely there. He invited her to a supper party, 'Just supper. Nothing grand. This isn't Paris!' She liked that. The slight teasing. She had visited the chateau briefly once before; they called in together one morning, Claude had forgotten his sunhat and they were planning to go into Toulouse. But she had waited in the car. This would be her first opportunity to see inside, and she was interested to find out how Claude lived. The supper was in large room on the ground floor, Claude took her jacket and led her in. He carefully introduced her to all the people in the room, there were about 10 guests, though more would come in during the evening. She looked about with interest, at the far end was the kitchen, she saw Luc, who appeared to be the cook for the evening. Hearing her voice, he waved without turning around, his hair had been tied back into a pony tail, he was wearing shorts. There was music in the background, nothing that Marthe recognized, it was modern jazz, Miles Davis. The centre of the room was dominated by a long table laid up with unmatched blue and white china and some fine glasses. It was lit by a low chandelier, and there were bowls of floating flower heads. Marthe thought it looked like a painting, a still life, the pool of light cast the rest of the room into a darker shade. At the far end was a huge brick fireplace with a fine walnut mantel, there was an eclectic mix of ornaments and above this an assortment of paintings hung very close together. Marthe had never seen such a beautiful room, it combined style and informality, in a way that she would never have managed. There was a fire burning quietly, apple logs she guessed from the scent. Claude led her towards a group of people mostly younger than her, and she recognised the young book seller from Auch.

My other son!' Claude said and Marthe smiled, 'Jerome.' She shook hands.

'Oh. We know each other! He plays jazz like you, and I browse in his bookshop. It's one of my favourite places.' Claude moved away and Marthe continued to glance about her; there were dark red comfortable sofas and low chairs, somewhat worn, and deep amber cushions and many rugs. Scattered about were several tables, some with lamps and one huge vase of lilies. And books everywhere.

At supper which appeared rather late, Luc served a salad from the garden, then a very good beef casserole, rich in wine and herbs. He was clearly a very good cook and Marthe praised him as he took away the plates.

'I should have gone to cookery school, I could find work then!' He said with a shrug.

Her attention was distracted by the man, who was seated to her right and who, like her, had moved from Paris. They discussed the challenges of living a rural life, after years of Paris, and Marthe found herself talking of her life with Xavier. Claude was listening as Marthe described concerts, restaurants, holidays in Italy. She stopped abruptly, 'But now,' she said, 'I have to find a new way to live. It happens to all of us at some point, the loss of a partner. But it gets easier, and one must accept what has happened. I've been lucky, as my son lives nearby in Toulouse, and I'm enjoying renovating our old family house. And I am making a garden, perhaps you will come and see it. We are opening it for one day in July. Please come if you can!' He said he would.

She remembered Claude, who had been listening, and turning to him, she said, 'You've the date?' He nodded. More people had now joined them, and the room was full of talk and laughter. There was cigarette smoke and a smell of brandy. Some continued to sit at the table, others had gathered around the fire. Jerome joined Marthe on one of the sofas and they talked about books, a conversation that drew in others. A lively discussion followed. It was the most enjoyable evening she had had for a long time and she was one of the last to leave. It was well past midnight as Claude escorted her to her car, he held her hand lightly on the uneven terrace. Opening the door he touched her shoulder and turned her towards him, 'Thank you for coming. You lit up the evening.'

Marthe stood still, then very slowly he leaned forward and kissed her. It was a moment of intense pleasure for them both.

'Stay.'

The prospect of a long drive home to an empty house was not appealing, and she found Claude interesting and attractive, but she looked at him and smiled,

'Not this time. Thank you for a lovely evening.'

They met for lunch in Toulouse a week later, Claude knew the city well and took her to a brasserie she had not seen before. It was in a tiny square, heavily shaded with plane trees, after eating they were going on to a gallery opening. Claude said, 'A friend of many years, more enthusiasm than talent! But you may like her work. She can surprise one!' Marthe and Claude had reached an unspoken agreement not to reminisce about the past; to avoid talking too much about previous husbands, or wives, or relationships. It made it easier for both of them; they talked about the present, the day they were sharing, or maybe a plan not too far ahead. It suited them both and Marthe really knew little about him, apart from his business, his home and his two sons. She had spoken of Felix, and hoped they would meet but had not planned any encounter. They had not kissed again.

Their lunch over they strolled towards the gallery, he took her arm as they crossed the busy narrow streets and she took his hand, the cobbles were difficult in heels and she had nearly stumbled, he smiled but said nothing.

'Look!' he had stopped, and was pointing. They were outside a hat shop,

'That would be perfect on you!' Marthe stared…it was a large summer hat, just a straw really but a soft colour with a grey ribbon around the brim.

'For your garden. You must be careful with the sun here, it will ruins the complexion!'

Marthe smiled at his comment,

'Let's go in!' Claude tightened his grip on her hand and pulled her towards the door. They went in. It was dark inside after the bright sunlight, and Marthe peered about. Claude lifted the hat from the window display and carefully placed it on her head, he turned her towards the only mirror, standing behind her, and waited. She liked it immediately, and could tell that it suited her small face. She rotated a little, glancing at her reflection, catching sight of Claude she smiled, it was an important moment of intimacy for them both. Ignoring Marthe's protests, Claude insisted on buying the hat, and carried it for her to the gallery.

They did not linger long, it was crowded and stuffy and it was impossible to see the pictures properly. There was cigarette smoke and young men with trays of rather warm white wine. Marthe wandered about, there were four small rooms and the paintings, mostly highly coloured landscapes did not interest her at all. Claude chatted to several people, he was clearly a familiar figure in this company. She observed him with interest, grey hair curling at his collar, a somewhat lined face, deep set eyes. He was handsome in an unconventional way, his clothes too worn and comfortable to be smart. On this day he was wearing a creased linen jacket and loose trousers, she wondered if he had once been heavier. He was very slightly stooped but tall none the less. She thought he was probably in his mid sixties, but it was difficult to tell.

Returning to les Palmes he knocked a peg into the wall by the kitchen door, 'You must keep your hat here. And always wear it from now on when you got into the garden. The sun...'

241

'Yes I know, will ruin my complexion.' She touched the hat. It really was quite elegant, for a garden. Claude stayed for a drink then left, he seemed to have an arrangement for the evening. Marthe waved as he drove through the gates, she was sorry to see him go, and wondered briefly what he was doing next. Felix was in Paris for two reasons; he needed to see his accountant for an annual review of his investments, and to discuss his overall financial position. He was also a guest at the wedding of a Conservatoire friend. The meeting did not detain him long, everything was doing well and after a lunch with the accountant, Felix enjoyed a long walk through the sixth arrondissement, where he had retained his small flat. It was a lovely afternoon, and he was in no hurry. The young women, he noticed were more chic, more original than those in Toulouse, stylish and confident as they walked often arm in arm on the narrow pavements. Several times he had to step into the road, causing cycles and cars to swerve. 'Merde!' shouted one, Felix waved his arm, this is Paris, it's how things are. He stopped at a very expensive shop to buy a wedding gift, emerging with a glass decanter, beautifully wrapped and tied with an elegant ribbon. He wondered idly if he had made a mistake in not returning to Paris with Valerie. But dismissed the thought rapidly.

The party after the wedding was followed with dancing on a tiny floor. Felix, who knew many of the guests, was soon enjoying himself. It had been a long time, he felt, since he had indulged himself and he determined to make the most of it. He removed his jacket and tie, and was soon dancing with a very friendly girl, who was clearly also looking for 'fun'. Like most of the guests they were drinking heavily, and well after midnight they left together. With little hesitation, Felix returned with her to her flat, a tiny space up some steep stairs.

Like a scene from La Boheme, he thought, undressing fast and looking out on to roof tops and chimneys. He could just see the two towers of Notre Dame, before falling onto her bed. She was an energetic lover, full of surprises. It was a long night.

The following morning, she led the way to a café. They sat recovering from their lack of sleep and excess of alcohol. She sipped her little coffee and rubbed Felix's ankle with her shoe.

' Shall I come to see you? In Toulon?'

Felix didn't correct her mistake. 'No. I don't think so.'

She was not offended, and they parted with a slight hug. Felix flew home that afternoon, it had been fun, but he did not want to live like that anymore.

CHAPTER 19

Marthe set about making a birthday cake for Charlie. She had overheard Annie talking to him the previous Sunday, outlining the plans for his 'big day'. He would be eleven. She watched the mixer head slowly turning, working the butter and sugar to a thick cream. It was to be a chocolate cake, with icing and blue decoration. Marthe enjoyed the late afternoon, the smell of baking, the table now dusted with flour and sugar. She glanced out of the window as the sun moved steadily across the garden – lighting up the plants and trees. Lowering her head she could just see the three palms standing together, very tall and majestic. She wondered who had named the house, and where the earlier palms had stood.

Having removed the cake, it stood on the rack cooling and smelling delicious, Marthe phoned Felix: 'Can you bring something for Charlie on Sunday?'

'Oh?'

'It's his birthday this week, he's going to be eleven.'

'Right! What are you giving him?'

'A chocolate cake for tea- I've got it cooling now. What about a nice leather music case? You had one... remember, soft, brown leather, a little brass clasp.'

'I still have it! In a drawer somewhere, with some early pieces.'

'Well? What about the same for Charlie?'

'He's just given up, I'm afraid. Not for him, Annie says. I'm disappointed, but, football has taken over.'

'Well that's sad. I thought- what with his chess- he had perseverance.'

'Maybe a fishing rod? He seems very keen to learn. He loves the river, beyond the gate.' Felix arrived at Marthe's on Sunday morning- carrying the rod, wrapped in brown paper, he looked around as he walked down the path, trying to locate Charlie. How green everything was. The change was extraordinary. The new plants, the cacti, the grasses, the young shrubs had merged into groups, the earth hardly showing. Above his head, along the walls, the roses were in full leaf, with a mass of blooms and buds reaching up and out for the sun. It was very quiet. Annie was nowhere to be seen, but Charlie, as usual, was in his 'camp'. the old shed. He was whittling at a stick with the penknife and seemed to be preparing a bonfire.

'Happy Birthday!' Felix called out. Charlie looked up with a grin, he was still full of birthday excitement. Felix, carrying the rod behind him, looked around the garden.

Charlie said, 'She's over there!' He pointed, waving the knife. 'Look!'

Felix spotted Annie, bent double, her bottom in the air. She was pulling up nettles, which had re-established themselves beside the back wall. He watched her briefly while Charlie went back inside his camp. He re-emerged wearing a bright red baseball cap. It was in the colours of the Toulouse rugby team, and was a present from Tony, who had bought a matching one for himself. It was rather large, almost down to his ears.

Felix revealed his present, 'Charlie! Happy Birthday!' Annie stood up hearing his voice and pulling off her heavy gloves walked over. She was flushed with effort. She watched as Charlie ripped off the paper, the boy stood open mouthed, speechless. He ran to Felix, clutching the rod, and hugged him. 'Thank you so much' he let Felix go, and began examining the rod, 'It's so great, I really want to fish in the river here- and now I can!' The rod looked very long beside him!

Annie looked at Charlie then came across to Felix; 'You're very kind! To think of such a super gift, he's, well, thrilled!' Annie touched his sleeve, and as Felix turned, kissed him softly on the mouth. She had acted without thought, Felix just looked so good standing there in his blue shirt, his sleeves rolled up.

Felix's heart took a leap as he looked at her, 'What does this mean?' was the thought flashing through his head. They stood for a moment, close, breathing. Charlie who was intent on his rod, broke the moment, 'Felix, let's go to the river now. Please.'

They drew apart, avoiding eye contact and occupied themselves with Charlie and his rod. Annie walked away, pulling on her gloves. 'I'll get back to my nettles. See you in an hour Charlie, for lunch.' Felix and Charlie walked down the path to the gate, and Felix found the key and carefully unlocked it. They went to the river.

Marthe later brought out the cake, which Charlie solemnly cut and then ate two very large slices. She found a tin, and Charlie carried it home sitting now on the front seat of the car, a new thing for him. Annie liked having him next to her; it was companionable and she had to resist touching his hair.

It had been a memorable day for them all.

Annie had surprised herself by kissing Felix. Driving back to Toulouse a feeling of excitement passed through her and she smiled to herself, I feel something has happened, but who knows? She was philosophical, love? It came and went had been her experience. She found herself thinking about Ralph, the early days, when they made love in their attic flat, their clothes flung on the floor, and a stew simmering on the little stove. How she had loved him, then. And now! She tried not to think about it. But she liked Felix, enjoyed his quiet company, his dry humour. She certainly found him attractive. 'He's on the rebound,' she reminded herself. 'This won't be serious. Who would date a woman with a child? There are plenty of pretty girls in Toulouse for him to have fun with!' But she thought about him again later that evening, he was unlike the other men with whom she had been 'involved'. He knew nothing about gardens, or children, or England, but he was interested in her. We have music in common, she thought, but that's about it! Would that be enough? Maybe not.

It was June, a glorious month. With long days of sunshine and heat. Toulouse buzzed with life; school would soon be over and holidays were being planned. The pavement cafes spilled almost in to the gutter as tables were filled with tourists and locals, all enjoying the arrival of summer. Striped awnings were pulled out and provided much needed protection, while the place du capitol took up its familiar role as the centre of city life. The cafes were kept busy as people competed constantly for tables; eager for breakfast: a coffee and a croissant or a pain au chocolat. Then lunch, tea, cocktails and supper, and everyone wanted to be outside. Harassed waiters, expert at avoiding eye contact, glided around the tightly packed tables, their black moneybags strapped to their waists. The noise of chatter was constant. It was not dark until after ten o'clock and children went moaning to bed. 'But it's still light! It's too early!' Annie grew tired of Charlie's complaining. She also found the heat exhausting, seeking shade as she worked in the public gardens, with her cotton hat soaked in sweat and her shirt sticking uncomfortably to her back. She longed for iced tea, a cold shower and somewhere cool at night. Sleep for everyone had become difficult.

The heat built up into great storms, a feature of south west France. Annie prayed that the tropical downpours were not damaging the young plants in marthe's garden. She watched the rain streaming down the windows of the kitchen, Charlie was counting the seconds between lightning and thunder, 'That was only five' he shouted excitedly, 'that means, wow, it's really close by!' The thunder rolled around for another hour, as the storm was trapped in the valley of the river Garonne. The flat which was normally cool and airy was now hot and humid, Annie could not bear to think about cooking, 'salad again,' she thought, 'how dull is that.' Charlie continued to watch out of the window. The phone rang, and Annie picked it up, it was Felix. 'How about supper, out of town? Away from this heat.'

'What a lovely thought' she hesitated, 'With Charlie?'

'Of course. Half an hour?'

'We'll be outside.' They put their phones down. Both were smiling.

'Charlie! We're going out with Felix. Change your shirt please, and perhaps your new shorts? I'm going to have a shower'. Annie put on a dress, a recent acquisition, purchased with Claire's encouragement. It was cool and sleeveless and red. It had been expensive, and Annie had not worn it before. She looked at herself in the long mirror behind the bathroom door, and cinched in the waist with a narrow gold belt. She added a pair of gold earrings, and felt pretty for the first time in ages. Felix saw her first; she was waiting at the square with Charlie, their heads rotating as they looked for his car.

'She is… lovely,' he thought and leaned over and opened the doors, ignoring the cars which were hooting vigorously as his car blocked the road. Charlie was looking up at the sky. Lightning still flashed across the buildings. He slowly got into the back. They set off.

'Pretty dress' he said, 'it's your colour.' Annie smiled, 'My mother chose it.'

'She has good taste!'

Annie acknowledged the compliments with another smile, she was not used to men noticing what she wore. Ralph had been oblivious to her looks, although he had been kind when she was pregnant and feeling enormous. She thought of him briefly, he was still angry about the divorce but less bitter. He seemed to be moving again, out of the flat, but she didn't have a new address. She hoped that it was not for financial reasons.

Supper was at a small restaurant in the foothills, an hour's drive, south of Toulouse. The thunder had stopped and the air was finally cooling. They ate beside an open window, there were few other diners. Charlie had brought a book on chess, which he read surreptitiously in between the courses. Annie and Felix talked easily of nothing in particular, and were happy to do so. He glanced at her across the table, they had drunk nearly a bottle of white wine.

Annie said, 'Stop looking at me! Felix.'

'Why? You look… Lovely! It's nice to see a woman looking pretty!'

She thought about that for a moment, had Valerie always looked pretty? She knew French women cared greatly about their 'looks', it had never been a matter of concern for her. It seemed that now she would have to make it so.

Charlie slept all the way back, and Felix took Annie's hand and held it driving with the other. As they turned off the motor way he put his arm around her shoulders, and kissed her as they waited in the queue at the toll booth. The adjacent car hooted and Felix grinned and waved, accelerating as he drove off.

Toulouse hit them with a wall of heat. The streets were crowded as people poured out of the airless apartments trying to catch a breeze. Annie fanned herself as she got out of the car, 'Wow, it's hot!' she said. Charlie woke up and gazed about him as he pushed the car door open, and staggered out onto the pavement. 'The pavements are burning in the evening,' he moaned. Annie sighed. Felix got out and, ignoring the protests of drivers who were forced to pull out and pass him, stood beside them. 'Shall I park? Come up? Help with Charlie?'

Annie paused, uncertain. 'I'll manage! Thanks. He'll be in bed in five minutes! But thank you for a really lovely evening, it was...' she repeated, 'lovely!' Felix looked at her gravely. He paused, bent his head and kissed her. Annie stood very still, while Charlie half asleep leant on her. Annie wondered whether he should come up, it was a bridge they seemed ready to cross, but the traffic was noisy and Charlie began moaning again, and that was that.

Annie put Charlie to bed, unwashed, it was late, but she didn't care. She hung the dress up carefully and thought about Felix for a long time and slept badly.

Marthe too found the heat of June oppressive. It was never like this in Paris, she thought, rinsing her face with cool water for the umpteenth time. Whilst she had learned the local trick for keeping the house cool: close the shutters all day, keep the sun out. Open them later in the evening, and the windows too. Let the night air in. Shut everything again after breakfast, still the house felt uncomfortable. With the shutters closed the house was plunged into a daily gloom, which she found depressing.

Outside the garden, with its high walls, lacked any breeze, the plants stood in a haze of heat, very still, motionless. The storms gave occasional relief- the rain making the sky almost purple. The sun came out, and the ground steamed. It felt like an endless cycle to Marthe. It was too hot to go out, except very early or late in the evening, the days felt long. The phone rang, it was a Tuesday morning. She recognized Claude's voice, 'Come with me to Collioure! It's too hot here, so I am going on a buying expedition. Maybe two or three days.' Marthe did not even think twice, 'That sounds like a very attractive idea. When are you going?'

'Today. Can I pick you up in, can you manage half an hour?

'I'll be at the door.'

'Don't forget your hat!'

Marthe and Claude spent four days down on the coast. A sea breeze welcomed them, and as Marthe stood on the balcony of their room overlooking the sea, she felt cool for the first time that week. The owner clearly knew Claude well; the two men chatted as he opened the shutters and then he showed her the view of the bay and the famous lighthouse. She was enchanted. She had never visited this part of France before, Xavier had always taken her to the Cote d' Azur with its stunning coast line, and mountains, and good restaurants. Collioure wasn't such a fashionable resort, but no less beautiful Marthe thought. It was famous for its anchovies, and for the artists of the Fauve movement, who had settled there and painted the town many times. Marthe planned to spend some of her time looking at their work, while Claude was busy with his buying. Claude was eager for lunch and they walked briskly to the harbour and into a restaurant, overlooking the harbour wall. Marthe knew that Claude was a regular visitor to Collioure, and she thought that she was probably one of several women that had accompanied him on his visits. But this would not stop her enjoyment. He chose a dish for both of them: some grilled fish of the day, bread and olives and salad, and a bottle of white wine. A siesta was needed, and they strolled back beside the harbour. Neither doubted that love-making should precede the sleep. They did not wake till after five in the afternoon, the sun had moved behind the hills that surrounded the town and the colour of the sea had changed from blue to silver. It was very beautiful, and Marthe took some photographs.

In the mornings Marthe explored quietly on her own, threading her way through the narrow streets, pausing at the many galleries, and resting on the benches that overlooked the sea. Claude foraged for his business and seemed content with several purchases. He took Marthe with him on their final day and turning south, they crossed into Spain and drove up into the Pyrenees. It was a long tiring drive, and by the afternoon they were both tired.

'Let's stay up here.' Marthe suggested. 'We can check into the hotel I saw in the square, and there's an antique shop. It might have something for you.' Her idea proved a good one. They took a room overlooking the shady square, and the antique dealer sold Claude two stone dogs that Marthe had spotted in the dusty garden. Later they ate in the square under the chestnut trees and watched the little town come to life. Marthe sighed with pleasure and Claude gave her hand a squeeze, and said, 'You're a good travelling companion! Thank you.' Marthe looked at him, Claude was not an effusive man and she liked his words of appreciation. She smiled in acknowledgement. 'It's been fun. I've fallen in love' she paused 'with Collioure!' It was an odd teasing moment. The following morning, while Claude organised the dispatching of the stone dogs, she took a short walk around the square, and bought a post card for Patricia. 'She'll wonder what I'm doing in Spain', she thought with a smile.

*

Marthe had been thinking for some time about Bertrand's personal papers, she had found nothing in her mother's desk that had been his. Did he have his own desk? If so where was it? Where did he store all the documents, bills, accounts, letters connected with the life of his family? She had returned from Collioure and was in the garden, in the orchard. She thought of what old Jean had said about how her mother enjoyed reading here, and being reminded of Jean, wondered, Could he remember any more about Bertrand?

Jean was living in the home for the elderly in St. Girou. She had visited him there several times, taking a little cake, or flowers from the garden. He was fragile and his attention had wandered as they spoke. On this day, she found him sitting in his chair, by the window in his room. He was dozing with a rug over his knees. The nurse told her that he was well, but confused, as were so many of the other elderly residents. He heard her steps and turned with a rather blank face. But, after several minutes, Jean became alert as she talked about Les Palmes and her father and mother, and his face became more animated. Marthe said, 'And do you recall the last time you saw them?' He answered slowly, 'Life was difficult then; we had to have passes, and food was short, so I killed several chickens...' she could see him drifting off into the war years. 'My father, do you remember the last time that you saw him? Or my mother?' Jean stared at her, 'There was a little girl,' he said, 'she didn't like the bonfire. It frightened her, it was so hot! She ran into the house…' Marthe wondered what he was remembering. He continued, 'It was very large; all the papers and boxes with documents. It burned for two days, left a pile of ash and all the smoke, everywhere. Nasty smell too. But the lady insisted, kept bringing out more and more. 'Burn it all!' she kept saying. So I did, but the little girl complained, said the smoke hurt her eyes.' He sat in his chair, thinking about a day long ago, and after a short while he drifted into sleep, and Marthe left him to his memories.

She had found out the answer to Bertrand's papers: her mother had had them all burned in the garden. What did they say? What did they reveal? What was she trying to hide? It seemed obvious. Her mother knew of the connection between Bertrand and the Nazi conspiracy to abduct the four men. She knew, maybe had known for some time, that he was a collaborator, so she determined to have all the evidence of his political activities, his pro- German sympathies destroyed. In a huge bonfire. It was the easiest way to get rid of them. Thinking further, Marthe wondered what else her mother had known… maybe also, the circumstances surrounding Bertrand's sudden death? Marthe thought of the sudden flight of her mother to Paris, was she fleeing from this death? Had she thought it was suicide? A grave sin in the eyes of the law and the church. It would have been a shocking thought for a young woman, who was now a widow, with a young child. Marthe felt weary with her reflections, but

she had now a much clearer understanding of the last months of her parent's lives at Les Palmes, though the story was not complete.

CHAPTER 20

Annie had arrived for work, the garden opening was only 3 weeks away, she now came in her car, which was already filled with garden tools and paper bags, empty water bottles, the odd cardigan. A pair of boots. But this day the car was at the garage for its first service and she had taken the train. Charlie was with a friend from school, they had been taken fishing. 'It's cooler here than Toulouse!' Annie commented as she stood with Marthe, under the palm trees. Marthe thought briefly of her stay beside the sea and in the mountains, she had returned home the previous evening, and buying lunch for Felix had been a rush. She had not decided whether to tell him of her trip with Claude.

'How do you manage?' Marthe replied,

'Well I don't really! Charlie and I live on salads, and we just open everything up at night. Sleep is the problem, Charlie is permanently tired, hot and grumpy.'

Marthe thought about that, 'What about the holidays. Is he going away?'

Annie almost flinched at the thought. She had been avoiding the issue for weeks. 'We're here- obviously- till July 14th- then well, I'll have to see- maybe to my mother and then his father.' Her voice tailed off...'It's not ideal. But, I'll work something out! It's a juggling act to be honest- my holiday allowance is generous for the teaching- all the students pack up in late June, but the City- they are not that understanding. I'll probably take a couple of weeks, that's all.'

Felix came in at the end of this conversation... hearing only Annie's last remark. He had not thought about July and August at all and suddenly realised how complicated Annie's life must be. He felt foolish, selfish. He only had himself to think about, while Annie had Charlie, an ex husband, a mother (who missed them) and two jobs.

He had brought with him the 'fliers' for the opening. One hundred had been printed off- he expected to find 'homes' for about half of them. Marthe was delighted both with the fliers themselves- clear and attractive- and to see Felix's enthusiasm for the day.

'I'll start putting them up later today,' Felix said. 'I thought around the town, obviously, then in a radius of about 20 miles. That should bring them in! Or do you think 20 miles is too ambitious?' He turned to Annie.

'I don't see why not. The more the merrier, really.'

'Goodness, can you manage all that? Marthe said doubtfullly.

'It won't take long- nail them on a tree or a post- fliers are everywhere in summer- there's so much going on- concerts, jazz festivals, car boot sales- you name it!'

It turned out to be a bigger project than Felix had expected, he spent nearly two hours that afternoon and still had only the town and approach roads covered. Annie had finished her work and was walking slowly back to the station- in the shade. She was tired and hot, but very pleased with her day- it was easier to concentrate without Charlie and whilst she missed his chatter, a day without him had its own rewards.

She saw with delight the 'fliers' in the small square and on the wall beside the church. She avoided looking at the plaque, it had too many unhappy memories. There was a third one beside the station. 'It really is going to happen,' she felt a surge of excitement and anticipation. 'I'll phone Mum when I get back. Make sure that she has bought her plane ticket. She waited on the platform for the train eating a very late lunch, and looking up the line expectantly. The baguette was already dry, so she pulled out the filling- salami and soft cheese and ate that with her fingers. Her water bottle was nearly empty and the water itself was warm. 'I'll stop for a beer in Toulouse, I deserve that', she decided. She brushed the bread off her shorts, stretched out her brown legs. There was a peach left in her bag, already bruised- she bit into it, juice dripped down her T shirt.

It was thus that Felix found her- having abandoned his afternoon's work. She looked up in surprise- wiping her mouth and grinned. 'Don't come near! I'm hot, sweaty and now covered in juice.'

'How delicious! I love peach juice,' he intended to kiss her but as he spoke the train came in and Annie stood up, grabbing her bag and picnic leftovers.

'No! I've come to give you a lift! The car is still full of 'fliers', but I've had enough. I'm on my way home. I need a beer.! How long have you got? Join me?'

'Charlie is due back about seven o'clock, so a couple of hours'. Maybe I could help you, two villages of 'fliers' on the way home?'

It was hot work jumping out of the car, sticking up a flier, and then doing it all over again ten minutes later. They were pleased to reach Toulouse and a café in the shade near the river. It was very quiet, as they stretched their legs and Felix ordered two beers. A few tourists wandered about listlessly, and some boys kicked a football against a wall. Some street traders, heavy bags on their shoulders passed by, heading home from the Sunday market around the cathedral. Felix and Annie sat quietly, recovering. But it was nearly seven o'clock and Annie had to pick up Charlie. She gathered her bag and rose from the table.

"How's Marthe? She looks well, and she has a very pretty new hat. But there's something else I think.'

'Really?'

'Yes. It's probably excitement!'

'I expect it's the Opening, she's full of optimism, and it's exciting, displaying her garden to strangers. It's given her a sense of pride in Les Palmes'

'Of course, it must be that.' They walked back to the car and Felix drove to the flat, keeping the traffic waiting in his usual way.

'I need a cold shower!' Annie said, as she lifted out her bags, 'It was a good day and your fliers were a brilliant idea. Not long now!'

She walked to the entrance of the apartment giving a wave. The heavy door slammed shut behind her as Felix, watching her go, put the car into gear and moved from the kerb. He too thought it had been a 'good day', but again felt that he had missed an opportunity with Annie.

The 'fliers' that Felix had put up in the town, did not survive for long. Henri, walking in on Monday morning spotted one on the church wall. He stopped and read it. Anger boiled up inside him, and his heart began beating dangerously fast. He read it again, then took it in his grasp and tearing and pulling, dragged it off the wall. He crumpled it up and threw it away. The flier lay on the dusty street, soon to be run over by vans and lorries. Henri continued his walk, but with a great intensity, his quick glances spotted a second, near the garage on a post. This too was rapidly destroyed. Forgetting his original intention- to purchase bread, a newspaper- he made a determined tour of the town. In all he found five of the eight fliers. He ignored the one in the square, fearing that he would be observed, the others were ripped and left torn up in the gutters. It was hot work. An internal rage consumed Henri; and he forgot his earlier promises to Sylvie, his fear of lawyers, his interview with the gendarmes. He thought only of Marthe, and her father, and the garden which he had seen.

'A garden opening, whatever did she intend with that? To win people over? to patch over the past? to pretend everything was forgotten… forgiven?'

Henri's mood was dark as he made his lunch- without bread. He could see Sylvie working outside, potting up plants near the old pigsties. She was frowning with concentration, her dark hair tied up, and her tanned face and hands, shining with sweat. She would be cross that there was no fresh bread for her lunch. He took note of the date- July 14th- a Saturday, less than three weeks away.

Nonetheless despite Henri's efforts word steadily spread in the local area. Marthe, Felix and Annie would have been gratified to learn that many people now planned to visit the garden. Some were interested in its 'dry plants' theme, and others by the offer of tea, and cakes, and a plant sale. The latter was consuming Marthe as much as anything else. The greenhouse, and the area outside it, was now full of little pots, which she watered assiduously, protecting them as best she could from the sun. They were all priced at two Euros. The profit, if there was one, was to go to Charlie's school. He had begged five fliers from Felix, and posted them inside the school. He was very hopeful that many of his friends (and their families) would come and support Marthe and his mum.

His excitement mounted as the day approached. He began looking anxiously at the weather map, 'Mum, what shall we do? If it rains?' Annie was equally anxious, remembering the sudden storms of June, she tried hard to calm him down.

'It won't. Unless grandma brings it with her from England!'

Charlie was aghast, 'Don't tease Mum. It's not funny! And you mustn't joke like that with Marthe!'

He saw himself as a key figure of the day. Marthe had entrusted him with several tasks: showing people the side door which led through to the garden, helping with keeping jugs of lemonade topped up, and most importantly, supervising her plant stall. There was to be a large pot for the Euros.

Claire arrived on Thursday, alone. It was too hot for Tony and gardens were not really his 'thing', though he had conscientiously visited several near their home in England. He was quite an expert on National Trust teas. He made his excuses to Annie, who was relieved to have one less worry- and looked forward to seeing her mother on her own for once. She would stay four nights and sleep in Annie's bed. Annie would move to a 'put you up' in the sitting room. This arrangement excited Charlie, they very rarely had people to stay, and he anticipated Claire's arrival as all part of the general break from normal life.

On Wednesday, a friend kept Charlie busy in Toulouse, while Annie and Marthe walked the garden; Annie looked at all the greenhouse plants, and gave the sheds a quick tidy. The labels on the plants, the gravel on the paths, the water in the basin, all the benches and urns were checked. 'They're bound to see all the bad bits!' Annie commented, 'our visitors are keen gardeners... they'll come to learn, hopefully, but also inspect!'

Marthe looked at her anxiously, 'You'll have to answer the questions! Explain what this is all about.'

'Of course, but this is your garden, not mine. What we have here celebrates your interest. My passion for 'dry' planting- well it's yours too now- isn't it? Just remember the key words for the design, dry and sustainable.'

It was a long morning, hot and sunny, and by lunchtime Marthe was exhausted! They shared a salad and Marthe then went to her room and slept! Annie worked on, she rarely had the garden to herself and she was thrilled to see it looking... Extraordinary! It fulfilled all her hopes and yet was so much more. She remembered her first visit the previous autumn, when she had seen an overgrown and neglected 'wilderness'. Even then she had seen its potential, and had not hesitated in taking on the challenge. She knew how lucky she had been to meet Marthe, who had given her such a free hand. She was the perfect employer. Annie hoped that Saturday would be the triumph that she deserved.

Claire flew into Toulouse on the Thursday before the Big Day (as Annie now called it)- she was full of excitement, antic- ipating a weekend with Annie and Charlie. She had brought a summer dress and large straw hat, as she expected to be in the garden all day and Annie had warned her of the strength of the sun. She took the train into Toulouse and a taxi from the station. Annie had left the key to the flat with the baker oppo- site, and she let herself in- feeling independent and important. The flat was dark, all the shutters closed against the sun, but she saw Annie's note on the table. 'Read me!'it said and there was a heart in red, the work of Charlie, she supposed.

Annie asked her to shop for supper for three. It was easily done; Claire returned to the baker and bought bread, savour- ing the smell! She walked down the street, keeping in the shade and bought a chicken, some salad and strawberries. She added some cheeses, though they were not on Annie's list. The range was extraordinary. Claire reflected that she and Tony would grow hugely fat if they ate like this every day, yet looking about her she saw slim women. 'They must be so disciplined' she thought, and walked back home, holding her stomach in.

They all enjoyed eating together. Annie gingerly opened the shutters and the big windows, but the air outside was still hot and she closed them again firmly.

Claire asked, 'So what is the plan for tomorrow?' She had taken a mere sliver of cheese, and had limited herself to only two glasses of wine, and was feeling very positive.

'Well. We'll go to Marthe's in my lovely new car, and finish the preparations, and take a picnic.' She looked at the chicken, 'not much there!'

'And supper?' Claire regretted this immediately. Annie would think her mother never stopped thinking about food.

'We can buy supper when we get back. The shops stay open till seven.'

Charlie asked, 'Can I take my fishing rod?'

Claire said, 'Fishing rod? Where did that come from?'

'Felix. It was my birthday present. And he has one too.'

'Where do you fish?' Claire asked.

'In the river, through the gate. I'll show you tomorrow.'

*

The following morning Claire watched the landscape through the car windows. There were scarlet poppies lining the roads, and the maize was tall and golden in the huge fields, so much larger than in England. 'There are no hedges are there.' She commented.

'No. They have rooted them out. It makes the land easier to work and so much more profitable, but they have lost their birds. Sad really, but here it's all about efficiency.' Claire regarded her daughter discreetly. 'Annie looks well' she thought, 'less strained, prettier, this is a big event for her, let's hope it all goes well.' Claire could not bear to think that anything might go wrong... in England it would be the rain, or a cold wind that ruined a garden opening. Here in France? She did not know, the heat probably.

Marthe was in the drive as they drove in- she was tidying up beside the gates and pulling up little weeds. Marthe greeted her warmly. 'She's an attractive woman.' Claire thought, 'Chic.' She and Marthe went into the house and Marthe showed Claire her newly refurbished rooms. Claire was astonished at the evidence of good taste and style. 'She is very wealthy,' she thought 'I had no idea.' They moved on and into the kitchen, where Marthe explained the arrangements for tea. They went out into the garden where Annie was already at work. Charlie rushed at her, 'Come! See!' he dragged her off.

'We've thought of everything, 'Annie said, 'nothing can go wrong! The weather is set fair all weekend, and the garden looks fantastic!'

Marthe looked around it was indeed wonderful, 'Thank you Annie, I've never really said that before. Thank you very much. I shall enjoy this garden for many years to come.' Marthe felt a little shudder of pleasure as she looked about her, it really was a transformation and all in less than a year. A little later Annie walked her mother around carefully explaining the plants and her design. Claire was impressed and proud too, they were standing in the centre of the garden, under one of the palms when Charlie interrupted. 'I'm going fishing.'

Annie said, 'Be back for lunch- we'll picnic sharp on twelve o'clock. And don't forget to put the key back on its hook!'

'Shall I go too?' Claire asked anxiously, 'Is he safe on his own?'

'He'll be fine. He likes the independence. He'll probably fish just the other side of the gate! And he can swim. Stay with me. I still have lots to do and can find you a job!'

It was already getting hot. The tables and chairs were delivered and set up in the shade, while Claire helped Marthe in the kitchen, preparing sandwiches, it was an easy task and as she put the last 'round' wrapped lightly in film in the fridge, she heard the door open and looking up saw Felix. He made her jump, while Felix saw how alike the family were. Charlie had his grandmother's eyes, wide set and grey, and mother and daughter the same springy hair.

'You must be Claire!' He laughed at her surprise. 'I'm sorry I disturbed you!'

*

Claire stood up and they shook hands. "No, No! I was busy." She moved to the sink, as she spoke, 'I'm a dogsbody today!'

'Where is everyone?' Felix took off his jacket, draped it over the back of a chair- his shirt looked cool and crisp Claire noticed approvingly.

'Charlie is fishing. Annie is in the garden, of course, and your mother is writing labels in the shade. We've been making sandwiches together all morning. I'm having a splendid time! We are about to stop for lunch.'

'I'll go and get Charlie then! Why don't you come too! The river's worth a look.' Felix suggested. Claire admired the orchard as they walked towards the gate, it was shady and cool, and the grass was nearly up to her knees. She stopped at the two urns, that had been positioned together under one of the older trees, it was a delightful place to linger, 'This is the only part of the garden that Annie hasn't changed, I suppose. The trees have been here for many years,' she ran her hand down the bark of one, it was covered in green lichen.

'Yes. You're right.' Felix said, 'Marthe wanted it left as it was, though some of the older trees have been cleared out. It balances the garden...'

'Yes I can see that. The mood is quite different here, calm and shaded. But I love the water feature best, it's...'she paused, 'somewhere to sit and reflect.' Felix thought about that as they continued walking to the gate in the wall.

'Goodness, it has a padlock.' She had noticed the lock which was hanging down where Charlie had left it. 'Are there wild men on the other side?' She joked.

'No! No! It's just a precaution, Annie keeps expensive tools in the shed. We couldn't risk her losing them.'

They turned on to the towpath and began walking slowly next to the river. They soon spotted Charlie, as Annie had predicted, he had not gone far, and had put himself in the shade of a weeping willow, almost hidden by trailing branches. He was sitting on the bank, fairly still, the rod between his knees.

'Lunch Charlie!' Claire took the lead. 'Have you caught anything?' She looked down the towpath, and asked, 'Where does this go?'

Felix explained. 'And the other way? Into town?' Claire pointed towards St. Girou.

'Yes, it flows all the way to join the Garonne nearer to Toulouse. There are a series of weirs and pools, it's popular with fishermen.' Charlie had packed up his rod. 'Let's go! Grandma. I'm hungry!' He took her hand, and they walked back to the garden, all three ready for lunch. By teatime they were tired and decided to call it a day. Marthe shewed Charlie all the food now carefully stored in the fridges, he was impressed. 'Now we can just sit back and see who comes!' She said.

' Lots of my friends are coming" Charlie claimed.

'Goodness,' Annie looked at him teasingly, 'are they interested in gardening?'

'Well some are, but really they want to see my camp and the fishing rod!'

'And the cakes perhaps?asked Claire.

They said goodbye, and Felix touched Annie's hand lightly. 'See you all tomorrow!' he said. Claire noticed and looked at Felix, 'Is something going on?' she wondered, ' Is he the reason that Annie is looking prettier?' she would ask later.

Driving home, Annie watched as both her mother and son fell asleep. It gave her an opportunity to think about the following day. She had assured Marthe that nothing could go wrong, and in regard to the garden she was confident. But would the villagers come? And from further afield too? It would be desperately disappointing if only a few families appeared... Annie suddenly felt very apprehensive. 'I need a drink' she thought, 'We may celebrate, but not yet!' A voice of caution warned her. They had a quiet evening at the flat and tried to talk about things other than the coming day.

After Annie and her family had driven away, Felix and Marthe sat in the garden together enjoying a glass of very cold white wine and some olives. It was cool on the veranda though the garden still shimmered in the heat. Felix was preparing to leave, he walked into the kitchen to retrieve his jacket and drink a glass of water, and was astonished, on looking through the window to see a grey haired man stooping over his mother and kissing her. Properly kissing her.

He watched. He was too surprised to move. They drew apart and the man, 'Who was he? What was this?' sat down on the seat that Felix had just vacated, he drew it nearer to Marthe and took her hand. She poured some wine into her glass and offered it to him. Felix realized with a sudden flash that this man was more than just a friend of Marthe he was more, much more.

Felix was right. Marthe and Claude had continued their relationship after their time in Collioure, and had slept together twice, once in his bed, which was very large and old with heavy hangings. and again here at Les Palmes, which was more comfortable. She felt' renewed' she told Claude as they ate breakfast on the second occasion, he had smiled his quiet smile and the next day, gave her a bouquet of roses that he had cut from his garden.

Felix went outside, and Marthe said, 'Can you fetch another glass? I want you to meet someone. And perhaps another bottle?'

Claude was amused to see the guarded of the man who he was sure was Marthe' son. 'You must be Felix. I'm Claude.' Coming forward Felix extended his hand as Marthe sat silently watching. She was glad that Felix had found them, here in the garden, it made the encounter easy for them all, the wine and the early evening atmosphere. They discussed the following day and Claude went to check the basin and its fountain. He moved a smaller urn turning it in towards the house, and placed another beside it. Returning he said, 'It all looks quite splendid. You'll be a great success!' He seemed to be staying for supper or was in no hurry to leave, and Felix said goodbye.

Driving home, he toyed with the idea of phoning Annie with the news of this unexpected development in his mother's life. But he felt it would be disloyal to discuss such a personal matter, so he could only mull over it by himself. He was pleased to see Marthe in the company of a man he immediately liked, but oddly apprehensive too. He had become protective of Marthe in the last year, and could not be sure whether this new man would be a short or long term addition to her life. He also felt mildly jealous that they had clearly moved into intimacy with such speed. He had a large whisky before bed in a state of considerable confusion.

Claude left very early in the morning. She was still in bed as he said goodbye,

'Good luck!' he said, with a gentle hug, 'Don't be anxious! You've created the loveliest garden in the whole of this area. And I know them all!' Marthe listened to his steps as he descended the stairs and heard the front door slam, she got up and went immediately to the window. It was a glorious morning, the sky already turning blue, the garden waiting for the day to begin. After a slow start, the day got going. Groups of varying sizes came through the gates, they were families mainly, and were directed by Charlie through to the garden, though some lingered at the plant stall. He sold several plants and was pleased to see the large pot filling up. He waited expectantly for some of his school friends to appear.

The morning went well; Annie was kept busy answering questions, and catching the eye in her white linen shirt and trousers. She had a professional air, as holding her plant lists, she explained her design and her ideas. A number of other professionals had arrived, also some local growers and two well -known horticulturalists who taught at the University. Claire, in a new yellow dress, tried to keep in the shade, while also handing out plant lists to those who wanted them. Felix kept the tables and chairs in neat groups, eyeing the mix of people. The garden became quite crowded, he kept a wary out for Henri.

At noon it quietened down, some 80 people had already visited, Charlie had counted everyone. Annie was thrilled by the positive response of so many people now she darted along the paths, checking her labels and pushing the gravel with her feet. She corrected several stakes and picked up some leaves that were floating in the basin. Many visitors had paused here, enjoying the play of water and the sound of the fountain. Felix closed the gates once the morning crowd had left and they joined Marthe in the house, pleased to get out of the sun. The house felt cool and dark. Marthe had wandered outside trying to listen to the comments but she felt that this was Annie's day, and anyway she had not the expertise to answer questions. But she had prepared lunch, which was in the dining room. 'A special day' she said to Charlie, as she propelled him, with hands on his shoulders into the cool room.

*

'Who wants a glass of wine?' Felix had come in last.

'Oh we deserve one surely?' Annie help up her hand, joined by Claire, and Marthe. 'What a morning!' Claire said as she sat at the table next to Charlie, and turned to Marthe with a smile, but before Marthe could respond the phone rang and she went to answer it. She returned after a few minutes and Felix glanced at her. She shrugged, and spoke quietly to him, 'It was Claude, he has gone to Bordeaux, something about a book fair and his son.'

'That's a shame, he was looking forward to it.' Felix replied, but before he could say anymore, Charlie who had overheard said, 'Who's that?' Annie put down her spoon, 'Charlie, apologize this minute to Marthe.' The boy blushed and stared at his bowl, but before he could speak, Marthe said, ' He's a friend of mine, who would have come if he could. Don't worry Charlie.' She smiled at him kindly, 'More icecream?' Chastened, Charlie shook his head. The moment passed.

Felix suggested a role reversal for the afternoon: Charlie would help with the lemonade and carrying out the tea,

Marthe and Claire, would serve the tea, cut the cakes and set out the sandwiches and he would stand at the entrance by the plant stall, though there was little left to sell. They knew that the afternoon was likely to be busy.

*

The next three hours were exactly that as they all kept to their tasks, though Felix regularly abandoned his post at the gate, eager to see everyone in the garden. He watched Annie who was now wearing a wide brimmed hat, much like her mother's, it was a beautiful sunny afternoon, she was talking animatedly to a couple of elderly ladies. She turned, and spotting him, gave a big wave and smile and put both her thumbs up. People came steadily through the gates staying for an hour or longer, finding a bench or seat to enjoy the tea that Marthe and Claire were serving. Marthe watched them admiring the garden, following the paths, reading the plant labels and talking to Annie. Many rested beside the basin, while others paused beneath the three palms which stood motionless in the heat of the afternoon. She recognised several from St. Girous: the pharmacist had brought his wife and elderly parents (who sat down very quickly), also the bakers' family, and she had seen the local garage owner, which surprised her. She put down an empty plate and stared about her, these ordinary people, enjoying ordinary lives in my extra ordinary garden. She was over whelmed with pride, tinged with the slight regret that Claude had not come, she wondered how long he was going to stay in Bordeaux. Later she spotted the man, who she had sat beside at Claude's supper party, and who, she remembered, had also moved from Paris. They chatted and shared the last slice of a piece of cake. 'A bold decision' he said, 'to move so far, but I envy you. This is a lovely house and garden.' He was with his daughter, a very pretty girl, who wandered off on her own. 'She studies in Paris, so this is a visit only.' He said, and Marthe realised that he was lonely. She decided to invite him to lunch, perhaps in the following week.

The garden shone in the afternoon sun, filled with movement and chatter. Claire now on her own at the tea table, called to Felix, 'I need a helper. Come!'

Felix joined her in serving food (there was little left) and drink. He grabbed the last slice of an almond cake, 'It's so busy! I am amazed! It looks great, doesn't it?' Before Claire could reply, Charlie and several boys rushed up, 'Can I go now?' He asked, 'Some friends from school are here, and I want to show them the river where I go fishing?'

Felix nodded his assent, he was not really listening, and Charlie made off towards the gate. Annie joined them, she was hot and flushed, and seized a cup of tea from Felix, he handed her the end of his cake which she took in one mouthful. Gradually the garden emptied, families drifted away, many came to find Marthe and to thank her for an interesting visit, and some asked if they could return later in the year to see how the garden looked. The two ladies who had engaged Annie for a long chat, had asked her to assist them in redesigning their garden, the first of several similar requests. Eventually Charlie and his friends returned, and swiftly ate up the last of the sandwiches, he was hot and excited. Marthe and Annie were sad to see the last visitors leave- the day was over. It was nearly seven o'clock.

Marthe was tired now and agreed that the clearing up could be left until Monday when the tables and chairs were to be collected, she went indoors, while Claire and Charlie walked towards the car. Annie took a last look standing on the path with Felix,

'Perfect,' she commented, 'Just what I wanted'. 'And that's how I feel about you.' Felix spoke almost without thinking.

Annie turned in surprise, 'Goodness! I've never been called 'perfect' before! It's kind, but untrue. Really Felix- you mustn't think of me like that!'

Felix refused to be put down, 'I shall think of you how I like!' He repeated 'Just what I wanted' and looked at her.

Annie smiled at him, 'Felix! You are trying to charm me...'

He spoke very quietly, 'And am I succeeding?' 'Well. Not here. Not now.' Annie stood looking at him. The question remained unanswered, and Annie gave Felix a light kiss, she wanted to touch him even momentarily. She set off for Toulouse with Claire, soon snoring in the front seat, and Charlie thinking about his day. They were followed by Felix through the gates, he accelerated past, waving as he went. His mind was very busy.

*

Marthe woke early the next morning, feeling ravenous. She had not eaten supper the evening before, having decided on an early bath and bed. Before she went to sleep, there had been a long telephone conversation with Claude who said he was exhausted, and sad to have disappointed her. He was still in Bordeaux with his son. Their drive had been slow and he had carried armfuls of books into the fair and arranged them on Jerome's stall. He was, he said, tired and eager to be home, but was needed for several days. He asked about the opening day and Marthe gave him a lively account. Claude repeated that he was very disappointed not to be there, 'I look forward to seeing you soon.' He assured her and then rang off.

Marthe drew back the heavy curtains, to enjoy the early light as it spread into the garden. She loved this time of day;

the garden resting before the sun warmed all the plants and shrubs and trees. It was very quiet and still. The sky was pale blue, cloudless. The garden lay below her, stretching towards the far gate in the wall. She blinked and stared. She stared for a long time- uncomprehending. Slowly her brain connected with her vision- she saw very clearly what lay before her. The garden was devastated! Plants torn up and thrown aside, slim stems kicked over, the shrubs had their branches hacked down, the paths were filled with debris. Her wicker chairs had been over turned, briefly Marthe thought of a tornado- but it was too deliberate and calculated for that. Marthe felt sure that the damage had been done by man not nature …a human tornado. She looked again. The honey- coloured, wavy grasses had been cut low haphazardly, the tall spiky cacti were untouched, but the lower ones had been trampled. Handfuls of gravel had been thrown onto the neat beds and- looking further she saw Charlie's shed, the window shattered. Both of the large urns that she had purchased from Claude were lying on their sides, the soil spilling out. Looking further into the orchard she could not make out any further damage.

She held to the curtain for support- feeling faint, her heart was pounding. 'Henri.' she said to herself, 'It has to be!' The sight of the devastated garden was overwhelming. She stepped back from the window and in her haste caught her foot on the rug. Clutching vainly at the small table, she fell, knocking her face as she hit the floor. She lay stunned, the appalling image stayed in her mind. Marthe rose carefully to her feet, her temple above her right eye was cut and badly grazed. She walked to the bathroom and holding the basin, gazed at herself in the mirror. 'Quite slight,' she thought, 'looks worse than it is.' Carefully she bathed away the blood, put cream on the graze, finishing with a plaster. This calmed her, but only briefly, as she caught sight again of the garden, with anger in her heart. 'I must phone Felix' was her immediate thought- 'He has to know.'

She dialled slowly, 'Be there! Please Felix be there!' She shut her eyes, holding the receiver, praying for him to pick it up. It rang and rang...

Marthe slowly pulled herself together. She dressed and made her way down the stairs, nodding as was her habit at Felix' ancestors. She made a pot of coffee, and found a bowl for her fruit, eating at the table with her back to the window. It was a beautiful Sunday morning.

Felix had started his day enjoying a quiet coffee and crois-sant with a morning paper in the square. He felt happy as he sat there, reflecting on the previous day. It had been a triumph, a real success. The garden was stunning and the many visitors had been full of praise. Marthe had enjoyed the afternoon, looking young in her dark blue silk dress, from her Paris days he assumed. He thought about Claude; he had certainly been a surprise, but he seemed a pleasant man, and Marthe could not live for ever without male company. He hoped to get to know him better. He lingered for some time, idly waching the many pretty girls who, like him, were enjoy-ing a summer morning in Toulouse. He thought about Annie, he wondered what she and Charlie and Claire were doing. Returning to his flat he found the phone ringing. He tried to make sense of what Marthe was saying, but she was extremely angry and difficult to follow. 'Start again!' he said, 'I need to understand you! Please... slowly.'

Felix sat at the table, his head resting on one hand- as slowly, Marthe explained again. 'Of course it was Henri! who else? He is a vindictive, horrible man. Oh you should see it! Everything damaged, and broken, and plants everywhere!'

She stopped suddenly, there was a silence. 'I am too angry for tears. And now I need to tell Annie!'

'Leave that to me. She is busy with her mother today. We cannot tell her yet. Try to calm down, it may not be as bad as you think.'

With a heavy heart, Felix returned to Les Palmes. He and Marthe spent the rest of the day together. They did a slow tour of the garden but neither had the will to examine it closely. It all looked terrible. Marthe went to look at the basin, and Felix walked through the orchard and paused, frozen. The gate to the towpath was wide open and, exploring further, he found the key and padlock on the grass, where Charlie had carelessly thrown them when he and his school friends went fishing. Felix blamed himself for having forgotten to check the gate, he could have wept with remorse, he had given Charlie permission. It was his responsibility. He closed the gate and locked it firmly. Marthe was resting beside the basin, she hadn't noticed. A hot day passed, they remained in doors for the remainder of the morning, and Felix tried to find some solace in playing the piano. Marthe sat and listened quietly, she was very pale, occasionally touching the plaster on her forehead. Later she said, 'I shall go to the gendarmes first thing tomorrow morning. I have no doubt they'll need to come and inspect the damage. We have to leave the garden as it is.' Felix drove home in a very dark mood.

News of the garden's devastation quickly spread through the town, the men who came to collect the hired tables and chairs were shocked by what they saw and passed the stories, such as they knew, around. By Monday evening it was common knowledge and many in St. Girou were appalled. On Tuesday morning several 'locals' walked up to the house, to offer their sympathy. One of them was a reporter form the local paper, he rang the door -bell vainly. But he learned the name of the owner, and took some photos of the façade and the drive way, he would write it up for his editor.

Annie knew nothing of this. She was preoccupied with her mother and Charlie, who were returning to England together on the Monday afternoon flight. They had all been tired on Sunday and somewhat at odds with each other, in the afternoon Annie began collecting Charlie's clothes, packing carefully. Claire and Charlie watched a movie on the TV, sitting side by side on the sofa, eating biscuits and drinking iced tea. Charlie was excited at the prospect of visiting England, and travelling with his grandmother. They took the shuttle train to the airport, Charlie pulling his suitcase on wheels, leading the way to the entrance. It was crowded and Claire was relieved to have Annie with them, they checked in and Annie walked with them to the security gate.

'Keep your eye on the departure board, and don't leave it too late, there's a long walk to the passport control here.'

'I know' interrupted Charlie, 'I'll show gran the way.' He was eager to be off and gave Annie a quick hug, Claire followed him, checking their boarding cards, and holding the passports. She gave a wave and disappeared, Charlie had already gone.

Annie was relieved to see them both go, she felt like spending some time on her own, digesting the events of Saturday. She walked back to the train station to pick up the shuttle for the Toulouse city centre, she hoped he would enjoy his first week with Ralph. Sitting in the train, she looked at her phone and saw, with surprise, four missed messages. 'Can't be work surely? I've only missed a week- it was all set up. Someone's panicking!' She held the phone to her ear as the train drew into Toulouse. She listened incredulously to Felix voice, her stomach sinking, unable to fully absorb what he was relating. 'Phone me, Annie. As soon as you get this!' Berating herself for not checking the phone earlier, Annie dialled Felix as she walked out of the station. They talked briefly, but Annie learned enough to understand that her year's work had been ruthlessly damaged. 'I'll come over early tomorrow. Tell Marthe, not to worry- it is very difficult to destroy plants and trees. It probably looks worse than it is. Felix was partially reassured, but Annie had not seen the garden.

CHAPTER 21

Sylvie had enjoyed her Saturday afternoon visit to les Palmes. She had wandered up and down the paths, taking notes, examining carefully the plant labels. 'I wish we'd been involved in this,' she thought angrily 'it could have been our names on all these labels. What an advertisement.' She had recognised several local growers and a renowned horticulturalist from Toulouse. 'Annie will build on this,' Sylvie thought, 'maybe she and I could go into business, her designing, me growing!' It was a dream idea, and opened up a different avenue, away from the existing business, which her father still controlled. Sylvie made some supper, and took it out to the narrow terrace at the back of the farmhouse. The dogs lay at a distance watching her. She went to bed. Sheard her father's car returning, it was a warm and still night and she got up to open the window wider. She looked at her watch- it was very late- nearer dawn than dusk, Sunday already. Puzzled, she went and lay down under the sheet. She shut her eyes and drifted back to sleep.

Henri had done much more that night than he intended. He had spent Saturday afternoon resting in the coolest room indoors, watching TV and dozing. He had heard Sylvie's little car set off down the drive; he knew where she was going, though nothing had been said at lunch. Slowly anger built up in him and he became restless- unable to sit quietly. He heard Sylvie return late in the afternoon, but he stayed watching the television apparently dozing.

After Sylvie had gone to her room, Henri became increasingly agitated and found it impossible to rest or sleep. Waiting for Sylvie to fall asleep, was almost torture to him. After midnight he rose quietly, and carefully drove off shushing the dogs who slept by the barn . They watched him go, then settled down again. 'I have to go and look,' he said to himself as he parked near the river and set off down the tow path. It was surprisingly light as the moon rose over the river. It shone like silver. 'Just look.' The open garden door was a gift and Henri entered, as he had before, but this time the garden was empty and silent. No women and no little dog.

He looked at the peaceful scene- making it out slowly as his eyes became accustomed to the dark. It was very beautiful, as a 'grower' himself he recognised that, in a different way too, which interested him. He looked up at the shuttered house, where Marthe, he knew, was sleeping. A single light came through the landing window. 'She has so much!' he thought, 'all this comes from her father! This house, this garden it all comes from him. She has no right to be happy here! He was an evil man and a murderer!' Looking around, he entered the shed, and found a spade - waving it like a maniac he lashed out and then methodically, almost calmly, he set about his task. It took some time and he was shaking as he finished. He was exhausted by the effort, without a backward glance, he walked to the gate, stopping briefly to hurl the spade at Charlie's shed, breaking the glass.

'Let her live with that' he thought, 'that should show her how unwelcome she is!' He went to bed and slept well, nor did his conscience prick him the following day. He spent a quiet

Sunday, and on Monday, opened up the garden business as usual. He had not spoken to anyone.

*

Annie was very relieved that Charlie and Claire had left France. She could not have borne them seeing what had happened. She drove out to Marthe as early as she could on Tuesday morning, the house appeared to have been shut up. She found Marthe indoors, talking on the phone. There was a nasty swelling on her forehead. They looked at each other, 'Felix is at the gendarmerie. It was Henri Carrere of course,' Marthe said, handing a cup of coffee to Annie, who took it and said, 'I'll go out now on my own, let me look carefully. I'll tell you then what I think!' Annie, more shocked than she wanted Marthe to realise, slowly examined the damage, she sipped her coffee and tried to order her thoughts. She felt very sad, almost overwhelmed by the senseless destruction. She didn't question Marthe's assertion that it was Henri, 'All my hard work!' she thought, and angrily kicked the gravel. She thought of the hours of pleasure the garden had given to her, how beautiful it had looked just three days ago; she remembered how proud Claire had been of her. She lifted the fallen plants checking each in turn, carefully stepping over those that now lay on the ground. She did the same with the grasses, and cacti and the shrubs. She pulled a small book out of her bag and jotted down notes, pausing as she studied the worst damage. The three tall palms were untouched, and she put her hand on their rough trunks looking up to their magnificent leaves. She saw Felix walking slowly towards her. He looked tired and pale. She spoke quietly, 'He did a pretty good job! How did he get in?' Felix turned away,

'Felix?'

'The gate was open.'

'Why? We didn't go out.' Then a horrible dawning thought, 'Oh my God. Charlie! He went out with his friends! He went fishing! And I never thought to check!'

'Nor I. We were tired and I should have checked. I told him he could go. I should have remembered.' They looked at each other, 'Does Marthe know?' Annie could hardly bear to ask.

'No. It seems irrelevant, knowing. We are both responsible and that is that!' Annie looked at him, 'This is very difficult for me.' He looked at the ground,

'Annie we share responsibility, we just have to get on with trying to put some order back into this,' he waved his arm, 'Destruction!' He took her hand and kissed her very lightly. 'Things go wrong. All the time. Come on, let's see what we can do.' Annie walked back towards the house, she felt slightly sick. The wonderful day now seemed far away. 'It's not impossible,' Annie tried to reassure him, 'a lot can be done. These plants were well established and their roots were unharmed. It's the roots that will help them now.' They returned to the kitchen and Annie told Marthe what she thought, 'I need to make a list, it won't be difficult- three columns- plants: ruined- restorable- untouched. It's not as terrible as it looks.' She and Felix returned to the garden and they set to work; Annie analysed the plants, while Felix listing them in the appropriate column. It was tiring, depressing work. Following up on Felix's complaint, a Gendarme appeared late in the afternoon. He was very polite and formal and looked gravely at Marthe. Felix escorted him around the garden, and he took notes in his pocket book. He seemed surprised at the damage and questioned Marthe, who insisted that the police visit Henri Carrere. He was noncommittal, but wrote down the name. He shook hands with them all, glancing carefully at Annie and left. Marthe sighed as she took Annie's arm, she said 'Enough for today.' It was nearly eight o'clock. Annie drove home, it had been a long sad day, and she had agreed to work all that week for Marthe, repairing as much of the damage as she could. It was not what she had planned.

Marthe talked later on the phone to Patricia, who was appalled at the news. She immediately promised to drive down the next day and stay 'until you're tired of me.' She arrived late in the afternoon on Wednesday, accompanied by Gaston who rushed into the house as though he owned it. Felix was pleased to see her, and warned her that Marthe had had a fall and her face was bruised.

'That's the least of her problems! Isn't it?' Patricia always went to the heart of a problem. Felix nodded, 'Keep off that, for the moment, would you? We are waiting to hear from the gendarmes!'

'Good. Let's hope they don't delay!"

Patricia hurried in and found Marthe at the kitchen table, studying a long list. She took one glance and said, 'You need a hot bath, a drink… and I've bought supper.' She held a bag up in her hand. Looking at Felix and Annie, who had been hard at work all day, she continued, 'You both look exhausted, go home! I'll look after your mother Felix!' Patricia's offer was impossible to resist.

The next morning Felix returned to the local Gendarmerie. A long wait in the small entrance, was followed by an interview in the run down office. The Gendarme, a young man who showed no emotion, wrote down in long- hand Felix's account of the preceding months. He made no comments apart from occasionally asking for more detailed explanations. So, the damage to your car? You did not report it? Why not?'

And 'You say that this man,' he glanced at his notes, 'Henri Carrere has entered the property before? When was that?'

For Felix it was a dispiriting morning. As he slowly recounted the events, he realized how serious Henri's behaviour had been, and how foolish, he, Felix, had been to ignore them. He bitterly, now, regretted his inaction. He read his statement through as requested, it was now nearly noon, and the Gendarme was eager to finish. He signed and dated it and left. The Gendarme had given no indication of what would happen next, his statement was to be passed to his Superior. Felix phoned his mother and told her of his morning, she was in the salon while Patricia prepared lunch. She said, 'When all this comes out, the whole town will learn of Bertrand and his Nazi views! And his role in the war. How will people then feel about this family, you and me?' Felix replied as calmly as he could, 'The town will see it for what it is. The past. You're having to live with it, as am I. Other families have secrets, things they do not want to remember, are eager to hide.'

Marthe found that difficult to believe, 'Well, I feel a terrible shame, and that's what I have to live with. The garden damage is nothing, compared with the damage that Bertrand caused. I'm not even angry with Henri now. Why shouldn't he hate us. This house. This garden. What are they?'

Felix listened aghast. 'Don't turn your back on everything, it's still our family home, and you've achieved a wonderful thing here, you and Annie. You've a right to live here, peacefully.'

Marthe interrupted him, 'You're right to report Henri, he's acted criminally. I know that. But I feel sad for him and Sylvie, their family's reputation will now be harmed, and all because of us. No good will come out of this.'

Felix replied, 'No. But it's out of our hands for the moment. Our task is to try and restore the garden, so that you can enjoy it again.'

Over lunch Marthe repeated this conversation to Patricia, who had no doubts, 'Prosecute the old devil! He's done you nothing but harm. Don't hesitate.' She looked Marthe in the eye, as she waved her knife, 'Really Marthe, the law exists to stop people like Henri. Use it!'

Marthe was grateful for Patricia's loyal support, but she didn't agree with her.

'I'll not go to court, I can't have the du Pont and Carrere history aired in public. It would be horrible, shaming! Let him be prosecuted for trespass, and criminal damage, but the harassment that must be set aside. I'll not give evidence.'

Marthe was adamant. There was a report of the damage to the garden, in the local paper later that week, and to Marthe's great annoyance, it included a photo of Les Palmes, taken through the gates. But it did not name anyone apart from Marthe and gave no details that could connect the story with Henri Carrere.

*

Annie worked steadily that week, a miserable task, aided by Felix, who found manual labour surprisingly rewarding. The sight of him, hauling broken plants and damaged branches down to the bonfire, was the only pleasure she could find in the day. The garden was slowly cleared and by Saturday with their combined efforts, it resembled something of what it had looked like, seven days before. Charlie's shed had been mended, Annie was concerned that he should learn as little as possible, and Felix planned to repaint it, when he had time, pale green with a blue window. Annie now felt she had done enough, and needed a break. She said goodbye to Patricia who was also ready now to return to Paris, and told Marthe that she was taking a holiday.

'I'll be away for a week.' She thought Marthe should take a holiday too, but said nothing. 'I need a change.' She said to herself on Sunday morning, 'but where to go?' Most of her friends were already away, their plans fixed around their children. She had earlier turned down several offers: to share a gite in the Pyrenees, to shares a villa by the sea. Both would get her out of the stifling hot flat and Toulouse which was full of tourists. But Annie had decided already that sharing a holiday with friends with children would not be much fun. 'So a week on my own!' she thought 'to do what I like! I've certainly earned it!'

The tremendous heat broke late on Sunday afternoon and a storm shook the city, thunder rolled around for the rest of the day and into the night there were flashes of lightening and sudden loud downfalls of rain. Toulouse became unusually quiet as people stayed at home, while the humidity made sleep impossible. Annie phoned Claire and told her that she was going away, 'What a good idea. You deserve a holiday. All that work for the garden opening.' Annie hadn't told her mother about Henri's visit and the days she had spent putting the garden back into shape. She changed the subject, So all went well at the airport when you landed? Ralph was there?'

'Yes. And on time too! But I didn't tell you, Ralph wasn't on his own! He has a new partner, a girlfriend !'

'Goodness,' Annie was surprised, it had never occurred to her that Ralph would 'move on', as she had suggested, and so quickly. The divorce was still not finalised, as if that made any difference.

'And Charlie looked really well when they brought him yesterday. His hair was washed and all his clothes too. Neatly folded in his bag and he brought us a box of chocolates.' Annie was pleased that her mother had some praise for Ralph and then she rang off. She was strangely put out.

Annie awoke on Monday to a clear, fresher day, it felt cooler and the streets and roofs shone wetly in the early sun. Annie packed a hold all, emptied the fridge and put out the rubbish. She glanced quickly around the flat, threw out some flowers that were beginning to droop, and picked up her car keys. She drove out of Toulouse with the window down and singing to herself, happy to be away, from Les Palmes and Toulouse, even Charlie . A sense of freedom infused her. She drove south to the mountains, towards a quiet town in the foothills, that had a hotel, and was off the beaten track. She intended to spend her week walking, and resting.

'Where are you?' It was Monday evening.

'Felix?'

'Yes! Where are you? You're not at home because I'm standing outside, and you're not answering!'

Annie smiled to herself. She was eating supper- excellent- at the restaurant, attached to her small hotel. She was beginning to feel more relaxed than she had for several weeks having enjoyed a good afternoon walk. A walkers' guide was propped up in front of her, and she was studying it as she ate, planning the next day. 'So where are you?' Felix sounded vexed.

'Oh! I'm a long way away!' She spooned a mouthful of crème caramel into her mouth,

'Are you going to tell me?'

'Maybe! Why?' she licked the back of her spoon, having finished the little pot.

'I want to see you- that's why!'

'Well, get in the car, take the auto- route for Bordeaux and stay on it until the turning for Bagneres de Louchon .Follow this road heading south, and into town. You'll find me- finishing a lovely supper at the hotel beside the church. Good luck! Oh and bring your walking boots!'

Felix looked at his phone in astonishment, Annie had rung off. An hour and a half later he found her, and following a late supper and a lot of wine, they fell into bed. Together.

Annie and Felix spent a quiet week, walking and exploring an area that was new to both of them. They were winding down from the emotional plateau they had been on the previous week. They fell into each other's arms every evening, drawn together in lovemaking. He found her intoxicating.

On Thursday, having studied the map carefully they decided to park high up at the Hospice de France. There was a long walk from there, the path led eventually over the frontier and into Spain. It was quite cold as they set off, but bright and sunny. They struck out along the High Pyrenees route, walking steadily uphill for more than three hours before resting for the picnic which Felix had carried on his back. They were well above the tree line now in the shadow of the north side, and surrounded by a line of irregular peaks some with snow. If they continued along the narrow and often steep path they would cross into Spain within an hour. It was cool, the wind blowing off the mountains in cold blasts. The view was magnificent; only mountains, grey and hostile and far below them a narrow river, full of boulders and crossed with occasional stone bridges. The sheep which grazed here all summer were far below. They had encountered several on their way up, grazing on the short mountain grass and were forced to shoo them off the path. They were surprisingly agile as they jumped aside, and ran off down the steep shaley mountain, until, stopping abruptly, they turned to stare. Their eyes were large and yellow, their coats rough and dirty. Felix and Annie stared back, and laughing continued their walk.

Annie huddled into her anorak- tearing off bites of bread- she held a big slice of cheese in one hand and waved the arm holding the bread, 'This is just wonderful! No houses, no people, nothing ugly or unnatural- no worries or responsibilities.'

Felix smiled, 'Just aching legs and a long walk back!' He had finished his bread and was trying not to 'eye' Annie's. 'No really Felix. These walks have really cleared my head. I feel more in control, can see things in perspective, Charlie, his Dad, Marthe...' She left the statement hanging in the air, and glanced at Felix, then swallowing the last of her bread, she leant across and put her cold hand on his cheek.

He looked at her, the wind whipped her hair around beneath her woolly hat, her face was sunburnt and her eyes clear and shiny. "I love you," he said and paused for a long time. Annie stared at him then reached over and kissed him slowly, 'And I love you Felix! This holiday has made me realize how happy I am with you.' They kissed again, forgetting even the cold wind. And sat leaning into each other.

Annie moved away slowly, the wind was reaching through her anorak. She turned and began packing away the picnic. Felix stood up, he looked at the sky, 'I think we should get going. Those clouds are building up and it will rain later this afternoon. We need to get lower, back to the tree line for protection.'

He held out his hand to pull her up. Shouldering the haversack, he tucked her hair inside her hat as Annie pulled up her collar, 'We can talk about Henri later,' he said. Annie began walking down the track it was slippery and she had to concentrate, 'Whenever you're ready.' Her words were nearly blown away in the wind. But they did not talk that evening. They drank a bottle of red wine and made love in the big lumpy bed, falling asleep soon after. The walk had tired them.

On Friday they woke early to the sound of heavy rain. Felix looked out of the small square window, pushing back the red checked curtains. The road outside was empty; rain was streaming down, the gutters were filling up, and water cascaded down the steep grey tiled roofs. A solitary figure emerged from the house opposite and hurried to the bakers hidden beneath a black umbrella.

'Time to go home.' He turned to face Annie, 'this will last all day!' It was the storm they had seen coming up from the West the previous afternoon. Annie packed her bags into her car and prepared to leave, as Felix came out and stared at the rain which had become even worse. 'I'll follow you,' he said 'Make sure we both get back safely.' Annie smiled, 'I'll be fine! You go off! In your fast car!'

'No. I said I'll follow.'

'Ok but …'

'Yes I know. You are an independent, grown up woman who can look after herself.'

'Exactly. And you are a kind, thoughtful man who is standing in the rain, and getting wet.' Felix nodded, 'Well that's agreed then. We can park in the St. Georges underground car park. I'll see you there.'

It was a tiresome drive until they got close to Toulouse where the rain eased. Annie liked glancing in the mirror, and seeing Felix behind her, it was pleasantly reassuring. She could see he was singing to himself. 'I do love him' she thought and not for the first time wondered how it would all work out. They parked and lifted out their bags. Felix came over and Annie spoke,

'Do you want to come up? I could fix us supper.' It seemed the most natural thing in the world that he should stay. Felix shook his head 'No. I don't think so. I left in rather a hurry and now I have some work to do …a concert review that is long overdue. When's Charlie back?'

'Tomorrow, he lands about lunch time. All on his own.'

Felix smiled. It was nice to think of Charlie, like Annie he had rather missed the boy. They went their separate ways.

While Felix was away, Marthe, resigned now to the intervention of the law, had been 'interviewed' by a gendarme from Auch- a stout middle-aged man with greying hair. He was very polite and formal, and asked to be allowed to inspect the garden, which, thanks to the hard work of Annie and Felix, no longer looked devastated. He was concerned with the two offences of trespass and criminal damage. Marthe had made very clear that she would not pursue the more complicated issue of harassment. 'I will not press further charges,' she insisted. He nodded, eyeing her above his glasses, 'I'll talk to my superior, but this matter of the harassment of which your son, Felix has spoken, cannot proceed further unless you want it to.' Marthe showed him to the door, she would not change her mind.

Sylvie had learnt about Henri's activities late on Monday afternoon, two days after the event. A client, who needed advice on how to treat her cankered fruit trees, inadvertently mentioned the story of the damage to a garden.

'Which garden?' Sylvie was not really paying attention, as she examined one of the wilted apple leaves the woman had brought, 'on the outside of town… I saw it on Saturday, lovely ideas, you were there I think.' the woman continued.

Sylvie stared at her, she had become very pale. She knew which garden now.

'Are you all right?' The visitor became anxious.

'What did you say? Damage?'

The woman hesitated. 'Yes, damage… The whole garden, apparently, knocked about, deliberately, why would anyone do that? It doesn't make sense.'

Sylvie turned away, muttering an excuse, she walked, almost ran, back to the office where Henri was sorting catalogues.

'We need to talk,' she hissed, grabbing him by his jacket, 'now!' The visitor was forgotten, and drove off perplexed. Her apple leaves returned to her bag.

A nasty half an hour followed for Henri and Sylvie. They were both angry and unforgiving. Nothing was resolved; Henri refused to change his position- and Sylvie's now familiar entreaties- 'The past is history, Marthe is innocent,' swayed him not a bit. She said, 'What of the business? What of our reputation? You will be seen as the perpetrator, then what?' She was nearly shaking him now. 'No one cares about the war, now. Your father and Bertrand. The betrayal. Every family suffered losses and hardships. We were not unique, but it's gone...over... finished.'

'You weren't there. It's easy for you. But I can't forget. I cannot.'

Sylvie stared at him, she spoke harshly, 'Cannot or will not? Which is it?'

Henri said, 'The men of the resistance were brave and patriotic, they risked everything for France and its liberation. In that cause my father lost his life. I can't forget that and I can't forgive the collaborators, and I make no apology for my hatred of the du Pont family This woman, Marthe, she has no place here, no place at all!' He picked up the catologues and walked back to the house. His head ached, and he felt old and unloved.

Sylvie took a long walk later that evening, she realised that she could no longer live with her father; she would have to move away and abandon her share of the business. Preparing for bed, she thought briefly of Annie. Perhaps there was a possibility there. It was the only comfort she could find at the end of a truly terrible day.

CHAPTER 22

The Gendarme drove back to the Gendarmerie, filed his report. 'An odd case,' he later told his superior, 'he will have to be charged.' It was the day after the row between Henri and his daughter, and Henri saw the gendarme enter the garden centre. Sylvie watched as the two men conversed. Having passed a troubled night, Henri was cautious as he spoke to the officer; he admitted the trespass and the wanton damage at Les Palmes, refusing any explanation. The Gendarme found him stubborn and uncooperative, and resolved to pursue the prosecution at the court in Auch.

It was Saturday evening and Marthe was exhausted after a tiring and emotional week. She was annoyed to hear the heavy locker of the front door being banged, firmly and repeatedly. Reluctantly, she opened it. Claude was standing there with a large bag in his hand. 'A present from Bordeaux!' he said, handing it to her, as he moved to come in. Marthe stared at him, he had been far from her thoughts. Silently she led him through the kitchen, putting the bag on the table, and into the garden, saying nothing as Claude looked about with astonishment. He stared at the ruined garden. Walking forward he found the damaged bench beside the basin, and then the two urns both badly chipped, the matching statues of the goddess seemed unscathed, but the whole garden looked as though a whirlwind had torn through it.

'We've had an intruder!' Marthe said simply. 'It looked much worse last Sunday!' They were standing under the three palms. Questions poured out of Claude, 'Who? When?' he asked as he gazed about, it was difficult to comprehend. Marthe turned towards the house and Claude followed, involuntarily smoothing the path with his feet. The bag was on the kitchen table and Claude opened it, and trying to be normal, asked, 'A lobster for supper. Would that be nice?' Marthe peered inside the bag, relieved to see that the two lobsters were already cooked, 'A lovely surprise! Thank you. They smell of the sea!'

Pleased, Claude said, 'We can prepare them together and then you can tell me what's been going on here.' Marthe arranged the lobsters on a dish, and Claude opened the fridge finding a bottle of white wine. They put together a green salad and there was some bread. They ate at the kitchen table, unceremoniously, and wiping their fingers on paper napkins. It was the most informal meal they had eaten together, and Marthe felt able to talk. Slowly she recounted the history of her father and the events of 1944, then spoke of the role of Henri Carrere right up to the previous Saturday evening. Claude listened in silence, he could see the strain on Marthe's face and her anguish. She seemed more concerned about her father and his role in the events of 1944, than the vendetta of Henri Carrere. He thought of his own father a Jewish bookdealer who had fled to England in the 1930's, and the accounts he had heard of the family members who had been victims of the holocaust. He said nothing of this to Marthe, but there was one thing of which Claude was certain, it had been his life's guide for many years: 'You can't be like Sisyphus! Struggling futilely all his life to push a bolder up a mountain. Your shame at your father's history, that can't be your burden. It can't weigh you down, for the rest of your life.' He paused, 'All of it… Let it go!' He took her hand and made her look at him, turning her shoulders almost roughly. 'Marthe! Let that be your mantra now. Or you will never find peace.'

Marthe stared at him, and knew at that moment that he was right. 'Sisyphus.' she said, and remembered the painting of the man struggling up the mountain, pushing a huge boulder, endlessly. A punishment. They sat silently, Claude finally rose and finding the coffee pot, he waved it at Marthe, who pointed at the tin. She stood up to reach the cups from the dresser.

'So this has been going on almost since you arrived here, this 'issue' with M. Carrere. And you dealt with it by yourself?' he said.

'Yes initially. Felix only learned of Henri when his car was attacked, then I had to explain to him. The whole town knows of the plaque and the names of the four men, but Bertrand's role was known only to Henri, I think. It was a secret he kept to himself, until he saw me in the café. But now he has spoken to others, his daughter and possibly a disgruntled man who was once a gardener here.'

'But it's not common knowledge is it? You haven't had trouble, hostility from others in the town? The whole of France, every City, town and village has its history, and there are secrets attached to each one of them,' he poured the coffee, 'France doesn't want to remember its dark past; the betrayers, those who were cowards, those who worked with the occupiers, the pro Nazis…' There was a long silence, neither spoke Bertrand's name. 'For the moment Marthe, you've done the right thing, you've handed him over to the law, and the law will punish him. And give you the protection that you deserve.'

They continued talking for several more minutes until Claude rose to leave.

"I hope to hear from the Gendarmes this week…' she said finally.

'And you'll keep me up to date.' She nodded. Claude drove home slowly, he felt an overwhelming sense of unease.

*

On that same Saturday Charlie returned to Toulouse. Annie, tanned from her week of walking in the mountains, watched eagerly at the Arrivals gate for his familiar face. He looked well as he walked towards her, his passport in one hand and pulling his case. He chatted away, as they negotiated the busy forecourt, and walked together to the car. Annie was delighted to have him home, and watched as he threw down his bag, and did a tour of the sitting room, then poured himself a glass of water and grinned at her, 'Grandma sends her love' he said, 'and Arthur is really well. It was nice.' He went to his room and she could hear him moving his stuff about. Charlie didn't tell Annie much about his week with Dad, it had been very different; Ralph had a new partner and was living with her in a flint cottage in the village where he now worked. Her name was Edna, and she worked in the local doctor's as a receptionist. They had met when Ralph limped in with a pulled Achilles tendon after a cricket match. She was unmarried, jolly and rather plump. She was also kind and gregarious. She saw Ralph as a man in need of love and 'tidying up'. They were well suited. Edna was an uncritical soul who didn't like living alone; her previous partner, a teacher, had had an affair and she had kicked him out. She liked Ralph's laid back ways and shared his passion for cricket and village life. They had been together now for several months and had become a regular feature around the village. Edna had little experience of children, she had none of her own, but entered happily into the task of entertaining Charlie. Ralph was delighted to see the two of them getting along well, as he was out at work all day, gardening for a living. The money wasn't great, but it came in every month, and Edna took his contribution with a smile. Ralph had finally settled down.

On the first day Edna took Charlie out to the playing fields, at the bottom of her garden. She pointed to a gang of local boys who were 'mucking about' on their bikes, 'You can play with them,' she said 'they're nice lads. I'll be at the surgery for a couple of hours. Come and find me if you need me' she pointed across the cricket pitch, ' or I'll give you a call when it's lunch time.' And that was it. Charlie wandered across to the gang and within a few minutes had joined in the game of 'wheelies.' The morning passed with bikes handed around, and an expedition into the woods beyond the field. Here they made a bonfire and Charlie showed off his expertise. He heard Edna calling and ran back. It had been a good morning, and Charlie ate all his lunch of baked beans and sausages, which he shared with Edna. There was ice cream to follow, and then they sat in the little garden together. Charlie had been given a catapult by Ralph and tried it out endlessly on the target which Edna set up. She read the Daily Mail, and then they did the crossword together. 'You should know this one Charlie,' she quoted 'A French river beginning with A or maybe S, I'm not sure!' The sun moved around the little garden, it was quite hot. 'We'll have tea outside,' she said 'Can you move the chairs into the shade?' She pointed and went indoors. Tea was as good as lunch, cake and little home- made biscuits. Charlie was settling in fast. They all had supper together, squeezed around the kitchen table, and Charlie told his father about his day.

The first day set the pattern for Charlie's stay. He played with the 'lads' and one of them lent him an old bike, and they cycled to the shops for sweets and crisps, and twice to the local river for a swim. 'I wish I had my rod,' he said to Ralph. 'Well next time you come, maybe we can get you one.' He replied.

Edna smiled approvingly, she felt she had a proper family for the first time.

During the course of the next days, the village boys taught Charlie all the swear words they knew, and he taught them all his French ones. The lady in the shop was surprised to hear a loud "Merde!" when one of them dropped his fizzy drink. 'Enough of that!' she exclaimed. They laughed and ran back to their bikes. On his last afternoon they played a hot and hectic game of football, 'Goodbye!' he said at the end of the game, as they lay sprawled on the grass next to the shed. 'I'm going tomorrow.' They didn't seemed surprised, but nodded and waved as he walked away. 'See you!' one called after him and Charlie held up his hand, 'Yeah. See You!'

Charlie looked forward to getting back to the cottage, he liked Edna and his father seemed much happier. He did not go to the pub anymore Charlie noticed, but spent the long summer evenings in the little garden where he was growing beans and tomatoes, and 'herby' things. Edna wanted Ralph to make her a small pond ,they spent a lot of time discussing this and Charlie hoped they would do it, and put fish in. On his last evening Ralph took him to a film and then for a pizza. 'Enjoyed your-self?' he asked as they got back into Edna's little car; Ralph still only had a van and his motor bike, which was now in the shed and not much used. 'You've made some friends?'

'Yes. It's different here, I can do what I like!' Ralph regarded him 'Don't you like France then?' Charlie was silent, 'I like France. But I like England too, staying here and then with Gran and Tony.'

'It seems to me that you have the best of both worlds! Lucky you !' They arrived back at the cottage where Edna was putting his clothes neatly in a pile. Ralph gave her a hug later 'Thanks for helping. He's had a great time. All due to you!' Edna gave him a push, 'He's a nice boy. No trouble. Not like you then!' Ralph was not sure whether that was a joke, but he gave her a kiss. It had been a good week.

In Toulouse Annie and Charlie had finished eating and Charlie was looking out his school bag. He was 'back' on Monday and ready for a new term. He was looking forward to seeing his friends and telling them all about the catapult and the bike rides and England. The phone rang, Annie who was washing up sighed, 'Can you pick it up Charlie?'

'OK. But it won't be for me! Hello. Oh! Hi Felix!' He listened, nodding his head. Annie watched Charlie as he spoke; Felix... 'Was there a future for her and Felix? And if there was, then second question, 'when should Charlie be told?' She had been worrying about this since her return from the mountains.

Charlie put down the phone, 'He's asked us to supper. Tomorrow night.'

'And?'

'I said Yes! We can go about 6 o'clock as I've got school. So he said not late.'

'Ok. That'll be nice.'

She turned back to the sink, smiling slightly to herself. In bed Annie reflected on her days in the mountains. She gazed up at the high ceiling and put several questions to herself:

Happy? Yes. Fun? Certainly. Were they 'in love'? Probably. But (there was always a but) wasn't Felix just looking for a fling? He had so recently been living with Valerie, was he simply on the rebound? She and Valerie were so different, was that the attraction? She counted the things that they shared: they liked walking, and both had an enthusiasm for music, he had supported her interest in the garden, and he was fond of Charlie. Was that enough? There was certainly a mutual attraction, and she was flattered by his attention, his compliments, she found him amusing company. They had both declared their love, but holidays were one thing, and daily life something else. In the meanwhile she and Charlie could look forward to having supper in his flat.

At Les Palmes Marthe received a letter from the Gendamerie. It confirmed that Henri would be prosecuted for the two offences of trespass and criminal damage. The case would be held in Auch and he was expected to plead guilty. Her statement would be the evidence for the prosecution. She was free to attend if she chose. She showed it to Felix, and he read it carefully, 'That is what you wanted, isn't it? he said and glanced at her. But for Marthe it was not straight forward; she had thought at length of what Claude had said: 'Let it go. Or you will never find peace.' She knew that he was right, and that she had to move forward, yet still there lingered a sense of guilt and shame. She could not understand why her father had been as he was, had acted as he did, it was beyond credibility. Marthe was now thinking very differently about Bertrand du Pont.

Felix left, and Marthe went into the salon and sat at her mother's desk, she found her writing paper, and very slowly, she wrote a letter to Henri, pausing regularly to find the right words, it was a difficult task.

Marthe, she wrote, could not atone for the crimes of
Bertrand du Pont, nor was she responsible. She acknowledged
the terrible impact of his actions, but she had played no part
in them. She was his only child, and she wished to express
her great sadness, and give her condolences for the loss of his
father; she realised that a great wrong had been done to his
family and that he, Henri, in particular had greatly suffered.
She felt only shame at Bertrand's actions during the war, she
did not expect forgiveness. She expressed the wish that the
past should be laid to rest, and that Henri could accept her
presence at Les Palmes. She requested that their two families
should live without further incident in the town. She posted
the letter the following day and felt better. It was an apology.

The supper in the flat was the first time that Felix had entertained Annie and Charlie and he had been strangely nervous.
He spoke to Annie, whilst Charlie was watching football on
the TV, and they were washing up together, 'I want to live
with you Annie. I hate this flat now. It feels empty, and I want
to be with you and Charlie.' He waited anxiously watching
her swift movements at the sink. She kept her back to him, as
she replied, 'Well, it's not just you and me is it? I have to speak
to Charlie.'

'Of course. I understand that.' She turned her head from
the sink 'Charlie is my first responsibility. He's adjusted to
leaving England, and rarely complains, but there are changes
back in England, his father has a new partner, and that's
something he may find difficult. His visits will be very different. But I'll think about it, I promise.' Felix had to be satisfied
with that. After they had left, Felix opened the letter from
Marthe, which had been waiting for him all day. It contained
a copy of her letter to Henri. Felix read his mother's words
quickly, his heart pounding, and then forced himself to read

it again, slowly. Felix closed his eyes, he was deeply shocked-appalled- angry. 'That it should come to this.' He thought, 'My mother apologising to that vile man, who has made her life a misery. Violated her, simple as that. Waging a campaign of hatred for nearly a year.' He reached for the telephone; Marthe was not surprised to hear his angry tone as he spoke to her, 'We can discuss this tomorrow, but not over the phone.' She said firmly, and suggested lunch. They were eating in the little parlour, and Felix was finding it difficult to keep back his disappointment, both with the letter, and also Marthe's failure to discuss it with him. He remembered an earlier conversation, when they had agreed to work together, and refer to each other; Marthe had either ignored or forgotten this. She spoke first, 'Well, my letter. I know that it's angered you, but I need you to accept what I've done. It's an apology; and that's what I have to do, apologise for my father. Felix tried to interrupt, 'No Felix, it's the only way forward, out of this…mess. I don't know if Henri will accept it, probably not, he's hated the family all his life, I doubt he'll change. But I've opened the door for him, and perhaps he will slowly forgive the events of the past, and as long as the law protects me, and you, well I can be free of him. That's all I want' she repeated, 'to be free of him. And I hope my apology will make it possible for him to put the past behind him!'

Felix sighed, 'I've never met him, only his daughter. She's the next generation, like me. It's all in the past for us, the war, the occupation, the resistance, the Vichy government- we learned about it in school. It was history.'

Marthe said, 'Well, history it is, but a sad and difficult period, for many.'

'I doubt that I'll get a response from Henri,'" she continued, 'and I don't really care now. By writing to him, I have made peace with myself.' Marthe refused to discuss it any further, fearing an argument with Felix could develop, she rose and began to clear the table. ' Let's go outside, shall we, take a look at the garden? I'll tidy up later.' They walked down the path to the basin and then on to the wall and the gate. 'I dream about this still, the open gate and the men walking in,' she put her hand on the bricks, they were warm and rough in the sunshine. 'But not so vividly. Memories and dreams linger, though we would like to forget. 'But I've some news for you,' she took a seat in the orchard and indicated a chair for Felix. 'I've decided to spend part of this winter down on the Mediterranean. I don't look forward to the cold, damp winter days here, the long dark evenings. I've thought about returning to Paris, which is what Patricia advises, but that's a step back into my past.' Felix was astonished, and felt a wave of disappointment, he said, 'I can see that the winter is difficult here, we all hate the short days, the damp weather.' He was trying to collect his thoughts.

'Yes, but for you, it's easier; you have your work and a city life! In Toulouse the evenings are lively; there are people about, lights from the bars, you have music and concerts, a choice of places to eat. Saint Girou is lifeless and dull, everything is shut up by seven in the evening. Nobody is about. The countryside is even worse, dark at night, the farms with their shutters all closed. I'm not complaining, it's rural life, and in the spring and summer it's wonderful here, but the winter? I dread it. So, I'll spend parts of this winter somewhere warm and sunny.'

'Have you decided where?'

'Yes. I think so.'

'And this house?'

'I'm going to rent a flat, this house will be my home, but a flat will give me a choice, an alternative. Maybe I'll be away for a week at a time, or longer if I feel like it. I'm free to decide.'

Felix was thinking hard, he looked at her, 'Are you thinking of…selling?' he asked,

'No, it's been in the DuPont family for many years, it's 'family', an asset that will be yours in time. I've grown to love this house and the garden too, I've put a great deal into it this last year, and it's changed out of all recognition!'

Felix nodded his head in agreement, Les Palmes was a very fine house indeed, the most charming of any in the area. He thought about the future, would he want to live here? He couldn't imagine that, for the moment.

'So where are you going?' Felix asked.

'I shall find something in Collioure, it's a delightful town and I've never lived by the sea. It's sunnier than here and warmer too, I think it'll suit my needs. A flat with a view, not large, something I can open up and close with no difficulty.'

'I've never been there. I know Perpignan, a little.'

'It's further south and much smaller, a bit touristy in the summer, but that's not when I shall be there.'

Felix felt that his mother would never cease to surprise him; first the move from Paris, then the renovating of the house, the changes in the garden, and now a plan to rent a flat by the sea. He looked at her, she was staring up through the branches of the tree, the sky was blue above their heads, would he ever really know her? 'I'll drive down next week,' she said, 'why not come too? I'd like that. You can help me choose.'

Felix was pleased and flattered by Marthe's suggestion, 'I'd like that too. Very much.'

'Good. Shall we say Wednesday from here? For a few days?

CHAPTER 23

Felix discussed it with Annie over supper, at her apartment. Charlie was very upset. 'But why? It's a lovely house and the garden is terrific, and what about my shed? And going fishing?' 'We'll still go there,' Annie said rubbing his back. 'I'm going on with my work in the garden, every other Sunday is the plan.'

'But it won't be the same,' Charlie had left the table and was staring at Felix, 'without Marthe!'

Felix said, 'If it's what she wants, then we should be pleased. It's just the winter months that she finds difficult. She may feel differently in the spring.'

Charlie was not convinced. 'Well I think it's a shame! And I am going to tell her so!'

Annie rose from the table. Privately she thought it a shame too, but she did understand that the house was lonely for Marthe. She also realised that the whole Henri issue had made the town a difficult place for her. 'Well, we must support her Charlie, I'm sure she has thought carefully.' He did not reply.

Later she and Felix studied the car map that Annie finally found under the bed, she had thrown it there after her mountain trip. 'So where is it? This town that your mother has chosen? And how do you spell it?'

Felix pointed to the South East corner on the map, 'There! Collioure.' Annie moved his finger away, and stared, 'Goodness! It's almost in Spain! Why has she chosen that? Has she been there before? With your father maybe?'

Felix shrugged, he had no idea. He would miss her, he knew, and while the year had been difficult, he had enjoyed her living close by. He thought of the day in July, and how lovely the garden had looked, and how proud he was of her. She had seemed very happy then. What was the reason for this new plan? Felix was unsettled for another reason; Annie had turned down his request that they should live together. She had been firm but kind, 'It's too soon, we need to get more used to each other,' she had said, ' and with Charlie having to adjust to Ralph's new partner, I can't add a further change here. He's very fond of you, but living here day to day is altogether different. I must take it slowly for his sake.' Felix had listened, but he felt frustrated, he thought back to their happiness in the mountains, and was impatient with Annie's hesitations. He felt rejected.

In Auch at the hotel in the Square, Claude was having lunch with Marthe. He was anticipating a leisurely meal, and then maybe a 'siesta' back in his bed. She was looking very lovely, full of life and energy, and he assumed that she was over the Henri business, and back to normal. He, like Felix, was astonished and disappointed at her news. Selfishly he could see that the equilibrium of his life was about to be lost. He had developed their relationship carefully, wooing her slowly, and had grown to like her very much, hopeful that their friendship would continue to develop, it enhanced his life, and hers too, he had thought. Claude was a man who valued female companionship. Was all this to be lost? Claude crumbled his bread, sipped his wine and questioned Marthe.

She had anticipated that he would be displeased and had her answers ready; nor did she want to hurt the man who had enhanced her life in recent months. She liked him too much for that. She argued that her move would not interrupt their relationship, it might even add a little spice to it! 'Think about it for a moment would you, please.' She held up a slim pink varnished finger, Claude noticed that it was a perfect match for her blouse, he liked that, it was stylish. 'I want a warmer climate, sunshine and a town which offers me diversions. I've been thinking about another winter at Les Palmes? it does not appeal! I'm only going to rent, and shall move between the two homes, I'm lucky that I can afford to do that.'

Claude struggled hard not to feel hurt by her words. She seemed to be rejecting the rural life that he enjoyed, and all that he had tried to share with her. He had tried to expand her horizons, introducing her to his friends, taking her to galleries. Apparently to no avail. Marthe sat silently, then in a moment of tenderness took his hand and held it to her lips, 'Claude, look at me. This can work for us too, for you and me. Collioure is no distance away, a lovely easy drive, less than 2 hours on a good day. The road won't be busy in the winter. You have business connections there anyway. We can walk in the sun, and have lunch down by the sea, drive into Spain, I would love to explore across the border.' She released his hand and waited for his response.

Claud began to feel better, he was recovering from the initial surprise, and was beginning to think that it might turn our well. He had always liked the little town, so the idea of regular visits was not displeasing. He looked at Marthe,

'What are your plans?' Can I help?' Marthe outlined her plans, and then they walked to the bookshop and Claude found her, with Jerome's help, a book on the Fauvist painters of Collioure. Harmony was restored and love making later in the afternoon confirmed the friendship that they both valued.

The only downside was Charlie's gloomy mood when he and Annie arrived the following Sunday. Marthe was secretly touched that Charlie so enjoyed his weekly visits, and sad that he appeared downcast. 'But I like seeing you,' he said, his finger tracing a wet spot on the kitchen table, where his drink had spilt. 'It won't be the same! Nothing ever is!' Marthe looked at him closely.

'Is there anything else that has changed then?' Charlie shook his head- his eyes still on the table. Marthe moved to sit next to him, 'It won't be so different, I'll be here lots, I'm not abandoning this house. You'll be coming with Mum, much like you have before, the garden will be here for you, and your sheds, and your fishing too.' Charlie wriggled on his chair and picked up his drink. They sat a little longer. 'Now, Charlie… Let's look out your rod and you can take me fishing!' They walked along chatting about Collioure, 'It's by the sea and has a famous light house. It's not large, has a pretty promenade and is lively with people and dogs. There are cafés and bars and small hotels.'

'It sounds nice.'

'Yes I think so.' she gave him a hug. He was feeling better. Charlie found his fishing spot and was looking out his rod, 'I can imagine you doing that, eating in cafes and looking at the people,' he said, and sat down on the bank and Marthe watched as he fitted his rod together. She took her place beside him.

'Now! Explain to me about fishing.

*

Felix and Marthe enjoyed their time together in Collioure, relaxing together without the pressures of the previous year.

His advice proved invaluable as they searched for a flat for the winter.

'Far too small,' he said of the first, 'impossibly dark' the second was condemmed, 'nowhere to park' was his comment on the third and fourth. They stopped for lunch and the young agent regarded them apprehensively.

'Collioure is difficult, the narrow streets are a problem...' he said.

'Show us something with a view, and space! That's what we asked for.' Felix replied. 'What else have you?'

Marthe was tired of wandering the town, climbing steps and being disappointed. She looked weary Felix thought. 'Go and sit in the sun on your balcony' he said, he turned to the agent, 'I'll look with you this afternoon, let's start.' There were two possibilities, they set off. Marthe walked back through the streets that were now becoming familiar, she turned a corner and was forced off the narrow pavement by a man she had met with Claude. He owned a gallery she remembered. 'Forgive me' he said, raising his straw hat, 'these pavements are impossible.' Marthe hesitated, 'We've met before, I think.'

He looked at her more closely, 'Forgive me again! A friend of Claude, of course.' They stood chatting.

'And what has brought you back? The sunshine? September is a perfect month here. But where is Claude? Off buying?' Marthe explained why she had returned and her frustration with the morning. 'Let me walk with you to the hotel, and you can tell me what you are looking for. Is it to buy, or rent?'

Felix spent a dispiriting afternoon, he was doubting Marthe's decision to spend time in Collioure even more. Entering the hotel, he was given a note by the owner, 'Have gone to look at a flat. Something unexpected!' There were brief directions. Felix was tired, and hot. He had been anticipating a drink, or even a swim, he had been glancing at the sea all day, it was blue and sparkling. He sighed, her directions were sketchy. 'Can you show me the way to…' he asked the hotel owner.' 'That's the big villa at the back, up on the hill, quite a walk!' he said, Felix sighed again.

Marthe had no doubts; the flat was on the top floor of an old villa, built to overlook the bay, set back on a steep slope. The owner was an old lady, she lived in Paris, coming down in the spring and summer. The flat was old fashioned, but sunny and spacious, it had outside steps to the entrance, and a wide wooden balcony, with glorious views. As Felix arrived, Pierre was phoning the owner, she was his cousin. 'Come and see!' Marthe called down to him, she was standing at the top of the steps. 'It's lovely!' Pierre introduced himself, 'It's been empty for a while, my cousin is very particular. But you, Madame,' he smiled, 'will be the perfect tenant!' They walked back down the hill, discussing arrangements, and celebrated with a drink in a café on the promenade. It was busy; Felix looked about, he liked it: the activity, the light house, the palm trees on the promenade. He could imagine his mother there in the winter months. Pierre was full of encouragement too, 'You will bring Claude with you? Next time? There are people that you can meet!'

They stayed for one more day and drove home. 'Thank you for coming with me.' 'But you found it on your own!' 'Pure chance.' He lifted her case from the car, and said, 'I think it's a very charming flat, and a pretty town, I can see you there.'

'It was a happy time, being there with you,' she replied, 'Now I can look forward to the winter months. You saw there was plenty of room, come and stay with Annie and Charlie too, if you want.' Felix nodded, he hoped they would want that.

*

It was September, Charlie had returned to school and Annie was teaching again at the University. Her timetable had thinned a little, and she was considering her future. She had received several enquiries from visitors to Les Palmes, and new possibilities were opening up, as a garden designer. Felix was busy; he continued to combine attendance at classical and jazz concerts, which with the attendant reviewing, and the travel, kept him out of Toulouse a good deal. He had acquired two new pupils both young boys, one of whom was very promising. He and Annie continued to see each other, and he stayed regularly overnight. Charlie did not seem to notice the change.

In St. Girou, the newspaper had reported the hearing at the court in Auch and Henri's offences were local gossip. Few people had any sympathy for him, there was no known explanation for his actions. The story behind the events of July was not revealed, Marthe had seen to that. No connection was made between Henri and the family at Les Palmes, and Bertrand's activities remained part of the unspoken history of the town. For a few weeks the Carrere business suffered, as people stayed away then customers drifted back. More serious was the departure to Bordeaux of Sylvie, who full of anger and shame, felt unable to live any longer with her father. She could not forgive him, and Henri struggled without her. Young Jean put in a few hours from time to time, he was no worker and the two men fell out within a few months. The business slowly failed.

It was the end of September, Marthe had been at Les Palmes for just a year. She was writing to Patricia, and had pulled one of Charlie's wicker chairs across from his shed to the orchard and was sitting in the shade. She recalled with pleasure the words of old Jean, 'Your mother liked to read in the orchard.'

She looked down the garden to the house, clouds were passing over and their shadows created a dappled light, which softened the brickwork and the lines of the windows. It was a pleasing façade, classic in its formality, and she had grown to love it. Had her mother? Loved it? she would never know. And Felix? Would he want to live here? it seemed unlikely, unless he married. It was a house that deserved a family, it offered so much; spacious rooms, a warm kitchen, she could imagine children's feet running down the stairs, their laughter.

Marthe rose from her chair and walked to the garden gate, securely bolted. 'Henri's way in' she reflected. He had used it twice. She thought of him, entering at night, in the dark, carrying his heavy stick, whilst she slept peacefully upstairs, exhausted by the efforts of her open day. It was a horrible image. She touched the old gate, recalling the memory of her father, as he was carried in and down the path. Turning away, and avoiding a heap of leaves, flower heads and other garden waste which Annie had swept up, Marthe returned to her chair, and finished her half written letter. She invited Patricia to join her in her new flat, 'whenever you like!' That will be a surprise, she thought, hoping that Patricia would approve of her winter plan.

Marthe left Les Palmes a few days later. The agreement for the flat was waiting for her in Collioure and she intended to stay there for a week. She waved at the portraits as she descended the stairs. Pausing on the bottom step, and reaching up, she tapped the nose of the nearest figure, 'Goodbye old man! I'll be back.' she said, and smiled at his stern face. She put her suitcase on the back seat of the car, added a thermos of coffee, and a basket containing her lunch. She picked up the last of her letters from the box at the gate, turned the car out through the double gates, glancing at the stone pillars. It would not be a long journey.

Marthe drove fast down the autoroute stopping for her picnic after she passed Carcassone. There was no one else about. Finding a bench with shade from the poplars that lined the river, she took the letters from her bag, they were mostly bills but there was a letter whose writing she did not recognise. Putting it to one side, she began to eat the cheese and bread that made up her lunch and took a bite from an apple. It was delightful sitting there, she felt very fortunate, and glanced again at the envelope. It had been posted two days previously, she opened it and read the letter. It was signed Michel Rinaldi. The handwriting was very precise, the ink black. Forgetting her lunch, she read it again.

Dear Madam,

'We have never met, yet your family is known to me. In 1944 M. Bertrand du Pont, betrayed my brother to the Nazis. His name was Jean Jaques Rinaldi, we lived in St Girou, and were the sons of a clockmaker. He was the eldest of four boys, I am the youngest. Jean Jaques was a member of the Resistance; a small local group, they made life difficult for the Nazis, and those who collaborated with them: sabotaging railway lines, hiding and smuggling arms, helping opponents of the regime, and using their knowledge to lead some, over the Pyrenees. Bertrand du Pont, your father, betrayed Jean Jaques to the authorities; he was arrested, and eventually died outside Strasbourg. We never recovered his body, he was twenty six years old.

Some months later my other brothers, Pierre and Andre, waited for Bertrand on the towpath outside Les Palmes. He was accompanied by a little dog. They blocked his path, calling him a 'traitor'. Your father protested at their manner, and there was a struggle, your father was assaulted. Blows were struck, causing him to stumble, lose his balance and fall...into the river. They watched his body disappear into the dark water. They did not help him. His

*drowning was unplanned, unexpected. It was kept a secret from the
family and the town. Many years later, Andre gave me his account
of the death; he was a sick man and I believe wanted to clear his
conscience. Recently I was told of your return to Les Palmes, and
have read in the newspaper that you have had trouble there, so I
think that you should know the circumstances surrounding your
father's death. Your father drowned, my brothers were responsible,
and whatever Bertrand had done, their actions were wrong. Revenge
is never justified.'*

The handwriting grew tired. He had no more to say. There
was a neat signature, Jean Jacques Rinaldi.

There was no address. Marthe sat on the bench for a long
time, staring at the letter, and the signature. She had read the
name on the plaque several times. 'They did not help him.'
The sentence was terrible. What would a court of law make of
it? It was deeply unsettling, and gave her fresh understanding
of the death certificate. 'Drowned.'

She packed away her lunch, threw the bread into the Canal
for the ducks, they were circling expectantly and turned
the car back onto the Autoroute driving on eastwards for
Collioure. Immediately she forwarded the letter to Felix.
She knew he would be angry. Two days later, Marthe took
the phone onto the wide balcony of her new flat. A warm
autumn sun shone. She could see the sea, and leaning on the
wooden rail, she said, 'Felix. Please let me speak, then you
can say what you want to say. This letter was a surprise and
a shock, I'd hoped that my struggle with Bertrand was over.
It's taken up so much emotion in the last year... and now
this! I've never heard of Jean Jaques, and I don't know how
he learnt of my return. But he has, and we have this information. It's an appalling story, and changes our understanding
of his death. We know that his death was not an accident, but

the result, perhaps unintended, of a violent struggle. What he did was terribly wrong, and its repercussions have caused us unhappiness and difficulty. I don't want to discuss Henri, or think about him.

There is nothing I can do to change the past, I have, like everyone else, to live with it.' She paused, still looking at the sea below the hill.

Felix listened, he had moved restlessly to the window while Marthe spoke, and was watching a woman with a push chair. She was struggling with a child, whose arched back and flailing arms made the chair rock from side to side. She lost her temper and pushed the child down forcefully, it screamed. Felix's thoughts were confused and disordered. Unhappy events seemed to surround him. 'The letter tells us that his death was… murder, in all but name, he quoted 'They did not help him'. And that's a crime, in war time as in peace time.' He turned away from the window, the woman had disappeared with her child still screaming. 'And for all we know these brothers, Andre and Pierre are dead. They've escaped the law, and that's difficult to accept. War or no war.' Marthe listened to his angry tone, 'I have to end this,' she said, 'we can't dwell on the past; there were wrongs, and lies, other families with secrets. Things kept hidden. Bertrand mustn't destroy us.' Felix listened, he knew she was right and that nothing could be changed. He heard footsteps outside the flat door and a gentle knock, 'It's open,' he called. A young boy walked in, his face eager and fresh, he smiled as he walked to the piano. 'I have a student,' he said to Marthe. 'Good, enjoy the lesson.' She replied.

Felix sat beside his pupil, 'Play me the Chopin first, the Nocturne, not too fast, there's a difficult passage on the second page…' he became immersed in the music, his anger faded.

Marthe stayed for a week, settling in and buying some things to make the flat more to her taste. She stopped herself thinking about Les Palmes and the dark days which Henri had caused. The letter from M. Rinaldi had been kept by Felix though she could not refrain from thinking about its contents. 'Bertrand's death …was it deliberate? It mirrored the deaths on the train. Who could say what the Nazis intended, when they loaded their human cargo onto cattle trucks? Theirs was an act of supreme indifference, as was the indifference of the two brothers to the drowning man. Later as she stood on her balcony, she looked out across the water to the light house, it's now familiar outline caught in its own beam. We are all the same in the end, she thought, victims of our emotions and prejudices; sometimes we're generous, forgiving, but many times we are not. The sun was setting behind the hills to the south, and the light in the bay had gone, it was growing cool, she turned back into the room behind her, the phone was ringing. 'Would you join me for supper tomorrow? I've some people I'd like you to meet!' It was Pierre. Marthe didn't hesitate, 'Thank you, I'd be delighted.' 'About seven in the evening, quite informal.' He lived near the fish market and explained how to find him, 'I look forward to it.' Marthe said. She opened a bottle of white wine, and took her glass onto the balcony, it was cool standing there, but the view was magnificent, it seemed a long way from Les Palmes.

The End.